Dear Reader,

In November of 1998, I was standing on top of a pile of laundry (yes, I was that far behind) trying to decide whether to do a load of whites or a load of darks, when the phone rang. It was an editor at Avon Books and she wanted to buy my manuscript for publication. Shocked, ecstatic, and disbelieving, I incoherently thanked her a million and two times and, as soon as I hung up the phone, I screamed and shouted and threw laundry in the air like confetti.

I will never forget that day.

That book was *The Abduction of Julia* and it sold like hot cakes, going back to print within a few weeks of being released. Since then, the book has been back to print many, many times.

To update the book, this reprint has two brand-new rewritten final chapters and a never-before-seen new epilogue. I didn't change anything else because, frankly, I love the book just the way it is. Julia and Alec will always have a special place in my heart.

I hope you'll enjoy the new final chapters and epilogue. And for the chance to win free books, read hot new excerpts, and find information about my Top Secret Book Release Schedule, please check out my website, www.karenhawkins.com!

All best!

Karen Hawkins

Karen Hawkins

Karen Hawkins

The Abduction of Julia

AVON

An Imprint of HarperCollinsPublishers

This is a work of fiction. Names, characters, places, and incidents are products of the author's imagination or are used fictitiously and are not to be construed as real. Any resemblance to actual events, locales, organizations, or persons, living or dead, is entirely coincidental.

AVON BOOKS
An Imprint of HarperCollins*Publishers*
10 East 53rd Street
New York, New York 10022-5299

Copyright © 2000 by Karen Hawkins
ISBN 978-0-380-81071-0
www.avonromance.com

First Avon Books paperback printing: April 2000

Avon Trademark Reg. U.S. Pat. Off. and in Other Countries, Marca Registrada, Hecho en U.S.A.
HarperCollins® is a registered trademark of HarperCollins Publishers.

Printed in the U.S.A.

10

The
Abduction
of Julia

Chapter 1

Hampstead Heath, England
May, 1812

It was a hell of a night for an elopement. After three miserable hours, the rain had finally ceased. A ghostly blanket of fog crept along the edges of the narrow one-lane road, glowing eerily in the scattered moonlight.

Alec MacLean, fifth Viscount Hunterston, pulled the coach to a thundering halt in the yard of the Black Anvil Inn. Mud splattered the inn door and sent wispy spirals of mist scuttering across black puddles.

His groom, Johnston, stepped from the dripping eaves. "There ye be, m'lord. Mite late, ain't ye?"

"Her ladyship apparently cannot tell time," Alec said with a shrug.

"A woman who'd keep ye waitin' at the altar will stop at nothin' to annoy the spit out of ye," the old groom prophesied glumly.

Alec ignored him and climbed down from the perch. Johnston was a family heirloom of sorts, with a Welshman's habitual sullen disposition. Though normally Alec argued against such a dour outlook, on this occasion he feared the groom was right.

1

The coach door creaked as his passenger tried to open it from within. Johnston grunted. "Door's stuck agin."

"A pity, but we've no time to linger." Alec consulted his watch. It was barely ten. Considering the condition of the road from London, he had made remarkable time.

The noise from the coach increased to a firm knocking that lasted an annoying length of time. Johnston eyed the equipage with an interested gaze. "Her ladyship seems a mite determined. Do ye think she's changed her mind 'bout marryin' ye?"

"With the amount of money I stand to inherit? Highly unlikely." Spoiled and vain, Therese had made her objectives plain from the beginning. She wanted money, power, and position.

The thought turned his stomach. He had eschewed polite society his entire life, hating its hypocrisy and vapid politeness, only to end up here, dragging his heels all the way to the altar with the catch of the season.

The coach swayed more furiously as the steady knocking was replaced by loud, determined thumping, along with a muffled demand for release. Alec sighed and replaced his watch in an inner pocket. "I suppose we can spare ten minutes, but no more. Have the horses changed, Johnston. They've had to fight this damnable mud the entire way."

The old groom shook his head. "Ye shouldn't have waited so long to plan yer nuptials. Pushin' yer luck a mite far, if ye ask me."

"It was Grandfather's wish I marry—not mine," Alec replied curtly, peeling off his gloves.

"As crusty as the old lord, ain't ye? There weren't nary a thing ye could do with him neither, once he set his mind on somethin'." The groom eyed the wildly rocking coach. "Though ye may have met yer match."

"I can handle Therese Frant," Alec said shortly.

Johnston snorted his disbelief. "I'll order ye a nice

stiff drink whilst the horses are bein' changed. Ye'll be needin' it."

Alec nodded and the old groom shuffled into the inn, wisps of night fog swirling about his boots. Steeling himself, Alec turned toward the coach. Better to get it over with, and quickly. Fortunately, he knew exactly how to deal with his bride-to-be.

Therese Frant was far from the demure innocent she presented to society. Too many times since she'd discovered the extent of his inheritance, the chit had attempted to drag him into a secluded alcove and plaster herself against him.

Therese's mother, a notoriously lax chaperone, did little to stifle her daughter's high spirits. Instead, the duty of keeping a watchful eye on the sensual Therese fell to a cousin of some sort, a plain dab of a female who took her duties so seriously that members of the *ton* had dubbed her the "Frant Dragon." Peering through her thick spectacles, the Dragon did what she could to quell Therese's propensity toward ruin.

A pity, Alec thought tiredly. Had Therese been involved in a scandal, he could have convinced the dry, dusty executors of his grandfather's will to overturn the requirements. But it was too late now. He would have to marry the tiresome girl.

He yanked open the carriage door and grabbed Therese by the wrist, pulling her into his arms. She tumbled from the coach, her bonnet sliding forward across her eyes. It was too dark to fathom her expression beneath the wide brim, but he knew what he would see— china-blue eyes glittering with petulant anger, a rosebud mouth twisted in rage.

To halt her angry tirade before it began, he pushed back the bonnet and covered her mouth with his. To his surprise, a trill of raw, sensual excitement jolted through him.

Therese must have felt something different, too, for

she stood as rigidly as a soldier braving a firing squad. Usually she moaned with pleasure at his embraces and clung with the stranglehold of a limpet. *Maybe she is nervous about the wedding.*

"Kiss me," Alec murmured against the silk of her cheek. She wore a new fragrance. Light and bewitching, it mingled appealingly with the rain-fresh air and swirled along his senses. His body tightened. Perhaps there would be some benefits from this arrangement, after all. "You smell like heaven. Kiss me, sweet Therese."

She kicked him. Hard.

"Owww!" Alec yelled, instantly releasing her. He bent to rub his shin.

And froze.

One of the many things his vain bride-to-be prided herself on was her dainty feet. The shoes that met his eyes were not dainty. Large and tightly laced, the heavy black boots reminded him of his old governess.

The implication hit him like a cannon shot.

This wasn't Therese.

He had eloped with the wrong woman.

He straightened abruptly, the pain in his shin forgotten. "Who in the hell are you?"

"I might ask you the same question," his prim attacker stated flatly.

Alec grabbed the impostor by the arm and pulled her toward the inn, where light flooded the yard. Her mouth thinned with annoyance, but she made no protest, merely stared back at him with a stern frown.

If Lady Therese Frant ever had an exact opposite, this woman would have been it. Instead of artfully arranged golden curls, the impostor's hair was light brown. The remains of a severe hairstyle fell in tortured loops about a narrow, angular face. Slim and flat, her figure offered a stark contrast to the lush, rounded curves Therese so delighted in flaunting.

All in all, the impostor was thin, brown, and plain.

The only good features she possessed were an appealing wide mouth and a pair of thickly lashed green eyes.

She squinted. "I had to take my glasses off." Her flat accent rubbed Alec's frayed nerves. "The coach ride was too bouncy by half."

"You're a damned colonial."

"I am *not* a colonial. I am an American."

There was something disturbingly familiar about that scowl. Alec frowned. If he imagined her with the missing spectacles, her mousy brown hair pulled into tight braids about her head, he could almost. . . .

He groaned. "Damnation! You're the Frant Dragon!"

An unbecoming red blossomed in her thin cheeks.

"Did she put you up to this?" he demanded furiously.

"Who? Put me up to what?" She leaned forward and squinted. "Are you bosky?"

"Am I *what*?"

"Disguised. Inebriated. Drunk." She regarded him speculatively. "Drunk or a bedlamite. You must be one or the other."

"I am neither drunk nor crazed," he said in a stiff tone, glaring at her.

"You must be," she insisted, "unless you normally kidnap women, then yell at them in posting yards."

To her dismay, Julia Frant suddenly knew why certain members of the *ton* called the viscount "Devil" Hunterston. His handsome face could harden into white fury on a moment's notice, his gray eyes glinting like liquid silver.

"You have just botched an elopement, not a kidnapping," he said in a chipped-ice voice. "Therese was supposed to be in that carriage."

Julia swallowed a surge of disappointment. Of course he had thought she was Therese. No one would ever bother to kidnap, then kiss, plain, simple Julia Frant. "I thought you were a hackney," she said apologetically.

"A hackney? Look at that carriage! Does it look like a hackney?"

She squinted at the blurry blob. "It did in the rain," she said finally.

He made a strangling noise. "Where is Therese?"

"At the Hadmores' musicale. She went with Lady Satterley."

"That damned little cat!"

"Perhaps she forgot," Julia offered.

"Not bloody likely. When I find her—" He stopped, clenching his hands.

A stab of pity clutched her. No doubt both his pride and heart were crushed. Her cousin enjoyed that sort of thing, making men suffer. Therese was probably at the musicale now, laughing behind her fan.

Julia peered up at him and stifled a sigh. Therese was a fool. Viscount Hunterston was beyond handsome. His was an unforgettable face, strong and aristocratic, with an arrogant slash of brows that gave him a darkly saturnine look.

Known as a reprobate, a scoundrel and a rake, he rarely followed the dictates of polite society. He freely discoursed with the most ragged edges of the demi-monde, frequented gaming hells, drank to excess, and engaged in a wide variety of sinful pastimes, all with a flagrant disregard for common decency. In fact, it was a shock to see him so obviously sober.

No man had ever needed reforming more than Devil Hunterston.

Julia cleared her throat, wondering what she should say to ease the moment. After a brief struggle, she blurted out, "It's a fine night, isn't it?"

His brow lowered. "Of course. It's rained for the last three hours nonstop, the roads are atrocious, and I've just lost the greatest fortune ever bequeathed on English soil. Other than that, I think the night is particularly fine."

Julia planted her hands on her hips. "Perhaps I should remind you that it has been a difficult evening for me, too. I've been kidnapped, tossed about in a poorly sprung carriage, rudely handled, and yelled at. It's enough to cause heart palpitations."

After an astonished moment, a reluctant smile tugged at the corners of his mouth. Her heart gave a strange leap at the sight.

"Forgive me," he said. "I am behaving abominably." He cast a swift glance around the yard. "Perhaps we should finish this conversation indoors."

"I really should—"

"I'm having fresh horses put to," he interjected smoothly, taking her elbow and propelling her toward the door.

"But I—"

"Lord Hunterston!" said the innkeeper, pouncing on them as soon as they crossed the threshold. "Yer man just announced yer arrival."

The viscount herded Julia into the front parlor. The innkeeper followed, reeking of garlic, his damp face ablaze with welcome. "Tom Bramble, at yer service. I've mixed up some hot rum punch. Now ye and her ladyship can rest yer pegs by the fire." He grinned with the air of one preparing to confer a long promised treat. "Would ye like some supper? We've rack of lamb, goose tarts, jellied calf tongue—"

"Goose tarts are her ladyship's favorite," the viscount interrupted. "She could speak of nothing else the entire way here."

"I did n—" Julia began only to be cut off by Alec's dark glance. "Oh," she said lamely, loosening her bonnet ribbons. "Indeed. Goose tarts. I just love them."

"Do ye, now?" said the landlord, eyeing Julia with an interested gaze. "Who'd have thought the gentry would be so fond of goose tarts?"

Alec held the door open and waved Bramble into the

hall. "Amazing, the things you discover. Pray inform us when supper is ready." Before the man could open his mouth again, the viscount firmly closed the door.

"Why did you tell him that?" Julia demanded, laying her bonnet on a nearby table. "I hate goose tarts." She glanced around the room, wondering what sort of romantic tryst the handsome viscount had planned for her beautiful cousin. Sparsely furnished, the parlor had the look of a hastily converted taproom. Julia didn't know whether she was relieved or disappointed.

The viscount strode to the table and poured himself a drink from the steaming bowl of punch. "If I hadn't told that fool you preferred goose tarts, he would have bored us all evening with a list of the indigestible fare offered at this posting house."

"Of course," Julia agreed, though her mouth watered at the thought of a tasty rack of lamb, with perhaps just a sprig of mint. She hadn't had time to eat, as she had already been running late before she'd even climbed into the viscount's carriage. At the thought of her missed meeting, she almost groaned aloud. The Society had met without her.

Stifling her impatience, she said, "I must return to London as soon as possible."

"Will they have missed you yet?"

The Society for Wayward Women would miss her badly. She was newly in charge of the Funds Committee, a position she had fought long and hard to earn. But the viscount had no way of knowing that.

He was really asking about her aunt and cousin. That was a simpler answer, though hardly to her credit. Neither would notice her absence unless a pressing need arose for a new packet of embroidery thread or a flounce came loose from a frock. But she wasn't about to admit such a lowering fact. "Of course they'll be looking for me," she lied.

A shadowed smile crossed his face. "I beg your pardon, Miss . . . er . . . Frant."

Julia pulled her spectacles from her reticule and set them firmly on her nose. She wasn't surprised he didn't remember her name. Few people did. "You may call me Julia."

He looked surprised, but quickly covered it with a rakish grin that sent a wave of weakness straight to her knees. "I forget you are an American. Allow me to introduce myself. I am—"

"Viscount Hunterston," she interrupted. "I met you before. At the Seftons' ball." He frowned as if puzzled and she added helpfully, "And the Montcastles' fête, the Markhams' breakfast, the Jollets' musicale, and . . ." She felt the heat rise in her cheeks at his amazed expression.

His soft laugh was the most beautiful sound she had ever heard.

"I am beyond reclaim," he said with a rueful shake of his head.

"No one is beyond reclaim."

His disturbing smoke gray gaze slid across her, lingering on her mouth and bosom. Julia felt the heat of his glance as surely as if he'd touched her. Her skin tingled at the thought of his hands sliding where his gaze had rested; up her arms, across her shoulders, and down her—

"May I get you a drink, Miss Frant?" he asked abruptly. "Perhaps I could take your pelisse?"

Julia clutched the buttoned front even closer and shook her head. "No, no. It is quite cold in here." Or it would have been, if she hadn't indulged her reckless imagination in the most wanton manner.

The viscount regarded her for a moment through half-closed eyes. His gaze darkened. "You may be chilled," he murmured, "but I find I am quite the opposite."

A delicious shiver traveled up her spine. Surely he wasn't flirting with her. No one *ever* flirted with her.

"You still have your coat on," she pointed out. "It's much thicker than mine."

After a surprised moment, he chuckled. "No doubt that is why." Setting his mug on the mantel, he shrugged out of his voluminous greatcoat and tossed it onto a chair.

Julia was immediately aware of her own frumpy appearance. Devil Hunterston might be a scoundrel, but he dressed with a quiet elegance that belied his immoral nature. An intricately tied cravat sported a single ruby that flashed wickedly in the careful folds. His coat of blue superfine stretched across his broad shoulders, while the excellent fit of his pale yellow breeches made Julia blush.

Though no supporter of male excesses in attire, she had to admit he looked handsome. Handsome and dangerous. "I should leave," she said, suddenly breathless.

The viscount recovered his tumbler. "Pray have a seat, Miss Frant. We'll leave as soon as I find a way to deal with this mess."

She thought about asking the landlord if she could hire a hack, but hesitated. Behind the viscount's rakish façade, she sensed a hint of desperation. Whether he knew it or not, he needed her. Besides, she told herself firmly, there was no sense in making a scene. She was seven-and-twenty years old, far too advanced in age to worry about sitting in a parlor for a pleasant half-hour with a known rake. Julia perched on the edge of the chair closest to the sputtering blaze.

The mantel clock chimed the quarter hour and the viscount stared at it as if transfixed. "Damn, damn, damn." Scowling, he downed his drink in one swift motion.

She lifted her brows in disapproval. "Whatever is bothering you, imbibing that lethal concoction won't help."

"Nothing can help now," he said with a faint sneer. "Thanks to your minx of a cousin."

Julia sniffed and he laughed, pouring another tumbler of punch. He crossed the room and held it toward her. The faint aroma of nutmeg and cinnamon made her stomach grumble eagerly, but she shook her head.

Amusement curved his mouth. "A prude, Miss Frant?"

"No. I can't hold my drink. It's a curse of the family, you know."

"An excellent reason, then, to drink more."

Without giving her time to remonstrate, he pushed the tumbler into her hand. Her fingers slid around the warmed metal and she welcomed the curls of steam that rose to tickle her nose. She would just hold it until it cooled and then set it on the table. Surely there was no harm in that.

The viscount sank into the chair opposite hers and stretched his legs toward the weak embers. A blackness hung about him that Julia had never witnessed. And she'd had many opportunities to observe the dashing and dissolute viscount. More than he would ever know.

"I can't help you if I don't know what's happened," she stated firmly.

His gaze dropped to his tumbler and he stared into it as if seeking answers. "There's not much to tell."

Her heart ached at the darkness she saw reflected in his face. "I might be able to help. Two heads are better than one."

He regarded her thoughtfully, then shrugged. "Why not? I have all the time in world now." He leaned his head against the high back of his chair and sighed. "My grandfather was determined to prove the error of my ways."

Apparently the viscount's grandfather was a man of some intelligence, Julia thought approvingly.

As if reading her thoughts, the viscount's silver eyes

glinted. "You may not know this, but some call me wicked."

"Among other things." At his astonished expression, she hurried to add, "Of course, it's probably all untrue."

The viscount chuckled. "Unfortunately, it's probably much too true." His amusement faded. "All of us, children and grandchildren, were a disappointment to my grandfather."

"Surely you are being overly harsh."

"Am I? Grandfather turned my uncle out without a penny for marrying a woman who had . . ." His gaze flickered over her. "Shall we just say she had unusual appetites?"

"Oh," said Julia, wondering what that meant. She caught the dark gleam in his eye and hastily asked, "And your mother?"

"My mother fancied herself in love with an impecunious Scotsman who possessed no land, no money; nothing more than a tenuous claim to a dubious title. She eloped."

"She must have been deeply in love."

He scowled. "She was seventeen and wild to a fault. When she disappeared, Grandfather was devastated. He searched everywhere. He finally found them, living in a state of poverty that defies description." His gaze dropped to the sputtering fire. "My parents died shortly afterward."

"So your grandfather raised you."

"Yes. Six months ago he died and left me his fortune. My cousin Nick inherited the title and the estate, though it is heavily tied up." Alec's mouth thinned. "Grandfather knew my cousin too well to leave it unprotected."

Julia wrapped her hands more securely about her mug. "What does all of this have to do with Therese?"

"In order to inherit the fortune, I have to marry before my next birthday and live in society for a year completely without scandal." His mouth curved in a self-derisive smile. "Grandfather feared I was too wild and restless."

"He probably heard about all your lightskirts," Julia said, breathing in the spicy steam from her own cup.

"Lightskirts?" he choked.

"Or the gambling," she said with a helpful nod.

A crooked grin tugged at his mouth. "You seem to be up on all of the gossip, Miss Frant."

"There's little else to do, sitting with the other chaperones. How much time do you have left?"

The viscount glanced at the clock. "Less than two hours."

She blinked at him. "*Two hours*? And just how long have you known of the conditions of your grandfather's will?"

"Since the day he died."

"But that was six months ago!"

"I kept hoping that something would happen to stave off this nightmare." He ran a hand through his black hair, one lock dropping back across his forehead. "But nothing did."

Julia curled her hands tightly about the mug to keep from reaching over and smoothing his hair back into place. "May I ask why you chose Therese?"

"The will is very specific. I am to marry the daughter of the late Earl of Covington if I wish to gain the fortune." His mouth curved into a faint smile. "Grandfather was certain marriage would settle my unfortunate tendencies."

"He must not have known my cousin," remarked Julia.

His eyes gleamed with amusement as he chuckled. "He didn't. The Covington lands march ours, and the earl had a marriageable daughter. For Grandfather, it was more than enough."

Julia tried to suppress the relief she felt at the news that the handsome viscount had not been head over heels in love with Therese. "Who inherits the money, if you don't?"

"My cousin, Nick Montrose."

"The new Earl of Bridgeton? He's been whispering to Therese a lot lately." She frowned, catching herself just before she took a sip of the punch. "It wouldn't surprise me if they were in it together. Forgive me for saying this, but Therese has always wanted to be a countess, and your title, while very nice, cannot compare to an earl's."

Alec slammed his fist onto the arm of his chair with such force, Julia started. "Damn them!" he snarled. "May they rot in hell for playing such a trick!" He cursed again and tossed back the remainder of his drink as if it were water.

Julia winced. If he became drunk, no mere kick in the shins would recall him to a sense of propriety. And empty the bowl he would, unless she did something. She lifted the mug and took a deep breath, the scent of cinnamon and cloves making her stomach rumble anew. The warm, spicy wisps of steam beckoned.

She would just drink this one cup. If nothing else, it would be one less cup he would devour. That decided, Julia took a large gulp. The rum spiraled through her and warmed her from head to toe in one delicious swirl. "My, my."

The viscount roused himself long enough to watch her take another sip. "Careful. It's stronger than it seems."

"I am no sheltered child, Lord Hunterston. I am very aware of the indelicacies of life."

"I'm sure you are," he said with a faint sneer. "You probably know every soiled dove in London."

She pointedly ignored his sarcastic tone and took a defiant sip. "I know a few. The Society for Wayward Women has—"

"Good God!" he said, revolted. "You're a reformer!"

"Call it what you like. I work to better the position

of those who are afflicted by the cruel hand of poverty."

"And what, Miss Frant, do *you* know of poverty?"

She gripped the mug with both hands. In the dark days following the deaths of her parents, Julia had come face to face with the realities of being a woman alone with no way to earn a living. The memory still twisted her stomach into a thousand knots, yet she managed to answer evenly, "I know enough to wish to see it ended."

He laughed, the sound jarring in the small room. "We make a lovely pair, don't we, Miss Frant? You, trying to help others, but without the money to make a real difference, and me, trying to help myself, yet with no more success."

She hid her hurt behind a shrug. "I do what I can." She looked down at her mug and wondered what had become of the rest of her punch. There was barely a mouthful left. She peered at the bottom to see if it had a leak, but could detect nothing. Reluctantly, she turned her attention back to the viscount. "Have you seen a solicitor?"

"Dozens of them, the damned leeches." With a bitter smile, he rose and refilled both their tumblers. "It is over. I played the game and lost."

His fingers brushed hers when he handed her the mug. Julia could feel the warmth of his hand through her thin gloves, the touch leaving her yearning for more.

To steady her erratic heart, she took a deep drink. Immensely fortified, she felt as if she could solve every problem. No wonder her father had been so adamant about the medicinal properties of rum. She wondered if anyone had ever thought to bottle it.

"There must be a way 'round this," she announced loudly.

This time his laugh had a touch of genuine humor. "Do all Americans believe they can work miracles, Miss Frant?"

"I was raised to value candor and hard work, Lord Hunterston."

"You *are* a complete contrast to Therese, aren't you?" He leaned a broad shoulder against the mantel, his eyes twinkling a silvery gray.

Julia looked down at her overly large feet with a twinge of regret. There were few things she envied her beautiful cousin, and the questionable attentions of the most notorious rake in London should not have been one of them. But there had always been something, a certain glimmer in his reckless smile, a certain wistfulness in his glance, that made her yearn to know more about him.

As if aware of her thoughts, he sighed restlessly. "We should return to London."

His words brought a moment of panic. Once they left the enchanted confines of the parlor, things would return to normal. He would become the unapproachable, faintly dangerous Devil Hunterston, while she once again faded to obscurity as a lowly chaperone.

Hastily, she downed the few sips left in her mug. "I need more punch."

The viscount raised his brows but agreed. "After today, I may not be able to afford such luxury." He walked to the table, pulled out a bench, and offered a graceful bow. "Will you join me, Miss Frant?"

She stood, noting that the room had taken on a swirling quality that made it difficult to navigate. Fortunately, she managed to make it without tripping over any of the wavering furniture. She sat beside him and held out her mug.

He refilled both tumblers. "We'll have to get more punch." He pushed her mug across the table and reached toward the empty bowl.

A rustling noise halted him and he frowned, removing a crumpled paper from his coat and tossing it on the table. "I won't need this now."

Julia rested her chin on the edge of her mug and

breathed in the spicy sweetness. A warm glow settled around her and the small parlor became cozier and more intimate. She squinted unabashedly at the viscount's profile, noting the length of his lashes and the proud curve of his mouth.

He looked up and caught her gaze. For a split second, she couldn't breathe. Then she found herself adjusting her spectacles and blindly reaching for the paper. "It's a Special License," she said stupidly.

Alec nodded, returning his preoccupied gaze to his mug.

The license was dog-eared and crumpled, with his name scrawled elegantly across the bottom. "Alec Charles MacLean, Viscount Hunterston," Julia mouthed silently.

She sipped her drink. It was, she decided, even sweeter when taken from the bottom of the bowl. The innkeeper must have forgotten to stir it. She swished the punch about her mouth, her idle gaze falling back on the paper. "You didn't write Therese's name out."

"I didn't have time to stop and ask her entire Christian name, so I just wrote 'Miss Frant.'" The viscount shrugged. "It served; the Archbishop did not question it."

Julia waited for him to say more, but he returned to his own dark reflections, his attention sliding away from Julia all too easily. She sighed and pulled her mug across the crumpled license. Maybe the heat from the warmed metal would iron it out.

Her father had always taught her the importance of neatness. She smiled wistfully. Though he had died over five years ago, she thought of him daily. She especially missed his ability to see right to the center of the most difficult situation and point out the one logical answer. It always angered Julia when Therese sneered at her father. It was true he had left England and ignored the position his own father had wished for him, but he had acted with the purest, most noble of intentions. He had acted for love.

Love. An idea slipped into her head with an almost audible *thunk.*

"I know how to help you," she said wonderingly.

Alec lifted his brows, his eyes the color of frosted glass. "How?"

"Simple. Marry me."

Chapter 2

Alec blinked.

"No need to look so astonished," Julia said gruffly. "It makes perfect sense."

He took her mug. "I'll have that fool of a landlord bring coffee."

"I'm not drunk." She lifted her chin with sudden dignity. "Just dizzy."

"Dizzy, eh?" Alec swung his leg astride the bench to face her. Her hair hung to her shoulders in wild disarray and her spectacles sat slightly askew on her nose. He chuckled. "You were right. You can't handle your liquor."

Absurdly pleased, she nodded, her spectacles sliding even further. "I told you so. Told you it was a family weakness, too." Her smile melted into a scowl. "You shouldn't have made me drink."

"I did no such thing."

"You did, too. You kept drinking it yourself. I had to stop you." She blinked like a befuddled owl.

He grinned. "Your concern is misplaced. I've had stronger libations with breakfast."

"Liquor for breakfast and rum for dinner. Bad thing to do. But that doesn't help you." She leaned forward, her cinnamon-flavored breath brushing across his mouth.

19

"You have to marry, and it might as well be me."

"Miss Frant—"

"Your grandfather's will says you have to marry the daughter of the late Earl of Covington, right?"

"Yes, but—"

"Does it expressly state it must be *Therese*?"

An idea glimmered. "The will doesn't mention her by name."

"I didn't think it had, or you'd have filled in the special license correctly."

Alec gripped Julia's arms. Her eyes widened, the green almost mesmerizing. "Julia, listen to me. Was your father once the Earl of Covington?"

Her generous mouth parted in a happy grin. "Yes. For two days." She held up two fingers and stuck them in his face. "Two. Count 'em."

Alec smothered his irritation and captured her slim hand. He'd never seen anyone succumb so thoroughly to alcohol. Under any other circumstances, he would have found it highly amusing. "Why only two days?"

Her mouth quivered, her happiness evaporating into a mist of misery. "He died." She swiped at her eyes with her free hand. "He never wanted the title anyway."

"Why not?"

"Grandfather said some very unkind things about Mama. Called her all sorts of names."

Alec absently stroked the hand that rested so trustingly in his. "He thought of her as an adventuress, did he?"

"Oh, no. As far as Grandfather was concerned, she was *worse* than an adventuress. She was a Methodist. He swore he'd never allow any in the family and threatened to disinherit us all. Papa refused to budge an inch, wouldn't even visit him, though Mama wished him to." Julia chuckled. "Mama used to say the only person more bone-headed than my grandfather was Papa." She lifted her face to Alec to share her amusement, her eyes brimming with merriment, her cheeks flushed a delectable pink.

It was a look Alec had never thought to see on the Frant Dragon. He cleared his throat, wondering how she had so thoroughly escaped his notice. "Are you certain your grandfather didn't disinherit your father?"

"Grandfather died before he could change the will, and Papa inherited it all. But he didn't want it." A shadow passed over her face. Behind her spectacles, her eyes slowly filled with tears, the green shimmering like a mossy stone beneath a crystal clear stream. "After Mama died, Papa didn't want anything."

The tears forcibly reminded Alec why he steered clear of virtuous women. He pulled a handkerchief from his pocket and handed it to her.

"Thank you." She tried to wipe her eyes without removing her spectacles and only succeeded in knocking them further askew.

"It's the rum," he said, slipping her spectacles from their precarious perch on the tip of her nose. Folding them neatly, he tucked them into his pocket. "Even sailors cry when they've had too much."

She gave him a watery smile and he realized how much her spectacles hid. Perhaps that was how she had remained invisible. When one looked at the Frant Dragon, one saw what one expected—plain clothing, an unremarkable face and figure, and little else. Her disguise effectively removed any further desire to discover the color and shape of her eyes, the smoothness of her skin, the firm chin. Truthfully, she wasn't a raving beauty like Therese, but there was a quality about her that was attractive . . . damnably attractive.

As if to belie his thoughts, she blew her nose into his handkerchief. "Papa was never the same after Mama died. He just sat in the dark for hours and hours and barely spoke."

An unfamiliar stirring of sympathy made Alec say,

"Your father must have loved her very much."

He was instantly rewarded with a tremulous smile. The wide mouth parted to reveal straight white teeth. He brushed her cheek and caught a single tear as it slid down the silken skin. Loosened tendrils of golden-brown hair gleamed in the soft light, framing her gamine face.

Of its own accord, his hand wandered down her cheek and hovered near the generous mouth. Just before he grazed the softness of her lower lip with his thumb, he caught her bemused expression. Her gaze glimmered, so innocent and soulful that he felt as if a noose had tightened around his throat. Though he knew the love he saw reflected there was for her parents and not for him, it was still unnerving to face such naked emotion. He dropped his hand.

Damn it, this was no brass-eyed paphian. Julia Frant was a straitlaced reformer who'd attracted his notice merely because she offered a way to fulfill the vow he had made his grandfather. If he so much as kissed her, an innocent gesture he had performed thousands of times with countless women, he had little doubt she would either swoon or indulge in a fit of hysterics.

As if she had read his thoughts, Julia blushed. "Sorry. I didn't mean to turn into a gudgeon."

"No need to apologize," he replied lightly, sliding away from her and standing. "If I'd had as much of that punch as you, I'd be muddled, too. I'll call Bramble and have him bring coffee." He went to the door and opened it.

A man stumbled into the room and sprawled headlong onto the floor, a tangle of muddied boots and livery.

Alec stared down with a stern frown. "Johnston! What were you doing with your ear against the keyhole?"

The groom stood and brushed himself off. "What did ye think I was doin' with my ear agin the keyhole? I was listenin' to ye gettin' caught in the parson's trap like a green 'un." He glanced at Julia from under lowered brows and shook his head. "It's a wild thing ye're about to do, yer lordship. Ye'll end up hobbernoled and not a whit closer to the money."

"When I want your opinion, I'll ask for it. Now, go and bring some coffee. We've only a little more than an hour left, and I don't want to begin this marriage with rumors the bride was too tipsy to stand on her own."

"I hope ye know what ye're doin'. I'd not bet on this scheme if ye franked me the whole amount." Johnston gave Alec a last warning glare and shambled out the door.

Alec knew the groom was right. There was no guarantee that this wild scheme would work, but he had run out of options. It was Julia Frant or no one.

"Who was that?" Julia asked, still staring at the door.

"My groom," Alec said shortly.

She peered at him suspiciously. "He didn't sound like a groom."

"Well, he is one, though he doesn't remember it as often as he should." He hoped Johnston would hurry with the coffee. He knew how to handle most women, but a slightly dizzy Julia Frant, her mouth folded in a prim line and her eyes still wet with tears, was a totally different matter.

"Are you going to marry me?" she asked.

He detected the slightest quiver of her bottom lip. "If we don't, Nick will inherit the entire fortune. I cannot allow that to happen."

For some reason, she appeared disappointed. "I see."

Alec frowned. "Nick is depraved, Julia. He would do irreparable harm with such a fortune." He dropped to the bench beside her and placed his hands on her shoulders. "I stand to inherit seventy thousand pounds a year, Julia. Just think of it."

"S-s-s . . ." She swallowed, looking more sober. "Pardon me. Did you say seventy *thousand* pounds?"

"It will be ours, Julia, if we make it to the vicarage before midnight."

A frown marred Julia's smooth brow. "But . . . the executors have to agree to the claim, don't they?"

"If your father was the Earl of Covington for so much as a second, they will *have* to agree."

She pinned him with a serious green gaze. "And if they don't?"

Alec shrugged, unwilling to say more.

She stared at him for a long, searching moment. "I suppose we could get the marriage annulled if it didn't work out," she offered.

"Of course," he agreed smoothly.

Her brows lifted into a perfect arch that would have matched the curve of her spectacles. She looked like an especially virtuous schoolgirl, unsullied by the greed and corruption of the world. An uncomfortable flicker of remorse rose in his chest. She appeared so virtuous, so . . . drunk.

Alec pushed away the unworthy thoughts. He would honor the pledge he'd made to his grandfather, and to hell with everything else. Besides, it wasn't as if he were forcing the chit into a life of drudgery. If anything, he was rescuing her. Hell, he would even allow her to use some of the funds for her charity work. In a way, that would almost make him as much of a philanthropist as her. He chuckled aloud at the thought of becoming a reformer. *Not bloody likely.*

At his laughter, Julia's color deepened. She stood and faced him, her chin squared in defiance. "This is absurd. It would never work."

The ticking of the mantel clock swiftly marked the time. There would be no soft seduction. Whether she knew it or not, Julia Frant's fate was already decided. "You will marry me, love. One way or another."

She frowned. "One way or another?"

"I could compromise you," he said softly, staring at

her tantalizing mouth. It was amazingly sensual, for all that she tried to press it into a straight, unexceptional line.

"You can't compromise me."

"Why not?" he asked, intrigued at her certainty.

"You don't have time."

He glanced toward the closed door. Somewhere down the hall came the firm tread of a heavy man. Alec pulled Julia toward him until her prudently buttoned pelisse fit smoothly against his waistcoat.

"What are you doing?" she asked in a breathless voice.

He knew what she wanted: soft words, a public declaration, all the noxious dance and parry that society demanded. It was laughable, really, when one considered how few members of the *ton* actually wed for love. Most were on the lookout for a title or fortune, and the practiced words and grandiose gestures were but a mockery.

Without warning, Alec sank his hand into Julia's tousled hair. It gleamed the color of the clover honey his grandfather had so loved, and smelled just as wondrous. Ruthlessly pushing such thoughts aside, he covered her mouth with his.

He expected her to fight, to push him away and then scream. Instead, she moaned and threw herself against him, almost knocking him off his feet. It took a stunned moment to realize she was not going to call for help. She was kissing him back just as wildly, just as passionately, as he could have wished.

Astonished, he almost stopped the kiss right then and there. But she arched against him, her hands pulling him closer and yet closer. A delicious tremor raced to his groin and he felt himself swell and harden. Pure, hot lust slammed into him, causing him to ache with need and desire.

Alec gave himself over to the kiss, running his hands over her back and cupping her intimately against him.

Heat melded them together as he captured and recaptured her sensual mouth. God, she was incredible. So hot. So sweet. So very—

The door thrust open. "Here ye are, m'lord," said Bramble in a cheery voice. "Martha'll have the goose tarts and a nice side of—" The landlord made a choking noise.

Julia's eyes flew open and she struggled to free herself, but Alec held her fast, his senses returning as a look of shocked dismay settled on her face.

The landlord's mouth opened and shut before he stuttered, "P-pardon me, m'lord, I'll just—" The door thudded closed and Alec released his captive, striving to still his harsh breathing.

With a muffled cry, Julia wrenched herself away. Gone were all traces of the rum punch. She shook with fury, her eyes flashing green fire. Putting a hand to her trembling mouth, she said accusingly, "You planned that."

Alec shrugged, running a hand across his own mouth, wondering at how quickly he'd responded to her. He'd just about devoured her where she stood, inheritance be damned. There was just a hint of the wild Frant blood hidden beneath her prim exterior and it was, frankly, exciting as hell.

She glowered, her earlier trust gone. "That proved nothing, except that you are a beast."

He adjusted his cravat with a deft touch, hating the glimmer of hurt in her eyes, hating these circumstances, hating himself. But he owed this to Grandfather, to keep the fortune from falling into Nick's vile pocket. Alec had almost ruined everything by allowing his pride to get in the way. He couldn't let this chance to redeem himself escape.

He met Julia's brittle gaze with a self-derisive laugh. "I've never claimed to be a gentleman, love. You know my reputation. You knew it when you agreed to stay alone with me in this room."

"You are a cad and a reprobate and a bounder," she said furiously.

He approached the fire, careful to keep a distance between them. "Whatever I am does not change matters. Think, Julia, of what you stand to gain."

Alec understood greed as he understood all the vices. They had been his closest companions for more years than he could count. "Think of how your life will change for the better."

"What do you know of my life?" Her voice held a hint of a child's wail that pierced him as thoroughly as any dagger.

He ignored it. While he didn't know her exact circumstances, it took no imagination to guess. "Your life is one of unappreciated servitude. Your cousin and aunt expect you to wait on their every whim, to give up what you have left of your youth. They spare no thought of you or your comfort. And for what? An attic room with no fire and a few cast-off gowns?"

"I don't have an attic room," she said stiffly, though her hand made a telltale motion toward her worn dress. "Aunt Lydia has been nothing but kind to me since I—"

"Kind? Being asked to sit among the chaperones, as if you were a little countrified nobody? A spinster on the shelf? How old are you, Julia?"

"Seven-and-twenty," Julia replied reluctantly, wishing he would stop. Her life was no fairy tale, but it was productive and useful. And with her new position in the Society, she could make even more of a difference.

He advanced on her, a heady combination of masculine beauty and bold determination. "You are young yet, Julia. Only think what it could be like. Gowns and jewels. Your own coach. Servants to wait on your every whim." His voice dropped to a seductive murmur.

"Think of all the projects you could fund if you had the money."

The man had a dangerous knack for finding one's weaknesses and exploiting them to the fullest. After a stilted moment, she asked, "How much will I get?"

A faint smile curved his mouth. "Ten thousand a year, to do with as you wish."

"No," she heard herself answer calmly. "I want half."

Alec's smile slipped. "What?"

"You heard me. Half." And she would spend every last penny on the Society. Her own pain lessened as she thought of all the good she could accomplish with such a sum.

Alec looked stunned. "But we will have a household to maintain, and a—"

"We can do nicely on fifteen thousand a year. More than nicely—lavishly, in fact."

"That leaves me only twenty thousand pounds!"

"And what do you need with that much?"

His face hardened, the lines about his mouth deepening. "You greedy little witch," he said softly. "You are not so different from Therese, after all."

The words flicked across her like live coals, but Julia held her ground. "Therese attempted to trick you from getting the fortune. I am helping you."

His mouth went white with rage. "Helping me? By taking half? This is ludicrous! I have expenses you know nothing about."

"I know enough." She regarded him through her lashes, suddenly struck by the enormous opportunity that dangled within reach. There were more lost souls in the world than those assisted by the Society. Julia had thought for many months now that perhaps, just perhaps, Alec needed rescuing as well. But just like many of the women from the Society, he didn't realize it.

Julia lifted her chin and prepared to do battle. "According to what you've told me of this will, you have to join the strict confines of the *ton* and live without scandal." Her heart pounded like a drum against her chest. "For an entire year."

His stare hardened. "So?"

"So you won't need money for gambling or any other disreputable activities."

"What disreputable activities?" he demanded.

"Opera dancers," she answered succinctly.

He looked as if his cravat had suddenly become too tight. "I cannot believe you listen to such vile gossip."

"Or actresses," she continued undaunted, "or mistresses of any kind."

"Who told you—what—" he sputtered, anger sparkling in his eyes.

"It doesn't matter. I heard it."

He leveled a glare that should have singed the edges of her pelisse. "For your information, I happen to be between mistresses at the moment."

"How convenient. In a year, you may have as many as you please." It was harder to say that one sentence than she would have thought possible, but somehow she managed to make it sound natural.

"Damn you," he swore, his eyes a stormy gray, as bottomless as the roiling ocean.

She could see he wanted to argue, but couldn't. And Julia realized that for once in her life, she was in control. Completely and utterly in control. It was a heady experience.

Still, she mustn't forget the real reason why she was agreeing to this wild scheme—to help the women of the Society and to save Alec. She would be in the perfect position to show him the error of his wicked ways. He was a man who eschewed honorable endeavors, a rake ruled by his base passions, while she. . . . Heat flooded her cheeks anew at the sudden memory of her reaction to his kiss.

Perhaps she wasn't much better. She fervently hoped

he blamed her wanton behavior on the rum punch. She certainly intended to.

But the memory served as a forcible reminder that she had to protect herself from his practiced blandishments.

Catching his cold gaze, she forced herself to say in an even tone, "I have one more term for this arrangement: it is to be a marriage of convenience only."

The viscount stood before her, dark and smoldering, angry enough, she was sure, to have happily shot her. "If I come to your bed, it will be at your invitation," he said icily. "And maybe not even then."

Hurt suffused her, but she managed to nod. "Of course. Do we have an agreement?"

"I don't know," he replied acidly. "Should I forgo whist? Perhaps confine myself only to country dances in case the waltz proves too lively for your tastes?"

"No, I don't think that will be necessary. I've spelled out my conditions."

"And what about *my* conditions?"

That gave her pause, but she managed to say in a credibly calm voice, "I can't imagine you'd have any. I'm not likely to cause a scandal, after all."

"I'm pleased to hear it," he snapped.

Julia glanced at the clock. "We'd better go, or we'll be too late. There's less than an hour left."

After a glowering moment, he swore and stalked across the room to gather his coat. Fury lent his graceful movements a lethal quality. He opened the door and bowed. "After you, my lady."

Clasping her shaking hands and wondering what imp of madness had possessed her, Julia marched out the door.

Chapter 3

The sofa was damned uncomfortable. Alec sat up and rubbed his neck, glad to see the sun streaming across the familiar carpet of his own room. Tired beyond belief, he eyed his bed with a ruminative gaze. The sight of Julia asleep, curled on her side with one hand tucked under her cheek, caused his anger to return in full force.

He wondered for the hundredth time what quixotic notion had made him hesitate to sleep in his own bed. The staff hadn't known to prepare the extra chamber, so his room had been the only one fit to inhabit.

At first, the thought of forcing his wife to sleep in the cold, empty bedchamber had held some measure of charm. But Julia had the benefit of being soundly asleep, not even waking when he'd lifted her from the carriage and carried her into the house. Holding her in his arms, he'd pushed open the door to a guest room and faced the black cold. Then he'd had the misfortune to glance down. Honey-colored hair wisped about her small, white face, her mouth parted in deep slumber. She slept as innocently as a babe, her wide, smooth brow untroubled. Only the deep shadows beneath her eyes belied her tranquil sleep for the exhaustion it plainly was. Without another thought, Alec had gathered her close and turned to his own chamber.

31

So here he sat, the devil of a crick in his neck from trying to fit his six-foot frame on a small sofa, while his wife slept in chaste luxury under his goosedown counterpane.

His wife. He said the words silently, as if tasting them. Whether he wanted to admit it or not, his life had changed drastically. Or at least, he amended, for the space of one year. Of course, with Julia's intolerable demands, that year would seem like a lifetime. Irritation tightened his jaw. Chaste and innocent Julia might be, but she bargained like a fishwife. Alec stood abruptly and jammed his hands into his pockets, disliking the feeling that he had somehow been tricked.

Of course, Julia's perfidy did not stretch to the length of Therese's. Therese had purposefully set out to ruin him, while Julia's only fault had been in taking advantage of a plum opportunity that was too good to resist.

Considering Julia's unfortunate situation, Alec wondered if he could fault her for wishing to better her circumstances, even if it was at his own expense. And despite his ire, Julia had been right in one thing: without her assistance, he would have been left with nothing.

She stirred and turned onto her back, nestling into the pillow. The edge of her skirt slipped from beneath the covers to drape to the floor. The threadbare muslin was a stark contrast to the elaborate material of the counterpane. A twist of disgust rose in him, dispelling his anger further. She was dressed like a commonplace chambermaid. Damn Therese and her selfishness.

Of course, he realized with a sardonic grimace, the same could be said for him. He, too, was using Julia for his own purposes. Though he had blithely promised her an annulment, he knew such a move would be disastrous; her reputation would be in tatters. Society would snicker behind feathered fans and enjoy her discomfort.

He crossed to the bed and looked at her sleeping face. Sighing in her sleep, she smiled, the shadow of a dimple racing across one cheek. Her hair rippled like golden brown satin across the pillows. Against his will, he touched a strand and marveled at the softness.

Her lashes rested on the cream of her cheeks, and her nose, clearly visible without her infernal spectacles, was narrow and patrician. Except for the undeniable sensuality of her mouth, Julia looked as fresh and unspoiled as a country maid.

But there was fire behind that prim exterior. Fire and passion, if her unexpected response to his kiss proved anything.

He rubbed his bottom lip thoughtfully. It was a good thing they were married in name only. A man could get burned by heat like that.

As if she heard his thoughts, she opened her eyes, blinking sleepily.

She had beautiful eyes, he thought idly. Startlingly so.

"Where am I?" she asked in a husky voice.

A smile almost slipped from him. Trust Julia to get straight to the matter of things. "My townhouse. You fell asleep as soon as we left the vicar's. I decided not to wake you."

She struggled to rise, only getting as far as one elbow before pressing a hand to her head, her delicate brows lowering. "Oww."

"I warned you about that punch." Her only answer was to cover her eyes and ease back onto the pillow as if her head was made of the finest crystal.

Alec crossed to the bellpull. He had barely tugged the embroidered rope when the door opened and his valet entered. Alec scowled. He hated it when the servants hovered, and Chilton was the worst of the lot.

The valet was aquiver with curiosity. "Good morning, milord. I took the liberty to request breakfast be served within the half hour." Though he addressed Alec, his bright gaze rested on Julia's prostrate form.

Alec moved in front of Julia. "Bring a bottle of rum."

Chilton hesitated. "I beg your pardon, milord, but . . . did you request *rum*?"

"A bottle of rum and two glasses."

The valet gaped. "Before breakfast? But the mistress . . . I mean, it is quite early and . . . you were just wed . . . surely you don't mean to—"

"Rum," Alec repeated. He opened the door. "And be quick about it."

Chilton's thin mouth pinched with disapproval. "Very well, milord." Outrage evident in every bone in his thin body, the valet marched out.

Alec sighed. What had he been thinking, to offer a place to Grandfather's old retainers?

Julia noted the crease between Alec's eyes, and an overwhelming urge to lay her head on her pillow and cry tightened her throat. It was silly and she knew it. But she was totally, utterly miserable. Her stomach roiled, her mouth was as dry as cotton, and it felt as if shards of glass had imbedded themselves behind her eyelids. She feared if she even moved, she would lose what little control she had. Still, circumstances demanded that she say something. *Anything*.

"The sun's too bright," she managed to croak, sounding so much like a frog that she wished the earth would rise up and swallow her whole, before she made more of a fool of herself than she already had.

Alec raised his brows and Julia placed her hands back over her hot, dry eyes and took deep, cleansing gulps of air. It was ludicrous. Here she was, her first morning as a wife, and all she could think about was how desperately she wanted to retch. "I'll never drink rum again."

Alec crossed to the window and closed the heavy curtains. "Yes, you will. It will settle your stomach enough to eat. I'll have some toast brought later."

Julia shuddered. "No. I don't want toast. Or rum. Especially not rum."

"Trust me. You'll feel better for it."

She didn't even bother to answer, just squenched her eyes closed and prayed for a swift end to her misery. But it was not to be. The longer she lay, the more the room swirled and danced. Nausea hit her in waves. Forcing herself to sit up, she opened her eyes and tried to focus on her surroundings instead of Alec's disturbing presence.

A welcome fire burned in the grate of the elegant room. A small sofa and chair flanked the hearth, a neat table between them. Julia noted Alec's jacket on the back of the sofa, the creased pillows pressed into one corner. It dawned on her that he had slept in the room with her. She looked down at her dress and noted that except for her boots, her clothing was completely intact.

Of course it was. Devil Hunterston had his pick of London's finest. Why would he bother with someone like her? She cleared her throat. "How did I get here?"

"I carried you."

Julia risked a glance at him and then wished she hadn't. His untucked shirt was startlingly white against his golden skin. His hair was in disarray, one inky lock falling across his forehead, while a day's growth of whiskers darkened the strong line of his jaw.

He had never looked so handsome. She wanted to trail her fingers along his jaw and kiss him like. . . .

Oh, God. Like she had before.

The memory of the kiss at the inn flooded back in glaring detail. He had swept her into his arms, determined to ruin her reputation, and she had responded like a seasoned courtesan, clutching him tighter and even opening her mouth beneath his. Her head throbbed anew. Julia groaned and covered her heated face with her hands.

"Do you need a basin?" Alec's voice came from beside her.

No matter how ill she felt, she would not admit to such a paragon of manly beauty that she was in dire danger of being violently ill all over his beautiful blue and gold carpet. She shook her head miserably.

A warm hand came to rest on her shoulder. "Take a deep breath, love. It will pass." Smooth and firm, his voice was as comforting as his touch.

An unfamiliar wave of heat rose through her, blood thrumming a painful tattoo behind her bleary eyes. She wasn't sure what hurt more, her head or her heart, but one of them was dying a slow and agonizing death.

"Damn it! Where is Chilton with that rum?"

Despite the irritation in Alec's voice, his concern was palpable. She wished he would do something evil or debauched so she would have a weapon to fight off her unrestrained reactions.

Instead, the hand on her shoulder slid up to rest on her head, sliding softly through her tousled hair. "Perhaps I should call someone?"

"No," she answered miserably. "Except for you, there is no one."

There was a moment of silence before he replied, "I meant a maid."

"Oh." Her cheeks heated even more and she wondered if a person could expire from sheer embarrassment. Darn the man for making her so ill at ease. Taking a deep breath, she lifted her head. If she were going to expire, she did not want to do it cowering beneath the covers like a ninny. Using every bit of composure she could find, she managed a shaky smile. "I believe I am feeling better."

Alec's silver gaze roamed across her, one brow lifting in polite disbelief. "We should send a message to your aunt. She'll be worried by now."

Julia doubted if either Therese or Aunt Lydia would do more than complain about the inconvenience of her absence, but she wasn't up to explaining such a thing to Alec. He would offer his sympathy and her tattered emotions would dissolve completely.

"I'll write a letter to your aunt," he said abruptly. "I realize this is awkward, Julia. I don't wish you to be uneasy."

The concern in his voice made her want him all the more. Tears welled and she pulled the covers to her face.

"Damn!" he swore. "Where is Chilton?" Alec moved away from the bed.

Julia waited with bated breath for the sound of his footsteps out the door. Instead, he startled her by returning to sit beside her. He thrust a bowl into her lap. "Here."

She dropped the covers to clutch at the porcelain basin and she found herself staring straight into Alec's amazing silver-gray eyes. He was so handsome, smiling down at her, that lock of black hair falling over his forehead. All thought of tears evaporated. "Th-thank you," she stammered.

A faint smile curved his mouth as his gaze roamed over her, lingering on her mouth before coming to rest on the spill of hair over her shoulder.

Julia knew it must look as if a bird had nested in it. If he was looking for flaws, he'd just discovered a treasure trove of imperfections. She was nearsighted, brown-haired, and square-chinned. Add to that mussed hair and horridly wrinkled clothes, and she knew she must look worse than death.

"The rum, milord," intoned Chilton, standing stiffly in the doorway holding a tray with two glasses. Barely a mouthful of liquid rested in the bottom of each.

"I sent for a bottle." Distinct reproof deepened Alec's voice.

The servant squared his shoulders. "Surely you didn't need more than this, milord. Especially since her ladyship has not yet risen."

Julia squinted at the man. Alec caught her look and said, "I should have introduced you. Lady Hunterston, may I present Chilton, my valet. I inherited him from my grandfather."

It took Julia a moment to realize *she* was Lady Hunterston. She managed a weak smile.

Chilton leaned toward her, his narrow face puckered. For a horrifying moment she thought he would cry. "My lady, allow me to be the first to tell you how much we have looked forward to the day when—"

"Master Alec!"

All eyes turned to the door. A stout woman, dressed in a neat, dark gown and carrying a laden tray, beamed at Julia. An impressive ring of keys proclaimed her to be the housekeeper. She bobbed a curtsey that set her brassy yellow hair into a frenzy of quaking curls. "I brought your breakfast, m'lord. I thought mayhap you and her ladyship would like to have it up here, all cozylike."

The housekeeper placed the tray on the table before the fire. The pungent aroma of fresh bacon wafted across the room, and Julia clutched her bowl tighter.

Chilton set his tray on the nightstand with an audible *thump*, his thin mouth folded in disapproval. "Mrs. Winston, I told you his lordship *preferred* to eat in the breakfast room."

The housekeeper sniffed. "So you did. But seeing as how his lordship is newly wed and all, I thought it best to bring it *here*." The housekeeper plopped her hands on her hips, a pugnacious challenge in her face. "You overstep your boundaries if you think to tell me when and where to set the table, Mr. Chilton."

Alec caught Julia's questioning gaze and gave a deprecating shrug. "The housekeeper, Mrs. Winston."

"Did you inherit her, too?"

He nodded morosely.

Mrs. Winston's broad front teeth appeared in a wide smile. "I've known Master Alec since he was a little thing, barely old enough to stand up and gnaw on the curtain tassels. He was a lovely child, all black curls and big gray eyes."

"That will be enough, Mrs. Winston," Alec said, his face as dark as a cloud.

Undeterred, the housekeeper launched into a catalogue of "Master Alec's" childhood escapades that made Julia's head swim anew. Under normal circumstances she would have loved to hear anything that had to do with Alec, but this morning all she wanted was a few minutes of privacy. Just her and her basin. Alone.

Mrs. Winston chuckled merrily. "Oh, Master Alec was as full of mischief as they come. Why once, he climbed into the coal shuttle, as naked as—"

"Thank you, Mrs. Winston," Alec interrupted hastily, his color suspiciously high. He stood and herded the servants toward the door. "I believe we should all retire and allow Lady Hunterston some time alone. She had a very hectic day yesterday and no doubt she would be the better for some solitude."

"Yes," agreed Julia fervently. "And a bath, please." She remembered how her father swore by the beneficial effects of a hot bath after a night of overindulgence. Right now, she could think of nothing more pleasant.

Alec halted by the door and glanced back. He hesitated, raking a hand through his hair. "Julia, I know you don't feel well, but we must visit the solicitors today."

"Julia?" said the housekeeper, turning on her heel and coming back into the room. Her wide gaze traveled from Alec to Julia.

Chilton peered over her shoulder, looking so like a goose, Julia expected him to begin honking. Instead, he said, "Good heavens! We thought you were to marry Miss Therese Frant. Isn't this. . . ." He trailed off as a bright red covered his cheeks. "Oh, dear."

Alec swore softly. "This is Miss *Julia* Frant, Therese's cousin."

Both servants stared at Julia with wide, astonished eyes.

She thought about putting the basin over her head and crawling out the door. If it wouldn't have made her ill to move, she would have done just that.

After a tense moment, Mrs. Winston gave a swift nod. "I never cared for the name Therese. Too French, to my way of thinking."

"I'm not French," said Julia. "I'm an American."

The valet gasped and clapped his hand across his mouth. The outraged gesture seemed to decide Mrs. Winston even more firmly. "American or no, my lady, I'm glad to have you here. His lordship needs someone who can take care of him. He's a bit lost, you know. Gambling and drinking and I don't know what else—"

"Mrs. Winston." Alec's frosty gaze narrowed on the plump housekeeper.

"There now, Master Alec, you know you've picked up some nasty habits since your grandfather died. A great pity it is, too."

Julia had to admire the way Alec held his temper. Considering one of his servants had just scolded him as if he were no more than six years of age, he showed remarkable self-control.

He merely glowered and said carefully, "Mrs. Winston, I'm sure Lady Hunterston would prefer us to leave her to her own reflections rather than burdening her with ours." He held the door wider. "You, too, Chilton. There must be duties that require your attention elsewhere."

Chilton looked wounded. "But, milord—"

"Elsewhere," Alec repeated.

The valet straightened his narrow shoulders and marched out the door. Mrs. Winston bustled about the breakfast tray, making minute adjustments to the placement of the silver and china before breezing toward the hall. She stopped by Alec. "Don't keep her ladyship from her breakfast. She'll feel more the thing after a bit of tea." The housekeeper flashed an arch look up at Alec before adding with a mischievous grin, "And we don't want her to go and tire herself, do we?"

Julia noted Alec's reddening cheeks as he nodded mutely. Satisfied she had finally reduced her charge to befuddled silence, the housekeeper whisked herself out of the room, humming merrily. Alec closed the door with such force, Julia winced.

An awkward silence filled the room. Julia cleared her throat. "You have very interesting servants."

Alec sighed and leaned against the door, crossing his arms over his open shirt. "Not one of them is capable of remembering I'm no longer a child."

"They're fond of you."

"Fondness like that can kill."

"I think they are charming."

"You haven't met Burroughs yet, my grandfather's butler. He waits up for me every night with a glass of warmed milk."

She pressed a hand to her stomach at the thought of warmed milk. "Do you drink it?"

"Never. I pour it out the window." The corners of his mouth curved, his eyes crinkling with sudden mirth. "The plum tree in the garden is dying a slow and agonizing death."

Julia offered a weak smile. "I'd rather die by warmed milk than rum."

His face softened. "Drink the rum and make yourself eat something. You'll feel better."

"A bath will help, too."

"Don't soak too long. We must meet with the solicitor today and present him with proof of our marriage." He pushed away from the door with a smooth gesture and opened it.

"Alec." Her call startled her as much as it did him.

He regarded her intently, his lashes shadowing his eyes until they appeared almost black. The sight sent a shiver through her that had nothing to do with the coolness of the room. Desperately, she cast about for a safe topic of conversation. "Must we meet the solicitor today? My dress is sadly crumpled."

His gaze lingered on her wrinkled skirts. "I'll send Mrs. Winston in to see what she can do."

Julia smoothed the creased muslin. "Perhaps it can be ironed."

Alec nodded, his distant expression telling her he had already dismissed her from his mind. "Then I'll meet you in the front parlor at noon."

He swung the door wide. As he stepped to the threshold, she blurted, "Alec, where are you going?" She regretted the words as soon as she said them.

His back stiffened. "You may possess half my fortune, my lady, but you do not possess me."

"No, of course not. I didn't mean to—"

"I will meet you in the front parlor at noon." Without another word, he left, closing the door firmly behind him.

Sobs threatened. Julia blindly reached for one of the glasses of rum and gulped. The liquid stung her throat, burning away the nausea and tears. She emptied the glass, then returned it to the tray and picked up the other.

The rum caught the sliver of morning sun that escaped through the drapes. An explosion of sparkles glittered deep in the glass. There was something mesmerizing about the beauty of the amber liquid.

With the greatest of will, Julia set the glass back on the table and rubbed her forehead. "Beautiful as those sparkles are, they make my head ache even worse."

Rather like Alec. Being with him was the most gratifying, exciting thing that had ever happened to her. But as with the amber sparkles, there was a price to pay. Though she wished it otherwise, she knew she was in danger of succumbing to his dark charm. And nothing would drive him away quicker than such a foolish action on her part.

The handsome viscount was an enigma. Despite his depraved ways, he had proved himself to be an honorable man. Nothing else could explain why he had slept on the sofa last night or allowed his grandfather's bothersome servants to inhabit his household.

Therein lay the problem, Julia decided. The Devil Hunterston she had secretly sighed over from afar had been safe because he was beyond her reach. But the Alec MacLean who'd surreptitiously poured warmed milk out the window to spare the feelings of an elderly retainer was another matter altogether. "An entirely, altogether more difficult matter, indeed," she said aloud.

Julia pushed the basin aside and stood. She would just have to keep her heart under tight control. The opportunity to help so many destitute women was not something she could let slip away because of a silly infatuation. She would drink her tea, soak in a hot tub, and gather her wits by the time the clock struck the noon hour.

Not that she had much choice, Julia thought wryly. She had, after all, made a deal with the devil.

Chapter 4

"**Y**ou don't look like a man who has just donned wedding shackles," drawled a deep, familiar voice.

"Lucien," Alec exclaimed.

Lucien Devereaux, the notorious Duke of Wexford, stood with one broad shoulder against the study door, an unlit cheroot dangling from his lips. His green gaze rested on the coat and hat Burroughs had just handed Alec. "On your way out?"

"Yes, to see you. I'm devilish glad you stopped by." Alec turned to the butler. "Why didn't you announce Wexford? It would have been damned inconvenient if I had gone to his lodgings only to discover he was here."

A pained expression washed over the butler's thin countenance. "I would never presume to tell you whom you should visit, my lord."

The duke chuckled. "Very proper, Burroughs. Are you sure I can't hire you away? I'd pay you twice the salary."

"Thank you, Your Grace. Though the offer is tempting, I feel his lordship would sorely miss my services."

Two pair of eyes pinned Alec—one calmly expectant, the other brimming with laughter. Alec tried not to scowl. "Of course I'd miss you, Burroughs. Though I'd not miss you forgetting to tell me when we have visitors."

The butler allowed a small smile to curve his mouth. "I apologize for any inconvenience, sir. His Grace arrived a half hour ago and let himself into the parlor, demanding brandy. As he was still attired in his evening dress and made no request that I notify anyone of his presence, I could only assume he was in no condition to visit and merely sought refuge from unwanted persons."

Lucien choked back a laugh. "As I said, very proper."

The butler's impassive stare never flickered. He inclined his head to Alec. "Shall I take your coat and hat, my lord?"

Conscious of the desire to pull his own hair, Alec merely nodded.

The butler took the garments and disappeared down the corridor.

"Don't be too hard on him," said Lucien. "It was inexcusable of me to appear thus attired." He held the door to the study wide. "Shall we test the quality of your brandy?"

Alec forced a smile and entered the room. "They are the worst trained servants. Yet every time I think to correct them, I remember all the times they helped me out of scrapes as a child."

"Noble intentions are a damned inconvenience." Lucien crossed to the mantel and leaned a broad shoulder against it, flicking Alec an amused glance. "Thank God I don't suffer from such a malady."

Alec lifted a brow. "No, you are completely untroubled by the plight of others, aren't you?"

"Hardly; I have three aunts and a sister who make incessant demands on my time." The duke flashed a lopsided grin. "That is quite enough, let me assure you."

Alec regarded Lucien thoughtfully. The duke's private life was something of a mystery. Within two months of inheriting his title and a heavily encumbered estate, Lucien had married an heiress who was as wild as she was beautiful. It had been painfully obvious from the beginning that the marriage was doomed to failure. Brazenly, and without regard for either her station or her husband's pride, the new duchess flaunted a succession of disreputable lovers and engaged in reckless escapades that had shocked even the most jaded of the *ton*.

Her behavior became more and more erratic until Lucien had been forced to take his volatile wife to the country and place her under the care of a physician. Two months later, news of the duchess's death reached London. Rumors abounded, though the accepted belief was that she had killed herself in a fit of madness.

Of even more interest had been the duke's unexpected reaction. Despite impassioned pleas from his many female relatives, Lucien never again appeared in any color other than stark, unrelenting black.

Alec caught the vexed glint in his friend's hard green gaze. "Lady Wexford after you to marry again?"

"My aunt exceeded herself last night. She invited not one, but three eligible chits, all smelling of flowers and sizable dowries, to what was supposed to be a family dinner."

That had been Alec's one advantage in possessing an unacceptable title and a lascivious reputation: no one attempted to force a dowdy daughter on him. Of course, all that had changed once it had become known he was to inherit a fortune. An astonishing number of highbrow mamas, who once had thought nothing of giving him the cut direct, now thrust their bony, freckled daughters into his path like the most brazen flesh peddlers.

He caught Lucien's frowning regard and forced a smile. "Were any of your dinner companions beauties?"

"None would be quiet long enough for me to tell. They all chattered like magpies. I didn't get to swallow a mouthful during dinner, what with this one asking me if I liked to ride and that one asking if I preferred to live in the country or in town."

"I'm surprised you stayed."

A faint smile curled the hard mouth. "I didn't. I made my escape out a library window when one of the young ladies began caterwauling at the pianoforte." Lucien scowled at Alec's chuckle. "Oh yes, you can afford to laugh, now that you are safely wed."

Alec's laughter died at the reminder. He was married. That fact had been borne to him all too well this morning when Julia had asked where he was going. He supposed it had been an innocent enough question, originating from genuine curiosity rather than a wish to curtail his activities. What had made it so unpalatable was the realization that as his wife, Julia had every right to make just such an inquiry.

Lucien pulled a tinderbox from his pocket and struck a match. With careless grace, he lit a cheroot and tossed the match into the fire. "Tell me, how do the wedding shackles fit?"

"Damned tight, and uncomfortable as hell."

"I warned you not to pursue that path." The duke's gaze darkened. "Marriage is a difficult road, even under the best circumstances."

Alec wondered if his friend was referring to the consequences of his own failed marriage, but the shuttered look on the duke's face kept him from asking.

"I had no choice. I promised Grandfather to keep the money from Nick." A flicker of distaste rose at his cousin's name. At one time, he and Nick had been inseparable and he'd thought the world of his older cousin. But those times were long gone.

Lucien blew a cloud of smoke. "You are too concerned about your cousin."

"Don't underestimate him, Luce. He can be deadly."

"So you keep telling me." The duke shot him a hard

stare. "You know, Alec, there are other ways to obtain money."

Alec took a chair near the fire and stretched his legs before him. "I didn't do it for the money, Luce. You know that. I made a promise to my grandfather."

"You are too stiff-necked for your own good," the duke growled, his brows lowered. "I hate to see you sacrifice your happiness for the misguided wishes of a dead man."

"You did the same thing."

"And regretted it. I have no desire to see you make the mistakes I've made."

Alec said nothing. How could he explain to Lucien, who possessed family, a respected title and an incontestable position in the *ton*, that all Alec had was his word? His word and now, thanks to his grandfather and Julia, a fortune. Of course, there had been a price for that fortune, one that he dared not examine too closely.

An expression of concern crossed Lucien's face. "You look as blue as a megrim. Though I imagined life with the demanding Therese would pall, I scarcely thought it would hit you quite so quickly."

"Therese is not the problem."

No, Julia was the problem. Every prim, frustrating, indecipherable inch. Alec slid a hand into his coat pocket and closed his fingers around her spectacles. He'd found them in his overcoat and had meant to leave them with her this morning, but had forgotten in his haste to escape.

Lucien flicked the ashes from his cheroot into the fire. "Your grandfather must have been touched in the head to want you to marry such a simpering flirt as Therese. Good God, the chit has been half a pace from ruin since she stepped out of the schoolroom."

The cool steel of Julia's spectacles warmed in Alec's palm. "Lucien, I did not—"

The door opened and Burroughs' thin form stood outlined against the light from the hall, his wispy hair forming a halo. He said in a voice of long suffering, "Lord Edmund Valmont."

A fashionable young man burst into the room, golden hair in disarray about a plump cherubim face. His bottle-green coat sat across ridiculously padded shoulders, the waist tightly nipped in until he resembled a stuffed sausage more than the well-dressed dandy he aspired to be. A florid waistcoat brightened the ensemble, while four rows of huge brass buttons twinkled merrily. Impervious to the stunned expressions of his companions, Edmund rushed forward.

Burroughs favored Edmund's attire with a pained stare before he pulled the door closed behind him.

"Alec!" Edmund cried. "I have been looking all over for you."

Lucien sighed. "What is it this time, halfling? Is the watch after you again? Or has yet another angry husband requested you meet him at twenty paces?"

Edmund waved his hand impatiently. "No, no, no. I have just returned from Lady Chowerton's, and—"

"At this hour of the morning?" Alec lifted his brows. "I take it Lord Chowerton is still repairing in the country."

The youth's round cheeks reddened. "That doesn't matter. Fanny . . . I mean, Lady Chowerton, saw Therese Frant at the Satterleys' musicale last night." He fixed a wide blue gaze on Alec. "She is telling everyone she duped you and left you standing at the altar."

Alec stifled the urge to curse. The little baggage had lost no time in holding him out for ridicule before the entire *ton*. Damn her black soul. If he got his hands on her, he'd shake her until the feathers that filled her little head puffed out her ears.

He caught Lucien's questioning gaze and forced himself to shrug. "That is why I was going to visit you this morning."

Edmund's jaw dropped. "You mean to say it is true? That you and Therese didn't. . . . But then the fortune . . . good God! You must be devastated!"

Lucien arched a dark brow. "Alec, before Edmund begins to imagine you are ready to put a bullet between your eyes, pray tell us what's occurred."

This wasn't the way he had thought to tell it, with Lucien looking as though he were ready to horsewhip Therese, and Edmund leaning forward, eyes aglow as if he sat at Ascot with his horse in the lead. Alec rubbed his neck, where an annoying crick lingered. Nothing about this marriage seemed destined to bring comfort. "I was trying to tell you when Edmund arrived. I didn't marry Therese."

"Then the fortune—"

"Is still mine."

Edmund blinked rapidly. "But how? You spoke with every solicitor in town and they all said there was no way to set the codicil aside."

"Quiet, halfling," Lucien ordered.

The youth sank onto the edge of the settee, his flamboyant waistcoat straining over his paunch. "Well?"

Alec raked a hand through his hair. "I married the daughter of *one* of the late Earls of Covington."

A faint flicker of surprise crossed Lucien's face. Edmund looked thoroughly confused. He tilted his head to one side, the height of his shirt points making it impossible for him to hold his chin at a normal level. "*One* of the late Earls?"

"Therese's father had an older brother who once possessed the title," Alec said shortly.

He hadn't thought to go into even that much detail before seeing the solicitor, but if rumors were already flying about town, he had to stop them and quickly. Marrying had been only one of the conditions of the will. He still had a year of hard labor left. Such an unflattering story as Therese was bandying about was sure to create a furor, and that was exactly what he didn't need.

Edmund scratched the bridge of his nose. "Strange. I wasn't aware Therese had a cousin. Of course, don't know all my cousins, m'self. Just the other day I ran into a gentleman at White's. Couldn't think where I'd seen him before, but I knew I had. It kept nagging at me. Finally, he demanded to know why the deuce I was staring at him. Rude of the fellow, but there it is. I told him I thought I knew him and he said, "You dashed well should, you imbecile. I'm your cousin Bertram." I hadn't seen him in, oh, two years. Not that he's changed much. He's thirty, you know, and—"

"I think we understand your meaning," interrupted Lucien, flicking him an exasperated glance.

Edmund looked relieved. "Good. Only meant to say I never heard of the Incomparable having any cousins other than the Frant Dragon, and there's no way Alec could have. . . ." He trailed off, eyes wide, his weak chin moving soundlessly.

"Yes, I did," said Alec grimly.

"Surely not! You couldn't marry the Frant Dragon!"

"I married Miss *Julia* Frant," Alec said with icy reserve. Though he himself had called her the Frant Dragon on more than one occasion, it was unexpectedly irritating to hear it from someone else.

Edmund's face pinkened. "I didn't mean to offend. She's not really a dragon. Unless, of course, she suspects you have been taking liberties with Therese, and then she can look exactly like a dragon. Once, when I was trying to convince the Incomparable to dance, the Dragon marched right up to me and—"

"Edmund!" Lucien silenced the younger man. "You have said more than enough, as usual." The duke turned to Alec. "Perhaps you can explain how this, er, fortuitous happening occurred."

Alec rose and poured himself a drink from the silver

tray. "There is nothing to explain. I married Julia Frant and that is that."

Lucien regarded him with a heavy-lidded gaze. "And you are convinced her father once held the title?"

Edmund frowned importantly. "Could be a hum to get you to the altar. At her age, she's bound to be desperate."

Not desperate enough to consent to marrying him without half his fortune, Alec thought grimly, returning to his seat with a glass of brandy. "Julia Frant has never been desperate a day in her life."

"She has always struck me as a young lady of singular determination," Lucien said, a quizzical gleam lighting his eyes.

Edmund shuddered. "One of those, eh?" He cocked a brow at Alec. "Mayhap she's fixed on you. You do have the devil of a way with women."

"God, no." Yet for an instant, Alec felt the heat of Julia's mouth beneath his. He shook his head and frowned at the heavy glass in his hand. His wife's prim exterior warred with a passionate nature. He wasn't sure why, but the thought depressed him.

Lucien lifted a brow. "So tell us of this mysterious earl."

Alec took a deep drink. "He left for America after a disagreement with his father and never returned."

"Not even when he inherited the title?" Edmund asked, startled.

The brandy left a bitter taste that perfectly fitted Alec's mood. "He inherited the title two days before his death."

Lucien pursed his lips in a silent whistle. "Playing it close, aren't you?"

Edmund absently tugged on his cravat, mussing the intricate folds. "Seems a havey-cavey sort of way to go about it, marrying a girl whose father was an earl for only a few days. Shouldn't think those high sticklers your grandfather put in charge of the funds would stand for that."

"They must," Alec said. He refused to think of the outcome if they did not.

The duke regarded the glowing end of his cigarillo. "You know, my friend, this may very well have been an act of providence. I can't help but wonder if Julia is not the better choice of the two."

"The Frant Dragon, better than the Incomparable?" exclaimed Edmund. He caught Lucien's minatory glare and added quickly, "So, ah, Alec, what are your plans now?"

Alec set down his glass. "I have an appointment to see the solicitor. I was headed to Lucien's this morning to ask what he thought I should tell the damned man. Pratt is a prosy old fool and I didn't want to shock him with the details."

Edmund grimaced. "He's right, Luce. I went with Alec to that fellow's office last month. Never saw a more Friday-faced individual in my life. When we returned, I was so blue deviled, I couldn't even look at the yellow sauce my new chef had cooked for my eggs, and I am usually fond of sauces."

"Alec, tell the man the truth," Lucien said.

"Even about Therese?"

"Especially about Therese. Perhaps if you can show her true nature to the executors, they will acknowledge that she is not the wife for you. Then, even if they fail to recognize your marriage to Julia, they might be willing to strike Therese's name from that damned will."

Alec leaned his head against the back of his chair and regarded the ornate plaster ceiling. He would never know how his grandfather had located such a parsimonious collection of drudges to serve as executors. Twice he had met with them, and both times he had left feeling as if he had been on trial for high treason. He sighed. "We can only hope."

Lucien raised his brows. "And if the will stands? What will you do then?"

"I will . . ." Alec trailed off, suddenly aware he hadn't really thought what his life would be like once the marriage had taken place. What *would* he do?

It was, he decided sourly, the culmination of a horrendous nightmare. His inheritance had instantly changed him from a carefree pariah to the most sought-after bachelor in London. People clamored for his presence. Earls, dukes, ladies, and lords, now eagerly sought him out, as though they had not previously treated him with ill-concealed contempt, mocking his lowly Scottish title and sneering behind their fans. As the richest man in England, he was suddenly worthy of instant approbation.

In the months that followed this disquieting change, Alec had become even more outrageous: bringing a retinue of soiled doves to the theatre, arriving drunk at every event, and even inviting a common prizefighter to dinner at Carlton House. It should have been amusing, but strangely, Alec found it flat. With such a fortune at his disposal, he could do no wrong. If he desired, he could probably walk naked down Pall Mall and no one would offer a single comment.

But that was not the worst of his problems. Thanks to the codicil on Grandfather's will, he was soon to join the ranks of perfumed pretenders he so despised, nodding and smiling with the best of them.

It was a lowering thought. He scowled into his glass. By God, he would not be the only one discomforted— for every pang and pain he suffered, so would Julia.

He raised his drink to the silent vow and caught Lucien's curious gaze. Alec managed a grin. "There is nothing simpler. Julia and I will set up house and live a life of social boredom for one year, beginning from today."

"But she's the Frant Dra—" Edmund caught himself,

a vivid red reaching to his sandy brows. "It won't be easy."

Alec shrugged. "Julia knows her way about. She was a chaperone."

"No, Edmund is right," Lucien said. "Julia knows how to keep amorous young men from pursuing her cousin. She knows nothing about comportment, conversation, and gentle etiquette. What was acceptable for a slightly eccentric chaperone will not do for the new Viscountess Hunterston."

Edmund leaned an elbow on one knee and rested his round chin in his hand. "Isn't she a reformer of some sort? Someone said something to me about that just last week." He frowned. "Wish I could remember."

"She works with the Society for Wayward Women," said Alec shortly. The quicker it was out in the open, the better.

Edmund sat bolt upright and snapped his fingers. "I remember! Dunston's sister, Lady Nottley, told it to me. Daresay you don't know Lady Nottley, but she is a sharp-tongued harridan, twice your size, Lucien. Used to be married to old man Nottley before she drove him insane. Dunston runs every time he sees her coming. He says she's got a deadly left hook, but I think he could take her on. He's not really fat, just big boned and—"

"Is there a point to this?" asked Lucien acidly.

Edmund looked affronted. "Well, yes. Lady Nottley said Therese was complaining that the Frant Dra—" He swallowed and cast an apologetic glance at Alec. "I mean Lady Hunterston—disappears for hours on end. Said she comes home dirty, her gown all mucked up, looking like a scullery maid. Apparently she visits the slums and don't come home 'til after dark. I don't care what you say, Alec, people're bound to talk if she keeps that up."

Alec scowled. "Nonsense."

"She'll have to stop," said Edmund, matter-of-factly.

"You can't have a scandal and you never know what will put people off."

Alec set his glass on the table. "How could Julia cause a scandal sponsoring a charity? Many members of the *ton* have favorite charities. Lucien's aunts have half a dozen between the lot of them."

"Yes, but they give money," Lucien said. "Much as I hate to say it, the stripling is right. Such odd behavior is bound to cause talk. Do you think you could speak with her? Perhaps warn her off about being so public with her ventures."

"By Jove, that's the very thing," said Edmund, beaming. "No need to raise a dust; just tell her to be more discreet."

From the little Alec knew of Julia Frant, he doubted she would take a hint any better than she took a direct command. He shifted in his chair. "She's very dedicated." Far more than he liked, now that he thought about it. Though he had been married to Julia less than twenty-four hours, he had already discovered she was a woman of incredible determination. From causes to kisses, she committed herself passionately or not at all.

Of all the things he knew about Julia, that scared him the most. For the first time, he wondered how much of his funds would be going to her charity. Far too much, he supposed, feeling glum. He wouldn't be surprised to find that she meant to squander half her portion on such things.

"I don't suppose she'd be willing to find another charity? One that meets in a better part of town?" Edmund saw the answer in Alec's flat stare and sighed his sympathy. "I know how it is. Once a female gets a maggoty notion in her head, there's no reasoning with her."

"There is also the matter of Therese," Lucien said. "She's bound to cause trouble once she realizes what's happened."

A pucker appeared on Edmund's smooth forehead.

THE ABDUCTION OF JULIA

"You should have seen her last night, crowing like a rooster and looking so smug it was all I could do to speak with a civil tongue."

"I'm not worried about Therese," said Alec impatiently. "Nick is the one to watch. He will stop at nothing to win the fortune."

Lucien blew a ring of smoke and watched it ascend to the ceiling in a lazy cloud. "What our Julia needs is a champion."

"A champion?" echoed Edmund. "Like one of those knights who used to run amuck, riding white horses and challenging people to duels and God knows what else?"

A faint smile curved the duke's mouth. "Nothing quite that drastic. Julia needs someone who has her interests at heart. Someone who will smooth the path for her entry into society."

Alec scowled. "I can do that."

The duke's eyes glinted with amusement. "You, for all your good intentions, have scarcely set yourself up as a model of the *ton*."

Alec swallowed his irritation. Lucien was right. He was not the one to offer Julia the advice she needed to navigate the perils of polite society. He had spent too many years avoiding that very path.

"Perhaps my mother could assist us," Edmund suggested.

Lucien shook his head. "Nay, halfling. As much as I revere your esteemed mother, she'd be hard pressed not to blab the whole to her friends."

"M'mother is a talker, all right. Often thought that's what drove my father to the grave. In his prime, he was as hearty as a horse. Mother was determined to—"

Lucien interrupted. "What we need is someone who knows the importance of being discreet, someone who is already established. Someone who . . ." He trailed into silence, a frown carving deep lines beside his mouth.

Alec leaned forward. "You've thought of someone."

The duke nodded slowly. "There is one person, though it will take much persuasion to win her to our cause."

"Who?" asked Edmund eagerly.

"Lady Birlington."

Alec frowned. "Mad Maddie?"

"What's my great aunt have to do with this?" Edmund demanded.

"If Lady Birlington took Julia under her wing, Therese would never dare sneer at her." Lucien lifted a brow. "No one would."

Edmund rubbed his ear. "Hate to say it, but it's true. I never could understand it. The old lady's rude to everyone and half a slipper shy of a pair, if you ask me. Just last week she called the Duke of York a simpleton. Right to his face, too. And when he attempted to remonstrate, she stared down that beak of a nose of hers until he turned purple and started apologizing as if he'd been the one who had—"

"Lucien, I think you may have something." Alec rose to take a few quick paces about the room. Lady Birlington was something in Julia's style. If anyone would know how to teach Julia to get along, it would be she. Alec felt a stirring of hope. "It just might serve. I'll take Julia to call on Lady Birlington first thing tomorrow."

Lucien rolled his cigarillo between his fingertips. "There's one thing you must do first."

"What's that?" asked Alec, suspicious of the humor that curved the duke's mouth.

"Buy the chit some clothes. The last time I saw the Frant Dragon, she was wearing a dress made of sackcloth."

"Surely Lady Birlington can—"

"Lady Birlington won't sponsor her if she thinks Julia can't carry herself off. The old crow delights in being eccentric, but only so far as it makes her a presence among the *ton*."

"And while you're at it, you really should secure a proper carriage," added Edmund. "That decrepit box you've got will never do if you're to make a splash."

"A splash? Who said anything about making a splash?" protested Alec. He had the feeling his life was beginning to career wildly out of control. "I just want to get through this next year as quickly as possible and get on with my life."

Lucien frowned. "You have to do this thing right, Alec, or you will be playing right into Nick's hands."

Edmund nodded. "You need entry to Almack's, a presentation at Court, and better lodgings." He cast a critical gaze around the room. "This is fine for bachelor quarters, but it won't do for a dinner party. Shouldn't think you could get more than four, five couples in here at most. And the downstairs is much too small."

Alec's exasperation rose. "Too small for what?"

"The new servants."

It was suddenly difficult for him to swallow. "Why would I want more servants?"

The duke's mouth twitched. "Though I know this will pain you, Edmund has a point. My aunt has no less than three personal servants just to keep her clothing in order and dress her hair. Your wife will need as many."

Alec groaned.

"Perhaps you would have been better off with the lovely Therese," Lucien said, a distinct challenge in his voice.

"Perhaps you would be better off in your own lodgings," Alec retorted.

Lucien grinned. "This marriage will either make you or break you, my friend. Care to wager which it will be?"

Alec didn't answer. With as much dignity as he could muster, he stood and crossed to the door, closing it behind him with a bang.

Lucien regarded the door thoughtfully. Alec was the

one person he counted as friend. Life had dealt them both unfair hands, yet neither one had bowed. He only wished there was some way he could prevent Alec from making the same mistakes he had made—mistakes that had ruined more lives than his own. Lucien sighed and shook his head. While he knew the old duke's determination to bring Alec to heel sprang from sincere concern, he had to deplore such heavy-handed methods.

"It'll never work," said Edmund into the silence. "If he doesn't come out strong and do the thing right, he'll be in the suds in no time."

Lucien pulled his attention to the younger man. "Tell me, halfling, have you ever spoken with the Frant Dragon?"

"No. Have you?"

"Once. She was seated beside me at the Melroses' dinner party last month. I spent three hours with her, and frankly, I don't know when I've enjoyed a conversation more. If she has a failing, it is that she is honest to a fault."

Edmund brightened. "Perhaps it won't be so hard for Alec, after all. I mean, if she's as charming as that—"

"Oh, I think he'll have his hands full. Julia Frant is a woman of great fortitude."

Edmund grimaced. "No wonder Alec looked so ill at ease."

"He is in for a perilous journey. He may have married by the deadline, but he still has a long year ahead."

"He will need our assistance. God knows he's helped me out of more scrapes than I can count." Edmund leaned forward eagerly. "What can we do?"

Lucien flipped his cheroot into the fireplace. "We have to help the lovely Julia become society's most dashing matron. It's the only way to counteract whatever evil Therese and Nick cook up."

A doubtful expression crossed the chubby face. "What do we know about married women?"

The duke lifted a brow. "Pray tell, did you not just leave the warm bed of the buxom Lady Chowerton?"

A dull red flush burned its way across Edmund's cheeks. "Yes, but—"

"And isn't there a Lord Chowerton lurking somewhere in the distance?"

"Tare and hounds, Luce!" Edmund exclaimed in a strangled tone. "Fanny is another matter altogether. Chowerton is twice her age and more. Besides, I shouldn't think Alec would want us to teach Julia about . . . well, I mean, dash it, we couldn't teach her how to—"

"Don't be a gudgeon, Edmund. Of course we couldn't. Now listen to me, stripling, for I will say this but once: we know the dressing, eating, and personal habits of at least half of the married women in the *ton*. All we need to do is teach those habits to Alec's young wife. That, along with Lady Birlington's sponsorship, will get our Julia in the door."

Edmund bit his lip. "If Maddie'll do it. I ain't saying she won't, mind you, for you never know what sort of an idea she might take to." He shook his head. "I still can't help but wonder if the women we know are the types Alec'd want his wife to emulate."

Lucien rubbed his temple and wondered why he had adopted this young cub. Actually, it was more the other way around. One never invited Edmund; he just appeared. Impervious to snubs, the lad wormed his way into their company so often, Lucien had actually missed the silly youth when Edmund had escorted his long-suffering mother to the country.

Sighing, Lucien said patiently, "Edmund, where is Lady Chowerton this morning?"

Edmund's brow furrowed in thought. "Visiting Lady Cowper. Then, she's off to the Winnifreds' tea."

"Where will she be tomorrow?"

"The theatre. Said I might see her there. She's wearing

an atrocious gown the exact pattern of my mother's window shades, gold with green stripes. I told her not to wear it, but—"

"Of course she will be at the theatre," Lucien interrupted. "The whole world attends the new play. And then, on Thursday night, you can be assured the lovely Fanny will attend the Seftons' rout. She is accepted everywhere. No breath of scandal has ever touched her name." He shrugged. "So long as one is discreet, one may do as one pleases."

Edmund bounded from his chair. "By Jove, you are right, Luce! I hadn't thought of it like that. All Alec has to do is show Julia how to get on and teach her to be discreet. You and I can see to it that he does the thing in style." He stood, wide-eyed and annoyingly eager. "Where shall we begin? Tattersall's, to look for a carriage? Or should we attempt to soften Lady Birlington?"

"First, you and I have an errand of a more delicate kind."

"Oh? And what's that?"

"We are about to start a rumor of our own."

Chapter 5

The solicitor examined the marriage license, his long nose flaring ever so slightly. Julia stared, fascinated, wondering if the little man could smell the ink.

Alec shifted impatiently in the hard chair. "When can you transfer the funds?"

Julia suppressed a sigh. Alec had been in a foul mood since this morning, no doubt regretting their hasty marriage. It was a great pity he felt that way, because once she had been revived by a hot bath and a swallow of rum, she'd felt only dreamlike wonder at her changed circumstances. Dreamlike wonder, and the tiniest bit of excitement.

Mr. Pratt's gaze lifted over the rim of his glasses as he placed the marriage license back on the desk. "It appears the document is legal."

"Of course it's legal," Alec growled. The chair creaked as he leaned forward. "The will does not specify which late Earl of Covington, so the conditions have been met. I expect the funds to be placed in my account by this afternoon."

The first thing she needed to do, Julia decided, was work on improving Alec's uncertain temper. She glanced at her impatient husband, then wished she hadn't. He looked wildly handsome, a scowl darkening his brow, his eyes snapping a frosty silver. Her heart quickened and a hot prickle traveled slowly up her arms and came to rest on the nape of her neck. She had to fight the urge to shiver.

The solicitor rested his elbows on the desk and pressed his fingertips together. "My lord, this is a very delicate matter. Your grandfather's instructions were explicit. I'm afraid it will take days, maybe even weeks, before the executors authorize the release of the funds."

"The executors be damned. I want the money transferred today."

"Just who are these executors?" Julia glanced from her scowling husband to Mr. Pratt. Thank goodness Alec had returned her spectacles. She wouldn't have been able to see the condescension in the solicitor's smile, and it was important to know just where one stood in matters like these.

"Lady Hunterston, the executors are men of value and worth, carefully selected by the late earl to oversee the distribution of his estate—"

"They are a bunch of prosy bores." Alec glowered. "Where in the hell did my grandfather meet up with such cheese-paring fops, anyway?"

The solicitor's nose flared in earnest. "I assure you, my lord, these sentiments don't become you. Your grandfather had your best interests at heart in selecting such honorable men."

Julia wished the man would just cease speaking. His pontificating was annoying Alec into a lather. Hands clenched around the arms of his chair, her husband tensed as if coiled to spring. Julia placed one of her hands over his and leaned toward the solicitor. "I'm sure the executors are exemplary men, Mr. Pratt."

He appeared mollified. "Thank you, my lady. They are indeed." The solicitor shot a sharp glance at Alec and sniffed. "I should remind you, my lord, that many an estate has been lost due to inexpert handling. There have even been cases where executors have lined their own pockets at the expense of others."

"I wouldn't mind sharing some of that blasted fortune if they would cease their warbling."

Before the solicitor could respond, Julia interceded, "How long do you think it will be before the funds are released?"

"Two, perhaps three months, if—"

Alec started. "That is unacceptable! If Julia and I are to live within the confines of society for the specified time, we will need access to the funds."

Julia nodded. They would, indeed. And she had no intention of sitting around for months doing nothing, when she could be assisting so many.

Mr. Pratt frowned. "I am sure, my lord, you understand how long these matters can take, but I assure you we will attempt to—"

"May I please see the will?" asked Julia. She'd had enough squabbling for one day. Her head was beginning to ache anew.

The solicitor lifted his thin brows. "It's an impressive legal document. I sincerely doubt you would be able to decipher it."

"I've read many legal documents, Mr. Pratt. Debtor's court, you know."

His mouth opened then closed. Finally, he managed to ask, "Debtor's court?"

"Paupers."

"P-paupers?" The solicitor looked as if he could no longer swallow.

"Lady Hunterston is a great believer in charity work," said Alec hastily, slicing a warning glance in her direction.

The solicitor's brow cleared. "Oh, charity work! That's very noble of you, Lady Hunterston, and quite a fitting occupation for a young lady of your station."

"I'm not noble, I just do what is necessary." She

started to request the document once more, but Alec's hand enveloped hers. Julia could only subside into the warmth of his grasp. She stared at his hand and noted how long and elegant his fingers were and wished she didn't have gloves on.

"Mr. Pratt, the will, if you please," Alec said.

The solicitor looked astounded. "You've seen the document several times, my lord. Surely you don't—"

"Until today, I have been very happy with the services of Pratt, Pratt, and Son. I *had* intentions of retaining you as my personal solicitor to oversee the disbursement."

The solicitor paled. "Your lordship! This firm has represented the Bridgeton family since—"

"If you insult Lady Hunterston, you will leave me no choice. She is my wife." Alec lifted Julia's hand in his and turned it over. With the care of a surgeon, he pushed the edge of her glove from her wrist and placed a lingering kiss on her bare skin. "You can understand why I would take offense at anyone who denies her such a simple request."

Even though she knew it was only a show designed to fluster the solicitor, Julia forgot everything . . . where she was, what they were trying to accomplish, why she had even wanted to see the blasted will in the first place. She forgot everything, that is, but the surge of heat racing through her at the feel of Alec's lips against her naked skin. Even after he released her, she couldn't look away from the spot where his beautiful mouth had touched her.

Mr. Pratt swallowed noisily. "I never meant to imply . . . of course I wish to assist Lady Hunterston in any way possible." He opened a drawer, pulled out a sheaf of papers, and slid them across the desk.

Alec glanced at the will indifferently before handing it to Julia. Silence settled in the room as she took the papers and began thumbing through them, so bemused by Alec's sensuous kiss that it took her several minutes before she could even focus. Little by little, the complex wording drew her in.

She reached the final page and lifted her gaze to the solicitor. "It says here that if the will is contested, the executors must release the funds to Lord Hunterston on the arranged schedule until all issues are resolved."

Mr. Pratt folded his hands together. "I am aware, Miss Frant—"

"Lady Hunterston," corrected Alec in soft warning.

The solicitor had the grace to look shamefaced. "Of course. Lady Hunterston, I realize you think you understand this situation, but—"

"Read it yourself," said Julia. She slid the document across the desk. "This page, last paragraph."

Mr. Pratt took the document. "I know the wording well. Lord Hunterston and I have gone over it many times."

"The executors must release the funds according to the schedule."

"Only in the event the will itself is contested." The solicitor's superior smile raked along Julia's nerves. "As I was saying—"

"Lord Hunterston and I contest the will."

"*What*?" asked Alec and the solicitor in unison.

"We have no choice." Julia looked at Alec. "If we contest the will, they have to release the funds. If we don't, they could debate the issue an entire year if they wished."

Mr. Pratt flushed. "Lady Hunterston, I assure you the executors do not—"

"If we contest the will, it will be out of the executors' hands." She tilted her head toward the solicitor. "Out of yours, too."

His startled gaze slid from her to the will. Slowly, word by word, he read the place she had indicated. Then he read it again, his brow lowering more each time.

"Well?" asked Alec.

Mr. Pratt placed the will on the desk and sighed. "It is true the executors could not withhold the funds under such circumstances, but—"

"Excellent." Alec turned to Julia. "What do we do now, love?"

"Pardon me, my lord!" Mr. Pratt said, eyes bulging in alarm. "I must urge you to reconsider this step! Such a move could tie up the settlement for months, even years."

"So? We would have the money."

"But the time . . . the expense! My lord, you've not thought of the time and trouble this could cause."

"Oh, it wouldn't be any trouble for me." Alec smiled, the flash of his white teeth startling. "But it would be quite irksome for my solicitor."

A look of confusion swept across Mr. Pratt's face and Julia experienced a moment of pity. She reached across the table and patted his hand. "Perhaps if you could arrange for the release of the funds now, Lord Hunterston will refrain from challenging the settlement."

"But if the executors find your claim spurious—"

"They will not. My father was the Earl of Covington, and I have legally wed Lord Hunterston. The executors must accept this marriage."

Mr. Pratt swallowed hard and rubbed a hand across his mouth. After a long moment that seemed to last an eternity, he sighed. "I will have the funds transferred immediately."

Alec relaxed in his chair and sent a heart-stopping grin toward Julia.

Mr. Pratt pulled a clean sheet of paper in front of him. "The executors will require an immediate investigation into the validity of Lady Hunterston's claim." He smiled at Julia with a touch of admiration. "In order to expedite this matter, it would help if you could supply some information."

"What do you need to know?"

"The approximate dates of your father's birth and death."

"He was born August 15, 1749, at the family estate in Derbyshire. He died October 7, 1807."

The solicitor wrote the dates in careful script. "Where did your family reside?"

"Boston."

The pen hovered over the paper. "Siblings?"

"No, I'm an only child."

"Hm. And your father's given name?"

"Jason Henry Frant. He was named after my grandfather." She frowned. "I don't know much about the details regarding the inheritance, but it should all be in my uncle's papers."

"I will call on Lady Covington this morning." Mr. Pratt read through the information. "One last question. Where were your parents married?"

"They eloped to the border." Julia smiled in remembrance. Her father loved to tell how he had swept his beloved Jane away during that wild ride to Gretna Green. "The third of June, 1778."

Mr. Pratt wrote a few more notes before returning the pen to its stand. "I will let you know if we have any other questions. The first installment of the funds will be released this morning."

"Good," said Alec, standing. "And now, if you'll forgive us, Lady Hunterston and I have some rather pressing errands." He assisted Julia from her chair and escorted her to the door, leaving the solicitor staring after them.

Alec settled in the corner of their carriage, his hat rakishly tilted over one eye, a mischievous smile on his lips. "Thank God for debtor's court."

Julia bit back an impatient sigh. "I didn't get to ask him to set up an account for my portion."

The smile disappeared as swiftly as it had appeared.

"Don't worry," he snapped. "You will get your fair share. More than your fair share."

She flinched under the sting of his words, and for an instant she regretted forcing him to give up half his fortune. After all, he had done nothing more reprehensible than to get caught in one of Therese's detestable ploys.

But had she not convinced Alec to give up part of his fortune, not one farthing would have gone for anything truly worthy. Julia smiled brightly. "I'm sure you will see to it I get my fair share. I am very excited about spending it."

His mouth parted in astonishment; then he chuckled. "At least you are honest. Shall I have Johnston go round to Tattersall's, or will Bond Street do?"

She waved a hand. "Oh, no! I have other plans for my portion of the money."

Alec pushed his hat back and sat up straight, his gaze narrowed on her. "Such as?"

"First, I plan on supporting the Society for Wayward Women. They just lost their biggest sponsor, and are in a terrible fix financially. After that. . . ." She frowned. "Well, I shall be very careful where I give the rest of it. Not all charities are well managed, you know."

His gaze wandered over her, his eyes shadowed by the brim of his hat. "Still the philanthropist, hm? All that will change, my innocent, once you've tasted champagne, felt raw silk on your bare skin, and wrapped a diamond necklace about your pretty little neck."

Julia patted the scarf at her throat to make sure it was still in place. "I've tasted champagne before, thank you. I didn't care for it at all." She rubbed her nose. "It made me sneeze."

He flashed a dark smile. "Then it wasn't good champagne."

"I was told it was the best, but you could be right. One never knows about those things."

Alec studied her as if he'd never quite seen her before.

"No," he said slowly, "I suppose one never does."

Julia was acutely aware of the burning sensation left on her wrist at his earlier touch. It heated anew as his enigmatic gaze roamed. She put a self-conscious hand to her hair and discovered that most of it had escaped from the neat bun. Long wispy tendrils curled over and under her collar. It must look horrendous. She attempted to tuck the annoying strands back into place.

"For the love of God," Alec said with a hint of impatience. "Let it be. It looks better down."

Julia's cheeks burned. "I beg your pardon," she said stiffly.

"Do you?" He reached across the distance that separated them. To her astonishment, he slid her spectacles off her nose, then leaned back in his corner, a faint smile curving his mouth.

"There," he said with obvious satisfaction. "Much better."

"Better for whom? I can't see a thing."

"Ah, but I can see ever so much more," he returned in a soft voice, his smile suddenly intimate. "According to our bargain, my dearest Julia, I cannot touch you, but I can look to my heart's content."

Julia's heart thudded so loudly she was sure he must be able to hear it. *He is a rake*, she reminded herself severely. *He says those things to every woman he meets.* She desperately cast about for a safe topic of conversation. "You told Mr. Pratt we had some errands."

Alec idly swung her spectacles to and fro. "We do."

"Such as?"

"We, my dear, are going shopping."

"For what?"

His gaze flickered over her attire, lingering on her outmoded pelisse and reticule. "Clothes."

She caught the censure in his glance and her heart contracted. Though Mrs. Winston had been able to press out many of the wrinkles, she knew she must appear dowdy. Facing Alec's shimmering gaze, she found herself yearning for a spectacular gown, one that would magically transform her into a beautiful temptress. One that would make his heart race as uncomfortably as hers.

Julia firmly took her wandering imagination in hand. "I suppose I will need one or two gowns," she conceded, though she thought it a great waste of money. For the price of one gown, she could fund an innumerable amount of work.

"You'll need more than one or two. We are about to cut a swath through society."

That astonished her. "Whatever for?"

"We don't have a choice. As the efficient Mr. Pratt so obligingly pointed out, the will is very specific. We have to take our place in society."

Julia smoothed her gray muslin gown over her knees. "I don't think I'm going to enjoy this."

"I'm sure it will be dreadful for both of us," he agreed easily. "The wealthy are like a pack of wolves. They like nothing better than to feed off the carcasses of those who have fallen."

She lifted her brows. "And I should purchase a gown for that?"

He flashed a lazy smile. "Several. The only way we can hope to come off is to enter the fray bedecked in our finest armor."

Julia reached over, reclaimed her spectacles, and sat them firmly on her nose. "It sounds like a childish game."

"So it does. Unfortunately, neither of us has a choice."

The coach slowed and came to a halt. Alec didn't wait for the coachman but opened the door himself and pulled out the step, holding out his hand. It amused him when Julia hesitated the briefest instant before placing her fingers in his and stepping down. The scent of lemon and spice rose from her hair as the breeze stirred the loosened tendrils and he caught himself leaning forward to catch the scent more completely.

Johnston arrived. "What are ye about, openin' yer own door?" he said in an injured tone. "The next thing ye know, ye'll be wantin' to polish yer own boots."

Alec took Julia's unresisting hand and pulled her toward a shop door. "We will be a while, Johnston. Lady Hunterston and I will be ordering a number of gowns for her debut."

The groom harrumphed. "And what should I be doin' in the meantime?"

Julia pulled her hand from Alec's and fished about in her reticule. She placed two pence in Johnston's hand. "There. Stable the horses and have some nice hot soup. You can return for us in an hour."

The groom, bemused by the sudden largesse, nodded mutely. Julia looked eminently satisfied as she turned toward the modiste's. With her hair falling about her face and her cheeks pinkened with the chill of the day, she was delectable. Alec regretted he had allowed her to reclaim her spectacles.

Watching the sway of her trim backside as she strode to the shop, he leaned toward Johnston and murmured, "Whatever you do, try to appear sober when you return."

The groom pocketed the coins and offered a cheeky grin. "I always *try*."

Alec laughed and joined Julia.

She met him with the grim air of someone about to face an unpleasant task. "Four gowns, but no more."

"You are not a chaperone any longer, Julia." She hesitated and he took her hands in his. "We may have managed to win a reprieve from Pratt, but it is only the beginning."

Julia wrinkled her nose. "I'm not going to enjoy this."

He had to laugh at her expression. "Neither will I." Alec placed a finger under her chin and tilted her face to his. "But we'll do it, or we will never see the rest of the funds."

She stepped away as if anxious to put some space between them. "Very well, but I insist on paying for my own gowns."

"No. *I* will pay for my wife's clothing. It is only proper."

Good God, what had made him say that? She already had half the money, and it wouldn't have been unreasonable to expect her to pay some of her own expenses. But looking down at her small upturned face framed by an unbecoming frayed bonnet, the ribbons faded and uneven, Alec was assailed by the desire to provide her with something—something more, something better. "Damn it, Julia. I will purchase your clothes and anything else I wish."

"I cannot allow you to—"

"Besides," he added, catching her hand and placing it firmly in the crook of his arm, "it will leave you more money to squander on your charity work."

Her eyes narrowed with suspicion. "You said we had several errands, not just this one. Where do we go from here?"

"Milliner, mantua maker, and then last, the jeweler."

She stared at him. "I don't think jewelry is necessary. My mother gave me her garnets. That should suffice."

"If you appear in something as trumpery as garnets, people will think I'm a nip-farthing or worse. You have no choice in this matter."

"It is a waste of money," she said flatly.

He scowled. Would she resist him at every turn? "Damn it! I will buy you jewelry and you will wear it."

Julia met his statement with silence, merely fixing him with a serious stare. Alec tried to glare her down, but she never so much as flinched.

After an unconscionable time, she sighed, though a

smile quirked at the corner of her generous mouth. "You are a stubborn man, Alec MacLean."

"So they tell me."

"Very well. I will accept your gifts. However, once this charade is done, we will sell whatever items we purchase."

He choked. "Sell?"

"And donate the proceeds to the Society for Wayward Women." She patted his arm. "That way you'll have the satisfaction of knowing your money has gone for a truly worthy cause." Having settled everything, she gave him a blinding smile and entered Madame Moulin's.

Alec watched her disappear through the door and wondered if any other woman of his acquaintance would have balked at his offer. Certainly none of them would have wished to sell any of her possessions for charity.

Sighing, he took off his hat and tucked it under his arm. He was coming to realize that having Julia for a wife was going to be a unique experience. Unlike life with the predictable Therese, life with Julia would be an adventure. Unfortunately, he was only now beginning to realize just how blasted uncomfortable adventures could be.

Chapter 6

"I said I do not wish to see any visitors," Therese snapped when the door opened. Damn the new footman. He was the seventh in as many weeks and as poorly trained as the rest.

"Oh, I think you'll want to see me," said a cultured masculine voice.

"Nick!" she cried, rising from the settee. "I was just about to send for you. Something has happened."

He closed the door and walked toward her with a casual, elegant grace. As always, she was struck by his golden beauty. Whereas Alec had inherited the acclaimed dark allure of the Bridgeton family, Nick had taken his fair looks from his mother, a notorious French beauty who had reputedly killed herself in a fit of rage.

Therese had heard it whispered the woman's family possessed a long history of madness and depraved behavior. Looking at Nick, she couldn't help but wonder. Surely someone so beautiful must have some hint of madness in his nature.

"You don't look well," Nick said calmly, setting his hat on a side table. "Perhaps you should lie down."

She flushed at the mocking tone. "I do not wish to lie down. Nick, we have lost the fortune."

He merely removed a piece of lint from his sleeve.

"Did you hear me?" she asked sharply. "We have lost the fortune!"

After a studied pause, he raised his gaze. His beautiful blue eyes, surrounded by long, sooty lashes, had more than once caused Therese an uncomfortable flutter of envy.

"I heard you the first time, my dear," he said. "That is why I came. Wexford and that fool Edmund Valmont dropped into White's this morning. They were spreading a most interesting tale about Alec and your cousin."

"Alec eloped with Julia last night."

Nick regarded her silently.

Therese allowed her lips to tremble ever so slightly. Normally such a move would have fixed the interest of any man on the fullness of her mouth, one of her best traits. But Nick's gaze never wavered. His expression was curiously dead, almost as if he'd sampled all the sins of the earth and found them wanting.

A delicious shiver stole through her. "I did everything just as we planned."

"Everything?" The gently spoken word hung in the room. "I beg to differ, my dear. You forgot one crucial thing."

She swallowed. There was something fearful in his very stillness. She allowed her eyes to fill with tears. "I don't know how you can say such a thing. I did what you asked. I risked it all for you."

"Such pretty tears," he murmured. "But I have no pity to give. Your efforts are wasted."

His indifference stung. "It is not my fault. I did everything we agreed upon."

He lifted a brow. "Oh? Is it possible you forgot to mention the dowdy Miss Julia was also a daughter of a late earl of Covington?"

Though spoken in a deceptively soft tone, the words cut like a whip. Therese eyed Nick carefully. She was never sure how he would react. It was one of the things she found fascinating about him. "In a manner of speaking, I suppose she is."

His blue gaze narrowed as he closed the short distance between them. "Explain."

Therese subsided once again on the settee. "Her father held the title once." She caught a glimpse of fury and hurried to add, "But I did not think it would matter. He died almost immediately."

Nick's face hardened. "You stupid fool. You should have told me."

"I didn't think it important. I would never have thought Julia capable of such deception. Good God, it is the most ridiculous thing in the world!"

A hint of cruel amusement curved his mouth. "Do you know what Wexford and Valmont are saying?"

She shook her head.

"They say it is a love match."

"No one would believe such drivel. Alec has been dangling after me for the last two months and everyone knows it."

"Not after Lucien and his babbling friend finish entertaining the entire *ton*. It really is a most romantic tale. Apparently Alec didn't care if the executors approved the match or not; he was determined to have her."

Therese's stomach tightened. "I told everyone at the musicale last night that I had refused to elope with him. Now they will think me jealous."

His eyes blazed. "I don't give a damn about you. The money is all that matters."

Heat flooded through her at his sneer. "I should have eloped with Alec when I had the chance. Why I let you talk me into such a preposterous plan I will never know."

"As I remember, you were the one panting to become a countess," he said, favoring her with a glance that made her wonder if her expensive morning gown of pale blue muslin had suddenly turned into sackcloth.

Her hand clenched the arm of the settee. Nick must have seen the gesture, for he favored her with a singularly sweet smile. "You know, my dear, if anyone comes off the worse for this incident, it will not be me. I may have lost a fortune, but I will still be an earl. While you. . . ." He gestured with a pale hand. "Once the laughter dies, perhaps some country squire will take you."

Without thinking, she stood to strike him. Nick caught her hand. For one long, endless second, he stared at her before capturing her against his chest. A brutal hand twisted into her hair, yanking her head back. She writhed against him, striking him with her free fist.

He covered her mouth with his. For an instant, Therese fought even harder. But his brutal strength, the rude, sensual thrust of his tongue inside her mouth, ignited the lust that coursed through her every time he was near.

She melted against him, passionately returning his kiss. She had longed for this, yearned for it. Twining her arms about his neck, she pressed her breasts against his chest. His hands left her hair and roamed over her body, cupping her roughly.

Therese grasped desperately at his lapels, rubbing herself against him. How she desired this man. More than any other, even Alec, whose dark good looks had more than once caused her mouth to go dry. There was something intrinsically forbidden about Nick, something untouchable that made her crazy with lust. She moaned into his mouth, and reached for the juncture between his legs.

Nick let her go, dropping her roughly onto the settee. Therese sprawled against the pillows, fighting to regain her breath. Her body throbbed with unfulfilled heat; her breasts ached for the touch of his hands.

He smoothed his jacket. "You really should do something about your unfortunate tendency to act like a bitch in heat. It is most unattractive."

Humiliation raged through her like a fire. "Damn you," she spat.

"Don't worry, my dear. I plan on taking you . . . eventually. I will need an heir, you know."

Therese swallowed a retort, knowing it would be wasted. She wasn't accustomed to being the one who wanted more, needed more. Everyone knew she was beautiful. It was reflected in the faces of the men who desired her, the women who feared her. There was something dizzying about the knowledge that one could, with a pout or a sidelong glance, get whatever one wanted. She had never failed.

Until now. But there was a reason for that, after all. Rumors were rife about the too-beautiful Earl of Bridgeton. "I suppose I deserved that," she said with a sly smile. "I keep forgetting you aren't a real man." She waited for his inevitable reaction.

His cold, serpent gaze lit to a vivid azure. "Oh, I'm a man, sweet Therese. Never forget that."

Some demon whispered her on. "But Alec—"

He yanked her up from the settee, his hands bruising the tender flesh above her elbows. "Don't," he hissed, his face contorted into a frozen mask of white anger. "Don't ever, *ever* compare me to my cousin. Do you understand?"

Mutely, she nodded, both terrified and thrilled at the same time. He dropped her back onto the settee, and as quickly as it had appeared, his anger slid behind the urbane, smooth facade. "Good. If I must marry, I would rather it be someone who understands me."

Therese rubbed her arms where his fingers had marked her. "I don't understand you at all."

"No? And here I thought you were as depraved as I."

She winced. As cruelly beautiful as a fallen angel, he

knew how to draw blood with his every word. "Nick, have you ever fallen in love?"

He looked at her for a long moment. "No," he said softly, placing a hand under her chin and lifting her face to his. "But if I ever do, I promise to share her with you."

"What do you mean, 'share'?" she asked, though a spiral of heat suffused her at the implications.

His smile whispered of forbidden pleasures. "Oh, yes," he murmured, dropping his hand. "We understand one another very well indeed."

It took the greatest of efforts to force her mind away from the tantalizingly erotic suggestion he had just made. "What do we do now?"

"Alec and your cousin must still live a year without scandal. Within that time, you and I will see to it that a scandal occurs to the lovely couple."

Therese frowned. "What will I have to do?"

His glance dismissed her. "Whatever I tell you to."

Briefly, Therese wondered why she hadn't just married Alec. He was certainly handsome enough and would be disgustingly wealthy. Had he been in possession of the earldom, he would have been perfect. But he was a mere Scottish viscount, whereas Nick possessed the venerated Bridgeton title. There was no comparison.

Her gaze fell on his pure profile and she wet her lips with the tip of her tongue. She had already savored his charms once. Her thighs dampened at the memory of that one impassioned tryst. He had been brutal, almost vicious, and she had cried out in her passion, something she rarely did. If she could just satiate herself, her interest would wane. It always did.

Yet she wondered if anything was the same with Nick. No man had intrigued her more. And no man had ever left her so . . . wanting.

He caught her gaze and frowned. "It appears the Frant

Dragon can indeed breathe fire when occasion demands it."

"Julia? She is the most boring woman in the world."

"Surely you exaggerate."

She shrugged. "Alec has met her many times and never paid her the slightest heed. No one ever does."

"Everyone will pay her heed, now that she is a wealthy viscountess."

"I doubt it. She's the drabbest creature, doing reform work and forever blurting out the most shocking things. Unless Alec can work miracles, they will never be able to avoid a scandal."

"Don't underestimate my cousin. He may be impetuous and quick to anger, but he is no fool. He managed to remain my grandfather's favorite despite my best attempts to separate the two of them."

She reclined against the settee and looked at him through her lashes. She knew the thin muslin outlined her form, hinting at the shape of her nipples. "I'm sure those efforts were drastic indeed."

"How very perceptive of you," he said dryly, collecting his hat. "You aren't quite the fool one would think."

Therese covered a flash of anger with a brittle laugh. "And Alec isn't quite the demon the world thinks him, is he?"

"I admit I've assisted in his fall from grace."

She watched him narrowly. It was unlike Nick to be so open. Unless, of course, he had a reason. "What did you do?"

"Don't look so excited, my dear. I did nothing ungenteel. Tongues do wag, you know. A word here, a word there. It has all been remarkably easy."

"Everything comes easy to you." She knew her words held a hint of bitterness, but she could not stop them. Eaten with frustration, Therese yearned to give him a taste of his own.

Nick crossed to the door, where he stopped and regarded her with a dispassionate gaze. "Not as easy as you imagine, my dear." His mouth curved in a half-smile that sent an uncomfortable flutter to her stomach and lower. "Unfortunately, this last venture proves it. We will have to plan something larger, more grandiose for the new bride and groom if we are to secure the fortune now."

"What should we do?"

He adjusted his cravat with a deft touch. "If your intriguing cousin left without her possessions, you can be sure she will return."

"I can't wait to tell that scheming little—"

"You will do no such thing. Instead, you will convince her you are her best friend."

Therese couldn't begin to count all the slights and snubs she had heaped on Julia's head. "She would never believe it."

"Convince her you have changed," Nick said sharply.

"And then what?"

"Then, my dear, we figure out how best to exploit her weaknesses." He donned his hat, nestling the sable brim atop his golden hair. "I want to know her thoughts, desires, and secrets, if she has any. Find out everything about her relationship with my cousin."

"What do I get in return?"

His lids shuttered his expression. "I will wed you the day I receive my grandfather's fortune and not a moment before."

"I want more than a promise." She crossed to him, laced her arms around his neck, and trailed her mouth along the smooth line of his jaw. His cologne laced through her like laudanum, causing a languorous heat to rise up her legs and pool between her thighs. "Announce our engagement, Nick. Send a notice to the *Gazette*." She put her lips to his ear and whispered, "I'd take you without the money."

He pulled away and opened the door. "There, my dear, is where we differ."

The portal shut behind him as Therese gave vent to a shriek of fury.

Chapter 7

Boxes upon boxes covered the foyer, some stacked so high they quavered as if the slightest jar would send them toppling. Alec had purchased his wife everything she needed to take her place in society. He should have been triumphant. Instead, Julia's somber stare had stolen the pleasure from the entire afternoon.

Refusing to be ruled by such prudery, he had bought even more than he'd intended. It had become a grim contest, a silent battle of wills. By the time she'd pleaded a headache, he'd suffered one as well. They had forgone the jewelers and returned home in silence, separating at the carriage with only polite, distant words.

He rubbed his neck wearily and wondered how a pleasant pastime like shopping could turn so sour.

Burroughs entered the foyer. "Welcome home, my lord."

Alec placed his hat and gloves in the butler's outstretched hand. "Where is her ladyship?"

"Resting in the front parlor." Burroughs cast a deprecating look about the foyer and added dryly, "It must be fatiguing to spend an entire fortune in one afternoon."

Fatiguing didn't begin to describe it. Alec gestured to the boxes. "Have Johnston carry these up to her ladyship's room."

"Yes, my lord." He hesitated. "If you'll forgive me, her ladyship seems subdued. I hope nothing is amiss?"

"Of course not." Alec refused to acknowledge the butler's concerned gaze. Frankly, he didn't think anything was bothering Julia other than an oversized dose of puritanical zeal.

The butler looked politely skeptical, but bowed. "Of course. Shall I bring tea?"

"No. Perhaps later."

"Very well, my lord." Burroughs turned and trod down the hall.

Alec randomly chose a box from the tallest stack and slipped through the open doors of the parlor. Julia sat on the edge of a settee, her pale skin startling against the dull gray of her shapeless dress. The kiss of the lingering sun as it slanted through the mullioned windows touched her hair with gold. She looked young and annoyingly innocent.

He walked toward her, the box tucked under his arm. She glanced up, clasping her gloved hands together in a nervous gesture, the leather shiny from use. There were eleven pairs of costly, delicate gloves in the boxes in the hallway. He had counted.

Maybe that was the problem. It was too much, too soon. God knew he himself felt a little staggered by the events of the past twenty-four hours. He couldn't begin to imagine what it felt like for Julia.

Alec set the box on the table, determined to be cheerful even if he died in the process. "It's rather like Christmas, isn't it?"

She stripped off her gloves with an economical motion and placed them on the table. "It's like no Christmas I've ever had."

There was no request for pity in the plainly stated fact, yet he felt as if he should say something . . . helpful. "Julia, I know this has been difficult for you. Your whole life has been wretched—"

"Wretched? Whatever made you think that?" She regarded him with an astonished gaze.

"I don't know. I just thought. . . ." Alec subsided into silence as the green of her eyes deepened. Good God, all he'd tried to do was offer the poor girl some encouragement, and she had flared up at him as if he'd grossly insulted her.

Julia's chin squared. "I had a wonderful childhood. Not much money, of course. But full of love and laughter."

"Then you had a better childhood than I," he retorted. "Grandfather was not a cheerful man."

"Yes, I heard. He was never the same after your mother died."

"Who told you that?" he asked, momentarily diverted by her knowledge. The only time he had ever seen his grandfather show anything resembling emotion was when the old man had gazed on the portrait of his mother that hung in the grand saloon at Bridgeton House.

"Mrs. Winston told me." Her lips quivered as if she would burst into tears at any moment. "She said he put fresh flowers on her grave every day until he died."

He must have looked as bewildered as he felt, for she bit her lip and added, "Of course you already knew that."

Alec didn't know anything of the sort. The housekeeper's constant chattering had never inspired him with the desire to listen. "I imagine Mrs. Winston knows quite a bit about the entire family."

A sudden dimple raced across Julia's cheek. "Oh, yes."

Fascinated, Alec wondered where the dimple hid when she wasn't smiling. She was a conundrum, this prim woman whose emotions ran from tearful sympathy to a mischievous twinkle in the space of a moment. "Did she mention the time I shaved the wolfhound?"

Her smile exploded into a full-blown grin, as enchanting as the dimple. "You wanted to make him into a lion."

"I failed miserably. Poor Ferdinand was mortified. He hid under the kitchen table for a week."

She laughed, the husky sound more suited to a boudoir than a parlor. "I hope you were properly chastised."

"Grandfather made me clean out the kennels every day for a week."

"Good for him. It is exactly what I would have recommended."

"You are a harsh taskmaster. But Ferdinand didn't look so horrible. In fact, he reminded me of Vicar Plumb." She looked uncertain and he added, "He married us."

All merriment swept from her face. "Oh. Of course."

He winced at the sudden change. That was the problem with trying to talk with a reformer, and a virgin at that. He wasn't sure what the latter had to do with his irritation, but it did.

Women like Julia were unreasonable and irrational, and fell to pieces at the slightest provocation, leaving men like him feeling like the biggest beasts on earth. He, for one, did not enjoy being made to feel so low. It was time she understood exactly what he expected of her. "Julia, we need to talk. Your behavior today was inexcusable."

She stared at him as if he'd suddenly sprouted horns and a tail. "What behavior?"

Damn her for being so particular. What behavior, indeed. He scowled and pointed a finger. "Today, while we were shopping, you pouted like a child."

"I was not pouting."

"Yes, you were." Color stained her cheeks and he relented slightly. "You must get over this hesitation you have about spending money. I know you—"

"I have decided to establish my own factory." Enthusiasm bloomed across her face, illuminating the pale angles with vivid color. "One of the major tenets of the Society for Wayward Women is to teach independence and self-reliance. I've finally figured out a way to do just that."

"I see," he said faintly. He didn't, but it was all he could manage at the moment.

"Most women who have taken up less than honorable professions have done so out of necessity. With the proper funding, we can train them to become productive members of society and—"

"Wait." He pinched the bridge of his nose and closed his eyes. "Do you mean to tell me that the entire time we were shopping, you were thinking about *spending* money?"

"Oh, yes."

He opened his eyes. "On *other* women?"

"Of course." She waved an airy hand. "But much more money than that paltry amount we dropped in the stores today."

"Paltry?" he heard himself echo hollowly. Here he had worried, actually *worried*, that she had been overcome by his generosity. Instead, she thought it paltry. His numb mind refused to calculate how much he had actually spent. It didn't bear consideration.

Julia wasn't even attending. "It all depends on what kind of factory we establish. It could be expensive." She brightened. "But think of the good it will do."

It suddenly seemed silly to have been shopping at all. He cleared his throat. "Julia, why are you so interested in the fate of these unfortunate women?"

Her bloom faded and her gaze dropped to her hands. After a moment, she said, "After my father died, I found out how few choices there are for women to earn their own way in life." She sighed heavily. "I don't watercolor, you see."

Alec struggled to follow her line of thought. "You wanted to earn a living as a painter?"

"Oh, no! I wanted to be a governess."

"You have to know how to watercolor to be a governess? What in hell for?"

She positively beamed at him. "That is a very good question and a perfect example of the shortcomings of modern education. I can speak three languages fluently, can do advanced sums, and know geography and philosophy. Yet because I do not watercolor, no one would even consider me an acceptable governess."

It was amazing how her face transformed when she felt strongly about something. Her eyes flashed, her cheeks warmed to a kissable pink, even her hair seemed to lift and curl with more vivacity, the honey gold threads gleaming. She went from plain and colorless to her own quiet sort of glowing beauty.

"I was fortunate Aunt Lydia wrote and asked me to come here to be a companion to Therese."

"Fortunate for Therese, perhaps, but hardly for you."

Julia looked at him and started to speak, but stopped, blushing profusely. "As uncomfortable as it has been, it taught me to be more aware of the needs of others."

Alec wondered at the size of her heart, to be in such desperate straits herself, yet only see it as a lesson about the difficulties of others. That thought prompted another: never in all of his debauched life had he been made to feel such a wastrel.

Damn the woman and her moralizing ways. He, for one, was glad he was both wealthy and irresponsible. If Julia harbored the false notion she could shame him into becoming a paragon of virtue like herself, she was sadly mistaken. If anyone was going to change, it would be she.

Alec reached for the box he had brought from the foyer and opened it, removing the bonnet that lay nestled among the wrapping paper. "Here, stand up and let's try this on."

She turned an abstracted gaze to the hat. "I tried it on in the store. There's no need to try it again."

"I beg to differ. It will look much different in this light. Besides, I paid twenty guineas for it." He offered his best smile, deepening his voice just slightly. "The least you can do is let me see it on you."

Reluctantly, Julia stood and held out her hand. "Very well, but it seems a silly thing to do. I really should go see Vicar Ashton from the Society and tell him the good news about the money."

"Write him a letter," he said, ignoring her outstretched hand and holding the bonnet aloft. "Allow me."

A frown pulled the corners of her mouth, but she didn't move away when he set the hat on her head. Indeed, she stared off into the distance as if he weren't even present. Never had any woman seemed so immune to him. The thought both irritated and tantalized.

He allowed his hands to linger on the softness of her hair as he adjusted the bonnet. "You know, love, it won't do for you to tell everyone about your charity work."

That caught her attention. Her brows drew together and she scowled. "The Society needs me. I won't give it up just to—"

"No one has asked you to, love. You should just be cautious, that's all. People sneer at things they don't understand."

Julia stared at him, her mouth pressed in a mutinous line. "It sounds very unfair."

Alec could tell her how unfair it was, how the sharp-edged banter of society could cut a person to shreds, but he didn't. Instead, he tipped up her chin to better regard the bonnet, shifting forward until a scant few inches separated them. She smelled of lemon and cinnamon. It made his mouth water.

"This is a silly sort of bonnet for me," she muttered

almost fiercely. "I told you that in the store, but you wouldn't listen."

The straw brim framed her willful face. The charming confection sported a wide, low crown trimmed with an outlandish profusion of artificial flowers and cherries. He had bought this one in particular because the deep green of the leaves echoed the startling color of her eyes.

But he was hard pressed to see her eyes now. She kept them fixed firmly on the floor as he took the ribbons and made a monstrous bow beneath her chin, his finger brushing her chin and throat.

"You know," he murmured. "It is usually polite for a wife to thank her husband when he purchases gifts for her."

"Thank you," she replied dutifully.

He touched one of the flowers on her hat and sent it bobbing. "Some wives might even knit their husbands a pair of slippers."

"I don't knit. I never could." She regarded him with a serious expression. "I can't embroider, either."

"Hmm," he answered, wondering how such a virtuous woman had come to possess such a sensual mouth. "Fortunately for you, I am not a demanding husband. I will settle for your 'thank you.' "

She hesitated, then looked down. One of the large flowers adorning the wide brim slapped him in the nose.

"I suppose that surprises you," she muttered.

He rubbed his nose. "What? That you can't embroider?"

The sprig of cherries quivered at her nod.

"To be honest, I'm *glad* you can neither sew nor embroider. Now I won't have to dread every holiday for fear you will sew some horrendous article of clothing I will be forced by politeness to wear." He lifted her chin with a finger, slipped her spectacles off, and tucked them in his pocket. "Here, love, let me see your eyes."

She made a noise of exasperation. "Why do you always do that? I can't see without them."

He leaned closer until their noses nearly touched. "Can you see now?"

Julia's mouth parted. Moisture glistened on the sensual slopes of her lips. His gaze drifted to her eyes. This close, he was amazed at the length of her lashes. Long and thick, they curled deliciously. Alec could tell from her rapid breathing that she was both frightened and excited. A sensual spell played between them, pulling them closer, making them yearn to touch and be touched.

Some inner voice he'd thought long dead whispered that he was taking this further than he should, but his body was too committed, his mind too focused to hear anything other than the luscious sound of her labored breathing.

"I think . . . you should. . . ." She swallowed and he watched, mesmerized by the movement of her graceful throat.

"I should what?" he asked, lifting a finger to trace the fall of a curl across her ear.

Julia closed her eyes and shivered.

Alec leaned closer so his breath fanned her cheek, her mouth. "Should what, love? Tell me."

A moan slid from her lips and then she fixed her gaze on his. Naked desire stirred in the black velvet centers, the verdant green eclipsed by passion. "Kiss me," she whispered unevenly.

Desire, hot and sugary, flooded his veins. Without another thought, he pulled her closer until the flowers from her bonnet halted him. He cursed, loosening the ribbons with impatient fingers. Finally freed, he dropped the offending hat to the ground and claimed her mouth with his.

Her generous mouth parted beneath his. She moaned and he took advantage of the moment to touch his tongue to hers. She gasped and would have pulled back, but he held her tight and deepened the kiss until she clung to him, breathless with desire. He slid his hands into her tousled hair.

Just as he remembered, the strands slipped through his fingers like heavy silk. He sank his hands into the honey brown curls, scattering pins and loosening tendrils. The silken strands clung to his fingers and urged him on.

She clutched him closer, her arms twined about his neck, her hands gripping urgently. He molded her lithe curves against him, savoring the feel of her firm body as he plundered the heat of her mouth. She surged against him in an unconscious motion that nearly destroyed him.

Alec ran his hands over her back, her hips, and lower. God, she was made for him, fitting against him as if some higher hand had crafted her curves to meld perfectly. A deep moan escaped her parted lips and he captured it, tasting her passion, reveling in her sweetness.

Through a barrage of uncontrolled desire, he was vaguely aware of a door opening. With heartrending clarity, Burroughs announced, "The Duke of Wexford."

Chapter 8

With a muffled curse, Alec broke the embrace and thrust Julia behind him. His cravat was ruined, his coat crumpled, and his desire agonizingly obvious against the smooth outline of his breeches. Damn Luce from now until eternity.

Burroughs choked and quickly removed himself from the room, his ears suspiciously red.

"Dear me," Lucien drawled, smiling like a cat facing a barrel of cream. "It appears the viscount and viscountess are occupied."

"So nice of you to stop by," Alec ground out through clenched teeth, trying to still his racing heart. His body thrummed with heat. Behind him, he could hear Julia's hurried breath as she attempted to put her hair to rights.

He couldn't believe what had just happened. He was a man who took his pleasures lightly. A man who enjoyed numerous dalliances with women who understood the ultimate goal of his flirtations. He eschewed the company of innocents the way some men ran from sin. Yet here he was, panting after his virginal wife like a love-smitten youth.

Lucien sauntered across the room, his eyes glowing with amusement. "I came to pay my respects to the lovely bride."

Alec risked a glance at Julia. Color stained her cheeks, and though she had retrieved most of her pins, one fat, satiny curl trailed over her shoulder. A stab of pure, hot lust ran through him at the sight of her kiss-swollen mouth. Unable to do more, he glared at Lucien.

The duke captured Julia's hand. "Since your husband refuses to make a proper introduction, I fear it rests on me to atone for his rudeness." He bowed, pressing a kiss to the back of her hand. "My Lady Hunterston, you probably don't remember, but I met you at—"

"The Melroses' dinner party. I remember it well," she said, her voice still breathless. She pulled free, swallowing nervously. "Would you care to join us for tea, Your Grace?"

"I would be delighted." Lucien's hard gaze lingered with appreciation on her mouth.

Alec scowled and reached for Julia. As soon as his fingers touched the coolness of hers, she snatched her hand away and cast a glance of such longing toward the door that he heard himself say, "Perhaps you should inform Burroughs we shall need some tea."

She nodded thankfully. "Of course. Pray excuse me." Bobbing a quick curtsey, she slipped quietly from the room.

Lucien retrieved the discarded bonnet from the floor. "My, my. And to think I was even feeling sorry for you."

"Shut up, Wexford. Why are you here?"

"A bit out of sorts, are you? I don't wonder. It is difficult to pull back from the edge of passion, just as—"

"Lucien." The warning in his tone was unmistakable.

The duke chuckled. "Very well. I will cease teasing you until you are in a better frame of mind. Judging from the bounty displayed in the foyer, I take it you've been shopping." He sauntered to the settee and perched on the arm, setting the hat on his knee. "Did Julia purchase finery to her heart's content?"

"If she had, we'd have been home hours ago. She didn't see the need to purchase anything." The ache in his groin subsided to a dull throb.

"Not an ounce of vanity to her, is there?"

"No, I had to remind her of the codicil a dozen times just to get her to buy even the most necessary items."

"You are a fortunate man. Imagine taking Therese on just such a venture."

Alec grimaced.

"Exactly." The duke flicked a careless finger at the flowers adorning the hat. "By the way, Edmund and I stopped by White's this morning."

"Did you?"

"Hmmm. Nick was there. He was everything affable. I mentioned how pleased I was at your wedding."

"And was he surprised?"

" 'Dumbfounded' would be a better term." Lucien pulled his quizzing glass free and examined the fake sprig of cherries. "Of course, I embellished the story a bit."

"Whatever for?"

"People might sneer at Julia if they thought she was anything less than your first choice as wife. I hinted. . . ." Lucien lifted his gaze. "Just hinted, mind you, that you and Julia had a longstanding attachment."

"Did anyone believe you?"

"Everyone but Nick."

"I told you he was not the fop you take him for."

Lucien opened his mouth to reply but Burroughs re-entered the room. With painful dignity, the butler announced, "Lady Birlington and Lord Valmont."

"Damnation," said Lucien under his breath. He stood, setting the bonnet on the table. "I told that fool to wait until we had time to set Julia to rights."

Alec swallowed his irritation and turned his attention to the lady who swept across the threshold. Angular and imposing, Lady Maddie Birlington dominated the parlor

as she did every room she chose to enter. It wasn't just
her towering height, but the sheer force of a personality
well used to gaining its own way.

She jabbed her gold-encrusted cane at Burroughs'
feet. "You there! See to my nephew. He is gathering my
things from the carriage."

The butler bowed. "Of course, madam." He cast a
telling glance at Alec before leaving the room.

Lady Birlington advanced. Her morning dress fluttered about her in fashionable purple and lavender folds.
Her hair, an improbable shade of red, curled from beneath a startling violet-colored turban. Shrewd blue eyes
narrowed on Alec.

"Well, Hunterston?" she said ungraciously. "Aren't
you going to welcome me? Not that I expect such cour-
tesy, but it's damned uncomfortable standing so near this
drafty doorway."

"Pray come in, Lady Birlington. It is a pleasure to see
you again." Alec was allowed to kiss her hand before
she limped past him.

She settled on the settee, her back as straight as a
board, then raised her thin brows. "Well? Why did you
wish to see me?"

Before Alec could reply, Edmund trailed into the
room. His arms overflowed with shawls, a tasseled pillow, lavender gloves, and a small, wheezing pug. The
young man fixed Alec with a desperate gaze. "Sorry, but
I couldn't convince her—"

"Don't be silly, Edmund!" Maddie interrupted. "I'm
sure Hunterston knows what's toward. He's not such an
idiot as you. Put Ephram by the fire."

Edmund grimaced, but did as instructed, settling the
dog on the pillow despite the fact that the animal tried
to bite him several times.

Lady Birlington cooed at the dog, "There, there, precious angel. Sleep until we get to the bottom of this
mystery." Satisfied the dog was comfortable, her gimlet

gaze flicked from Alec to Lucien. "Ah, Wexford."

The duke bowed. "How wonderful to see you, madam. May I say you look beyond compare, as usual."

She waved a dismissive hand, though a pleased smirk curved her mouth. "Save your Canterbury tales for your lightskirts. What are you doing here?"

"I am a frequent visitor at Hunterston House."

"Seems too respectable of a place for you. Not a gaming hell by night, is it?"

Lucien's mouth twitched. "No, but I intend to visit one or two before the morrow."

"Ha! Spoken like a real man. Did you hear that, Edmund? No mealy-mouthed platitudes from him."

"Yes, ma'am," replied her nephew miserably, sinking into a chair with his burdens.

"You could learn a lot from Hunterston here, as well." She gestured to Alec with her cane. "He reminds me of your great uncle."

"Oh, God," muttered Edmund, clapping a hand over his eyes.

The old woman ignored him. "Daresay you don't remember. Uncle Timothy was before your time. But it was a cold Sunday in August that you didn't find him without at least two incognitas perched on his knee. Quite a man for the ladies. At least, he was before he drank himself into a hole."

"Thank you," Alec said with what he hoped was a properly meek expression. "You are most gracious."

Maddie gave a bark of laughter. "No, I'm not. But then, that's one of the few virtues of being old." She placed her hands on the cane's gold knob and leaned forward. "What do you want, Hunterston? All I could get from my silly grand nephew was that you needed my help."

Alec bowed. "I'm pleased you—"

"Poppy seeds. You may well wish me to the devil before we're through." She poked Edmund's foot with her cane. "Bring me a shawl. It's cold enough in here to freeze the Thames."

She waited until he scrambled to settle a startling red and gold shawl about her lavender-clad shoulders before turning back to Alec. "I'd have thought you could afford a decent fire, now that you've inherited that fortune everyone is gabbing about."

"Grandfather was very generous."

Her gaze softened ever so slightly. "John was very fond of you."

"I know." However misguided his grandfather's attempts to secure his happiness, Alec never doubted the old man had cared for him in his way.

Silence reigned until Edmund blurted, "We might as well go ahead and ask her. Aunt Maddie, Alec needs your help with a problem. Not that Julia is a problem. At least, not exactly. She's more of an inconvenience." He caught Alec's scowl and flushed. "I mean, not an inconvenience at all, but—"

"What happened, Hunterston? Get some girl in trouble? Not a serving maid, was it?" When Edmund made a choking noise, she scowled. "If it's not that, then what is it? Spit it out, one of you. Never met such a bunch of velvet mouths in my whole life."

Alec stepped forward. "Lady Birlington, I was hoping you could assist my wife."

"Don't tell me you married that gel with that ungodly French name."

"No, I married her cousin, Julia. She is an American."

A look of supreme distaste crossed Maddie's face. "Good God! No wonder you need my help. Most stubborn people in the world, Americans. Don't care what anyone says, they have no finesse."

"Exactly," interjected Lucien smoothly. "What Julia needs is polishing." A smile curved his mouth. "In fact, Hunterston here was attempting to do just that when I arrived."

Heat crept up Alec's neck and spread to his ears. He cast a fulminating stare at the duke before turning to Lady Birlington. "It is a requirement of my grandfather's will that Julia and I reside within society for a year without a scandal. We need your assistance."

"Ask Edmund's mother. Smart gel, Eugenia, though you'd never know it to see the lummox she married," the old woman said ungraciously.

"No, Julia needs you. She is . . . unusual."

"Unusual? She hasn't got three heads or the like, has she?"

"Aunt Maddie," Edmund said, scandalized. "Of course Alec's wife doesn't have three heads!"

Maddie looked disappointed. "Well, you never know. I saw a man at a fair once that had two heads. No use in that. Now if he'd had two p—"

"Please!" interrupted Edmund in a strangled voice. "Alec was speaking of his *wife*."

"I know what he was saying, you empty-headed dolt!" She stared down her nose at her great nephew until he tugged uneasily at his cravat. Then she turned her gaze to Alec. "Tell me about this chit. Is she pretty?"

He hesitated before answering. "No, but there is an undeniable quality to her."

"Quality? Then what's she doing with you?"

That stung. Julia *was* far better than he deserved, but he'd freeze in hell before he'd admit that to this outspoken old woman. "Julia and I reached an agreement."

"Didn't compromise her, did you?"

"Of course he didn't," said Edmund loyally. "Julia's a reformer."

"Eh?"

"I said," said Edmund, speaking more loudly, "Julia's a reformer."

Maddie stared at him until he turned beet red. "You know," she said with painful clarity, "you remind me more and more of your father every day."

Edmund opened and closed his mouth.

Alec took the opportunity to turn the topic back to Julia. "Lady Hunterston feels very strongly about helping others. She's the most generous person I know."

"I met her father years ago," Maddie said. "Handsome man with a nice leg. Met his wife, too. Couldn't imagine what he saw in her. Plain little thing."

"We need your help to launch her. She will be torn to shreds if it is not done right."

Edmund nodded earnestly. "Aunt Maddie, you have to—"

"I don't *have* to do anything." She scowled. "Impertinent bunch of sapskulls."

Anger tightened Alec's jaw. To hell with it all. He would dress Julia in the finest silks, cover her with jewels, and dare anyone to treat her with less than respect. If they dared to so much as frown at her, he'd answer them with the end of his pistol at twenty paces!

Then his gaze fell on the bonnet, and an image of her impish smile rose before him. No matter how he wished it otherwise, he and Julia were committed to this path. And Julia, for all her belief that she was immune to such things, would take every cruelty to heart. As eccentric as Lady Birlington was, she was the only one who could help.

Feigning a sigh, Alec nodded. "You are right, milady."

Her eyes narrowed with suspicion. "Right about what?"

"It is too much to ask. At your age. . . ." He shrugged.

"Age? What's age got to do with it?" Her voice crackled with hostility.

Alec met Lucien's cool gaze for the space of a second.

A faint smile passed over the duke's face. "Hunterston is right. It would be too much for you, madam. I can only think of one or two people who could carry it off.

Even then, it is bound to set all of London on its ears."

Resolutely suppressing the urge to laugh at Maddie's outraged expression, Alec sighed. "Yes, it would be a shocking thing. Daresay the prince will give the cut direct to anyone who tries to foist a plainspoken colonial onto society."

Maddie stood with imposing dignity. "The prince is a mawkish idiot! Let him dare cut me."

"Quite so, madam," Alec agreed mildly.

A reluctant twinkle sparkled in Maddie's blue eyes. "You're a fool, Hunterston, but you've your grandfather's charm. I never could say no to a man with a sense of humor. Very well. Bring the gel 'round tomorrow. God knows I've been bored lately. If she's the quality you say, this could be just the thing to keep me from dying of ennui this season."

Edmund jumped up and retrieved the forgotten shawl. "By Gad, that's capital! I knew you'd come through, Aunt Maddie."

"I haven't decided if I will help or not. Won't, 'til I've met Alec's wife for myself. Now, quit standing there like a bumpkin and get Ephram."

Her great nephew gathered the scattered objects, eyeing the snoring pug with distaste.

"Don't forget his pillow," reminded Maddie. She looked pointedly at Alec. "I expect you to come in the morning with your lady wife."

"I look forward to it."

Maddie snorted. "Edmund, stop loitering. I promised Admiral Hutchins I'd bring him some of my gout remedy."

As her "remedy" included some of his late lordship's best brandy, Alec had little doubt the admiral was anxiously waiting.

She limped to the door, stopping long enough to point her cane at Alec. "Ten in the morning. Don't be late."

"You may count on us." Alec swept an elegant bow. "You are an angel."

Maddie's mouth twitched in a reluctant smile. "A good thing, too. From the sound of it, divine intervention is exactly what you are going to need."

Chapter 9

Julia shut the door to her chamber and leaned against it, one hand covering her lips that still tingled from Alec's kiss. Though her knees quivered like newly formed aspic, she managed to walk to the settee and collapse against the cushions.

"You are supposed to be reforming *him*, you wretch," she muttered to herself. Pulling one of the pillows closer, she hugged it to her. It was the very pillow *he* had slept on the night before, when he had so chivalrously allowed her the use of his bed.

Darn the man. She wished he would just decide what he was: a hardened rake in need of reforming, or a pretender with a generous heart. He couldn't be both.

Pressing a shaking hand to her temple, she leaned her cheek against the pillow. All this sensation from a simple kiss. No wonder the man was attracted to libertine activities. One could easily get addicted to the thrill of such sensations, wanting more and more, until thinking became an impossibility, and—

"Stop it," she chastised herself. "He is a rake. A kiss means nothing to him and should mean nothing to you."

She caught sight of her blurred reflection and put aside the pillow to stand in front of the beveled mirror. Confound the man for taking her spectacles. He seemed to be making a habit of it. Julia leaned across the gleaming wood surface until she could see her reflection.

Her hair was a mess, one curl drooping piteously over her shoulder. Yet for all her disheveled appearance, she looked amazingly alive. Of its own accord, her mouth, bruised-looking from the force of his kiss, curved in a tremulous smile. Even her eyes, her only good feature, gleamed with secret warmth. Tousled hair and all, she nonetheless appeared dazedly happy.

"Rakes are known for their lack of decorum as well as their determination to exceed the boundaries of polite society. What you need is to cease mooning about. Alec will not appreciate such a reaction to a simple embrace," she scolded her reflection.

Yet she couldn't quite banish the image of his gaze just before he kissed her. He was so incredibly handsome . . . so beyond her reach.

"He's your husband, ninny," she told the dreamy-eyed woman in the mirror. "The man is within *easy* reach— that's the problem. Now, wash your face and fix your hair. You've work to do. If he ever saw you with such a bird-witted expression, he'd run as though his coattails were afire."

That much was true. An unmistakable flicker of relief had crossed his face when Burroughs had announced the duke. Already regretting his impulse, he had shoved her behind him, as if embarrassed to have been caught kissing his own wife. Julia refused to admit how much that impulsive gesture had hurt. She rubbed a finger over her still tingling mouth. How could she help him if he kept her in such a muddle she couldn't think?

Pushing the uncomfortable thoughts aside, Julia tried to repair her fallen hair with the few pins she had left. It wasn't easy, but she managed a simple arrangement. If she hurried, she would have time to visit the vicar before dark. She couldn't wait to see his face when she told him about their new funding.

The idea of establishing a factory gleamed before her, bright and beckoning. The Society needed to find an industry that was neither too difficult to establish nor too physically demanding. Charity was an anathema for most of the women they helped. They desired nothing more than to provide for themselves and their families in a respectable way.

As Julia imagined how many women would benefit from Alec's fortune, her spirits lifted. "Nothing soothes an uneasy heart like a sense of accomplishment," she said aloud.

A knock on the door startled her. Before she could reply, Mrs. Winston opened it and peered around the corner, her round face beaming pleasantly.

"Whomever were you speaking to, my lady?"

Julia turned from the mirror, hoping she had hidden the ravages of the kiss from the sharp-eyed housekeeper. "I was just, ah, humming."

"Speaking to yourself, were you?" The housekeeper opened the door further and marched in with a tray. "It's no wonder, what with the last few days you've had. I brought some tea to help calm your nerves."

"Oh, how thoughtful. But I really should rejoin—"

"Now, don't you fret. I told Burroughs to make your excuses to the gentlemen as you would be resting." Mrs. Winston favored Julia with a motherly beam as she set the tray on a small table before the fireplace. "Johnston is carrying up your things. I had him put them in the guest room."

"But . . ." Julia looked around the room. Unmistakably male with its dark blue carpet and draperies, naturally this chamber was Alec's. Of course he would prefer her in the guest chamber and not here. She caught the housekeeper's curious gaze and her cheeks heated. "I'm sure it is a lovely room."

Mrs. Winston's brows lowered. "Well. I wouldn't say that; the dressing room is scarcely big enough to turn around in. I don't know where we'll put your new things as it is. La, I've never seen such bounty. You must have emptied the shops."

"We spent much more than was necessary." Her own weakness was to blame for that. Alec had taken such delight in buying things, she hadn't had the heart to protest.

Julia noticed the conspicuous placement of two fine china cups beside the plate of pastries. Mrs. Winston was obviously hoping to stay for a chat. Julia had to tamp down a flicker of impatience. The Society waited, but her new duties as mistress called. She indicated the tray. "The pastries look lovely, Mrs. Winston. Perhaps you'd care to join me?"

The housekeeper's rosy cheeks bloomed into a pleased pink. "La, I wouldn't think of it."

Julia poured tea into a cup and held it out to the housekeeper. "I would appreciate the company. It will keep me from having to talk to myself."

Mrs. Winston's face creased in a smile. "If you insist." She sank onto the sofa and sighed with pleasure, stretching her tiny feet in front of her. Small and round, she reminded Julia of a hot cross bun fresh from the oven.

Julia sat down across from her and couldn't help but return the warm smile. Alec's adopted servants were delightful. Gruff Johnston, the groom, had made her laugh aloud with his glum predictions, earning her a grudging smile. He was not nearly as fearsome as he pretended. She had already warmed to Burroughs by the simple knowledge that he brought Alec an evening glass of milk. Such devotion earned her highest regard. And Mrs. Winston was so warm and motherly that Julia felt very comfortable indeed.

The housekeeper slid the plate of pastries toward Julia. "You need to eat something, my lady. Thin as a rail, you are." She patted her own rounded stomach. "I'm trying to thin down, myself. Lucy Cockerel, the house-keeper at Lord Walcott's, next door, told me to drink a half cup of vinegar every night afore I went to bed and I'd be as thin as a wisp in no time."

Julia grimaced. "Pray tell me you don't do such a noxious thing. It makes me ill just thinking about it."

"I did try it, but only once. I couldn't get more than a sip down and then I had the strangest dreams. I dreamt I was a potato floating in a sea of creamed sauce, sprin-kled with rosemary and thyme." The housekeeper blinked, her eyes wide. "What do you think that means? They say dreams tell the secrets of the soul."

Julia chuckled. "I think it means you shouldn't drink vinegar before bedtime. I certainly hope dreams are nothing more than simple imagination gone astray. I once dreamed I was a shoe someone had thrown away. An unpleasant dream, I assure you, and one I refuse to give any credence to whatsoever."

"I suppose you are right." Mrs. Winston looked long-ingly at the cakes. "Dreams or no, I simply could not continue drinking that vile stuff."

"Good for you. You don't need to thin down. Women should be proud of their figures, however they look," Julia said bracingly.

Mrs. Winston looked down at her pudgy body with a doubtful eye. "Do you really think so?"

"Of course." Julia patted the housekeeper's hand. "You look lovely."

The housekeeper beamed. "I hope Master Alec appre-ciates what a gem he's found."

Julia placed a pastry on a plate and handed it to the housekeeper. "We had a bit of a tiff this morning."

Mrs. Winston clicked her tongue. "Being difficult, is he? Well, give him some time. Master Alec can be a difficult man, but you're sure to bring him 'round." Mrs. Winston poured tea into a cup and handed it to Julia.

"He has a way of sneaking into your heart just when you least expect it."

As if she didn't already know that. She sipped her tea. "Tell me, Mrs. Winston, does Alec look like his mother?"

"Oh, yes. Miss Anna was a beautiful child and the old lord doted on her. It nigh broke his heart when she ran off with her Scotsman."

It was inappropriate to gossip with the servants. Julia also knew she should not shamelessly encourage them to tell her every nuance of Alec's life. But some inner voice chided her for such silly, prudish thoughts. If she wished to help her wayward husband find the error of his wicked ways, she needed all the ammunition she could get. "If the old earl was fond of his daughter, you would think he'd allow her to marry wherever her heart led."

"Ah, but the old lord thought Miss Anna's beau was a brazen fortune-hunter, and he demanded that she have no more to do with the poor lad." The housekeeper sighed. "Miss Anna would not listen. She declared that it was to be her Scotsman or no one."

"Now I see where Alec gets his stubbornness."

"All of them, as stubborn as they can hold together. The old lord was livid when Miss Anna refused to heed him and he threatened to lock her in her room."

"What a silly thing to do! I've often noted that men, when faced with a situation they cannot control, over-react and thunder orders as if they were field marshals in some huge battle."

"That is exactly what happened. The old lord ranted and raved like a madman." Mrs. Winston took a sip of tea. "To give him credit, he had Miss Anna's best interests at heart. He was just a bit overprotective."

"Sole parents usually are."

"La, yes. He alternately coddled and bullied her. As

a result, Miss Anna was more given to her feelings than most."

Julia refilled the housekeeper's empty cup. "I've no sensibilities at all. One of my failings, I've been told."

"That's a whisker and no doubt about it," declared Mrs. Winston stoutly. "I think you possess a very sensitive nature."

"Oh, no. My father used to say I was all bones and no blood." Julia chuckled. "He was right, you know. I couldn't work up a fit of vapors if I tried. I cry only if I'm tired." She looked at her cup and added, "Or drunk."

The housekeeper started. "Drunk?"

"Rum punch. Deadly stuff, but quite tasty."

Mrs. Winston laughed uncertainly. "La, my lady, how you do go on! I'm sure you are as sensitive as any lady should be." The housekeeper absently helped herself to another cream cake. "Just like Miss Anna. When the old earl brought her back from Scotland after her Scotsman died, she moped about the house for months, draped in black and playing the most dismal music on the pianoforte."

"That must have been difficult to stand. I can't abide dark music, myself." Julia scooted the teapot under the housekeeper's searching hand.

"Those were sad days, they were. Miss Anna couldn't look at Master Alec without crying, saying he had his father's eyes. His lordship was an active mite even then, and he had no time for such silliness as tears. It wasn't long before he would take to running the opposite way whenever he happened to see his mother coming."

Julia nodded. It confirmed her notions exactly; Alec was not a man to welcome clinging affections. She would do well to keep that thought firmly in mind.

The housekeeper dabbed at a spot of cream on her chin. "To make matters worse, the old master got the notion that nothing but a season in London would help

Miss Anna, so he packed her and the babe into a carriage and off they went."

Julia thought of all the parties and routs she had attended. Being relegated to the corner of the room with the other chaperones had at least one advantage. One could dispassionately observe the proceedings with very few distractions. "The bustle of the season would not have answered a grieving heart."

"Isn't that the truth!" declared Mrs. Winston around a mouthful of pastry. She swallowed noisily. "Miss Anna was more miserable than ever. What the old lord didn't know was that rumors had already started circulating. People knew she had run away to Scotland with her handsome young man and returned with a babe." The housekeeper's broad face puckered in a scowl. "People said Master Alec was naught but a by-blow of Miss Anna's degenerate connection with a groom."

Julia replaced her cup in the saucer with a smart snap. "People can be such idiots! I hope the old earl put a speedy end to such nonsense."

"No one dared tell him. But Miss Anna found out and seemed bent on proving the rumors true. She became wilder and wilder, slipping away with the most ineligible men and staying out past dawn. It all happened so fast that the old lord was at a loss. When he finally realized what was being said, he was so furious he packed up Miss Anna and Master Alec and left town."

"Without setting things straight?"

The housekeeper took another bite of cake. "There is no halting wagging tongues, my lady. Within the month, Miss Anna fell ill and died. The doctor said it was measles, but I think her heart was broken."

Julia didn't bother to ask how measles could be mistaken for a broken heart.

Mrs. Winston sighed. "Poor Master Alec has had to bear his mother's shame. And children can be the cruelest of all. They called him names and made remarks about his parentage—all sorts of evil things. Poor Master Alec was sent home from school I don't know how many times for fighting."

"I can imagine." Julia rubbed her bottom lip, where she could still feel the pressure of his kiss. "The poor man," she murmured. Catching Mrs. Winston's bright gaze, she hurriedly added, "What a burden for a child. It's a good thing he no longer has to deal with such foolishness."

"Oh, but he does. No one would have thought it, but those nasty rumors seem to follow him. It's almost as if someone stirs those stories every so often so no one will forget them. And Master Alec has just enough of Miss Anna in him to prove them all true."

"I don't blame him," Julia said stoutly. "Why should he make a cake of himself, trying to win the approval of a bunch of old rattles with nothing better to do than sit around and repeat a lot of nonsense?"

Twin dimples appeared in Mrs. Winston's chubby cheeks. "Master Alec needs someone like you, bless me if he doesn't."

"I'll do my best," said Julia. No wonder he seemed determined to offend polite society with his debauched actions.

The mantel clock gently chimed the hour. "La! Will you look at the time?" The housekeeper scrambled to her feet. "I had best be about my duties."

"Of course." Julia replaced her cup on the tray and stood. "I believe I will be going out as well." If she hurried, there would be just enough time to visit Vicar Ashton.

Mrs. Winston gathered the tray. "Very well, my lady. I'll have Johnston bring the carriage 'round."

Julia shook her head. Alec had been harmed enough by wagging tongues. She would be discreet with her work and none would be the wiser. "I don't need the coach. I'll call a hack."

"Lud! It won't do for you to be riding about town in a hack. Whatever will Master Alec say?"

"I'll be back before he even misses me. I just need to stop by my aunt's house and retrieve my belongings." That much was true. She possessed remarkably few things and it would take only a minute to pack them into a bandbox.

Mrs. Winston's plump face folded in doubt. "I still think you should let me call Johnston. But I suppose you'll be all right." She crossed to the door, stopping just long enough to beam at the empty pastry plate. "At least I know you won't be leaving hungry."

Chapter 10

Julia pulled out her last remaining pence and placed them in the hackney driver's outstretched hand. The richest woman in England, indeed.

The man peered at the coins, his lip curling over black teeth. " 'Tain't enough."

"It's a reasonable amount, considering the distance you traveled." She fought to keep her shoulders from slumping. It had been a long, arduous day and she longed for the comfort of a bed.

"I come all the way down Fenders' Road, I did—"

"And went out of your way to go that route, too. Chattingham Street is closer and you passed right by it without so much as slowing." She pulled the drawstring on her reticule and looped the ends over her arm.

The driver's dirt-streaked face registered resignation as he eyed her threadbare purse. "I'll be damned if I ever help a nabob acrost town agin."

"A great loss to us all." Julia watched the lumbering hack wheel down the road before turning to her aunt's house and hurrying up the walk. The setting sun cast long shadows across the fashionable street, covering the neat hedgerows and walkways with a touch of spring chill.

The visit to Vicar Ashton had taken much longer than

she'd intended. She had announced their unexpected largesse from an "anonymous donor" and her idea to sponsor their own industry. She should never have succumbed to the vicar's invitation for a cup of tea, but he had been so excited she hadn't the heart to refuse.

Once Julia realized how late it was, she'd hailed the first hackney available and ordered it to her aunt's. She still had to gather the few things she deemed precious and return to Hunterston House before anyone missed her.

Even through her tired haze, excitement buoyed her. There was so much to do, so many good works to achieve. The vicar was calling an emergency meeting of the Society to discuss the new funding. They were dear old men, with generous hearts and a sincere commitment to their important work. Julia was glad none of them chose to move within the social circles their birth and position allowed, or her plans for anonymity would have surely failed.

Lord Kennybrook, an active Member of Parliament, eschewed society entirely as a frivolous waste of time. And Mr. Tumbolton, a noted theoretician who had published several books on metaphysical philosophy, rarely left his home on High Street except to attend their meetings.

The only worry she had was Lord Burton. A noted philanthropist, he refused to attend any function that did not promote one of his many causes. But his new wife was another matter. The daughter of a minor noble, Lady Burton was an active social climber.

But Julia had met the hard-eyed woman only once and had been peremptorily ignored, so there was little chance Lady Burton would recognize her if they met at some function. Or so Julia hoped.

"You can cross that bridge when you have to," she mumbled, reaching the front door and thumping the brass knocker. The oak panel swung open almost immediately.

The gray-haired butler bowed. "My lady. Pray come in."

Julia stepped into the foyer. "Good evening, Roberts. How are you?" When she had last left the house, she'd been a poor relation. Now she returned a viscountess, wealthy beyond her wildest dreams. It should have been exhilarating, but all Julia could dredge up was mild embarrassment, as if she'd overdressed for a party.

The butler shut the door behind her, his impassive face softening slightly. "I am fine, Lady Hunterston. I trust you are the same?"

At the mention of her title, Julia grimaced. She had hoped to break the news to Therese herself. "I'm as well as can be expected. I suppose the household is in an uproar."

A twinkle appeared in the butler's brown gaze. "One could say that, my lady. Your aunt has taken to her bed with a megrim, while Lady Therese has just now received Lord Hunterston in the parlor. Shall I take your pelisse?"

Alec was here. Julia swallowed, wondering if she should have left him a note on her departure. Since she had thought to only be gone an hour or so, she had not bothered. She caught the butler's lifted brows and shook her head. "No, thank you, Roberts. I don't expect to stay long."

"Of course." He led her through the wide hallway to the parlor door. There, he hesitated. "If I might be so bold as to congratulate you on your new station, my lady. It could not have happened to a kinder, more worthy person."

Tears filled her eyes, surprising them both. Darn her tired brain. She dug into her reticule and produced her handkerchief, hastily wiping her eyes. "Pray do not say such kind things to me. I've had a long day and I'm in danger of turning into a watering pot."

His mouth twitched. "You are not a watering pot, madam. You are, as ever, our kind and deserving Lady Julia."

She chuckled and sniffed. "I don't know what I am, lately. But thank you anyway. I do hope you will come and visit."

"I hardly think that would be proper," the butler said in a tone of gentle reproof.

Julia folded the handkerchief into a neat square. "Proper? What could be more proper than visiting an old friend?"

He smiled. "I will announce you, madam." Waiting until she had tucked her handkerchief away, he opened the door and said, with the same reverential air with which he would have announced the crown prince, "Lady Hunterston."

Julia forced herself not to look at Alec, though it was her first impulse. Vibrantly aware of his dark presence by the settee, she forced her unruly gaze to Therese. Her cousin leaned against the pianoforte and Julia silently congratulated her on contriving such an artful pose. The dark gleaming wood showed her pale coloring to advantage, as well as serving as an entrancing background for her elegant blue silk gown.

Despite Julia's intentions, her disobedient attention slid to her husband. Dressed in formal evening clothes, he was, as always, heart-wrenchingly handsome. A quiver of something other than hunger rose in her very empty stomach.

Therese held out her hands and glided across the room. Small, fair, and graceful, she looked like a picture-book fairy. "Julia! How glad I am to see you!"

Bemused, Julia allowed her cousin to embrace her. "Oh, yes. I'm very happy to see you, too." The words rang flatly beside Therese's gushing acclaim. In the three years she had resided with her cousin, this was the first sign of affection she had ever received.

The china-blue eyes glistened. "Julia, I know I have been unfair to you in the past . . . Alec has made me see . . . I only hope you will forgive me." Golden curls framed Therese's perfect face as a lone crystal tear slid down her cheek. No angel could have appeared more penitent.

To Alec's extreme irritation, his wife did not look at all put out by such an obvious gammon. Instead, she patted Therese's shoulder awkwardly and said, "There, there. No need to hug me quite so tightly. I'm not angry with you at all."

"Oh, Julia! You are so kind! And after all the times I slighted you."

Another tear rolled down Therese's face and Alec felt an impulse to toss the chit headfirst out the window— lace, lies, and all.

Red faced, Julia mumbled, "Oh, no! You and Aunt Lydia must visit soon."

Therese pulled back from the embrace, dabbing at her eyes with a scrap of lace that had miraculously appeared in her hand. "You don't know how much that means to me."

"Oh, I think we can guess," said Alec caustically, wondering what the little minx was up to now. It was amazing that he had ever thought Therese a beautiful woman. Though there was no doubt her form met the brief requirements of beauty, it was now painfully obvious her eyes were somewhat narrow-set. Furthermore, he decided critically, her small, cruel mouth lacked Julia's sensuality.

As if reading his thoughts, Julia shot him a hard stare before returning her attention to her cousin. "You will always be welcome at Hunterston House."

"You are such a dear!"

Alec saw the triumph flit through the blue eyes. Even

for Therese, this was a bit much. Not that he was surprised she wanted to continue her connection with Julia; who wouldn't? Julia now had more money than any sane person could rightfully spend. Still, he couldn't shake the thought that there was more to this little charade than met the eye.

He crossed to the door. "While I hate to interrupt such a charming scene, Julia and I need to return home."

"Alec!" Therese reproached, "we've barely had time to speak. I want to hear about the wedding." She cast a sly glance at him from under her lashes. "Mother and I are Julia's only relatives. We want to know *all* the details of the wedding."

That made him pause. The quicker he removed Julia from her cousin's poisonous clutches, the better. "Come, Julia. Mrs. Winston is holding supper."

Julia flushed. "I'm sorry I'm so late. I'm not used to having anyone wait on me." Her wide mouth hinted at some strong emotion, and he thought he detected the shimmer of tears behind her spectacles.

Alec's irritation evaporated instantly. The last few days had been hell. He took her hand in his. "Come. Home awaits."

For one horrified second, he thought she would cry. Instead, she gave him a tremulous smile that made his chest swell with an inexplicable ache. To cover his discomfort, he said sternly, "From now on, I expect you to take Johnston when you go out."

"Oh, were you visiting your charity again, Julia?" Therese asked with deceptive sweetness. Despite her attempt to play the part of devoted cousin, she could not resist flicking him a malicious glance. "Julia has always been so generous with her time. I fear, Alec, you will have to get used to sharing your new wife."

Though the hand that lay quietly in his never moved, he was aware Julia had tensed. He tucked her fingers into the crook of his arm and led her to the door. "I don't think I could get used to sharing my wife with anyone."

Therese's mouth tightened.

Alec hid a grin and bent solicitously over Julia, whispering, "I asked Roberts to gather your things when I arrived. He should have them by now."

He opened the door and nodded to Therese. "I appreciate your hospitality, but I fear I must rush home to tuck my wife . . . back into bed." At Therese's outraged gasp, he pulled Julia into the hall and bustled her to the carriage. She offered no resistance, murmuring her thanks to the graying butler as he pressed a worn bandbox into her hand.

Within moments, they were on their way home. Alec took the opposite corner from Julia and lounged in the seat, taking up more than his fair share of space. Since he had discovered her missing, he'd had to fight off the damnedest thoughts. Julia, trying to find a hackney in the dark. Julia, lost in the dark streets of London. Julia, changing her mind about their marriage and going back to the only home she knew.

The last thought had sent him posthaste to the Covington household. The flood of relief that flowed through him when she'd appeared had been almost overwhelming. And strange. He pulled his hat low so he could watch his wife in the gathering darkness.

Julia leaned her head against the worn squabs, and shot an apologetic glance his way, barely visible in the approaching night. "I meant to return before supper. The time just slipped by."

"Mrs. Winston wouldn't serve anything until I'd found you."

Her wide mouth curved into a tired smile. "Mrs. Winston is a charming woman."

"Not when she's holding an entire basted ham hostage."

She chuckled and he was assailed with an instant desire to taste her laughter. Low and rich, it would trail down his throat and heat his empty stomach. God, she was a taking thing, even for an avaricious reformer. "You should have told someone where you'd be." He almost winced at the petulant note in his voice. He sounded far too much like a jealous husband.

Fortunately, she didn't think his comment misplaced, for she gave a nod. "Was Mrs. Winston upset?"

"She was weeping over the bread pudding when I left."

Julia laughed. Her white throat caught the light and he allowed his gaze to wander down the graceful column to the long row of tiny buttons that adorned her pelisse. Her breasts pressed against the material, small and firm, perfectly made for a man's hand. His mouth watered and he pictured himself bending over her shapely body, his mouth fastened on her ni—

"Did you hear me?"

Alec blinked. Good God, what was he doing? He glanced down and placed his hat across his lap. "No, I didn't hear you. Forgive me; I seem to be wandering."

"Tired to death? Me too. I merely mentioned how pleased the vicar was at the donation." She continued to expound on the vicar's reaction and the possibilities that awaited the Society.

He nodded absently, noting how animated she became as she talked about her charity work. She was unlike any woman he had ever known. He admired her determination and intelligence, but the ease with which she made him stiffen with desire was disturbing. How on earth could he lust after such a prim woman?

Of course, he'd been without a mistress these past two weeks. The little charmer he'd enjoyed had become too demanding, and that was always a sign a change was in order. Perhaps his reaction to Julia was a combination of his unsatiated urges compounded with the tantalizing knowledge he couldn't have her.

He'd given his word and she was, after all, an innocent. Her reaction to his kiss this afternoon had proved to him how easily her innocence could be taken advantage of. It strengthened his resolve to keep his promise that the marriage be one of convenience only.

Alec had always enjoyed the company of women, particularly those who loved life. He had lounged in the beds of many a high-priced lightskirt, laughed through the raucous comedies at Vauxhall with doe-eyed cyprians who encouraged him to slip his hand under their skirts, and driven more than one somewhat married woman to distraction in a dark carriage. He reveled in their softness and indulged himself between their thighs. But he had never been even remotely interested in a woman like Julia.

Innocent and virtuous, she represented the exact type of female he avoided. Interested only in commitment and the boring necessities of life, women like Julia enjoyed the closed confines of Almack's, desired nothing more than a home in the country, and dreamed of babies. Alec wanted no part of any of those things. He knew what he was: the son of a questionable union between a landless Scottish nobleman and a hellion. A man branded by sin to sin.

Julia, with her rows of buttons and sensible spectacles, should have had no more effect on him than the money-grubbing Therese. Yet somehow, all his prim wife had to do was part her generous mouth in a smile and he instantly thought of those soft lips parting for other, less chaste reasons. His groin tightened uncomfortably and he shifted, suddenly aware she was looking at him with an expectant gaze.

He adjusted his hat on his lap and thought furiously. What had she been talking about? "Uhm. Yes."

"Good."

The relief in her voice worried him. He cleared his

throat. "Perhaps you should explain again what I just agreed to."

After a prolonged silence, she asked flatly, "You weren't listening, were you?"

"No. I'm afraid not."

In the dim light, he could just make out her squared chin. "Too bad," she said. "You've agreed and I refuse to allow you to take it back."

She sounded so much like an outraged governess that he almost chuckled aloud. Instead, he crossed his arms and stretched out his legs so they brushed the side of her skirts. "I'm a man of my word, Julia. Enlighten me to the extent of my folly."

She pulled away and tucked her skirts back. "I asked if I could hire a few servants for the house. Not many, but one or two. Mrs. Winston is woefully short-handed."

More servants? Damn his inattention. He had better get his lust under control before he ended up agreeing to something far more costly.

"A wonderful idea." Even in the darkness, he could feel the force of her smile. He cast about for a safe topic of conversation. "Where exactly does the Society meet?"

"Whitechapel. We own a house. It was once a brothel, but the building is sound. With a few repairs, it should serve us well."

He sat up straight, his hat slipping to the floor. "*Whitechapel*? Good God, don't tell me you traipsed through that hellhole without so much as an escort?"

"Very well, then; I won't tell you. But I do it all the time and have never come to any harm."

"What you did before you became my wife is of no concern," he replied frostily. "You will remember you are Viscountess Hunterston now. In the future, Johnston will accompany you."

In the occasional flicker afforded by the streetlights, he could see her face, colorless against the squabs, her mouth pressed into a straight line. After a long moment, she nodded. "Very well, but I will not curtail my visits. There's much work to be done. Besides," her glance pinned him with deadly accuracy, "we have a bargain."

"I am beginning to believe our bargain was very one-sided," he snapped.

"That is no fault of mine. When we first struck our agreement, I asked if you had any conditions you wished to mention, and you couldn't think of any."

"Well, I can think of some now." He stretched his legs out even more until the warmth of her knee pressed against his.

She attempted to pull back further, but she was already pressed into the corner as far as her slim body would fit. "I'm sure you can. Unfortunately, it would be very unfair of you to insist on new conditions at this point."

His anger sparked anew. "If you risk a scandal with your trips to Whitechapel, my lady, I will be well within my rights to demand a new agreement."

Julia sniffed. "There will be no scandal. After all, I am merely helping those less fortunate."

With deliberate menacing intent, Alec leaned forward and placed his hand on her knee. "And if there is?"

Her fingers tightened about her reticule. "If for some unthinkable reason I cause a scandal, then we will speak again about our bargain." She turned to look out the window.

Alec grinned, feeling inordinately proud. It wasn't the assurance he'd wanted, but it was all he would get. And from Julia, it was more than enough. The woman was nigh bursting with prudish honor; she'd keep her word or die.

Julia was the most exhilarating challenge he'd ever faced. He burned to wrap his hands about her trim waist and pull her across the hard leather seat. He dreamed of sliding her sensible skirts up to her waist, parting her tender thighs, and plundering every delectable inch of her.

Alec stifled a moan at the hot images flickering through his mind. God, he needed a drink. A drink, and his hat back in his lap.

As he bent over to retrieve it his arm brushed against her skirt. Julia started as if he'd run his hand up her thigh. Muttering to herself, she hunched a shoulder and looked steadfastly out the window.

She was not immune to him. With one or two well-placed kisses, he could ignite the fire that smoldered beneath her primly buttoned exterior and win any assurances he desired. She possessed the wild Frant blood, despite her belief to the contrary.

The only problem was, there was more than mere honor at stake. Alec wasn't at all sure he would be able to stop a simple kiss from progressing into something far more dangerous to his own peace of mind. If he were to compromise Julia in such a way they would be married in more than name only, and that was a commitment he was not about to make. Especially not to a woman who had wed him for no other reason than to secure a hold on his purse strings.

For that very reason, he would turn Julia over to Lady Birlington with his blessing. He needed some time to adjust to the fact there was at least one woman he could never have and that he'd been foolish enough to marry her. For now, he would remain on his side of the carriage, his entire body achingly stiff, his disposition lowering with every passing moment.

Sighing heavily, Alec decided Lucien had been right. Noble intentions were a damned inconvenience.

Chapter 11

～⌒の⌒～

"**E**dmund!" Maddie thumped her cane on the carriage floor. "Wake up! How do you expect us to get out of the carriage with you sprawled across the doorway?"

Startled from a comfortable doze, Edmund jerked upright, his head cracking against the low roof. Shawls and books tumbled to the floor as Ephram barked hysterically.

Edmund clutched his chest, wrinkling the gaudy green and yellow waistcoat. "Tare and hounds, Aunt Maddie! I'm having heart palpitations!"

Julia choked back a laugh. Edmund possessed a natural sweetness of temperament that had won her instant favor. For the past fortnight he had been everything polite and charming, escorting them everywhere and offering her numerous suggestions on how to wear her hair, which color best suited a rainy day, or what type of half-boot complemented her new pelisse.

As his own taste seemed somewhat questionable, she usually listened politely and did the opposite. So far, her instincts had not erred.

Maddie patted Ephram on the head. "There, there, precious angel." When the dog's barking had subsided into satisfied grunts, she poked her nephew in the stomach with her cane. "Cease your wailing and open the blasted door."

"The coachman—"

"Is older than I. It will take him an hour just to climb from the perch."

Edmund gathered the strewn articles and dutifully opened the door. "Don't know why you keep him on if he's so blasted slow. Took us almost a half-hour to get here. I can make it in ten minutes in my curricle."

"That's because of the way you drive your cattle." Maddie took her great nephew's arm and climbed from the carriage.

Edmund blinked his surprise. "Why, thank you, Aunt Maddie. I can't understand why they won't let me in the Four Horse Club. I am a fair hand at the whip, if I do say so myself."

She snorted. "Bound to say it yourself—no one else would. Most cow-handed fool I ever saw." Maddie glanced over her shoulder at Julia. "Once saw him tip over right in the middle of Bond Street. Biggest green 'un ever to handle the ribbons."

"I say, Aunt Maddie," sputtered Edmund, his face deep red. "It's cursed unfair of you to remind a fellow of the things he did years ago."

"Hmph. You'll be as wet behind the ears when you are forty as you are today."

Julia climbed out of the carriage. With a reassuring smile at Edmund, she relieved him of some of his burdens, taking a book and shawl that seemed in imminent danger of toppling to the ground.

"Thank you, Julia," he muttered. "I vow, some days I want to throttle my aunt. She can—"

"Edmund?" Maddie called over her shoulder. "I'm too old to stand out here in the sun all day. Might wither and look worse than I do now."

Julia chuckled as Edmund spared her a smiling shake of his head before he hurried after his aunt. Though Julia had been apprehensive at meeting Lady Birlington, she had warmed to the cantankerous woman from the beginning. Julia suspected Maddie's crusty exterior hid a soft heart.

The old lady settled her shawl around her shoulders and led the hapless Edmund toward the subscription library. "Come, Julia. I wish to find that new book Lady Castlewaite was telling me about at the modiste's."

Julia grimaced. For the last two weeks, she and Lady Birlington had spent a good portion of every morning shopping. Julia had been pinned, primped, and pressed until she felt like a paper doll. Yet even she had to admit the transformation was amazing. Now, when she looked in a mirror, an astonishingly fashionable woman stared back.

Her hair, artfully cut and arranged, emphasized her eyes and made her appear younger than her twenty-seven years. Her face, framed by soft tendrils of hair, seemed less angular, and her eyes appeared even larger. But the most astonishing change of all had been in her figure. She'd always considered herself sadly flat chested and much too short ever to command attention. But now she was beginning to see she was perfectly suited for the current fashion.

Not, she thought peevishly, that Alec noticed. Since the night he had met her at Therese's, he had studiously avoided her. Although he appeared each morning for breakfast, looking shadow-eyed with fatigue, he offered nothing in the way of polite conversation. He seemed totally uninterested in her progress and had scarcely noted her changed appearance. Yet she treasured those morning visits, silent as they were, for they were among the few times she saw him.

She knew the servants whispered. Mrs. Winston had taken to the annoying habit of patting her hand with an expression of tearful concern, while Burroughs had begun to bring her an obligatory glass of milk every night.

Julia accepted it all with stoic silence. Though she was very fond of them both, they were Alec's retainers, not hers.

Night after night, Julia lay awake hour after hour until she heard the sound of his measured tread in the hallway, followed by the soft thud of his door. In her own way, she was every bit as assiduous as Burroughs.

It was a silly thing to do and she knew it, but no amount of stern lecturing seemed to make her able to sleep until she heard him return. She wondered where he spent his evenings. Though she knew he would never break his word, she could not help but picture him in the arms of some painted Cyprian, his arms about her slender waist, his face buried in her neck.

Julia usually stopped the image right there, before she dissolved into tears.

Distracted by her thoughts, she stumbled as her new half-boot caught the bottom step. Books slipped from her arms as she tried to regain her balance.

Strong hands clasped about her waist. "Easy, love," murmured a deep voice.

Julia clutched at the broad chest and looked up, her heart in her throat.

It wasn't Alec. Instead, she found herself staring into the faintly smiling face of the Earl of Bridgeton. She flushed and pulled away, aware she had leaned against him much longer than was proper. "Pardon me. I thought you were someone else."

The amused glint in Nick's blue eyes deepened. "Did you?" He released her and bent to retrieve her scattered books, glancing at the bindings as he straightened. "Novels, Lady Hunterston? I am surprised."

"You shouldn't be. I've been able to read since I was a child, you know."

His finely carved mouth quirked into a smile. "That's not quite what I meant." He tilted his head and favored her with a considering gaze. "I'd never have thought you, of all people, a romantic."

"Nonsense." She took the last book from him and tucked it under her arm. Truthfully, Julia had never indulged in novels before her acquaintance with Lady Birlington, but she had to admit there was enjoyment to be had in reading a story one felt reasonably certain would have a happy ending. "All people are romantics, one way or another."

"No person would ever condemn me as a romantic. Lascivious, yes. But romantic?" He replaced his curly brimmed beaver with easy grace, the sun glinting off his golden hair, his slow, deliberate movements as sensual as a snake's.

There was something compelling about the aura of forbidden maleness of this man. It was almost as if the perfection of his face and form was at constant war with the scarred blackness of his soul. A flash of pity softened her irritation. "Maybe you should try a novel. Love is good for the soul."

Disbelief and humor mingled in his gaze. "Love is an illusion." He glanced around the crowded street. "Speaking of which, where is my worthless cousin?"

Any pity she may have felt evaporated in an instant. "Alec is not worthless."

Nick's smile hardened. "Ah, yes. Thanks to your timely intervention, he is now worth a great deal."

"He's rich as Croesus," Julia said bluntly.

His blue gaze narrowed. "As are you. Tell me, Cousin, did you plan to place yourself so conveniently in Alec's way, or was it a mere twist of fate?"

Julia recognized the spite behind the polished tones, but she supposed Nick was due. "Upset to have been cut out, are you? I don't blame you. It's a lot of money."

A faint crease appeared between Nick's eyes, though his smile never ceased. "Touché my dear. May I ask what plans Alec has for his wealth?"

Julia wished Nick would move from her path. She was to meet with the solicitor today to sign for the final transfer into the Society's account. Her days with Lady Birlington were so full of morning visits, fittings, dancing lessons, and other nonsensical things that she'd had to move the Society's weekly meeting to an unseemly hour of the morning. Everyone had grumped, but there had been no help for it.

All they needed now was an idea as to what business to establish. Lord Kennybrook had suggested a sausage factory, but Julia couldn't see the women undertaking such a hideous job. Unfortunately, no one else had any other suggestions and, for now, they were at a standstill.

Julia caught Nick's interested gaze and flushed. "Alec does whatever he wishes with his money." Just as she did what she wished with hers.

"Does he? I wonder."

Her hand tightened about her book. She'd like to slap it across Nick's too-handsome face, leaving a lasting imprint of the title, *The Evil Knight of Thebes*, on his cheek. It was frustrating, but she had to be content with lifting her chin into the air and saying stiffly, "Alec's affairs are none of your concern, Lord Bridgeton."

He chuckled. "No need to breathe fire, my dear. You took me by surprise with your little maneuver, stealing Alec away. You are to be congratulated on what was the neatest trick it has been my privilege to witness." He shrugged at her surprised expression. "Why hide it? You knew well enough what your lovely but empty-headed cousin and I had planned, didn't you?"

"Perhaps."

Nick lifted his quizzing glass. "You continue to surprise me even now. Who would have thought such a stunning creature existed behind the colorless rags of the Frant Dragon?"

Julia supposed he could be forgiven for saying that. After all, she *was* dressed in her favorite new pelisse.

Of pearl gray merino, the heavy cloth was accented with rich ruby velvet trim. Her bonnet was one of the many Alec had chosen for her, wide brimmed and adorned with ostrich feathers dyed to match the edging of her pelisse. Despite her determination not to be affected by such fripperies, she had to admit it was thrilling to suddenly find oneself all the crack.

She brushed a hand over the cloth. "To tell you the truth, I almost don't recognize myself. It is shocking what clothes can do for a woman."

He regarded her with astonishment before breaking into a genuine laugh, his eyes crinkling with amusement. "You are an unusual woman, Cousin Julia. I can see Alec won more than a mere fortune." He pulled one of her hands into his and bowed. "Allow me to beg your forgiveness. Alec and I have been competing since we were born. It was a favorite pastime of our grandfather's, and we seem determined to—"

From somewhere down the street a blood-curdling yell sounded as a boy, covered with filthy rags, ran heedlessly into the path of a cart full of cabbage. Cursing loudly, the driver tried to avoid the small figure, pulling to one side at the last minute. The horses lunged, overturning the cart into the street.

Mayhem ensued. Cabbages rolled across the narrow road, followed quickly by a horde of urchins who grabbed as many cabbages as they could before disappearing into a startling number of alleyways. The driver yelled and tried to chase down his missing produce, enlisting the help of every bystander he could.

Forgotten, the barefoot urchin who had started the whole mess slipped through the crowd and swiftly maneuvered his way up the street. A bullish looking man gave a startled shout and charged after the urchin. Desperate, the boy dodged between two carts and ran right into Julia's outstretched arms.

"Lemme go! Damn ye to 'ell, lemme go! Pribble'll kill me, 'e will!"

"Easy, child," Julia soothed. "I won't let anyone harm you." She wrapped both of her arms about the thin, wiry body and held on with all her might.

Dank and odiferous, the child squirmed. "Ye 'as to lemme off! 'E'll strap me if 'e catches me!"

Ash, dirt and grime mired her new pelisse, but Julia only held tighter. Stench wafted from the trembling body and closed her throat. She loosened her hold enough to grasp the boy's head between her hands and tilt the woefully dirty face to hers. His face was a mask of bloody bruises that made Julia's heart burst into righteous fury.

"No one will hurt you," she said firmly. "Not without dealing with me, first."

Some amount of reassurance must have reached the child for he stopped struggling, though he regarded her with a suspicious scowl. "An' what would ye do? Ye ain't nofin' but a girl."

"I would call the constable," Julia replied promptly. "That or hit him with my reticule."

The child eyed her wispy-looking purse with a skeptical eye. But before he could reply, the bullish looking man stormed up.

"There ye be, ye lil' weasel." Small ferret eyes set in a round, flat face shifted from the boy to Julia. The man's gaze lingered on her fine dress before he reluctantly removed the greasy cap from his matted hair. " 'Ere, now, missus. Thank ye fer catchin' me boy. I'll take care he don't bother ye no more." He reached for the child.

The boy shrank from the grimy hand. "No! I won't go wif' ye, ye soddin' prig!"

Nick noticed the Frant Dragon didn't even flinch at the obscenities. Instead, she soothed a hand across the filthy head and said bracingly, "There's no need for that.

Wars are not won with vile words, but with strong deeds."

The boy looked at her and blinked, utterly confused. "Eh?"

Julia chuckled and cast a laughing glance up at Nick.

For a second, he held his breath. Gone was the prim, sedate woman who exuded virtue and honor with every breath. In her place was a woman of passion and humor, alive with warmth. Her piquant face lit with shared amusement as her generous mouth curled in a beguiling smile. Most entrancing were the green eyes that brimmed with laughter behind the concealing spectacles. Nick could not have been more surprised if she'd dropped to her knees right then and there and serviced him.

His gaze narrowed. There was more to the new Viscountess Hunterston than he'd expected. Much more.

Julia straightened the boy's torn shirt. "What's your name?"

The urchin regarded her with a suspicious stare.

"Answer her la'ship," said the sweep, scowling. "Or I'll pummel it out o' ye."

"There's no need for such violence. He's only a child." Julia shot a hard glance at the man, then turned back to the boy, her face softening. "Won't tell, eh? Very well, I'll just make one up. How about Tommy?"

The boy regarded her somberly and then shrugged. "Good as any, I s'ppose. I don't haf no real name. Lest, not one I can 'member."

"Surely you were called something," Julia said. When the child gave no reply, she turned to look at the sweep. "What is his name?"

The sweep scratched his ear with a soot blackened hand. "His ma never tol' me nofin' but that he was a wisty worker." A scowl lowered the man's brow. "Course, that was jus' her way o' gettin' rid o' him."

"Most of the time, Pribble jus' calls me 'Muck,' " offered the boy with a black-toothed grin. "That, or fu—"

" 'Ere now," exclaimed the sweep with a hasty glance at Julia. "Her la'ship is none too interested in what I calls ye, ye little bugger."

Nick watched the scene with growing amusement. Beside Julia's radiance, the child resembled a thin, wasted gutter rat. Sandy lashes framed small, close-set eyes in a sharply featured face that boasted huge ears and a squat upturned nose. The child's mouth sported a number of crooked black teeth and Nick had no doubt the little vermin's breath was as foul as the rest of him.

Yet to see the Frant Dragon with her arms about the thin body, her face warm with reassurance, one would believe the child a prince at the very least. She seemed not to notice the ugliness or grime. Instead, she gazed at the child with a gentle smile that belonged on a painting of a madonna.

It was the most remarkable thing Nick had ever beheld.

"Good God! What is that?" Resplendent in orange velvet, Lady Birlington stepped from the library and cleared a path through the crowd that had gathered.

Julia rose to her feet, one hand firmly grasping the child's. "Lady Birlington, I would like you to meet Muck. He will be going home with us."

"*What*?" exclaimed both the sweep and Lady Birlington at the same time.

"Ye can't do that!" said the sweep angrily. " 'E's mine!"

Maddie stared down her hooked nose at the ragged child. "I won't have that filthy child in my carriage, Julia. Ephram is sensitive to odors."

"Madam! This man is a sweep and he cruelly misuses the boy. Just look at the bruises on the child's face. We must rescue him."

Maddie's mouth pursed in a frown. "I daresay he fell

down the steps or some such thing. But it does not matter. The child cannot go with us, and that is that. Come now—we have much to do."

It was obvious Lady Birlington expected immediate acquiescence. It was equally obvious Julia was not going to give one inch. Hugely amused, Nick noted that the crowd had grown. He couldn't remember when he had been so diverted.

"Julia, we must leave," Maddie repeated sharply. "The boy is none of your concern."

Maddie's censorship encouraged the sweep to new boldness. He grasped Muck's bony arm with both hands and pulled. "Aye, listen to the ol' crow. Muck is none o' yer concern."

Maddie's cane cracked on the sidewalk, her frosty blue gaze pinioning the hapless sweep. "*What* did you call me?"

Nick stifled a laugh at how quickly the sweep let go of the boy's arm. The full force of Mad Maddie's gaze had made crown princes sweat beneath their corsets. He imagined that the force of that gaze on the sweep was nothing less than astounding.

"B-beggin' yer pardon, missus, but I paid a fiver fer the boy, and. . . ." The thought of the lost five pounds seemed to imbue the sweep with courage, for he straightened his shoulders. "I'm not leavin' wit'out 'im."

Maddie's face reddened until it matched her wig. "You landless jackanapes! Is that the way you speak to your betters?" She turned her gaze to Edmund, who stood beside her, a stack of books under one arm, her wheezing pug under the other. "Edmund! Did you hear what this person called me?"

Edmund swallowed and shot a nervous glance at the burly sweep. "Ah, yes, Aunt Maddie, but, ah . . . I don't think he . . . he did pay for the child, so surely—"

"Demme, that's not the point," Maddie said. She ges-

tured with her cane. "That ignorant fool called me a
crow! An *old* crow!"

"That doesn't matter!" Julia exclaimed, eyes flashing.
"What matters is the child. If it bothers Ephram to sit in
the carriage with Muck, then he and I will ride beside
the coachman."

Nick lifted his quizzing glass to regard Julia. By God,
she was magnificent. Here was Therese's incredible
beauty touched with something else, something warm
and alive.

Edmund's weak chin dropped. "Dash it, Julia. You
can't ride with the coachman; bound to attract attention.
People'd stare."

Maddie smacked the tip of her cane on the sidewalk.
"Forget the child! That hurly-burly man called me an
old crow and I demand satisfaction!"

Her nephew gawked. "Surely you don't expect me to
call him out? You can't have a duel with a chimney
sweep."

A martial light entered Maddie's brilliant blue eyes.
"Why not?"

"It's not done, is all." Edmund's miserable gaze fell
on Nick. "Bridgeton! For the love of God, tell her it
isn't done."

Nick was hard pressed not to laugh aloud, but he managed to assume an expression of serious consideration.
"You are quite right, Edmund. It is never done." Edmund relaxed and Nick continued relentlessly, "At least
not in England. I believe, however, there is some pre-
cedence for such matters in Italy. Especially if the honor
of a woman is concerned."

Edmund looked like a fish gasping for air.

"There," said Maddie with a satisfied nod. "I don't
usually hold with Italian manners, but that makes more
sense than your namby-pamby English rules, Edmund.
Now challenge the man. Julia and I have an appointment
at eleven with Madame Rousard for her final fitting."

"B-but . . . I, ah, don't have my gloves." Edmund looked relieved. "I left them in the carriage."

"What do you need gloves for? Just challenge the man and be done with it. Julia and I haven't got all day."

Edmund gulped, then whispered loudly, "But look at him! He's filthy."

Maddie eyed the sweep, her gaze lingering on the dirt and mire.

The sweep's brows knit in confusion. "Pardon me, missus, but—"

"Stay out of this," Maddie said with an impatient gesture. "We have to decide what to do."

"Edmund may borrow my gloves," said Nick smoothly, holding out his own.

Maddie nodded her approval. "There! Very good of you, Bridgeton."

Edmund shot him a dark look and mumbled, "I can do without your help."

"Can you?" Nick replied with a gentle smile. "And here I was going to offer to be your second."

"Capital!" Maddie turned to her hapless nephew. "What are you waiting for?"

Edmund sighed and deposited his burdens on the sidewalk. With a disgusted glare at Nick, he took the proffered glove and walked up to the bemused sweep.

"Sorry, old chap," said Edmund, offering an apologetic grimace. Holding the glove in one hand, he gently slapped the man across the cheek. "I challenge y—"

The sweep punched Edmund in the nose, and the plump young man toppled head over heels into the street.

"Lud!" Maddie exclaimed.

Julia pressed Muck's hand into Nick's, stepped up to the sweep, and delivered her own punch. As quick as it was, Nick had to admit she had excellent form, her feet widely stationed, her whole arm behind the hit.

The sweep, caught unaware, staggered backward,

tripped over the curb, and fell heavily to the ground.

"Gor'," cooed the child. Nick looked down at Muck's filthy hand and suppressed a shudder.

Julia gathered her skirts and stepped across the loudly moaning sweep to where Edmund lay.

"Did you see what that fellow did to me?" Edmund allowed Julia to help him up, blood flowing from his nose and onto his cravat.

Maddie turned a furious gaze on the sweep, who was gingerly clambering to his feet. "You insolent cur! You have just attacked the only son of the Earl of Littleton! Your head will rest on the pikes at Tyburn for this!"

"But he punched me first," protested the sweep, his eyes wild.

Julia handed a handkerchief to Edmund and retrieved Muck's hand. "Perhaps we should send someone for the constable." She glared at the sweep. "I'm sure he has broken some sort of law treating a child in such a way."

The sweep cast an uneasy glance at the gathering crowd. "I didn't do nofin' to 'im. I only wants what's comin' to me. That lil' monkey is mine."

"No, he is not," Maddie said in a freezing voice. She looked down her prominent nose at the sweep. "You are not fit to associate with children."

"But who will I git to clean the chimneys?" asked the sweep with a cautious glance at Julia. "I paid fer 'im, I did, and I wants 'im back."

Nick couldn't have planned a better, more disreputable scene than this, and among the crowd he saw several of society's more rigid matrons, their faces avid with interest. Yet to his immense surprise, he heard himself say, "Perhaps I have the solution."

Every eye turned on him, but he was aware only of Julia. He withdrew his purse, took out a guinea, and tossed it at the sweep's feet. "There—consider yourself compensated. The child now belongs to Lady Hunterston."

The man scrambled for the gold coin and clutched it with both grimy hands. "Thet's more like it, guv'nor. I thank ye." Turning to Julia, he offered a brown-toothed grin. "Ye're welcome to the little bugger. 'E's nofin' but trouble."

"I'm sure he will continue that fine tradition," agreed Nick pleasantly. "Now, leave before the watch arrives."

Glancing furtively over his shoulder, the man melted into the crowd. Nick didn't notice, mesmerized by the luminous gaze Julia turned on him. Never had he seen such beautiful eyes.

She grasped his hand and held it to her, her fingers warm against his. "That was quite the nicest thing I've ever seen. I have misjudged you, Lord Bridgeton."

Nick could have told her she had not been wrong, that he was as evil as rumored and worse. Instead, he lifted her hand and pressed his lips to her fingers. "It was nothing compared to your efforts, Cousin. I stand in awe."

She blushed and retrieved her hand. "I shouldn't have lost my temper."

"Demme," exclaimed Maddie from where she was instructing Edmund on how to stem the flow of blood. "Amelia Cornwall just passed in her carriage. She was gawking like a mongoose, her eyes popping out of her head. It'll be all over town within the hour."

Julia bit her lip, a worried pucker between her brows, though she said staunchly, "We had no choice. Someone had to rescue the child."

"I cannot believe that dangerous man attacked Edmund in such a brash fashion." Maddie handed a fresh handkerchief to her nephew before locking her gaze on Julia. "There's no help for it. I had planned on launching you at the Seftons' ball, but I see we need to speed things up a bit. We will use the Bastions' rout instead."

"But that's only a week from now," echoed Julia, a hint of concern in her voice.

"It will be perfect." Maddie sniffed the air and grimaced. "Julia, the next time you decide to rescue an urchin, pray choose one who is better washed. This one reeks of a water closet." She bent to pick up Ephram, who sat wheezing by her feet. "Put that child up with Jeffers and help me get Edmund into the carriage. He cannot stand the sight of his own blood and is likely to faint at any moment."

Nick wasn't sure what he had just done, but watching Julia assist the ugly child onto the perch with the ancient retainer, he thought that perhaps his impulsive gesture had been the right thing after all. He only wished he could be a witness to Alec's dismay on discovering the newest member of Hunterston House.

Within minutes the carriage rumbled off, Maddie's loud voice still audible as she instructed Edmund on the various ways he could have protected himself from the sweep. Perched on the top of the coach, a bright silk shawl wrapped around his ragged brown clothes, sat Julia's urchin.

Though he hadn't thought of it in years, Nick remembered a time when he had believed love could indeed produce miracles. Watching his beautiful, depraved mother slowly descend into the pit of madness, daily growing more virulent and spiteful, Nick had hoped with every ounce of his adolescent soul that God would see fit to send her the love she needed, for his was plainly not enough. But no love had come, and one fateful night his mother had thrown herself from the roof. If he listened closely enough, he could still hear the echo of her scream as she tumbled through the air.

Nick watched the coach as it disappeared from sight. It was just possible, he reflected dispassionately, that a woman with Julia's ability to love might indeed save his lost soul . . . had he one to save. With an easy shrug, he turned and made his way back to his lodgings.

He might not have a soul, but he did have debts.

Mounds of them, all run up at the expectation of receiving an inheritance that should have been his for the taking. It would take far more than a dab of a woman with an unexpectedly beautiful smile and a punishing left hook to turn him from his ultimate goal.

Whistling a jaunty tune, Nick began to plan his next encounter with the intriguing Lady Hunterston.

Chapter 12

Alec blinked fuzzily at Burroughs' long white
nightrail. "Why in thunder are you dressed like
that? You look like a damned ghost."

"It is four o'clock in the morning, my lord. Most *respectable* people are to bed by now." Reproof lingered
in the cultured tone.

"Not true. You are one of the most respectable persons I know, but you haven't gone to bed yet." Pleased
with his masterful logic, Alec crossed his arms and
rocked back on his heels. Even filled to the gills with
Lucien's best brandy, he was capable of clear, concise
thinking.

Burroughs set the silver tray bearing a glass of milk
aside and assisted Alec in removing his greatcoat. "I
always wait up for you, my lord. It is a tradition for us."

Alec slung an arm around Burroughs' thin shoulders.
"Yes, by God, that's exactly what it is. A tradition. Like
. . . like Christmas." He might be a wastrel and a laggard, but he could handle his liquor with the best of 'em.

Burroughs gently disengaged himself. "Allow me to
escort you to bed, sir."

Alec waved him off. "No, no, no. Need a little something to calm my nerves. Something to give me pleasant
dreams." Or at least, better dreams than the disturbing

ones that had haunted him the last fortnight. Between disreputable visions involving his prim, untouched wife, and nightmares where pocketwatches, teapots, and other mundane household items tangled about his neck like iron shackles, sleep had become little more than an elusive memory.

He had attempted to amuse himself with a variety of activities, including boxing, fencing, and riding, in the hope that sheer weariness would cause him to drop into a restful slumber. Even those diversions had proved unsuccessful.

Worse yet, as he descended into this sleepless hell, his wife had begun to blossom before his very astonished eyes. Fashionably dressed and coifed, she appeared to his weary brain as alluring as any siren from an ancient Greek myth.

He sighed heavily. All he wanted from life were simple joys: wine, women, and a little mirth. Yet he was married to a woman who thought only of the suffering of strangers and had no interest in anything pleasurable.

Alec turned his blurry gaze on the impassive butler. "Tell me, Burroughs. Do you ever laugh?"

"Yes, sir. Quite frequently." The butler took Alec's arm and led him to the stairs. "But I have trained myself to refrain until you have left the room."

"I'm glad you—" Alec halted, one foot on the bottom step. "That was a joke."

"A small one, my lord. Shall I attempt another?"

"By God! You are quite the fellow, Burroughs! Damned if you aren't."

"Thank you, my lord. Shall we proceed to your room? Her ladyship has been quite worried."

Alec's grin faded. His freedom was gone. Nevermore would he be able to seek any kind of enjoyment from life without the nagging thought that Julia would not approve.

Though he told himself there was no reason why he

should care, he couldn't stop imagining how her gaze would change from breathless admiration to condemnation. And for some reason, he wanted to keep that admiration all to himself.

Yet he could not deny that she was a passionate woman; he'd seen it in her gaze, tasted it on her lips. But it was an innocent passion, chaste and pure, rendered by a lifetime of denied affection. He would be foolish to think her reaction solely for him. Had any other man possessed the audacity to kiss her, she would have responded in the same sensual way.

The thought hurt like the constant dig of a splinter. Alec shrugged from the butler's hold and headed for the library. "One more drink."

Burroughs sighed and retrieved his tray. He followed Alec into the library and strategically placed the milk glass beside the brandy decanter.

Alec ignored the glass and crossed to the fireplace, where the dull glow of ashes flickered restlessly. He added another log and straightened, his boot crunching on something on the hearth. The light from the newly banked fire flickered over a shard of glass. Alec picked it up and held it toward the light. Milk white, with a touch of blue, the thin sliver gleamed with the unmistakable texture of fine porcelain.

Burroughs was beside him in an instant. "I'll take that, my lord."

Before he knew what the butler was about, Burroughs plucked the shard from his hand, cast a quick glance across the hearth, and left the room with a murmured goodnight.

Alec stared at the closed door. What was that all about? He searched the hearth for other pieces of porcelain, but none came into view.

Dizzy from bending, he straightened and crossed to the sideboard. This was what his life had been reduced to—looking for stray pieces of broken glassware in his own home. He sighed and pushed the glass of milk aside.

The truth was, he was bored. Nothing amused him anymore, and while he tried to tell himself it was because he had been forbidden his usual pursuits, he knew it was untrue. The restlessness that stirred inside him had been there for as long as he could remember. He had managed to subdue it with mindless pleasures, but now the darkness had been stirred to life by dreams of Julia, half-clothed, her wide, sensual mouth opening to him, her arms clasping him closer as she. . . .

"I need a drink." Alec poured a measure of brandy and silently toasted the gaming hells and painted women of his past. Thanks to that blasted will and Julia's strident rules, even those poor diversions were gone. He was alone once more—only now he was plagued with a wife he could never touch. Why had he ever agreed to such an impossible stipulation?

"Because you were desperate and she knew it," he muttered, finishing off the brandy. He set the glass down and untied his cravat, tossing it to the floor. Then he loosened his shirt until it hung open and he could once again breathe.

He poured himself another drink and crossed to his favorite chair. Sighing deeply, he dropped onto the cushioned seat with the ease of long familiarity.

And promptly fell onto the floor.

He lay there staring at the ceiling, as brandy soaked across the carpet in an ever-widening stain. By Jove, he was drunk, but not *that* drunk.

He lifted his head to regard the chair with a suspicious glare. Louis XV in style, with rocaille ornamentation, it had once held a position of honor beside the fireplace in his grandfather's library. Alec liked it because the stripped velvet seat was thick and cushiony. With its high back and carved arms, it was easily the most comfortable chair in the—

"Damnation," he muttered and struggled to sit upright. Bleary-eyed, he squinted at the chair. The arms were missing.

"What happened to you?" Alec climbed to his feet and tilted the mangled chair to one side. He was still examining the broken, splintered wood when the door opened and Julia stepped in. Alec dropped the chair into place and stared.

She appeared nothing like the half-nude wanton who had visited his dreams of late; her lithe, supple body was covered from neck to foot in yards and yards of hideously ruffled cotton.

Through the shadowy opening of the robe he could just detect the lace nightgown he had purchased for her during their first shopping venture. It was scandalously sheer and he had thought to tease her into a reaction, but Julia had been too busy thinking of her charity work to pay any heed. Now, she added further injury by covering the costly garment with a monstrosity of a robe.

Alec told himself that his sigh was one of relief.

Her myopic gaze drifted from him to the chair and back, stopping to note his undone shirt. Her cheeks flushed warmly. "I'm sorry to bother you. Perhaps tomorrow would be a better time." She turned to the door, the robe trailing on the floor.

Alec wondered if she had borrowed it from Mrs. Winston. "Wait. I suppose you know what happened to my chair?"

She halted and turned. "Oh, that."

The light caught the shine of her hair, plaited into a thick rope. The honey strands flickered gold and red, as alive and warm as a fire. The silken end of the braid curled around the slope of her breast.

He should send her away now, before his growing lust took control. Yet he found himself waving to the chair opposite his. "Pray have a seat. Unless, of course, that one has been demolished, too."

Julia made no move toward the chair. "No, it was just that one. I hope it was not a favorite." She bit her lip and looked at him, seeking reassurance.

Alec was too enthralled with the sight of her white teeth worrying her full lower lip to do more than nod. He burned at the sight. He wanted to release that tortured morsel and lave the wounded lip with a kiss. He wanted to find her curves, hidden in those frustrating yards and yards of material, and caress her into mindless pleasure.

But it was not to be. Though Julia was more than willing to take his money, she wanted nothing whatsoever to do with him. She had made that abundantly clear in setting her terms for their marriage. In her own way, she was just like the rest of polite society, accepting him only for the sake of his fortune. The thought rankled, sparking a flame of discontent.

She peered at the chair as if to ascertain the damage herself. "Burroughs seems to think it cannot be fixed, but I believe a bit of glue will repair it well enough."

Alec looked at the raw, broken edge and instantly sympathized with it. "It is probably ruined."

"Then we will get you another."

"Of course," he agreed, wondering sourly if she thought to replace him as easily, once this year was done.

She rewarded him with a blinding smile that caused his breeches to tighten even more uncomfortably. He ground his teeth into a semblance of a smile. For the rest of his life, he was doomed to suffer the torments of hell at the hands of an innocent.

"Alec, I came to tell you about the chair . . . and one other matter." Julia walked toward the closest chair, the multitudinous folds of her robe flowing like water over a statue, alternately hiding and emphasizing the curves beneath. With each step, the outline of her leg would appear, deliciously long and slender against the white fabric before melting back into the obscurity of the graceful folds. Even in a gown comprised of more material than any six he had seen, she looked delectable.

Alec watched as she took her seat and arranged the folds about her until she sat in a pool of white ruffles. He managed to sit in his wounded chair without falling in the floor. What in hell was he thinking? She was in his care, his trust. He had made a promise, and he would keep it or die.

Unaware of his turmoil, Julia smiled, all chaste flesh and sultry eyes. "Lady Birlington, Edmund, and I went to the lending library today."

"Oh?" The word came out like the warbled cry of some lovesick canary. Alec scowled and hoped she hadn't noticed.

"Do you remember when you said I might hire some new servants?" She grasped her chair and pulled it to face him more directly. The chair leg caught at the folds of her gown, and for an agonizing instant, one sweetly rounded hip was outlined in stark relief.

Alec clamped his hands onto his knees, beads of sweat gathering on his lip and brow. Unperturbed, Julia perched primly on her seat. The layers of cotton drifted back into a sea of complex folds, once more concealing all. Alec had to swallow twice before he could even speak. "Well?" he snapped. "Did you hire someone?"

"Not quite. It was more in the way of a purchase."

He must have looked as confused as he felt for she added, "Actually, Nick did the purchasing. I wouldn't have sanctioned it at all, except that appalling man refused to relinquish the boy without—"

"Nick?" In the wavering light, Alec thought he detected a faint blush.

"He was outside of Hookham's circulating library. We met him quite by chance."

Nick. At a library. And his own wife, defending the bastard. "My cousin has never been to a library a day in his life."

She raised her brows. "Well, he was there today. And it was a fortunate thing, too. Edmund didn't want to fight, but Lady Birlington was in an uproar over—"

"Wait." Alec rubbed his temple where a small throb beat out a steady pulse. "Start at the beginning and tell me everything."

"Lady Birlington and Edmund were in the library when a small boy darted into the street. He overturned a cart. Cabbages rolled everywhere and stopped traffic and caused quite a ruckus. The sweep. . . ."

Alec watched, mesmerized, as her lips formed each word. He liked the way she spoke, so firmly and matter-of-factly, as if she stored up her words for a time when they would really matter. His pragmatic Julia. But where on earth had she gotten such a sensual mouth? Was it a reflection of the wanton Frant blood? He wished his chair still had arms so he could find a place to put his hands. With a concerted effort, he made himself listen.

". . . And then the sweep insulted Lady Birlington and she demanded that Edmund call him out—"

"Lady Birlington insisted *Edmund* call out a *sweep*." Surely his brandy-numbed ears had misheard that bit of information.

"The sweep called her an old crow." Julia tilted her head to one side, her braid swinging gently, the feathered end splayed like fingers against the white material. "Lady Birlington was very angry. I can't say as I blame her; it would have made me angry, too."

"All this occurred in front of a library? In Bond Street?"

She suddenly became immersed in threading her fingers through the end of her braid. "Yes."

"Damn it, Maddie is supposed to keep this exact sort of thing from happening. And as for Edmund! I shall have a few choice words to say to him, the fool."

Julia's eyes flashed. "Edmund attempted to dissuade

Lady Birlington." She faltered and frowned. "But Nick overruled his objections."

"I'm sure he did," Alec returned shortly. "I take it Edmund is meeting this sweep at dawn like a crack-brained idiot?"

"No, the sweep drew Edmund's cork and knocked him head over heels."

He shut his eyes for a moment, imagining Nick's amusement. "Who, besides Nick, witnessed this debacle?"

"Aunt Maddie said she recognized Amelia Cornwall."

"It'll be all over town before morning. That woman is a known gabster." He rubbed his neck, wishing some of his earlier drink-induced euphoria remained.

Julia folded her hands in her lap, momentarily distracting him. Her hands, slender and white, nestled in the gathered material. He wanted to be a bird and nest in the curls those folds hid. He wanted to—

"There's more," she blurted out. "I hit him."

Alec blinked. "Who?"

"The sweep. But only once," she said with evident regret. "I should have followed with a knock to the chin, but I didn't think of it in time."

"Oh, my God." Alec's head began to pound. "Oh, my God. You hit a sweep in front of the lending library."

"You should be thankful Nick was there. Despite his improper behavior in urging Edmund to fight, he dispensed with the sweep. It could have been much worse."

"*How*?"

She flushed, the rosy color sweeping across her cheeks to her forehead. "The man could have pressed charges. Edmund did hit him first. But Nick bought him off." She sighed. "I should have thought of that myself, but I didn't. I was much too angry by then." Her dark gaze settled on him. "So you see, your cousin was not to blame for this incident."

The hell he wasn't, Alec thought viciously. Nick had

stood aside and waited until the little drama had produced a sufficient amount of attention before riding in
and saving the day like a knight on a white horse.

Julia leaned forward, her gown smoothed across her
breasts as lovingly as any hand. "Alec, I'm sorry I lost
my temper, but you should have seen him. The burns
on his feet, and the bruises." Tears glistened in her green
eyes.

"Nick?" Alec asked, astounded.

"No! The boy we saved from the sweep. That's what
I wanted to talk to you about. That and your chair." She
took a deep breath. "You see, we needed to give Muck
a bath, and—"

"Wait. Who in the hell is Muck?"

Julia sighed in exasperation. "That's the boy's name,"
she said. "And a very uncomplimentary one, at that.
Though it did rather fit him at the time—I never saw a
child more in need of a bath."

Alec looked down at his armless chair. "I take it he
did not wish for a bath and thus found it necessary to
break my chair."

"He didn't break your chair, but. . . ." Her gaze drifted
toward the mantel. An empty space loomed between the
silver candelabra and the ormolu clock. "He is very sorry
about your vase."

"I'm sure he is," Alec bit out, though he could not
remember what treasure Mrs. Winston had placed in the
distinctively empty space. His housekeeper's fondness
for useless rattle was a source of constant irritation.

"Muck dropped it on the hearth. It depicted a Greek
battle scene," she added as if that explained everything.

"Before or after he broke it?"

She ignored him. "But the poor thing was frightened
Mrs. Winston would punish him for his carelessness, so
he decided to flee."

"By throwing my chair?"

"Oh, no! He just ran. We attempted to catch him, but

he was much too quick, so we asked Johnston to assist us."

Alec tried to straighten in the chair, but it was impossible without the arms. "So Johnston broke the chair," he said through his teeth.

"He tripped over the carpet and went crashing into it. Muck took the opportunity to dash into the kitchen." A faint frown curved her generous lips. "The cook was not pleasant."

Though his whole life was in shambles, he managed to say pleasantly enough, "We don't have a cook, love. We have a chef. Antoine would be very upset to hear you call him a cook."

She sniffed, unimpressed. "He won't hear me call him anything. The man was horribly rude to Muck and called him all sorts of names." She scowled, fingering the end of her braid. "It's a good thing I speak French."

"Are you saying Antoine quit?" Alec asked carefully, thinking of the months it had taken for him to woo the temperamental Frenchman from Lady Birchley's house. It had been a coup for him, of sorts. Lady Birchley was a society matron of no small consequence, and one of the leading voices in stirring up the whispers about his mother. It had made acquiring the chef's exquisite culinary skills all the sweeter.

"He didn't quit. I dismissed him."

"*What?*"

She winced at his roar. "Alec, I had to."

"Damn it, Julia! You cannot dismiss the servants without consulting me first!"

"He did not know how to deal with children."

"And that is important in a chef?" he asked, incredulous, his anger suspended in disbelief.

"It is to me." She hesitated before saying in an uncompromising voice, "I suppose I should also tell you about the stables."

"Let me guess," Alec snapped. "Burroughs broke

down the stall doors. Or perhaps he just set the entire building afire."

As impervious to his sarcasm as she was to his lust, she waved an airy hand and chuckled. "Oh, no. Nothing like that. Muck tied a spoon to the cat's tail and she ran into the stables among the horses. A child's prank, no more. Johnston says it can be fixed within the month."

Before Alec could do more than open his mouth, she continued, "Muck really is a sweet boy, Alec. He just needs some attention. No one has ever cared for him. Children left alone without anyone to show them affection find other ways to get the attention they crave."

Looking at Julia's glowing expression, Alec could almost picture the child. Soft blond curls about an angelic face, a cupid bow's mouth set between two plump cheeks, all hiding the evil spirit of an imp.

And of course his tenderhearted wife championed such a paragon. Julia spent her time and precious care on all manner of worthy causes. Even Nick merited attention. Alec's smoldering frustrations flared to life. She expended her affections on everyone but him.

"We'll send the child to an orphanage. There is a good one in Asbury." He caught her minatory gaze and added remorselessly, "I will contribute a sizable amount to ensure he is well cared for, Julia. But he cannot stay here."

Her hands curled into fists, the knuckles white. "You can't mean that."

"Have you forgotten our circumstances, Julia? You will set the entire *ton* against you with such hoydenish behavior."

Her color rose with her anger. "That horrid man hit Edmund. You would have done the same thing. I know you would have."

"What I can do and what you can do are entirely different matters." God, was that him, mouthing platitudes like a country vicar?

Julia stood, her hands firmly on her hips. "I should

remind you that ours is a marriage of convenience. I am not bound by your wishes, just as you are not bound by mine."

Alec flung himself from his chair and crossed the small space that separated them. "If I am not bound by your wishes, then I will have you to bed this very night."

She gasped, her hand automatically clutching her robe protectively to her throat.

"You expect too much of me. You deny me the services of a mistress, while you waltz into my study dressed like—" He gestured toward her, then realized she was actually covered from neck to toe in Mrs. Winston's robe. "Julia, you forget I am a man."

Her color high, she said in a low voice, "I have never forgotten that."

For a second, he thought he detected a flicker of raw passion in her eyes and his heart thudded to a halt. But she looked away, her thick lashes casting shadows across her cheeks. "I should never have come here. I only wanted to tell you what had occurred. But whatever you say, I cannot send the child away."

"And what if the executors catch wind of the incident? This will cause exactly the sort of gossip we cannot afford. I warned you about becoming too involved with your projects, Julia."

"If you had seen the child—"

"We made a bargain, my lady." He caught her wrist and pulled her forward until he could see directly into her eyes. "If you wish to renegotiate, I will not be the only one making concessions."

She met his gaze without flinching. The firelight caressed her face, molded the graceful line of her throat and warmed the curve of her cheek. "I wish to keep the child. Whatever your price, I will pay it."

With those few words, she placed him back where he belonged, with the unclean, the ungenteel. And why not, he thought harshly. Wasn't that who he was? He was not now, nor had he ever been, a gentleman. "What are you willing to pay?"

She eyed him warily, as one would a mad dog. "I don't know what you. . . ." She stopped, her face pink with color. Slowly, ever so carefully, she placed her hand on his chest.

His skin burned where each of her fingertips rested. Alec shut his eyes and willed himself to continue breathing as she slowly slid her hand down his chest. Sweet Jesus, but she was going to. . . . The hand stopped at his stomach, hovering as light as the brush of a feather. Breathing heavily, he opened his eyes.

Julia stared up at him, her mouth parted, her face flushed, her eyes dark. "I will give you a kiss."

He wanted more. But for now, he would take whatever she had to offer. Take it and use it to end some of his frustration, quench his insatiable lust. Without giving her time to reconsider, he swept her in his arms and kissed her just as he had kissed her in his dreams every night since their marriage. He covered her mouth with his and devoured her like a starved man given a bounteous feast. He plunged his hands into the folds of her nightrail and found the lithe curves below, molding her to him, rubbing against her so she could feel how he wanted her, desired her.

At first she was stiff and unyielding, but as his hands curved about her, his mouth plundered hers, she moaned and joined in, her hands no less demanding, her passion matching his.

He kissed her until she lay limp and panting in his arms. Then, with the last strand of control he possessed, he released her and staggered away. Julia sagged against her chair, hanging onto the back for support.

Panting, she regarded him with eyes that sparkled with anger. "There. I have paid your price. Muck will stay."

She rejected him even as she quivered from his touch.

Alec turned away, his whole body aching as if bruised. Trying to control his thudding heart, he sank into his chair. "You have only begun to pay, madam. For each and every day that urchin is in this house, you will pay the forfeit."

Julia stilled, one hand on her cheek. "Every day?" A husky quiver warmed her voice like velvet.

Alec didn't trust himself to reply. He just stared. Stared at the white, smooth skin of her neck, at the rounded curve of her breasts, and at the incredible length of her legs, so evident in the folds of her robe. "There is no going back, Julia. You are mine to kiss whenever and wherever I desire."

Her eyes sparkled with anger. "Whatever you may say of your cousin, Nick is at least a gentleman."

Damn Nick. All he had to do was toss a coin and he came out smelling like a rose, while Alec would be forced to adopt some hell-born babe to satisfy Julia's notions of responsibility. For one wild instant he thought of renouncing his inheritance and retreating to his old life, of following the path of ruin offered by the demimonde and allowing Nick free access to the fortune.

But he could not. He might be a cad and a rakehell and possess fewer principles than any man to ever walk the earth, but he still had his pride. And for a brief year, he had Julia. "You know nothing of my cousin."

Julia gave an exasperated sigh. "You are drunk. I will speak with you in the morning, when you are more yourself."

She turned and walked toward the door, crossing in front of the fireplace as she did so. For one heart-stopping second, the firelight revealed her legs and the dark triangle of hair at the juncture of her thighs.

Alec's heart slammed to a stunned halt. Did this woman have any idea what she did to a man? No, of course she didn't, he told himself grimly. It was yet another problem of being married to a virtuous woman.

She reached the door and yanked it open, leaving without a backward glance. The tension dissipated as the door shut. Alec slumped in his armless chair and sourly regarded the ceiling, waiting for his heart to resume a normal pace.

His only hope was to convince Julia that he was worth her attention. Yet how could he manage such a transformation when he'd just proved himself the greatest beast on earth? He rubbed a fist against his forehead and cursed his impetuous temper and unbridled passions.

Yet he could not totally regret the outcome of this evening. Julia had agreed to kiss him every day. A slow smile curved his mouth. Yes, every single day she would submit to his embrace, chaste though it would be. It was a beginning.

Suddenly, the future seemed brighter. Humming softly, he stood and crossed to the decanter, methodically filling every glass on the tray.

He would have to do something about Nick and his meddling. It was barely two weeks after the wedding and already he had involved Julia in a possible scandal. Julia might wish to believe his cousin as innocent as a kitten, but Alec knew differently. Nick never did anything without reason.

Alec lined the glasses in a row and lifted the first, tossing it back quickly. As surprising as it would be to the *ton* and everyone who knew him, his life was about to change. He was about to turn into the season's most devoted husband.

He picked up the next glass and tossed that one back as well. It was fortunate he could afford good brandy. He had the feeling he was going to need every drop.

Chapter 13

J ulia scooped up her bonnet from the side table and quietly opened her door. Breath held, she stared silently at the door across from hers.

No sound of movement escaped Alec's room. With a mingled sense of relief and disappointment, she slipped from her room and tiptoed down the narrow passage.

She wasn't surprised he was still abed. He'd been deep in his cups when she'd visited the library last night. The brandy had amplified his passions completely out of proportion. It had shown in the glitter of his silver eyes and the way he'd watched her as if she were a lamb and he a starving wolf. But Julia had ignored the signs, determined to explain about Muck.

That had been her first mistake. Her second mistake had been to forget how witless she became when he was near. And when he'd kissed her . . . she shivered as a treacherous sense of pleasure filled her, and she closed her eyes, savoring the memory.

Somewhere in the distance a door opened and closed, and Julia firmly called her giddy emotions to order. She should have been outraged at Alec's demands. But she wasn't. In fact, it had been rather exciting, bargaining with a kiss. If she were truthful, she might even admit she had wanted more. It was a good thing she was in no mood to be truthful.

She sighed and forced herself to the task at hand: escaping the notice of Alec's overzealous servants. After last night, she needed some time to sort through all of the feelings her wicked husband's kiss had stirred to life.

Julia leaned over the top banister and peered down into the entryway. Dust motes danced in midair, golden sparkles against the dark paneling. Bright splashes of sunlight warmed the polished wood floor and filled the air with the faint scent of beeswax. From belowstairs, Mrs. Winston called to Burroughs to help her carry up the breakfast tray. Without wasting any more time, Julia looped her reticule over her arm, ran lightly down the steps, and slipped out the door.

Glorious sunshine greeted her. Closing the door carefully, Julia lifted her face to the warmth. Birds chirped, the trees rustled pleasantly, and the steady, comforting clop of horse's hooves rang on the cobblestone road. It was a perfect day.

Smiling, she settled the chip straw bonnet on her head and found the bright cherry ribbons that dangled to each side. The only thing that would make the day more perfect would be Alec, claiming his kiss.

If she closed her eyes again, she could imagine his touch where the sunlight warmed her cheek. He would take her in his arms and kiss her until she fought for breath. For a long moment, she allowed herself to float in the dream until the clattering of a carriage brought her back to reality.

"Enough of that," she muttered to herself, adjusting the shawl of Spanish lace across her shoulders. "You'd do well to forget last night even occurred."

Alec would awaken this morning with a raging headache and no memory of her visit, anyway. Julia sighed and began to tie her bonnet, mulling over her lamentable tendency to yearn for things she did not have.

"And where are we off to, this bright morning?" A deep, masculine voice broke her reverie.

Julia froze, hands mid-bow. Alec leaned against the wheel of his phaeton, his handsome face shadowed by the brim of his hat. Freshly shaven and immaculately dressed, he looked sinful, dangerous, and handsome.

Her first instinct was to turn and retreat into the house. Or at the least, change into the cherry muslin morning dress she'd just bought. Why, oh why, had she worn the green striped cambric? She caught his questioning gaze and blushed. "I thought you'd still be asleep."

"Is that why you were sneaking out of the house like a thief?"

"I was not sneaking."

He lifted his brows in polite disbelief. The sun lit the sensual curve of his mouth—the same mouth that had so easily claimed hers, stealing her every thought, her every breath, until there was only the drugging taste of Alec.

Julia discovered she had tied her bow far tighter than she'd intended. She loosened the ribbons hastily. "I didn't wish to bother the servants." Or to allow them to bother her, which was much more to the point.

"Were you going unescorted?"

The deceptively polite tone put Julia on edge. She eyed him warily. "I was going to call a hackney."

In one lithe, fluid movement, he pushed himself away from the phaeton and stood before her, the very picture of towering masculine impatience. "You are not to travel alone, Julia."

She took a prudent step back. "I always took Johnston whenever I visited Whitechapel, but I am not going there today." At least, not now.

Alec stared down at her, his jaw taut. This close, Julia could see that his eyes were faintly shadowed, the lines by his mouth carved deeper than usual. Yet the marks of dissipation did little more than sharpen his already handsome features.

Julia thought of how she would have looked had she had as little sleep and as much brandy as he. It was not fair. She sniffed. "If you think to intimidate me by glaring, I should warn you it will have no effect. I am quite used to glaring. In fact, hardly a day goes by that I am not glared at by someone."

"I am not surprised," he returned grimly.

Well, that was rude. Glancing up at him through her lashes, Julia wisely decided not to pursue it. "I really must be off. Please summon a hackney." She was proud of how cool and commanding she sounded even though her pulse beat wildly. "Lady Birlington is to arrive at two and I have dozens of things to do before then."

Alec's gaze narrowed. "Then we, madam, will do them together. In the future, you will not leave the house without an escort, or you will answer to me."

At his proprietary tone, Julia glared back. "You cannot tell me what to do."

He leaned forward, and six feet of delectable male blocked the sun. "Don't tempt me, Julia."

She opened her mouth, but nothing came out. She just stared, her heart fluttering like a caged bird, her entire body agonizingly aware of his.

Her expression must have given something away, for Alec's gaze darkened. Heedless of where they stood, he reached out and grasped her arms, his fingers pressing into the tender flesh above her elbows. "Julia, why did you marry me?"

The question seemed to surprise him as much as it did her, for he dropped his hands and took a startled step back.

Every move he made to distance himself confirmed Julia's fears. She only prayed he had not seen too much. "You know why I married you." She forced a light laugh. "The same reason you married me—for the fortune."

For a long instant he stared down at her, his gaze shadowed by the brim of his hat. Then, without another word, he turned and opened the door of the phaeton and pulled out the steps. "Get in."

Her chest felt as if a huge rock had been placed upon it. Julia twisted the strings of her reticule and wondered miserably how things had gotten so muddled. "Perhaps I should find Johnston." Though the old groom might be dour-faced and grim, she'd prefer him to this too handsome stranger who scowled at her as if for two pence he'd happily wring her neck.

"Johnston is attempting to set the stables to rights." Alec reached out and unceremoniously lifted her into the phaeton.

Julia snatched her hand away as soon as she was certain she would not tumble to the ground. "I should get a hackney. I have dozens of things to do before this evening and you'll—"

"Accompany you," he said briefly and climbed in beside her. His thigh brushed against hers as he loosened the reins and flicked at the lead horse with the whip. The horses sprang forward and soon they were bowling down the wide lane.

Julia clasped her hands in her lap and searched desperately for a safe topic of conversation. "I'm surprised to see you looking so awake. Last night you seemed. . . ." She wondered what the polite term would be. "Ill," she finally said.

"Drunk," he said with a dark glance.

"Edmund calls it 'a trifle to let.' "

"I was more than a trifle, Julia. Trust me on that score."

Trust him? Of course she trusted him. Hadn't she married him, helped him regain his grandfather's fortune, and dedicated herself to helping him defeat his rakish tendencies? Though if last night was any indication, she was failing miserably.

A dog darted into the street and the horses reared, kicking against the traces. Alec half stood, his feet planted wide as he forced the bays to settle. Gripping the edge of the seat, Julia found herself at eye level with Alec's thigh, marvelously encased in fawn-colored breeches.

Heavens, Aunt Maddie was right. Men *were* wearing their breeches tighter every year, and it certainly was a disgrace. Yet somehow Julia could not dredge up a single morsel of regret, only a breathless admiration and an overwhelming desire to touch that beautiful thigh, to splay her hands across the rock-hard muscles that flexed within inches of her mouth and taste the warmth of his skin and—

Alec resumed his seat and set the horses back in motion. He turned the phaeton off the main thoroughfare. "I assume you wished to visit Bond Street first."

It took all of her powers of concentration to remove her gaze from the rippling muscles of his thigh. "Oh, yes. Shopping," she said, her voice sounding husky even to her own ears. "I am going shopping."

He glanced sideways at her, his silver gaze curious. "What item do you so desire that you would rise at dawn?"

Glad for the excuse to turn her face away, Julia tilted her head back to look at the sparkling sky. "It is at least nine o'clock, to judge by the sun." She smiled, the beauty of the day warming her to her toes. "My father used to awaken at six every morning."

Alec noted how her eyes shimmered behind her spectacles, the verdant green flecked with gold. The lashes curled lushly and cast shadows over her cheeks and the sun kissed the honey of her hair to gold. God, but she was lovely.

She turned those amazing eyes on him. "My father

and mother would sit on the front steps every morning and watch the sun rise." A dimple hovered in her cheek. "I think it was just an excuse to be alone, but Father would never admit it."

Alec tried to remember something of his own mother, but all he could recall were tears and clinging arms that weighted his shoulders even now. He shrugged the uncomfortable feeling aside. "Your parents were unique."

"They loved one another," she said simply.

For the barest instant, Alec found himself envying the love Julia's parents had shared. He grimaced. He was just tired from yet another sleepless night.

Blithely unaware of the turmoil she caused, Julia pulled a list from her reticule. "I need blue ribbons and a rose-colored scarf." She glanced up at him and chuckled. "The scarf is for Aunt Maddie. She won't admit it, but she has a tendre for Admiral Hutchins. Just yesterday I heard him say how lovely she looked in her pink pelisse, and I thought this would be just the thing to thank her for her help."

Alec could only smile at such an enchanting confidence.

Color bloomed in Julia's cheeks and she hastily turned back to her list. "Oh, and we must choose some livery for Muck. It will make him feel much more important."

"Important?"

"Oh, yes," she replied, earnestly. "Children are not so very different from adults. We all need a purpose, something to believe in and work toward. It keeps us from becoming selfish."

Alec frowned and turned the horses toward Bond Street. Frankly, he couldn't think of a single thing he believed in. His gaze fell on Julia's bent head as she tucked her list back into her reticule. The straw bonnet sat crooked, and she'd tied the ribbon in a huge, lopsided bow that threatened to come undone at any moment. To his surprise, he heard himself say, "Perhaps there is one thing I believe in."

"Only one?" She looked disappointed. "I believe in all sorts of things."

"Do you?"

"Oh, yes." She counted off on her fingers. "I believe there is good in all people, if they only have the opportunity to show it. I believe everyone has a duty to help their fellow man. I believe children are the most precious resource of society. And I believe in lo—" She halted and bit her lip, her face flaming bright pink.

"Love," he finished for her. "Like your parents'."

She nodded, the bow slipping completely free. Twin cherry ribbons framed her face as her generous mouth curved in a tender smile. "They had true love. The kind you read about in books."

He looked at her and his heart squeezed painfully. "There is no such thing as true love."

With the quiet dignity he had so come to admire, she answered, "It is the only kind I will accept."

Fighting back an absurd sense of disappointment, Alec fell silent and concentrated on guiding the phaeton through traffic.

For the rest of the day he was careful to keep the conversation light, though he was annoyingly aware of her. Every move she made served to remind him of the scene in his study the night before—of the feel of her in his arms, the scent of her, the taste of her mouth beneath his. She, on the other hand, seemed to think nothing of the incident, for by neither word nor action did she betray any hint it held some meaning for her.

By the time Alec pulled the phaeton to the curb in front of the house, he was grimly determined to remind her of her promise. With great restraint, he handed her down from the carriage and followed her in.

Once in the foyer, he closed the door and leaned against it, watching her intently. She untied her bonnet and pulled it from her head, shaking her curls free. One lock of hair stayed mashed to her head while another looped out in a messy bump.

It was, simply, too much. He shoved himself from the door. "You've forgotten something, love."

She looked down at her reticule, then checked the bandbox that swung from her other hand. "No, I have everything here."

He stepped closer, placing a hand on the wall just above her head. "There is the little matter of your daily forfeit."

Her eyes widened, and Alec witnessed something akin to fear in the velvety depths. He almost took a step back, chagrined to have inspired that look. Had he been more violent last night than he'd thought? Perhaps his passion had overwhelmed her, though that seemed impossible when he remembered her response. Mayhap she feared both his passion and her own.

Strangely, the thought encouraged him. Taking his galloping lust under firm control, Alec lifted a hand to her face. He lightly traced the curve of her cheek, allowing his fingertips to linger just beside her mouth.

Her lips parted and her eyes half closed, her breath sliding between her white teeth in shallow gasps. With a *thunk*, the bandbox hit the floor and rolled to the corner.

Alec trailed his hand from her mouth to her chin. Leaning forward ever so slowly, he slid his lips across her smooth jaw to the delicate skin right below her ear. She shivered, one hand coming up to clutch at his lapel. Alec closed his eyes and forced himself to end the tortuous kiss with a soft touch of his lips and no more. Then he stepped away, fighting with every breath to maintain his control.

Julia's hand fell to her side and she stared at him, her gaze filled with yearning.

It was exactly the expression he had hoped to see. He

would woo her slowly until she came to know and trust him. He would show her that there was more to life than the illusion of true love. There was the release and beauty of passion.

For now, that would have to be enough. "You had best change before Lady Birlington arrives."

Julia blinked as if she'd just awakened from a deep, dream-filled sleep. "Who?"

"Lady Birlington," he repeated gently. He took her hand and pulled her forward, stopping to gather the lost bandbox. He placed it in her hand and led her to the bottom of the stairs. "Shall I send Mrs. Winston to your room with some tea?"

Like a sleepwalker, Julia nodded and began a dreamy climb up the steps, weaving ever so slightly as she went, one hand still on the place his lips had just left. Alec watched her go, admiring the hypnotic sway of her hips. At the top, she stopped and looked down.

Their eyes met and color flooded Julia's face. Then she whirled and disappeared down the hallway.

Chapter 14

L ondon's bawdiest slum rang day and night with
the sounds of gin, sin and filth, yet the Society for
Wayward Women remained a haven of safety. No untoward attacks or robberies occurred within its hallowed
walls. Ruffians and robbers alike gave the locale a respectable berth, mainly out of a reluctant respect for the
kindly Vicar Ashton.

Julia climbed the narrow steps leading to the front
door. She loved this building. Once a brothel spattered
with filth, it now gleamed, sparkling under a new coat
of paint in startling contrast against its grime and soot-
covered neighbors.

Stepping into the gleaming entryway, she smoothed
her dress. A simple round gown, it had been divested of
bows and trimwork and seemed startlingly plain when
compared with the costly garments that now filled her
wardrobe. Here she was once again plain, simple Julia
Frant. The transformation did not lighten her spirits.

It was time she faced the truth: she was a total failure
as a reformer. Not only was the Society still without a
project to help the women, but Alec was just as sinful,
just as seductive, just as prideful as he had been the day
they had wed. Oh, she had managed to win a few com-

promises, but he'd undergone no real transformation of character.

Unfortunately, she could not say the same for herself.

Julia brushed a hand over her mouth and shivered. She never knew when Alec would appear to demand his forfeit, and she spent each day and the better part of each night wondering when the next kiss would come and how wantonly she would react. To her dismay, there was no predicting either.

She was both fascinated and terrified, dreading and yearning for his touch, and all the while sinking ever more under his spell. Of course, a spell of Alec's weaving was hardly the stuff of nightmares; it was more that of dreams—hot, sensual dreams that left one lying awake in the middle of the night, yearning and trembling with raw lust.

Julia fanned herself with a limp hand. She was weakening. Every day brought her a step closer to begging for more than a mere kiss. And Alec had let her know by look and touch that he would be more than willing to comply.

If she didn't come up with another way to reach her stubborn, lustful husband soon, she would be just as lost to sin as he. Refusing to dwell on such unhappy thoughts, she gathered herself together and entered the office.

The vicar rose from his chair at the head of the table, his thin, patrician face creased in a welcoming smile. "There you are, my dear. We were just about to begin."

"About time you arrived," growled Lord Kennybrook, shooting her a sharp glance from under gray, bushy brows. "Late. Just like a dratted female. And after making us move our meetings to this ungodly hour of the morning."

Julia smiled. "Are you trying to raise my hackles, Lord Kennybrook? I should warn you it won't work."

His brown eyes twinkled from beneath fierce brows. "Why not?"

"I don't have the energy. I didn't get much sleep last night." Or the night before. Or the night before that. Actually, she hadn't had one good night's rest since her wedding night.

"Trouble sleeping, eh?" asked Lord Burton, full of bluff sympathy. "You're just in time, then. Tumbolton here was just about to explain one of his queer philosophical notions."

Kennybrook snorted. "That's enough to put any soul into a trance, listening to such drivel before the sun's fully up."

Julia regarded the small group about the table with a fond smile. The disparate assemblage that made up the Society's Board of Directors had come together under the gentle persuasion of Vicar Ashton. Men of position and wealth, they freely gave of their time and expertise for the simple reward of helping others. Julia loved them dearly and considered them the closest thing she'd had to a family since leaving Boston.

Vicar Ashton picked up a sheet of paper and peered at it through his spectacles. "I am pleased to announce that the Society for Wayward Women currently has enough money to establish any number of businesses."

Mr. Tumbolton leaned over to read the sum at the bottom. "I vow, but that is a lot of money." He coughed, the shallow, racking sound plunging the meeting into momentary silence.

Dr. Crullen shook his head. "You should not be in London, Augustus. It is poisonous to someone with your lungs."

Julia caught the faint scent of peppermint. The doctor kept a store of candy in his pockets for his younger patients, though Julia believed he ate more than he ever gave away.

Tumbolton pressed a handkerchief to his colorless lips

before taking a shuddering breath. "I can't leave yet, Marcus. I'm in the middle of developing my new theory. It's due at the publisher next month."

"You won't be around to do anything if you don't take heed," warned Lord Burton, his heavy jowls quivering with each word. "But I must admit we need your help if we're to decide how to fix this sum from the new sponsor, whoever he is."

Kennybrook narrowed his gaze on Julia. "This new sponsor bothers me. Something smoky about him, damn if there isn't."

Lord Burton nodded. "Shame we lost our last sponsor. He was a great man. I always thought John was the—"

"He was, indeed," interrupted Lord Kennybrook with a meaningful glare.

"Oh, yes," replied Burton hastily. He cast a guilty glance at Julia. "No more to be said about that."

Vicar Ashton favored the assembly with a sad smile. "We still haven't found a solution to our problem. I begin to fear we may never find one."

"Humph. I still think a sausage factory is the thing," Lord Kennybrook said. "There's a huge demand and not enough suppliers. My own chef told me so. Perfect time to go into the business."

Julia shook her head. "It is much too unsanitary."

"Nonsense," he scoffed. "All that fresh meat. What could be better?"

She wrinkled her nose. "Just about anything."

Kennybrook's face folded into a scowl and Dr. Crullen interposed, "I cannot think of a large scale project for the women, but I do need a housekeeper. Mrs. Jenner has decided to return to the country to be with her daughter. Perhaps I could hire one of the women to take her place."

"It's hard to find good help," Mr. Tumbolton commiserated. "I need someone to do my laundry."

Julia wished Hunterston House were larger. At the

most she could employ two or three women, and then she would have to deal with the fact that they were untrained. Of course, she and Mrs. Winston could instruct them, just as they had Muck.

"Heavens!" Julia cried. "That's it! Mrs. Winston has been looking for a cook for weeks, and Lady Birlington is short a maid, and the Duchess of Roth said she'd give her left eye for a maid that could braid hair!"

Lord Kennybrook snorted. "What good is all that? Even with Tumbolton's laundress, that places only four women and we have hundreds to see to."

"Exactly! We will set up a company to train the women of the Society to become the best servants London has ever seen. We'll run a servant referral service!" Julia drummed her fingers on the table, excitement buoying her spirits. "I know of a dozen matrons, the best of the *ton*, who are looking to hire maids, cooks, housekeepers—oh, all sorts of servants."

The vicar stroked his chin. "Julia, I believe you have something there."

"It is a healthy, respectable occupation," Tumbolton said, giving a thoughtful nod. "And it certainly would not take much effort to begin." He beamed with growing enthusiasm. "We should start immediately."

"There's only one flaw," Dr. Crullen said. "In order for this effort to succeed, we will need a spokesperson who will vouch for us. Preferably someone within the *ton* itself."

Kennybrook waved a hand. "We'll get Lord Burton's new ball and chain to do it. Have her blow it about town a bit. Won't take long once the females start chattering."

Julia looked hopefully at Lord Burton.

He folded his hands over his stomach, his fleshy mouth pursed into a frown. "I doubt Marie would be able to do much. She hasn't quite 'taken' as she'd hoped." He gave a self-deprecating shrug. "I suppose I should escort her about more. But all that gadding about makes me bilious."

Frustrated, Julia turned toward Lord Kennybrook. "Surely *you* know someone."

"I know lots of people, my dear. But most are well past the age of changing servants. Unless, of course, one of theirs die." He brightened. "Perhaps there will be a shocking influenza season this year."

"I hope not," interjected Julia hastily. "Surely someone—" She stopped. Could she? Dared she?

"What is it?" asked the vicar.

Perhaps if she were discreet, all would be well. She simply could not allow her wonderful idea to fall by the wayside. "I know just the person to help. Leave it all to me."

"Wonderful!" Vicar Ashton exclaimed, his gentle face wreathed in smiles. "I knew we could count on your ingenuity."

The rest of the assemblage agreed heartily, beaming at Julia with pride. Perhaps that was why Muck had been placed in her path—to show her the way for the Society. Everything made perfect sense.

At the thought of Muck, Julia glanced at the clock. The tailor was due at Hunterston House within the half-hour for the final fitting of Muck's page uniform. She had taken great delight in ordering the child's clothing for his grand debut this evening—more than she had in her own.

Her stomach tightened. How she dreaded this evening. Swallowing her nervousness, she stood. "I hate to leave, but I've pressing duties."

The gentlemen rose, Mr. Tumbolton reaching the door first. "Allow me to escort you."

"That is quite kind, but there's no need. I have a carriage waiting."

Kennybrook and Burton converged on her with all the pompous assurance of old age.

"Let the boy escort you," Kennybrook said.

Burton nodded. "Can't forget you're—"

"Too young to be traveling without an escort," Kennybrook finished with a stern glare at his companion.

Color tinged the end of Lord Burton's bulbous nose. "Yes, yes, of course. Too young."

"Sapskull," Kennybrook muttered under his breath. He limped forward to take Julia's hand and pat it fondly. "We're just concerned for your welfare, my dear. Allow us to walk with you."

Julia was forced to allow the gentlemen to see her out, hoping against hope they would not notice anything untoward. Luckily, the open door of the carriage hid the Hunterston crest, and after Mr. Tumbolton assisted her inside, the men turned back toward the building, arguing over something. In relief, Julia motioned to Johnston to be off.

As the carriage rumbled over the cobbles, away from the sights and smells of Whitechapel, Julia settled into her seat and began making plans. Perhaps she wasn't such a failure as a reformer, after all.

Chapter 15

An ear-splitting scream emanated from the upstairs window of Hunterston House and echoed against the stately homes of Mayfair.

Johnston jerked around just as Julia stepped down from the coach. "What in thunder was that?"

Julia regained her balance by clinging to the open door. She bounded to the ground with a very unladylike hop, her bonnet tilting haphazardly to one side. "It couldn't be the French cook. He left last week."

"I never did like that Antoine. Too high in the instep, even fer a Frog." The shrill yell sounded again and Johnston glared at the house. "Sounds like yer hellion has gone and murdered the whole household."

Julia straightened her bonnet. "Muck has done no such thing, Johnston. I would appreciate it if you didn't speak such nonsense." But even she winced when another blood-curdling scream resonated, this time followed by a masculine shout that sounded very much like Alec.

"Now ye're in the suds," Johnston said with grim satisfaction. "The little rat has gone and woken the master. I wouldn't be in yer shoes fer twenty quid."

"My shoes are perfectly fine, thank you," Julia said tartly. She gathered her skirts and marched up the front

walk. The noise increased, screams and thundering footsteps preternaturally loud in the crisp morning air. Julia
rushed through the doorway and halted.

Muck scrambled down the main stairway, his pale
body in sharp relief against the dark wood. Naked, he
took the steps two at a time. His skinny white arms and
legs bore a shocking number of bruises, none debilitat-
ing, as evidenced by his rapid descent. With each thudding step, he screamed anew, the sound echoing
throughout the entryway.

Julia approached the stairs, her arms outstretched, and
Muck launched himself toward her with all the grace of
a cat seeking sanctuary from a pack of wild dogs. Gar-
bling unintelligible phrases, he tangled himself in her
skirts and tried to disappear into the folds.

Hard on his heels came Burroughs. The butler's cravat
was wildly mussed, the center mashed together as if
someone had tried to swing from it. Soapy water trailed
from one elbow onto the floor.

He skidded to an undignified halt, his stocking feet
sliding on the waxed floor. "Your . . . ladyship," he said
between pants, managing a very credible bow though his
hair splayed about his head like a rack of feathers. "Pardon me."

Alec was not far behind. He came to a halt a few
steps from the bottom stair, regarding her with a silver-
edged glare.

Julia's mouth dropped open and she was suddenly bereft of speech. Alec was completely drenched. His white
linen shirt was unbuttoned, the sodden material almost
transparent across his muscular frame. It outlined his
broad shoulders and clung to the ripples of his stomach.
Even more disconcerting was the state of his soaked
trousers. Molded across his powerful thighs, they left
very little to the imagination.

Heat pooled in her belly, igniting a steady burn
through her limbs as a flood of wildly improbable

thoughts jumbled together in her muddled brain. God help her, but he was a magnificent specimen of male virility. Magnificent—and *all hers*.

Her hands splayed across the surface of her reticule as she imagined touching him, running her fingertips over the planes and angles of his shoulders, his chest . . . his thighs. Julia's knees weakened to the consistency of bread pudding.

She wondered for a dazed minute if perhaps she'd taken ill. She certainly felt as if she had a fever.

Unaware of her turmoil, Burroughs caught his breath. "Forgive my appearance, my lady. An unfortunate mishap with a bag of flour made it necessary to bathe the young person. His lordship and I were assisting Mrs. Winston when he escaped."

Julia nodded absently. No amount of persuasion could have pulled her attention from Alec. Bubbles slid with caressing slowness down one side of his face and threaded across his unshaven chin. She lifted a hand to her own chin and wondered how his shadowed jaw would feel beneath her fingertips. The tiny whiskers would scrape and tease. She closed her hand over the imagined feeling.

Alec swiped at the wet trail, brushing aside the bubbles, his shirt stretched across the muscles of his arms. Julia swallowed convulsively. He dropped his arm, the half-buttoned shirt opening further to reveal the most fascinating trail of dark, crisp curls across the wide expanse of his chest. The path directed her eyes down to his waistband.

There her gaze halted, though her mind churned busily on.

Alec crossed his arms. "We must discuss your brat, Julia."

Julia's heated mind cooled at the sight of the brush he held in his hand. "What were you going to do? Hit the child?"

His gaze followed hers. "Good God, no! I had this in my hand when the screams from that"—he gestured to the hump on the side of her skirt where Muck lurked—"boy drew me to your room. When he escaped the bath, I attempted to help Burroughs catch him."

The butler nodded. "You were of immense assistance, my lord. A pity you were unable to keep the small person contained. I trust you did not hurt yourself when you fell in the—"

"I'm fine," Alec returned curtly. He pinned Julia with a steady stare. "Don't ask."

She bit her lip, struggling to contain an undignified giggle. "Fell in the tub, did you?"

His scowl grew until it encompassed both her and the butler. "Burroughs didn't come off any better than I. The brat attempted to climb him like a tree."

The butler put a hand to his ruined neckcloth. "Yes, it has been quite an invigorating morning. The house is topsy-turvy."

"It is unacceptable." Alec's glare fastened on Julia, leaving no doubt where he placed the blame.

Burroughs interjected smoothly, "If I may suggest a change of clothing, my lord. Shall I call for Chilton?"

Alec did not move his hard gaze. "Have him lay out fresh clothing in my room and inform him I will need a towel."

The butler bowed and strode from the hall.

Alec leaned an arm on the newl post and said sourly, "It was fortunate you came when you did, madam. I was well on my way to chasing your hellchild all the way to St. James, if need be."

The idea of a naked Muck leading a thundering Alec and a mussed Burroughs through town was more than she could bear, and Julia gave in to laughter.

Alec's scowl softened. "What are you laughing at, wretch?"

She caught her breath, a chuckle still escaping. "I

wonder what Edmund would say if he saw you dash by like that."

"Nothing worth repeating." His gaze dropped to where Muck's wet head soaked her skirt. "You should rethink your plans, Julia. There is no way you can take such a poorly behaved urchin to tonight's rout."

His words sobered her immediately. Here was her chance to show Alec how well the Society's servant referral effort would work. She patted Muck's shoulder and smiled with far more confidence than she felt. "You are wrong. He will be perfectly behaved; you'll see."

Alec muttered something under his breath.

Julia frowned. "Pardon?"

He regarded her glumly. "I don't see why this is necessary."

"Despite Aunt Maddie's best efforts, there is still talk about the confrontation with the sweep." Embarrassed heat climbed her neck and face. "I shouldn't have lost my temper, but I did."

He appeared slightly mollified at her confession. "I hold Edmund at fault as much as you. I will never understand how he came to be cajoled into calling that scoundrel out."

"Maddie says everyone will be overcome with sympathy once they see Muck, and it will turn the tide in our favor."

"I certainly hope so." He eyed her with a ruminative gaze. "Just how do you propose to pull this off?"

Julia smiled and leaned over. "Muck, the tailor will be here soon. Remember what I told you?"

There was a second of silence before a freckled, bucktoothed face appeared. "Thet I'll haf me own uniform, like a soldier?"

"Just like a soldier."

Muck's face creased into a fierce scowl. "Ole Boney'd be afeared to see me in a uniform, wouldn't 'e?"

"Bonaparte would turn tail and run." Julia affected a

loud sigh. "A pity you won't be dried off when the tailor arrives. I so wanted you to serve as my guard at the party this evening."

The child's thin nose quivered with interest. "I'm to be yer guard?"

"Oh, yes. You'll stand at attention, fetch supplies, and all manner of things. Just like a real soldier." She shrugged. "I suppose I'll have to get someone else to do it."

The boy shot a glance at Alec, eyeing the brush with a dubious stare. "I'd go if'n this 'ere bloody stiff'll keep 'is 'ands off me arse."

Alec's knuckles whitened about the brush while Julia tried to contain a chuckle. He shot her a fulminating glare before setting the brush on the step. "There, you ungrateful little romp. I promise not to give you the whipping you so deserve, providing you behave yourself from now on."

Muck scampered past him, stopping just long enough to peep up at Alec through a sweep of sandy lashes. "Ye run fast . . . fer an old bloke." The boy didn't wait for a response, but clambered merrily up the rest of the stairs.

Alec eyed Julia without remorse. "I suppose you think I should be flattered by that."

"Oh, no. It must be unpleasant to be considered old." She blinked at him with her most innocent expression.

His mouth curved into a smile, made all the more devastating by his drenched attire. Seeing such perfection of both face and form sent her thoughts galloping into places no sane, virtuous woman would dare go. Julia shifted, uncomfortably aware of the growing warmth in her lower limbs. It was as if the heat of summer had slipped between the folds of her muslin dress and caressed her bare flesh.

"You're very wet," she blurted.

Alec quirked a brow. "You possess the most irritating habit of stating the obvious."

"So my father used to say."

"I suspect I would have liked your father."

Her father would have liked Alec, too. "He was a very sensible man. I always try to do what he would have wanted."

"Like taking in street urchins who thrust themselves upon you in the street?"

And handsome rakes who hide their kindnesses beneath a blanket of sin. "Something like that."

His eyes softened to a smoky gray. "I must admit, Muck's presence has certainly enlivened the household. If I didn't know better, I'd swear he was a weapon planted by Napoleon to dismantle London brick by brick."

"He's just a boy."

"He's a very naughty boy."

She brushed at the wet spots on her skirt, realizing how mussed she must look. "Mrs. Winston said you used to run naked through the house all the time, riding a broom and waving a wooden spoon like a—"

"Besides an annoying tendency to state the obvious, you also possess a lamentable memory."

"Lamentable?" She blinked at him. "I remember everything."

"Exactly my point."

His smile seemed to go awry and Julia noted how shadowed his eyes appeared. She wondered if his weariness sprang from something other than dissipation. Perhaps he was worried about the conditions of the will, too. "Having trouble sleeping?" she asked with sympathy.

His eyes rested on her, hooded and intent. To her increased discomfort, they traveled slowly over her, resting for a brief minute on her breasts and hips. "I cannot sleep at all."

Julia rubbed her throat where a heated blush had left

a trail of prickles. "You might want to try Burroughs' warmed milk."

He moved closer. "I'm not that desperate, Julia. Not yet."

Oh, God. He was going to kiss her. Alec might not be desperate, but Julia was rapidly coming to the conclusion that she was just that—and not for sleep, either. She didn't know if she could handle another kiss. Not now, not with his clothing clinging to his powerful frame, emphasizing every delectable inch. She stepped back, her knees quivering as if someone had boiled her bones into jelly. "Warmed milk sounds very healthy. Perhaps I should try it myself."

That stopped him. He frowned and stared at her carefully, as if just seeing her. "Haven't you been sleeping well, Julia?"

How could she, when the man of her dreams lay across a narrow hallway, all sensual flesh and dangerously heated blood? She colored even more, almost afraid she'd blurted the thought aloud. Relieved her unruly tongue had been silent for once, she replied, "The rout is tonight. I never sleep the night before a big event."

His brow creased and he took another step closer. "There is no need for concern. I'm sure everything will go well. Lady Birlington won't allow it otherwise."

If she reached out her hand, her fingers would rest on the strong plane of his chest, now beckoning through his gaping shirt.

He clearly took her silence for doubt, for he repeated his assurance, "Truly, Julia—everything will be fine."

"Of course." Even to her own ears, her voice rang hollow and thin.

Alec rubbed his jaw, his hand rasping across his unshaven skin. Julia watched his hand, long-fingered and well formed, as it stroked his chin. The air thickened with a languorous heat. Unable to stay still, Julia worried the braids of her reticule until they were hopelessly twisted into knots. The very fact Alec would assist his servants in bathing Muck, even going so far as to chase the recalcitrant child, spoke volumes for her husband's capacity for kindness. Despite Alec's protestations otherwise, he possessed a generous nature.

It made her want to throw her arms around him and. . . .

Forcibly stopping her runaway thoughts, she plastered what she hoped was a cool, friendly smile on her face. The last thing Alec wanted was any show of affection, however well intentioned. But propriety urged her to at least thank him for his endeavors. Giving up her efforts at untangling her fingers from the reticule, she raised her gaze to his. "You were a great help with Muck. Thank you."

"It was no bother." Alec raked a hand through his still wet hair, his fingertips parting the thick strands in a way that left Julia breathless. A drip of water ran down his cheek and he grinned. "Well, it was a *bit* of a bother."

Julia nodded dumbly, realizing she must resemble a witless sheep. But no woman could have looked upon Devil Hunterston, drenched with bath water, and remain any more composed than she.

He suddenly chuckled, his eyes glinting silver. "Perhaps we should offer to train Muck as a footman for Burroughs. I think he'd like that, don't you?"

Julia opened her mouth. To her horror, she heard herself murmur, "You are wonderful."

He recoiled as if she'd struck him. "*What?*"

Embarrassment seared through her, but Julia forced a shrug. "You are wonderful, to help with Muck."

His brow lowered. "Don't make me into a saint. It's a good thing I didn't catch that brat this morning. I may not have used the brush on him, but I sure as hell would have boxed his ears."

To Julia's relief, Burroughs entered the foyer. "Breakfast is served," he intoned.

The butler had regained his usual state of propriety, his hair combed, his cravat neatly tied. He turned to Alec. "I believe you have a meeting with the executors this morning, my lord."

Alec glanced down at his sodden appearance. "I need to change. It wouldn't do for the old windbags to see me like this."

"Yes, my lord." Burroughs bowed and withdrew.

"What do the executors want?" Julia asked.

"My thoughts exactly, love."

Love. She knew he said the word without meaning, a flippant caress he gave without thinking, yet her heart danced with excitement.

"If I were to guess, they wish to reiterate the conditions of the will." A bitter smile flickered for an instant before disappearing. "As though I need a reminder."

Julia almost winced. Thanks to Muck, Alec had received plenty of unpleasant reminders of his wedded state. "Perhaps I should accompany you. It doesn't seem fair you should have to face such curmudgeons alone."

"I hardly think that necessary."

"A pity. I've never met an executor before. It might be interesting."

A smile lifted the corner of his mouth. "They aren't elephants, love. They are just a bunch of philanthropists with no appreciation for the finer things in life."

Though his words were not directed at her, they stung nevertheless. Irked, she asked, "What do you mean by 'finer things'?"

Alec regarded her with a spark of amusement. "I mean those things that bring pleasure."

Her brow creased. "You mean happiness."

"No. I mean pleasure. Physical pleasure."

A delicious flood of pink swept her cheeks. "Oh," she said. "That kind of pleasure."

With her bonnet askew, gloved hands clutching her
reticule for dear life, Julia could not have appeared more
innocent. Or more delectable. For some reason, he felt
an absurd need to strip away her primness, to rattle her
composure beyond their kisses—kisses that tortured him
more than she would ever know.

Alec's control was thread thin and ready to snap at
the smallest instance. Yet he could not stop dreaming of
possessing her. He dreamed of her by night and burned
for her by day. He took a step closer. "Tell me, Julia,
what brings you pleasure?"

She stepped away until her back was against the
newel post. Twisting the cords of her reticule nervously,
she regarded him with a wary expression. "Well . . . I
had a maraschino jelly at the Comptons' ball once that
was quite nice."

Alec had to smile. "That's not what I meant and you
know it."

Her clear green gaze fastened on him, sending a hum
of warmth through him. "My Aunt Lydia said you were
a man devoted to empty pleasures, the kind no honest
woman should know about."

He wondered that she could make him laugh even as
he burned with yearning. "I hate to tell you, love, but
that wasn't meant as a compliment."

"I didn't think it was. Aunt Lydia never says anything
nice unless she is speaking about Therese. Horrid
woman, my aunt."

It always amazed him how dispassionately she spoke.
Amazed—and, he admitted, not a little challenged.
There she stood, calm and self-possessed, a confirmed
virgin with no stain on her conscience. Meanwhile he,
a blackened sinner, felt as if he were tied in a thousand
knots, a prisoner of his own unbridled lust. How many
times had he halted outside her door, wondering what
she would feel like, writhing beneath him, her long legs

locked around his waist as he took her to the heights of passion?

The urge to punish her for the discomfort she'd caused welled within him and silenced the lonely voice of his conscience. Disregarding anything but his increasing desire, he closed the space between them until she had to tip her head back to meet his gaze. "Do you know pleasure, Julia? Real pleasure?"

She gave a jerky nod, regarding the stair behind him as if planning her escape. "I have if you count maraschino jelly."

He reached out and captured one of her golden brown curls. The strands clung to the roughness of his hands like a silken net. "Pleasure is something far grander than maraschino jelly, love."

"Oh." Her mouth trembled ever so slightly.

Alec leaned forward until his mouth drifted a scant inch from hers. "Pleasure is so many things, Julia. A waltz on a balcony under the caress of the moon. The thrill of placing a bet you know will win." His voice lowered. "The hint of mint in the air after a spring rain."

"Mint . . . spring rain," she repeated. Her tongue appeared between her lips, running across the sensual slope and leaving a fascinating trail of glistening wetness.

He brushed the back of his hand across her jaw, lingering on the curve of her neck. She swallowed, her graceful throat moving with the effort. As elegant as a swan, her every gesture resonated with economical beauty.

"There is more," he said, lowering his voice to a husky whisper.

Her gaze fluttered upward. "I was afraid there would be."

The sensual heat in her eyes whispered to him of dark pleasures. He wondered how she would taste today. All prim and sugary? Warm and soft, like innocence melted with desire? Or would she surprise him with heated passion so raw and overwhelming that it threatened to consume them both?

Heedless of his wet clothing, he pressed against her, allowing the evidence of his desire to rake along her hip. She gasped and he threaded his hand through her hair, holding her in place. Her scent wafted to him. "Pleasure, my sweet Julia, is the scent of lemons and cinnamon in a place you least expect it."

Tension flowed between their bodies like the tide at full moon. The rapid pulse that beat in the delicate hollow of her neck told him she felt it, too—and fought the urge just as he did.

But why? Why fight such an attraction? Julia had denied him the physical release that would lessen his yearning. Perhaps she yearned as much as he. If he possessed any nobility of character whatsoever, he would do what he could to remedy both of their frustrations.

Pleased with his reasoning, he smiled and cupped his hand over the smooth cream of her cheek. Cool and silken under his fingers, her skin warmed. He whispered, "The highest form of pleasure makes your heart thrum so hard, you wonder if it will expire from too much feeling, too much sensation. It is more than a kiss."

"More than a kiss? Heavens," she said faintly.

Behind her spectacles, her eyes seemed unfocused, her breathing rapid and shallow.

Alec trailed his fingers along the line of her cheekbone just below the rim of her spectacles. "As you can see, maraschino jelly doesn't even compare."

She closed her eyes and shivered, swaying toward him. Her breasts brushed his chest through the opening in his shirt, and Alec gritted his teeth. He was taking this much too far. He knew it, yet could no more stop than he could capture the sun.

Julia clutched at the newel post with both of her hands, the hopelessly mangled reticule dangling between them. "You . . . you can stop now."

The husky tones of unrelenting desire trembling in her voice pulled him closer. "No, I can't," he answered, slipping her spectacles from her nose. She didn't protest, her eyes fixed on his with silent pleading.

"Julia, let me show you how delicious, how fulfilling passion can be. Please," his voice slipped into a whisper, "come to my room."

Her eyes widened ever so slightly, her lips parting. "I—"

"Pardon me, yer lordship," came Johnston's strident voice.

Cheeks flooded with color, Julia clutched her reticule to her chest like a shield.

Alec clenched his teeth as waves of intense frustration pounded through him. He fixed a fiery gaze on Johnston. "*What?*"

The groom looked at the ceiling, his ears suspiciously red. "Burroughs said ye needed the carriage."

Julia's gaze lifted to Alec. Her eyes glowed an incredible green, the black center expanded to a velvet sea of lingering desire. She silently pleaded for things she could not possibly understand. A twinge of conscience nipped at him and he scowled. What was he doing? Kisses were one thing. Seduction was something else.

He turned to Johnston, guilt reducing his desire to a lonely ache. "Walk the horses until I have changed."

The groom nodded and left.

Alec's stomach knotted in frustration. He would gladly forgo breakfast this morning.

From upstairs came a wild screech, and Julia cast a relieved glance at the landing. "Mrs. Winston needs some assistance." Before he could stop her, she darted past him, racing up the stairs as if hell hounds nipped at her heels.

Alec started to reach for her, but Mrs. Winston's round face peering over the banister stayed him. He halted and scowled. If he didn't know better, he'd almost think his servants had set themselves up as Julia's protectors. A ridiculous thought, knowing how devoted they were to his interests, but one he couldn't quite remove.

He watched his wife ascend the stairs, her damp skirts clinging to her long legs with each step. His discomfort already beyond endurance, he remained where he was until she disappeared from the landing and into her room, the door closing with a soft thud.

Alec let out a breath and slumped against the railing. Julia had burst into his life, forced him to the life of a monk, then transformed into a siren right before his eyes. He wasn't a man used to being denied and was even less used to denying himself. He raked a hand through his hair. He was faced with the most damnable dilemma: his wife, every dewy, innocent inch of her, responded to his caresses like an avowed wanton, and yet he was honor bound not to proceed beyond a simple kiss.

Had he any sense, he would cease demanding the daily kiss that had become sheer, agonizing torture. Alec stared up the stairs where his wife had just walked.

But he would not relinquish his right to claim her lips. Not yet.

Chapter 16

❧

To say that no one recognized Julia in her new finery would be a misstatement, but several people openly stared and at least one young couple came to a complete halt on the dance floor, mouths agape. A hum of excitement rose as the gossips pointed and whispered.

"It appears we are the topic of conversation tonight." Alec cast a quick glance over his shoulder. "Of course, we would be."

Julia followed his glance to where Muck followed in silent awe. Ferret-faced, with two great pointed front teeth and a thin nose that quivered like a rat's, the child's unattractiveness was made all the more memorable by a pair of ears several sizes larger than they should have been.

Resplendent in a uniform of blue velvet, Muck was on his best behavior and had done nothing more irritating than asking nine or ten times in the carriage how long it would take them to arrive.

Alec bent to Julia's ear. "Nervous?" His breath stirred her hair and sent a shiver dancing down her back.

She nodded but refrained from looking directly at him. She was weakening. For his sake as well as her own, she needed to keep some space between them.

Somehow, she must show Alec the error of his wicked

ways, how he wasted his innate talents on futile pleasure seeking. If only she could find a way to do it without succumbing to those pleasures herself.

She nervously fingered the soft edge of her cashmere shawl. "Today was rather frantic, wasn't it?"

"Yes, it was."

Something in his tone caught her attention and she cast him a quick glance, then instantly regretted it. Dressed in formal evening attire, a lock of dark hair shadowing his silver-gray eyes, he was as disturbingly handsome as an angel.

Only he was no angel, she reminded herself. She could still hear his sensual voice, husky with meaning, as he described the earthly pleasures he so enjoyed. All he had to do was touch her and she melted like a pat of butter on a piece of well-toasted bread.

Alec glanced over her head to the other side of the room and frowned. "Damn. There's Nick."

Julia followed his gaze. Nick stood beside Therese, both looking as if they had just stepped from the pages of the fashionable *La Belle Assemblee*. Nick caught their eye and made an elaborate bow, murmuring something to Therese that caused her to laugh behind her fan.

"One day," Alec muttered, his jaw clenched. "One day he and I will settle our differences, once and for all."

"Why are you so against him?"

Alec raised his brows and said coolly, "Surely Mrs. Winston has already told you about Nick. She seems to enjoy divulging family secrets."

Julia supposed it must be galling to have a servant repeat your every fumble and foible over cream cakes and tea. "She hasn't gotten to Nick yet. She's painfully chronological. The last time I spoke with her, you had just had your twelfth birthday and had infuriated your grandfather by kissing the milkmaid."

"Good God," he replied, a startled look on his face. "Is it as bad as that?"

"Oh, worse than you can imagine. She has to repeat every last detail." Julia gave an exaggerated sigh. "I'd like to hurry her up a bit and get to the good parts, but I'm afraid she'd forget where she was and start over at the beginning."

He chuckled and her lips quivered in return. She was relieved they seemed able to put the tensions of this afternoon behind them. "I didn't mean to offer you a setdown. I just wondered why you are so set against your cousin when he seems determined to garner your favor."

Alec's brow creased. "He wants something." After a long moment, he murmured, "It seems like a hundred years ago, but at one time I thought of him as a brother."

Julia looked from one to the other. Where Nick gleamed the gold of a newly minted coin, Alec's dark looks fascinated and tempted. Yet they both had the same chiseled handsomeness, as if a master sculptor had crafted them from marble. "Except for your coloring, you look remarkably similar."

"Most people think us opposites."

Despite his casual tone, she detected an underlying bitterness. "What happened to cause such a rift between the two of you?"

"Nothing that concerns you."

Julia lifted her brows at his clipped tone. "You might as well tell me now. Mrs. Winston will get to it sooner or later and heaven knows how she might exaggerate it. I'd hate to have to quiz you for the real story."

His mouth curved in a heart-stopping grin. "Wretch! It is a wonder someone hasn't strangled you before now." His amusement faded and he regarded her somberly. "Why do you wish to know about Nick?"

"Because you keep warning me away from him. It would help if I knew why."

"There is no other reason?"

"What other reason could there be?" she asked, surprised.

"None, I suppose. And you are right. Mrs. Winston will eventually get to Nick and she does not know the whole of it." He led Julia away from a large matron who seemed determined to intercept them. "When I was ten, my cousin came to live at Bridgeton House. Grandfather had discovered that his mother had left him behind with near strangers while she traveled to Europe with her lover."

"What a horrid woman!"

"That's not quite what my grandfather called her, but you are close. Nick had just turned thirteen and was furious at being brought to rot in the country." He glanced at her. "Those were his words, not mine."

"He was angry at being left behind; a very normal reaction."

"Perhaps. I was just glad to have a companion, even a surly one. I followed him around like a pup. He'd done so much, traveled to so many places, while I had never been further than London."

"I felt the same about Therese when I first met her. It didn't take me long to realize I was wrong."

"You, love, had the benefit of age and experience. I was a child and believed my dashing cousin infallible." He paused. "For several months, it appeared all would be well. I think he even came to enjoy it there; Bridgeton House has its own charm. But then, a considerable amount of money disappeared from Grandfather's study."

"Was it lost?"

"Stolen. Apparently, I had erred in my estimation of my cousin. Nick was all too human."

"How do you know?"

"Grandfather taxed him with the evidence. Nick didn't even attempt to deny it." Alec stopped by a table and poured some lemonade into a crystal cup. "Of course, there wasn't much he could say. He was guilty and we all knew it."

Julia absently accepted the cup. "Hmm."

Alec quirked a brow. "What do you mean, 'hmm'?"

"Just that it seems very unlike your cousin to admit to such a thing. He is far too clever."

Alec's face darkened. "You seem to know Nick very well."

"I've seen him any number of times these past four years, though we've rarely had the opportunity to talk." She glanced back at Muck and saw his eyes fixed in wonder at the huge chandelier that hung from the ceiling. She smiled and turned back to Alec. "What happened after your cousin admitted to stealing the money?"

"Grandfather was devastated. Having opened his house to Nick and given him the benefit of his protection, he felt he'd been cruelly betrayed. Fortunately Nick's mother had just returned from Europe. Grandfather ordered her to come and fetch him. They had a great row, for she didn't wish to be burdened with him, either. But Grandfather was adamant and she took Nick to France with her the very next day."

Julia decided she needed to hurry Mrs. Winston along—she was missing all the important details. "The first time I met Nick, he had just returned from the Continent."

"We are blessed with his presence because his mother's family was forced to flee from Napoleon's troops."

Julia sipped her lemonade, grimacing at the sour taste. "Part of the French aristocracy, were they?"

"Yes." Alec took the cup from her hand and set it on the table. "Perhaps ratafia would be more to your taste."

Though Julia longed to pursue the topic, she could see Alec's confidences were at an end. "No, thank you. How did your meeting with the executors go?"

"They were surprisingly well reconciled to the fact that I married you and not Therese."

"I feared they might argue that point."

Alec had feared the same thing, and had gone to the meeting prepared to defend the circumstances of his marriage. Yet the executors had done no more than glance through the documents proving Julia's claim before subjecting him to a humiliating examination designed to highlight his every fault.

One of the executors, a pompous ass who'd provoked him at every turn, had even gone so far to suggest that if Julia were to become "in the family way," the issue of the inheritance could be settled immediately. Alec had felt as if someone had slipped a noose around his neck and slowly tightened it, inch by bloody inch.

As the executors had taken great delight in pointing out, Julia was in his care. Anything that befell his wife rested directly on his shoulders. He thought of their encounter in the foyer this morning and winced. Before he could protect Julia from Nick, he'd have to find a way to protect her from himself and his own damnable desires. Yet just a hint of her distinctive lemon and cinnamon scent caused his manhood to lift and swell.

He glanced down at his wife and the pressure around his throat increased. Though she would never possess Therese's outstanding beauty, Julia was an undeniably attractive woman. The additional presence of a sensual elegance and a sharp wit that could startle a reluctant laugh from him under the worst of circumstances allowed her to easily outshine her less fascinating cousin.

Julia caught his gaze, a faint blush touching her cheeks. Dressed in a simple creation of white gauze over a mint green slip, her hair piled on her head in a series of tumbled ringlets, a pretty fan hanging from her wrist, Julia appeared as innocent as springtime—and just as luscious. No, she didn't *appear* innocent. She *was* innocent.

Her delicate brows pulled low. "Perhaps I should meet the executors. Maybe if I—"

"No," he interrupted, shuddering at what those staid and repressed gentlemen would make of Julia's forthright manner. "There is no need."

"Well," she said in a doubtful voice, "if you don't think it's necessary. I just hate for you to face them alone."

Try as he might, Alec could picture no other female of his acquaintance offering to accompany him into such a den of lions. "Julia, you are—"

"Hunterston!" Lady Birlington's strident voice reached them. "Come over here. I wish to see your wife." Outlandishly attired in a bilious green silk gown and a bright yellow shawl, she beckoned imperiously.

Fighting a sigh, Alec guided Julia to where Maddie sat. A long-suffering Edmund stood behind her chair and cast yearning glances in the direction of the game room.

Maddie pointed her cane at Muck. "So this is the boy from the library, eh?"

"Tare and hounds, Aunt Maddie," exclaimed Edmund. "Who else could it be? Can't have two urchins with the same face. Least, not 'less they were twins, and even then I'd lay you a monkey they wouldn't look exactly alike. Though I did see a set of twins at a fair once who—"

"Demme, Edmund! Cease your prattling." Maddie placed her hands on her cane and leaned forward until her nose was even with Muck's. The urchin jutted his chin and scowled. Apparently satisfied, Maddie drew back and nodded. "Good thing he doesn't have dark hair, Hunterston. Wouldn't want anyone to think he was one of your by-blows."

"Aunt Maddie!" Edmund's anguished gaze fell on Julia. "Sorry. She don't always think about what she's saying."

Julia examined first Muck, then Alec. "I can't imagine

anyone thinking such a thing. There's almost no resemblance."

Alec looked at the homely child. Muck obligingly stared back. "What do you mean, 'almost'?"

Julia tilted her head to one side. "Same nose."

Had he not seen her mouth quiver with suppressed laughter, he might have been taken in. "If that child's nose looks like mine, then he has your hair." He chuckled and reached out to tug on one of her locks, the back of his hand resting against her cheek. A sharp prickle of awareness ran the length of his arm.

Julia stepped away from him so swiftly she bumped into a chair, her color fluctuating alarmingly. "Sorry," she mumbled.

Alec's hand dropped back to his side, irritation curling his hands into fists. Did she truly hold him in such aversion? Were her kisses the result of uncontrollable passion and nothing else?

He looked at his wife's profile, noting the delicate sweep of her brow, the long splay of her lashes, the gentle slope of her mouth. She deserved a courtly suitor, one who wrote poetry to her beauty, appreciated her spirit, and dedicated himself to her charity efforts. Not a man who was so selfish he couldn't even stand beside her without wondering how the smooth, perfumed skin of her thighs would feel against his mouth.

Disgusted at his lascivious thoughts, he turned away. "You look lovely this evening, Lady Birlington."

Maddie patted her red hair, set with a haphazard arrangement of sapphire and emerald pins. "Thank you, Hunterston. Good of you to notice." She turned to Edmund. "Don't you have something to ask Julia?"

"What? Oh, yes. Care to dance, Lady H.? Been anxiously awaiting the opportunity."

Julia sighed regretfully. "I'd rather not. Two left feet, you know."

"Nonsense," Lady Birlington said testily. "You've seen that French dance master no less than four times this past week alone. Should be able to dance like Princess Charlotte by now."

"It didn't help. Monsieur Armonde said I was as graceful as a cow in slippers."

"No!" Maddie declared. "What a rude thing to say!"

"Perhaps Monsieur Armonde did not realize Julia speaks excellent French," said Alec shortly. He missed his chef's way with crepes.

Julia's brow knit. "Very useful thing to know, French. One can learn all manner of things."

A plump blonde went dancing by, wiggling her fingers over her partner's shoulder at Edmund.

Edmund grasped Julia's hand and said urgently, "The quadrille. My favorite dance. Come, Julia."

She grimaced. "Oh, very well. I suppose it would look odd if I didn't dance at least once."

Alec noticed she didn't even look toward him. The omission bothered him more than he cared to admit.

Julia laid her reticule on a chair then bent to look Muck right in the eye. "Will you guard this for me?"

His face puckered.

She patted his hand. "I'll only be gone a moment. Master Alec will be here, if you need anything."

The boy cast a suspicious glance at Alec before establishing himself by the chair, rigidly at attention. "I'll keep me blinkers peeled fer ye, missus, in case there be any knobby ones about."

Alec tried to suppress his irritation as his wife blithely left with Edmund. After a few false starts, the pair made their way through the quadrille with more enthusiasm than grace.

Leaning against a pillar, Alec watched Julia. Who would have ever imagined such a gamine creature existed beneath the dull exterior of the Frant Dragon? He tried to remember what she'd looked like before her amazing transformation, but couldn't. She was simply

Julia—elegant, attractive, and irritating, all in the same breath.

It was comical to watch Edmund as he attempted to place himself by the plump Lady Chowerton. He eventually succeeded, making obvious gestures to her over Julia's shoulder. Julia glanced behind her and frowned.

After a few passes through the dance, her frown changed to a scowl. By the time the music came to a close, Edmund and Julia appeared to be involved in a lively argument. As they neared, Alec heard Julia say in her distinctive accent, "Bonehead."

Edmund, coldly furious, favored her with a stiff bow, "I won't deign to reply to that." He then proceeded to ruin the effect with a decided pout.

"Who is a bonehead?" asked Maddie, her blue eyes bright with interest.

"No one." Edmund glared at Julia as if daring her to defy him.

Her chin firmed. "*Edmund* is a bonehead."

"La, child," Maddie said, disappointed. "Everyone knows that."

Julia turned to Alec. "Edmund has been flirting in the most outrageous manner with a married woman."

Maddie tsked. "Serve you right if Lord Chowerton called you out, Edmund. If I were a man, I wouldn't hesitate to put a bullet right through your heart."

Edmund's face reddened. "Surely you wouldn't."

"Would, too. That or spatter your brains 'gainst a wall," Maddie said thoughtfully. "Depends on how angry you made me."

He sputtered, but before he could say a word, Julia poked him in the chest with her fan. "You should find some nice unattached girl. There are so many of them— and without dance partners, too." She looked about the room as if she expected to pluck some unfortunate girl from her chair and place her in Edmund's waiting arms.

Knowing her penchant for organizing other people's

lives, Alec would not have been surprised to see her do just that.

Edmund turned to him, his gaze wild. "Tell Julia it's deuced improper to discuss such things."

"Not in my day, it wasn't," said Maddie, adjusting her shawl. "Used to talk about worse things than that. Spent hours trying to figure out who was slipping off with whom. Kept us amused for days."

Julia nodded. "My father said that a truth not spoken can cause as much damage as the vilest lie." She glared at Edmund. "You should *always* tell the truth, no matter the cost."

Edmund dropped into a chair and tugged at his cravat. "May we *please* speak of something else?"

Alec took pity on him. "Lady Birlington, I meant to thank you for assisting Julia with her transformation."

Maddie examined his wife from head to foot and said grudgingly, "She'll do, but she'd have made more of a stir with the bronze gown."

Julia caught Alec's questioning stare and blushed. "It was very indecorous and was cut down to here." She gestured with her fan.

Alec stared where she had indicated, right where the modest lace of her gown covered the provocative swell of her breasts. He cleared his throat. "Surely Lady Birlington did not mean for you to wear anything so revealing."

Maddie snorted. "Of course I did. I suggested she dampen her skirts, too, but she wouldn't have any of that, either. Pity. Would have been more fun to launch a dashing matron instead of such a sedate one. But then, life is never perfect."

"You told her to *what*?" Alec wondered if he was hearing amiss.

"You should follow fashion more closely, Hunsterston. Everyone is dampening their skirts. I'd do it myself," Maddie said with unimpaired calm, "if I weren't afraid of catching my death. May look like a hag, but I still have the figure of a girl. Least, that's what I've been told." Something amazingly like a simper crossed her face.

"Who has been saying such improper things to you?" demanded Edmund.

"Oh, hush. We were talking about Julia, not me."

The conversation between Edmund and Maddie quickly degenerated into an argument, and Alec turned to Julia.

He took her hand. "Let's dance."

"But that's a waltz."

"All the better." Without giving her time to remonstrate, he swept her into the dance.

Within moments he began to understand Monsieur Armonde's frustration. Besides having no sense of timing, Julia showed a disconcerting tendency to lead. By holding her tightly and dancing slower than the music demanded, Alec managed to settle into a reasonable facsimile of the waltz.

Yet there were compensations for her inability. For one thing, he had to hold her considerably closer than the prescribed twelve inches. Each time they turned, her breasts brushed against his coat, causing her to flush an adorable pink.

He found himself holding his breath in anticipation, his gaze inexorably caught by the sight of her silk gown sliding against his lapels. Alec could almost picture her breasts reacting, the rosy nipples tightening as they circled the dance floor, sending vibrations of sensation throughout her body.

Damn the will, damn the executors, and damn the entire ordeal. God help him, he was surely destined for Bedlam.

After what seemed an interminable time, Alec ventured a comment. "Shocking crush, isn't it?" He winced at the triteness of it.

"Hmm."

"I don't suppose it will rain any time soon, do you?"

She didn't even pretend to answer this time.

"It has been an incredibly chilly spring." He tightened his hold the tiniest bit more. "The roses are sure to die horrible, painful deaths. Their little petals will shrivel, their leaves twisting in agony as they—"

Her startled gaze flew to his. "What?"

"I was merely commenting on the weather."

Julia's mouth quivered with amusement. "Dancing like a bumpkin, aren't I?"

"I wouldn't say that. I'm just not used to being ignored by my partner."

"I can't help it. I have to mind my steps, you know. I'd hate to break your toe."

Alec chuckled and pulled her even closer. "Let me count the steps for you, love. I am generally held to be a creditable dancer."

"Oh, yes. I know that."

He frowned. It bothered him to think that he might once have danced with her and couldn't remember it. "Have we danced before?"

Her dimple appeared, resting on one cheek with all the audacity of a caper merchant at a funeral. "You'd have bruises if we had. Therese said it was one of the things she liked about you. That and the way you kiss. Of course, I know how you ki—" Julia broke off, a deep blush staining her cheeks.

Entranced, he wondered what she would do if he traced the line of her blush with his lips. "Why shouldn't you know how I kiss? We are married, love."

Her gaze dropped back to the floor. "Edmund is right. I need to watch what I say."

Had Alec been a true gentleman, he would have allowed the matter to rest. Instead he brought her body flush with his, ignoring the outraged gasps of the other dancers. "Do *you* think I kiss well?"

"That's not a fair question," she said gruffly. Her color flared brighter, but she made no move to disengage herself.

"Why not?" She had the loveliest skin, like the spill of cream, smooth and translucent.

"I can't really compare it. I've never kissed anyone else."

"And I suppose you need a comparison?"

"Oh, yes." Julia tilted her head to one side. "Perhaps Edmund would do. He seems to have a penchant for married women." She met his astonished gaze and chuckled.

Her laughter trailed through him like fire and he immediately loosened his hold. Alec managed a perfunctory smile, but no more. One touch, however innocent, and he would have lost all control and yanked her to him right there.

Julia noted his withdrawal and her liveliness fled. But other than casting an abashed glance at him, she did not offer any comment. Alec had never been so thankful when a dance ended. He escorted Julia to Lady Birlington as the last note died.

Maddie was deep in discussion with the Dowager Duchess of Roth, an imposing, gaunt woman with a prominent nose who was well known for her charity efforts. The two welcomed Julia and immediately drew her into conversation, exclaiming over Muck, who stood stoically by her chair, guarding the abandoned reticule.

Alec decided it would be far less worrisome to watch Julia from afar. If he saw Nick approaching, he would simply rejoin Lady Birlington's party. He stationed himself in a strategic location that afforded him a good view of his wife and consigned himself to an evening of unalleviated frustration. Oblivious to his presence, Julia talked and danced with an endless line of callow youths.

He decided it was a good thing his wife was such a wretched dancer. No man could wax poetic while the lady in his arms trod upon his feet every chance she got.

Only when waltzes struck up did Alec return. Yet each dance was more torturous than the previous one. By evening's end, Alec's mood fell just short of foul. Returning home, he placed a chaste kiss on Julia's hand and consigned himself to the library with a bottle of his best brandy.

He poured himself a hefty drink and tossed it back in one gulp. There wasn't enough liquor in the whole damn house to cool his blood, but it was all he had. Pouring another, he turned to sit in his favorite chair but pulled up short at the empty spot. It was still being repaired. Consigning all reformers and their troublesome charges to the devil, he dropped onto the settee and positioned the meager cushions to attain some semblance of comfort.

Glancing at the ceiling, he wondered if Julia were already asleep above, comfortably ensconced in her virginal bed, the covers pulled to her chin. But as his thoughts had a disturbing tendency to peer beneath her chaste covers, he quickly dismissed the image and forced himself to concentrate on his brandy.

He sighed heavily and glanced at the mantel to check the time, but no clock rested in the center of the ornately carved shelf. Yet another of Muck's casualties. Alec cursed and rose to cross to the sideboard. Abandoning all pretenses, he opened another bottle of brandy and carried it to his lumpy settee.

It was going to be one hell of a night.

Chapter 17

Two weeks after the rout, the Dowager Duchess of Roth appeared at Almack's with a page even homelier than Muck. She further astounded her friends and family by graciously announcing that the child was a former pickpocket, plucked from the gutter and trained by her own tender care. The gossips clamored. No one seemed to notice that the dowager was also a distant, but fond, relative of Lady Birlington's.

Within a fortnight, bewildered footmen from all across London were sent into the streets and alleyways to rescue homely children for the employment of their mistresses.

Julia's success was assured. Therese, startled by this unexpected coup, immediately sent for Nick.

It took him three days to reply, but when he did, she had the coveted pleasure of riding out with him in his high-perch phaeton, an honor he afforded very few. After assisting Therese into the carriage, he climbed up beside her and set the horses to a smart trot down the tree-lined street.

Therese waited until they had left the fashionable confines of Park Lane before turning to him. "You must do something about Julia."

"What do you suggest? Kidnapping? Torture?"

The amusement in his voice stung. "You cannot mean to sit idly by and allow Alec to inherit the money."

Nick directed the horses around a halted coach-and-four before returning his attention to her. His blue glance fell just short of boredom. "Never fear, Therese. I have everything well in hand."

A sudden breeze sent the skirts of her blue silk gown into a graceful flutter, catching the eye of a young cit exiting a shop, his arms filled with parcels. On seeing Therese, he stopped, his mouth dropping open. She rewarded him with a blinding smile that caused him to drop his burdens into the street.

She peered at Nick, hoping he had noticed.

He didn't so much as spare her a glance, tooling the phaeton across the bustling square, the great wheels coming within scant inches of a tanner's lumbering cart.

Therese regarded his strong profile with a wistful sigh. Dressed in a multicaped driving coat of moss green that complemented the wonderful fit of his pale yellow trousers, Nick could not have appeared more handsome. He represented wealth, position, and more. Once they married, she would be the wealthy Countess Bridgeton and Nick would be hers.

Though it frightened her to admit it, she was almost certain the yearning she felt for him was love. It had to be, for she could not stop thinking of him. She wanted the taste of him in her mouth, the feel of him beneath her hands, the smell of him on her sheets. Therese allowed her gaze to wander across his broad shoulders down to the hard muscles of his thighs beneath his fitted trousers.

As if reading her thoughts, Nick flicked her a contemptuous glance. "It is rude to stare, Therese. Even for you."

Her cheeks heated to match the rest of her body. She forced herself to return his cool stare with one of her own. "I was not staring."

His lifted brow told her he knew her lie for what it was. "I suggest you lift your gaze from my lap long enough to acknowledge what few admirers you have left." Nick's amusement doused her desire as effectively as sand over a fire. "We just passed Lord Marshton, who favored you with a very elegant bow. He appeared quite crushed you did not notice him."

Therese shrugged. "He will call on me later. He is very devoted."

"And up to his ears in debt." Nick smiled down at her. "But he may be all you have left. Just how many admirers have abandoned your court for the elegant Viscountess Hunterston? What is it now? Five? Six?"

"None," Therese snapped, though a feeling of unease sifted through her. In truth, she had lost at least one admirer to Julia.

Lord Bentham had been pursuing Therese for almost a year, his declarations most passionate. But though he held an acceptable position, his portion was only adequate. Therese had held him at bay, enjoying him as an acceptable companion, but never intending to give in to his persuasions. Still, his defection had hurt, especially as he had promised to paint her portrait.

All the *ton* clamored for a Bentham painting and he was notoriously selective about his subjects. Therese suddenly wondered if Bentham had consented to paint Julia. It did not bear thinking of. She tossed her head and glared at Nick. "My cousin is *not* elegant."

"I must disagree. Your cousin is elegant, intelligent and. . . ." He frowned, his gaze narrowed thoughtfully.

"Julia is a countrified little colonial with no pretense at fashion."

Nick laughed. "How excessively ill bred. No matter what you say of the intriguing Julia, you must admit she presents herself without fault. You would do well to discern what is so fetching about your cousin and emulate it as best you can." His cool gaze flickered over her dismissively. "You aren't getting any younger, my dear. Such fair beauty will not age well."

It took all her efforts not to strike him. "You are cruel. You should be thankful I have your best interests at heart."

"You, my little charlatan, have no heart. For us, everything is about money. It is what we crave, what we dream of."

"If I simply wanted money, I would have already wed."

"And just whom would you have married?" A touch of true amusement lit his eyes to the blue of a summer sky. "Who possesses enough of a fortune and a lofty enough title to satisfy your extravagant needs?"

The truth of his statement chilled her. Thanks to her father's mismanagement of their fortune, her dowry was woefully inadequate. Though she had attracted more than her fair share of attention in her first season, each year her suitors numbered less. Sadly, few men were both wealthy and titled.

Besides Alec, only two men had proposed to her in the last year. One of them had been so old and doddering that she had shuddered every time he'd kissed her hand. The thought of his shriveled, wrinkled body next to hers made her ill.

The other had been a wildly handsome but impoverished youth she had taken a fancy to and allowed to kiss her with far more passion than decorum allowed. His callow attributes had quickly palled, and she had been mortified that he had thought himself enough her equal to ask for her hand.

Nick turned the phaeton into the park. The light perfume of the flowers alleviated the dust and grime of the city. "Look about you, Therese. Name one man you would be satisfied with." He chuckled, the sound low and rich. "I cannot see you lying beneath a wealthy cit as he sweats on your delicate skin."

Other than Nick, Therese could no longer see herself gracing the bed of any man. "Since you and I will be wed within the year, it is not a matter for concern."

"There is more to be concerned about than you know." No emotion touched his voice, yet she was aware of an undercurrent of tension in both his face and tone. "If we do not do something, and quickly, there will be no fortune. And if there is no fortune, there will be no Countess Bridgeton." The blue of his gaze sparkled dangerously. "At least, not for you."

Her throat constricted painfully. Nick would have no compunction about abandoning her. "What do you want me to do?"

"I must see Julia alone. Find out if there is anywhere she travels without Alec." Nick's handsome mouth straightened. "My cousin has become very wary. If you haven't noticed, he shadows Julia like a dog guarding a particularly juicy bone."

She had noticed and it had piqued her ire. It was humiliating to stand by while her old suitor paid court to another woman, even though Alec had never been more than a reluctant admirer, at best. A sudden improbable thought made her turn to Nick. "Do you think Alec actually cares for Julia?"

Nick urged the horses into a trot. "No."

"You don't know him as I do. Only the greatest devotion would send him dancing attendance on any woman."

"Poor Therese. He was never attentive to you, even after he knew the contents of Grandfather's will." Nick grinned. "Feeling slighted?"

She smiled tightly. "Alec is a bore. I'm glad he had found such a worthy mate in Julia. No one deserves her more."

"You desired him more than you admit."

"Perhaps I did." She lifted her eyes to his. "Until you came along."

Nick turned away, flicking the tip of the whip to the leader's ear and then catching it neatly in his gloved hand. "You know, it is one of the few pleasures I have, stealing what once belonged to my cousin. That was one of the things that drew me to you."

She placed a gloved hand on his arm, but he ignored her. "Alec is not in love," he said dismissively. "The fool merely seeks to protect his interests."

The rebuff was plain. Therese removed her hand and stared at the passing scenery. "Alec may not be in love with Julia, but it is not so the other way around. She has always had a partiality for him, even before they wed."

The horses lurched. Nick cursed and spent the next few minutes controlling the spirited bays. When they finally settled back into their rolling pace, he said in a low voice, "It does not matter. We must find a way to ruin them."

"We still have ten months left. Surely in that time Julia will do something to—"

His gaze stopped the words in her throat. "I'm up to my neck with the cent-percents. If we don't do something soon, I will be forced to flee the country."

"You are not so done in as that."

He stared straight ahead.

"But . . . the estates, surely they are worth something."

His mouth twisted into a bitter grimace. "Not to me. The whole property is so entangled with provisions, I can barely touch it. I, the earl of Bridgeton, receive a paltry allowance like a schoolboy, while Alec—" He broke off abruptly. They turned from the park and back onto the cobblestone streets. In a calmer tone, Nick said, "All that will change once I get my hands on the fortune."

"I will take great delight in seeing Alec without a feather to fly with." He had made her a laughingstock more than once, first with his elopement, and then flaunting his own cousin in the face of the *ton* as if Julia were actually someone. Therese had seen the amused glances and heard the titters as she walked by. The whispered comments burned like a festering sore.

Nick slowed the horses to a walk. "In the meantime, I have to get near Julia." He scowled, his brow creased. "I *must* see her."

Therese regarded his profile with a sense of growing unease. There was something different about Nick today. He looked unaccountably anxious, as if the idea of not seeing Julia actually caused him physical discomfort.

The thought caught Therese and held her. "You want her," she said wonderingly.

His mouth curved in a slow, sensual smile. "Your cousin is a challenge. I would enjoy conquering her."

Therese's mouth dropped open. She could not mistake the admiration in Nick's voice. "My God."

He did not pretend to misunderstand her. "Julia is the most intriguing woman I've ever met."

"She's a prude!"

"No," he said harshly, the lines about his mouth white. After a moment, he continued in a milder tone, "There is passion there, a great deal of passion. Yet I would vow she is untouched."

"Untouched? With Alec for her husband?" Therese gave a harsh laugh. "Julia is well used by now."

His anger suddenly blazed like a blue flame, and she drew back.

"Sometimes, Therese, you manage to disgust even me. My cousin has not touched her. You have but to look at her to know it."

A crushing weight forced the air from her chest. "You *care* for that little nobody."

Nick regarded her with a closed expression. "I admire her. It is a different thing altogether."

"Not different enough. I know you, Nick. You want that little bitch, no matter what lofty tone you wish to use!"

He guided the horses between two approaching carriages.

"Well?" she demanded as the silence lengthened.

His amused glance eased her suspicions somewhat. "Rest assured, my interests lie more with the fiscal than the physical. And frankly, my dear, I do not care who or what gets in my way."

She regarded him narrowly. "Not even Julia?"

His beautiful mouth curved into a smile. "Not even Julia."

Therese adjusted the blue ribbon beneath her chin, not entirely satisfied but calmed. "I want that little baggage so discredited that no one will ever say her name again."

"Then discover when I may find her alone."

"What do you intend to do?" she asked suspiciously. "I won't stand—"

"Listen, you silly little chit," he hissed. "If I am forced to flee to the Continent, you will be left here to breed with whatever country squire will have you."

Therese sat silent at the thought. She couldn't allow that to happen.

Nick pulled the horses to a halt in front of Covington House. He tossed the reins to the waiting groom and jumped down.

As he assisted her from the carriage, Therese clung to his arms. Sun filtered through the trees above to light his hair to glistening gold. Framed by the sweep of dark lashes, his eyes deepened to a mesmerizing blue. He removed his glove and tilted up her chin with a careless finger. To anyone who might see them, he appeared to be paying her a compliment.

"Don't try my patience. I am not a man who takes failure well. I would hate to break that pretty neck of yours."

This was the Nick she knew. Strangely reassured by the threat, she clasped her hand around his wrist and rubbed her moist lips across the rough edge of his fingers. "I love you, Nick." Her breath caught in her throat as she waited for his response.

He pulled his hand from her grasp. "Don't waste yourself on me, my sweet. I'm not worth your love, or anyone else's."

Without a backward glance, he climbed into the phaeton and set off down the street.

Therese watched him disappear from sight, humiliation and disappointment vying for expression. But she gave in to neither. She didn't know how she could love such a cold man, but she did. She would do as he asked, but her pride would not allow matters to continue as they were.

Aware of the interested eyes that might be staring through the curtains of the surrounding houses, Therese plastered a smile on her face and trailed her fingers through the fringe of her shawl. She needed a plan—one that would bring Alec to his knees. One that would ruin Julia in such a way that no amount of trickery could save her.

One that would win Nick completely.

Down the street, Therese caught sight of Lord Bentham's thin frame. There were ways of causing a scandal, and then there were ways. She smiled wider and bent, pretending a stone had slipped into her shoe, and waited.

Chapter 18

❧∽◦◗◖◦∽❧

Julia hurried to her waiting carriage, a leatherbound ledger tucked securely under her arm. Vicar Ashton's genius lay more in delivering inspiration than in recording expenditures. While no lamb under his care went without his tender attentions, the books often collected dust as expenses went unrecorded.

Conscious of his failing, the vicar had asked Julia to put the blotted pages into some sort of order so all would be in place when they finally established a business with their new funds. Though not sure she could offer much assistance, Julia had agreed to attempt it. At least it gave her something more productive to do than wear silk gowns and make idle conversation, both of which were beginning to pall.

The Society had met twice in the last week and had finally consolidated their plans, though there were still many details to work out. Julia sighed, her shoulders drooping with fatigue. Their venture must succeed, whatever the cost. The women of Whitechapel were counting on them.

"There you are, Cousin."

Nick stood before her, exquisitely dressed in fashionable buff trousers and a close-fitting blue coat. She wasn't really surprised to see him. He'd tried several

216

times to speak with her, but between Alec and Maddie, they'd managed to keep him at bay. They apparently thought him dangerous, but for the life of her, Julia could not figure out why. She knew exactly who and what he was. "What are you doing here?"

His mouth curved in amusement as his deep blue gaze slowly traveled over her. "You should always wear that shade of green, my dear. It becomes you admirably."

Green might suit her, but a flirtatious Nick did not. "Thank you. It was nice seeing you, but I really must go." She nodded pleasantly and tried to walk around him.

He moved into her path, forcing her to retreat a step. "You seem to be in a hurry. Tell me, where is my overly protective cousin?" He glanced up the street toward the carriage. "Ah, I see it is not Alec, but the estimable Johnston who awaits."

Julia shifted the heavy ledger to a more comfortable position, misliking the way he looked at her as if she were one of Mrs. Winston's pastries. "What do you want, Nick? I've a busy day today."

"What makes you think I *want* anything?"

"Because it is highly unlikely you'd be in Whitechapel unless you wished to see me." She frowned and realized that wasn't entirely true. There was one other reason a man of Nick's standing would visit this part of town. "You aren't casting lures to the local lady-birds, are you?"

His eyes widened before he threw back his head and laughed. "The devil, Cousin! You are blunt to a fault. Actually, I came on an errand of mercy."

Julia eyed him doubtfully.

A rueful smile curved his mouth. "Nonplussed by a chit with spectacles." He placed a hand over his heart and sighed. "My reputation is ruined."

Despite her mistrust, Julia chuckled. When Nick laughed with genuine amusement, he looked even more like Alec. "You may as well come clean and tell me what you want, Nick. It will save us both a lot of time."

He opened his arms in a gesture of defeat. "I will admit all. I came looking for you, Julia."

"Why not just come to Hunterston House? Mrs. Winston makes an excellent cream cake."

"And visit you amongst your flocks of admirers? There's not enough privacy for what I have in mind." He regarded her with a lazy gleam as he removed his gloves. "Besides, Alec has made it abundantly clear he does not want me near you."

The idea unexpectedly lifted her spirits. "Oh? Has he said so?"

"Yes," Nick said, a sudden crease between his eyes. "Several times, in fact, and in such a way as to imply he meant me violence if I ignored him." He slipped his gloves into his pocket. "Such husbandly devotion is rather unfashionable. He will make you a laughingstock if you do not contain him."

"Alec doesn't do anything to be fashionable. He's worried I'll make an error and then you'd inherit the fortune."

"Would that be so bad?" He reached out and retied the bow beneath her chin, the blue of his eyes darkening to midnight. "You, my sweet, would not be left destitute. I would be a most generous donor to your beloved charity."

"Would you give me half of the fortune?"

His hands stilled beneath her chin. "Half? That is a bit steep. What do you say to five thousand? That is more than generous."

"Alec gave me half."

An inscrutable expression crossed Nick's face. "Did he, indeed? And just how did you manage to charm my hard-hearted cousin?" His gaze lingered with insolent intent on her breasts. "Or need I ask?"

Julia stepped away. "All you need to know is that I

will do what I can to keep you from getting the fortune."

He chuckled. "You are a delight, Julia. Even the sordid truth sounds palatable tumbling from your mouth." His gaze rested on her and he murmured, "Such a lovely mouth, too."

She tried to stifle her annoyance, smoothing a hand over the cool leather of the ledger. Lately, her days were so filled with frivolous social activities that she had been excited at the prospect of spending a few hours engaged in a truly useful industry. Bantering with Nick seemed an additional tedium. Yet Julia could not dismiss the hurt she'd witnessed in Alec's eyes when he'd spoken of his cousin. Perhaps here was a way she could pay back some of Alec's generosity.

Julia tilted her head. "Alec told me you and he were once close."

Nick's smile thinned. "I am surprised he mentioned me at all."

"You shouldn't be." She patted his arm. "Every family has its quarrels."

He broke into an astonished laugh. "My God, you want Alec and me to cry friends?"

"Why not? Neither of you has any family to speak of." She frowned. "Though I did hear you had relatives in France."

His face closed. "A few."

"Very volatile sort of people, the French. We had a French cook once. It didn't work at all." She leaned forward to say earnestly, "If I were you, I wouldn't count anyone from France as family."

Nick chuckled. "I don't. I met them only once, and it was not a pleasant stay. They were all as mad as my mother."

"Mad?"

"Ah, Alec didn't tell you everything, did he?"

"He told me some money disappeared."

Nick nodded pleasantly, as if she'd just mentioned the possibility of rain. "So it did."

"Did you take it?"

His smile melted into silence. After a long moment, he said, "You are the first person to ever ask me that question."

Julia frowned. "Surely not. Alec said you admitted to stealing it."

"I'm sure that is how Grandfather saw it."

"Ah—he didn't give you a chance to speak, did he? I've noticed Alec has a tendency to engage in that same sort of high-handed behavior."

"He is remarkably like Grandfather. But I cannot blame either of them. Grandfather hated my mother and feared I would be a disruptive influence on Alec. My fate was decided the instant I set foot in Bridgeton House."

"You were only thirteen. Everyone makes mistakes."

His hooded gaze flickered across her. "Only thirteen, and yet more debauched than any whore you have ever allowed in the doors of your Society."

Julia almost shivered. "I think you'd like everyone to believe the worst of you. It keeps them from expecting more."

He looked amused. "Do you always involve yourself in the lives of the people you meet, or is this an honor you bestow only on the misfits of society?"

"You are not a misfit."

Nick stepped closer, deliberately crowding her on the narrow sidewalk. Julia stood her ground, tilting her head back to regard him sternly. "I am not afraid of you, Nicholas Montrose."

He smiled and relented, moving back a pace. "Then you trust me?"

"No," she confessed. "But everyone can become a better person. Even you."

Nick's smile did not quite reach his eyes. "Sometimes,

Julia, a wolf is just a wolf. No more and no less."

She nodded, shifting the book in her hands until it separated them like a wall. "Even wolves deserve a home."

"And lost souls—don't forget them." He withdrew a card from his pocket and held it out. "Which brings me to my purpose."

She stared at the card but made no move to take it. "What is it?"

"The address of someone in need." He slipped the stiff card into the pages of the ledger. "She is in desperate straits. If you do not help her, no one will."

Suspicious of his bland expression, she asked, "What kind of assistance does this woman require?"

"Miss L'Amour is an actress, though her skills in that area are lamentable. The theatre manager has been hinting he will entertain bids for her company for a certain type of private performance. I doubt she realizes her intended fate; she is indeed an innocent."

Julia felt a blaze of excitement. It would be the perfect experiment for the Society. "I shall contact her immediately."

"I knew you would. But hurry, Julia. One man in particular is pursuing her with less than noble intentions. If someone does not interfere, he will win her." He leaned forward and dropped his voice to an intimate level. "I know this man, Julia. Once he has her in his bed, he will quickly tire of her and toss her away like soiled linen."

It was all Julia could do to meet his gaze. "How did you come to know this woman?"

He caught at one of the ribbons that trailed from her bonnet and pulled on it, slowly untying the large bow. "How do you think?" he asked softly.

Julia yanked the ribbon from his grasp. "*You* are the man making the improper advances."

He bowed.

"It is not very chivalrous of you."

"I would pay her well."

Julia pinned him with a hard stare. "Why are you telling me this, Nick? You cannot care what happens to this actress."

"Had I not thought it might amuse you to save yet another soul from ruin, I would not have bothered. Indeed, I would have deflowered her, used her well, and left her for the next ragged soul." He retrieved his gloves from his pocket and pulled them on. "I still might. She is a thoroughly delectable piece."

Her brows lowered. "You're not given to kind gestures. You must have another motive for doing this. I don't suppose you'd tell me if I asked."

"No, I would not." Nick gently disengaged one of her hands from the ledger and placed a lingering kiss on it. "I must be off. Pray give Alec my best." He tipped his hat and sauntered off.

Several women on the street stopped to brazenly stare as he passed, but he ignored them all. Whatever Nick was about, Julia knew it boded ill—but she had never been one to turn from a challenge.

Tucking the card into her reticule, she hurried to join Johnston.

Chapter 19

~~~∽◯◯∽~~~

Julia sat at Alec's large mahogany desk and opened the ledger. She carefully selected a pen and settled in for a satisfying hour of genuine labor. One page at a time, she slowly worked her way through the labyrinth of numbers, deciphered the vicar's spidery handwriting, and wrote corrected tallies in the columns. As time wore on, her neck began to ache, but she doggedly continued.

She was a quarter of the way through when she lifted the pen from correcting a total. Black ink dripped from the nib and soaked into the paper, blotting out the carefully written figure. "Confounded ledger," she muttered, frowning at the frayed nib.

"What was that?"

Startled, she dropped the pen. Ink splattered across the page in a decorative spray.

Alec's smile hinted at devilment. Arms crossed, he leaned against the doorjamb attired in the tailored coat and knee breeches required by Almack's.

At the sight of his clothing, Julia turned to where the ormolu clock should have been. "Is it eight already?"

"Past that. Lady Birlington will be wondering what's become of us." Shoving himself from the door frame, he came to stand at her shoulder. "What has so absorbed your attention that you have forgotten the time?"

She sighed. "Vicar Ashton asked me to take a look at the records, but I'm not sure if I'm correcting them or just making them worse."

He leaned forward, one hand resting along the back of her chair, the other placed flat on the table. His hip brushed her shoulder and the subtle aroma of sandalwood and leather encircled her.

Her stomach quavered and she leaned away. If she didn't put some distance between them, she would become a babbling idiot. "I'm not very good at accounts, but the vicar seemed to think I could do it." She looked at the blotted page. "He was wrong."

Alec turned the ledger to face him, his sleeve brushing against her cheek. "Perhaps. Let me see what is to be done."

With unsteady fingers, Julia tucked a few stray wisps of hair behind her ears, reminding herself that such casual contact was a commonplace occurrence, and she should accustom herself to such happenings. Yet she couldn't resist leaning ever-so-slightly to one side until her cheek just grazed his arm. She held her breath, but he didn't move, apparently immersed in the sea of blots and figures. Julia savored the moment, closing her eyes and absorbing his warmth.

After a moment, his stillness seemed unnatural. Julia opened her eyes and swallowed, casting a glance up at him. He stared at her, his eyes dark with some swirling emotion. "I was planning on saving our kiss for the coach ride home. But if you wish, I could deliver it now."

Mortified, she managed to squeak, "No, thank you."

Smiling, he watched her through half-closed eyes, then shifted forward to point at an entry on the page. "That should be listed in this column here." His hard thigh pressed against her arm. As far up in her seat as she was, there was no escape from that steady, licentious pressure.

Her chest constricted. She forced her unseeing gaze to the page. "Oh. That." Despite her determination not to succumb to the sensual lassitude spreading through her limbs, the air thickened with unspoken meaning. As if to tempt her further, he subtly increased the pressure of his muscled thigh against her arm.

A welter of desire radiated into her chest and lower limbs. Any moment now, she would toss caution to the wind and wrap both her arms about his tempting thigh and hold onto him with all her might. She closed her eyes and fought a flood of unladylike impulses until Alec muttered an imprecation and moved to the other side of the desk.

Bereft, Julia stared at the forgotten ledger. Numbers danced and swayed, blurring together until she could no more add than read.

It doesn't mean anything to him, she reminded herself, in as calm and orderly a fashion as a woman on the brink of indiscretion could manage. *You forced him to give up his mistress, and now all his heated impulses are collecting, pooling within him, simmering like a volcano ready to erupt.* But no matter the result, she could not regret having made such a demand. "If he had a mistress, he would never even look at you," she muttered, forcing herself to return to the ledger one more time.

"Pardon?"

The hint of disbelief in his tone left her with no doubt he'd heard every word. Drat her impulsive tongue. Smiling brightly, she said, "Just talking to myself. I said, uhm, 'If he had a seamstress, he would never heave a book at you.'"

"*What?*"

Clinging to her pride, she added doggedly, "It's a child's song I learned in Boston. I daresay you don't know it, but it's quite common there."

He answered this with a skeptical lift of his brow, a

hint of laughter in his gaze. "Sing it for me," he said softly.

Julia blinked. "I can't. It is bad luck to sing the same song twice. Indoors. On a Thursday."

He chuckled. "It is even worse to lie to your husband."

She assumed the most innocent expression she could and waited.

"Stop that." His mock scowl was as endearing as his grin. "You are as bad a liar as you are an accountant."

Alec returned to her side and opened a drawer and pulled out a large leatherbound book. He set it before her. "Let me show you a better way to set up your accounts, love. If you enter the income here with expenses listed so, you won't have so many errors. As bills come in and are paid, you just move the amounts from this column to this column. That way you know at any date how much you owe and to whom."

His ledger had nary a blotch nor blot on it. Every number beamed up at her, orderly and legible. Julia regarded the neat tally with a sinking heart. "I could never get our books to look like that. I suppose we'll just have to hire someone." It was disheartening how little she'd been able to contribute to the Society lately. She no longer had time to work with the women and she had thought that here, finally, was a way for her to contribute something.

Alec's hand rested on her shoulder, his fingers brushing against the skin at her neck in a most disquieting way. "If anyone can make the Society productive, Julia, it will be you."

The quiet confidence in his tone brought tears to her eyes. It was all she could do not to throw herself in his arms. She cleared her throat. "When did you learn to do accounts?"

After the slightest hesitation, he removed his hand. "Grandfather was determined that I possess some useful skills. He believed that any man who would trust another to watch over his funds deserved to be cheated of them."

"Sounds like my father. He was forever telling Mother she shouldn't trust every soul who came through the front door. She would just laugh and say Jesus didn't dwell with the saintly, and neither should he."

Her smile quavered and fell. At times she missed her parents more than she could bear. Slipping off her spectacles, she swiped at a stray tear with the back of her hand.

"Julia, what's wrong?"

She sniffed and slid her spectacles back on her nose. "I was just thinking of this mess."

"I can see where that would make you cry," he said in a dry voice.

"Well, it does. I hate to leave things undone."

Alec handed her his handkerchief, his gaze never wavering as she blew her nose. "Would you like me to take a look at the books? I'm not sure I could help, but I'd be willing to try. Meanwhile you can go and get dressed."

Julia looked at him over the fold of his handkerchief. "Can you fix them?"

His mouth quirked into a lopsided smile. "Yes, if you have the original bills."

"I can get them from the vicar tomorrow." She blinked down at the blotched accounts. "We need it done by Friday, though. You'll have to work fast."

"Yes, madam," he replied, his meek tone belying the laughter in his eyes.

Ignoring everything but his offer of help, she nodded. "Excellent."

Alec gave her a wry smile and pulled a chair to the desk, sitting far closer to her than necessary. "Let me see how bad they are." He slowly turned the pages, stopping now and again to shake his head when he came across an especially blotted entry. "I'm not sure who was worse, you or the vicar."

"Probably me. I couldn't get the nib on my quill quite right."

Alec didn't answer, already lost in the sea of numbers. The silence grew as he began adding rows of figures. Julia admired his strong profile. His long lashes fanned across his cheek, at odds with the strength of his jaw.

She really should go and dress. The Duchess of Roth wished to consult her about holding a charity ball, yet spending the remainder of the evening making idle small talk held no appeal. What she really wanted was to stay here, beside Alec, and watch him as he helped her with the accounts. For this one instant, it was as if they were a family.

Julia propped her elbow on the table and rested her chin in her hand. Perhaps she could use this time to her advantage. She regarded her silent husband through her lashes and waited until he had finished adding a particularly long column of numbers. "I had a very busy day today."

He turned a page and began a new column. "Oh?"

"Yes." She slid the inkwell and a silver engraved paperweight in front of her. "I hired a maid to assist Mrs. Winston."

Alec lifted his gaze from the ledger, a hint of unease in the smoky depths. "She's not some misfit, is she?"

"Heavens, no. Whatever makes you think that?"

He didn't look especially convinced. "Is she from the Society?"

That irked her but she let it pass, spinning the paperweight on the desk. "No. She has never even been in Whitechapel that I know of."

"Good." He returned his attention to the ledger. "We don't need another incident like Muck."

She thumped the paperweight on the desk. "Muck was not an incident."

"No, you were," Alec said implacably, moving the paperweight from her reach and placing it back into the proper position beside the inkwell. "Fortunately, most people seem to have forgotten your scrape with the sweep."

Julia regained possession of the paperweight and added a box of sand to her collection of objects, arranging them in a triangle. "Muck is an excellent page. He has worked hard."

Alec pinned her with a stern stare that reminded her of the portrait of his grandfather that hung in the morning room. "I shudder to think of the amount of furniture that child has broken in this house."

Now would not be a good time to mention the sadly bent silver epergne Mrs. Winston swore was a special favorite of Alec's. The poor child was really not at fault, having fallen on it when he was trying to reach a spider hanging from the chandelier. "He is improving."

"That boy is a hellion and deserves to be horse-whipped on a regular basis," Alec said firmly.

Julia prudently held her tongue and tried to balance a silver-handled letter opener across the inkwell. Despite Alec's grumbling, she had already seen him sneaking Muck candy on two occasions. Julia suspected her husband was more like his grandfather than he knew, all grumbly and gruff on the outside and soft and warm on the inside.

If she could only convince Alec to open his house to one Miss Desiree L'Amour. To Julia's amazement, she'd found Nick's estimation of the actress entirely correct; Desiree was as innocent as she was simple. Worse, the young girl was not more than seventeen, with a fatal addiction to trinkets that could only be described as vulgar.

To anyone familiar with the ways of the world, it would not be long before Miss L'Amour was importuned into a life of sin and corruption. And Julia would not put it past Nick to be the one to do it. Thus she had no choice but to offer Desiree immediate employment in the Hunterston household.

Convincing the girl to give up an exciting career in the theatre had taken some doing. But once Julia had promised a genuine diamond bracelet for her efforts, Desiree had agreed, arguing only that she could not possibly leave the theatre until the current production ended its run. Julia suspected the girl's loyalty sprang more from admiration for the silver costume she wore than anything else, but Julia had agreed, knowing she needed time to alert Alec to the arrival of this newest addition to his staff.

She glanced at Alec. "The new maid will be of immense help with the dinner party."

The quill hovered over an especially blotched page. "What dinner party?"

"Lady Birlington seems to think we should hold a small gathering here. Nothing large, just five or so couples. I thought next week would serve."

"If she says it is important, then I suppose we must. Be sure to invite Lucien, would you? He returned yesterday."

"Of course." Julia turned her efforts to balancing the letter opener between the inkwell and the paperweight and said casually, "It would be very small, just the thing for Desiree."

Alec frowned. "Desiree?"

"The new maid."

"Oh, yes." He turned the page. "Sounds French."

Actually, she suspected Desiree was from Cornwall. Julia frowned. Despite her belief that the new maid was a complete innocent, she could not rid herself of the idea that somewhere lay a trap. Nick was not the type of man to assist anyone, no matter how beautiful they happened to be. Still, it was gratifying to be able to help the poor girl and soon Julia would be in a position to help others like her.

Her heart swelled at the thought of hiring more servants. If all went well with Desiree, Julia would hire a cook, a kitchen maid, and maybe even a lady's maid. Of course, she would choose only the worthiest candidates. It would be difficult, as they all deserved another chance. Deep in thought, Julia propped her chin back in her hand, her elbow jiggling the table.

The box clattered off the makeshift bridge onto the table and sent a spray of sand across the ledger. "Oops. Sorry."

Alec regarded the trail of white grains that crossed the page and sprinkled the front of his black coat. "You, madam, are worse than Muck." His gaze rested on her for a moment, traveling slowly across her face, resting on her mouth. "Only much, much prettier."

Despite her determination to remain unmoved by his casual flirtation, Julia's face flushed. "I meant to say something about that."

He lifted his brows, a faint smile hovering over his mouth. "About how pretty you are?"

"No. About the new maid. Desiree was cruelly persecuted for her appearance at her last place of employment." Julia scraped the loose sand back into the box, careful not to meet Alec's gaze. "I just thought you should know."

Alec sighed, already seeing where she was heading. Before Julia was through, they would be forced to remove all of the mirrors in the house lest they crack in horror. "Everyone suffers from something, Julia."

"You don't know how it is to be judged by your appearance."

Hurt darkened her green eyes. Alec stared at her for a long moment, trying to discern whether she referred to herself. It was difficult to remember that the elegant woman who now sat across from him had once been a poorly turned out, dowdy chaperone. Dressed in a pretty pink-striped muslin ornamented with cherry ribbons and a graceful fall of lace, she would appear perfectly at home in the most elegant salon. He wondered if she even realized how attractive she had become.

Julia caught his gaze and offered a tentative smile. "I know you don't like a lot of servants falling over themselves and getting in the way, but Mrs. Winston needs some assistance."

"I hope your protégée is thankful you put her in the way of such a respectable position."

"Oh, she is!" Julia stared at the paperweight, as if mesmerized by the lights playing across the silver surface. "I don't know if you are aware of it or not, but there is a lamentable shortage of good help in town. Aunt Maddie and I alone know of three households desperate to find trained servants." Julia folded her hands, met his gaze, and announced, "That is why the Society is opening a servant referral service. It is the perfect solution for the women."

Alec caught the inkwell just before it, too, tumbled across the ledger. He placed it firmly out of reach. "Nonsense. You cannot pass those women off as virtuous housekeepers and maids."

"Pass? Heavens, no. By the time we get through training them, they *will* be virtuous."

"But how—" He caught sight of her expression. "You are serious."

Julia's eyes gleamed with excitement. "We had the most horrible time trying to find the proper employment for the women." She chuckled, a delicious, throaty sound. "We even thought of opening a sausage plant."

"Good God!" he said, realizing what a close escape he'd had. The idea of hiring out servants suddenly seemed more reasonable. He noted her flushed cheeks and sparkling eyes. It was amazing, really. His wife was thrilled at the prospect of teaching a group of soiled doves how to make scones and serve tea. Nothing delighted her more than her charity work.

In a way, it was a very lowering thought.

Julia propped her elbow on the table and leaned her chin into her palm, a glowing smile lifting the corners of her wide, sensual mouth. "We will hire existing servants, excellent ones like Mrs. Winston and Burroughs, and pay them to do the training. Perhaps I should invite a few leaders of the *ton* to see how very well the servants perform and then—"

"Invite them? Invite them *where?*"

She turned a bewildered face to him. "Here, of course."

Alec shut the ledger. "Julia, you cannot bring your Society work into this house."

"Someone must sponsor this project, and it may as well be me."

He pushed away from the table. "We cannot afford a scandal."

"There won't be a scandal. All we have to do is find one or two genteel women and train them to—"

"They are not *genteel women*, Julia. They are prostitutes and whores. You cannot change that."

She stiffened. "They are *reformed* women, Alec. Forced by circumstances to do what was necessary to survive."

For a second, a pang of something uncomfortably close to jealousy pinched at him. He wondered what would happen if she ever committed her heart to him with the same fervor she spent on her reform efforts.

Sighing, he leaned back in his chair. "I am not saying these women didn't have a reason for what they did, nor am I suggesting they don't deserve your compassion. It's just that you cannot continually foist your projects onto the *ton*."

"But the Society—"

"The Society knows you as Julia Frant, not Viscountess Hunterston." He frowned. "I must have been crazed to have allowed even that. If I'd thought you would carry this so far, I would have put an end to your association with the Society from the first."

She stood, eyes flashing sparks of outrage. "Of all the insufferable. . . ." Her hands balled into fists. "I should remind you that it was my idea to keep my identity concealed. And that was only because you were concerned there would be talk about my visits to Whitechapel."

Alec's determination rose to meet hers. The season would be over in less than a month and the majority of their social responsibilities would be at an end. They were too close to success to take chances.

He shoved back his chair and faced her, hands splayed across the desk. "If the Society decides to pursue this path, Julia, it will be without you. The cost is too high. You won't be able to help anyone if we lose the funds."

That froze her in her place. He sat down, pulling the ledger to him. "Get dressed, madam. Lady Birlington awaits us at Almack's. The doors close at eleven."

A frosty silence met his command, but he forced himself to keep his gaze on the ledger before him, holding the quill so tightly that it bent.

Finally, when he'd begun to believe she would flout him, she sniffed. "I will be ready within a half-hour." With a flip of striped cherry muslin, she disappeared out the door.

As soon as it closed, Alec tossed down the broken quill and raked a hand through his hair. He had little doubt he could have won the argument based on sheer logic, but it was a relief not to have to engage Julia in battle. She would fight to her last breath and confound him with emotional appeals until he forgot his purpose— something he could not afford to do.

Sighing heavily, he pushed the ledger away, the leather cover grating on the sandy surface of his desk.

Life with Julia was filled with unexpected twists and turns—not all of them pleasant, but at least there was never a minute of boredom. Between her disrupting his household with street urchins, firing his chef, and blithely stumbling from one potential scandal to the next, Alec was never sure what each day would bring.

But he had dealt well with her this evening, he thought, suddenly proud he had stood firm. She had presented him with one of her outlandish ideas and he had told her no, just as a husband should. An odd feeling of triumph flittered through him, and yet . . . he glanced at the door.

He could not reconcile himself with Julia's sudden acquiescence. Somehow, he knew he hadn't heard the last of this.

Chapter 20

His face pinched with disapproval, Chilton replaced the stack of neatly starched cravats in the wardrobe. "Someone has applied too much starch to the linens." He shot a telling glance at Alec. "Of course, considering everything Mrs. Winston has had to deal with, it is hardly surprising to see such an error occur."

Alec continued to tie his cravat. He had enough on his mind without worrying about Chilton's tendency toward high drama.

Julia had been noticeably cool to him following their argument, not speaking a word the entire way to Almack's and studiously avoiding his presence in the days that followed. It had been almost a week now, and still his stubborn wife showed no signs of relenting.

He was not surprised; Julia was a strong, independent woman and it must be galling to admit defeat. He placed a sapphire pin in the folds of his cravat and smiled at his reflection in the mirror. Julia might be able to maintain a frosty silence for an entire week, but she could not control her response to his touch.

Of course, he'd made a point of making each kiss the zenith of seduction, pushing both his control and her passion to the pinnacle of pleasure and frustration. Perhaps today he would see if he could move past a mere kiss. Perhaps today, he would discover how much of her anger he could fan into the hot blaze of passion. Humming softly, he buttoned his waistcoat.

Chilton shut the wardrobe with a sharp snap. "My lord, I *must* say something. The entire household is in an uproar and it is unbearable. Things simply cannot continue, or I. . . ." He stopped, unable to continue, his mouth quivering with emotion.

"Are you threatening to leave, Chilton?"

"No, my lord! I would *never* leave your employ." The valet waited a telling moment before adding, "Regardless of the number of vulgar persons allowed into your house."

Alec offered no comment. He shrugged into the coat the valet held ready and then smoothed the sleeves, waiting.

After an apparent struggle, Chilton burst out, "It is the new maid, sir. Lady Hunterston brought her yesterday afternoon and she is unfit. *Something* must be done."

Ah, Julia's homely maid had arrived and offended Chilton's delicate sensibilities. For some reason, the thought amused Alec. Just to goad the stuffy valet further, he remarked, "Lady Hunterston mentioned her. Taking thing, isn't she?"

Chilton met his gaze reproachfully. "I would venture to suggest many would find her so. However, her conduct makes one question—" He broke off, his long nose quivering in outrage.

Alarm raised the fine hair on the back of Alec's neck. Julia had promised that the maid was not one of the Society's misfits, and yet. . . . Frowning, he dismissed the valet as soon as he was able, and went in search of Julia.

She was nowhere to be found on the upper floor, so he proceeded to the front drawing room. There he stopped short. A female attired in the strict black uniform of a maid stood on a small stool, watching out the window.

"Pardon me," he said.

She started and turned, regarding him with wide blue eyes. Alec stepped backward as if someone had just thrown him a leveler. Far from the homely creature he had imagined, the new maid was a vision of female loveliness. Shining ringlets of dusky black framed a heart-shaped face while the stark lines of her uniform emphasized her enchanting figure.

As guileless as a lamb, the beauty fluttered long, thick lashes and obligingly climbed off her perch. "You must be the viscount."

"And I suppose you are the new maid," he said, hoping against all hope he was wrong.

She favored him with a blinding smile, enchanting dimples appearing in each cheek. "I am so thankful Lady Hunterston found me." She clasped her hands together, the dozen bracelets adorning her slim wrists jangling noisily.

He raised his brows at the sparkling array. Silver and gold, some set with costly gemstones, they bedazzled the eye and gleamed against her sober uniform. "Where did you come from?"

"The Lowdry Theatre, off Fleet Street." Her innocent gaze fastened on him, wide and unblinking. "I was an actress, you know."

"Is that the new euphemism?" he asked dryly. "*Actress*?"

The maid's white hand flew over her mouth. "Oh! Lady Hunterston said I was never to speak of that again." She frowned, her pretty mouth curling down at the corners. "But I do think it is a pity. Mr. Bibbs, the theatre manager, said I was on my way to becoming his most popular attraction."

Things were becoming clearer by the minute. "Pardon me, Miss . . . ?"

"L'Amour. Desiree L'Amour."

Lovely. A soiled dove with a name to match. "Miss . . . er, L'Amour, how did Lady Hunterston meet you?"

"She came to my room after a performance. I lived over the theatre, you know." A frown marred the perfection of her brow. "Well, it wasn't really *over* the theatre, more behind it."

Alec could see it clearly—a whore's squalid room in a filthy back alley, the stench of sin wafting through the air, and Julia, girded for battle, come to save the day. God, was there ever to be an end to his wife's antics?

The maid must have mistaken his appalled silence for interest, for she smiled and jangled her trinkets. "Aren't they beautiful?" She lifted her arm so the collection showed to advantage in the waning sun. "I love London. The gentlemen give me such handsome things."

"Do they?" Alec asked grimly.

Her smile melted into a frown. "All except one. He gave me a bracelet that turned green after only a week." Desiree tossed her glossy ringlets. "I refused to speak with him after that."

"I'm sure that was wise."

"I cannot afford to be cheated. I am very poor, you know," she confessed with artless candor. "It is the most dreadful thing."

Nonplussed, all he could do was murmur an agreement.

She fingered a gold bracelet that reflected a bevy of dancing lights across the carpet. "I would dearly love to have a real diamond bracelet. Lady Hunterston says I may have one if I work hard."

"Did she indeed?" He had underestimated his wife for the last time. There simply were no bounds to her audacity.

"Oh, yes. And as soon as I have enough money, I am going to purchase my own cottage, too. I had thought to earn my way on stage, but it was frightfully uncomfortable."

"Uncomfortable" was hardly the word he would have chosen.

Desiree heaved a regretful sigh that pressed her plump bosom against her modest bodice. "I did get to wear the loveliest costumes, though. I do wish you had seen the silver dress I wore in the last play."

Alec regretted a lot of things, but seeing his maid perform on the open stage in a silver dress was not one of them. He'd reluctantly allowed the reprehensible Muck into his household, but this—a woman of sullied character—was beyond the acceptable. Alec couldn't wait to get his hands around his wife's slender, entirely too busy, neck.

Just then, the object of his ruminations breezed into the room amid a rustle of blue silk. Her gaze fixed immediately on the maid.

"There you are, Desiree! I've been looking all over for you. The guests will be arriving any minute and Mrs. Winston needs you in the kitchen. We've no cook, you know. You'll have to help where you can."

Desiree nodded, then blushed, sinking into a deep curtsey. "Yes, Your Grace."

Julia waved an airy hand. "No, no, no. That's for the Dowager Duchess of Roth. For me, it's just 'my lady.' And you don't have to call me that if no one is about."

The maid's face puckered, tears threatening. "I do hope I don't ruin your dinner party. I was just telling His Grace—" She clapped a dimpled hand over her mouth. "Oops, I should say 'my lord.' "

Julia turned a startled glance in his direction. "Alec! What are you doing hiding behind the settee?"

To his fury, he felt a flush lift up his face. He hurriedly stepped from behind the settee. "Nothing! I was conversing with Miss L'Amour. She was telling me of her adventures on stage."

Telltale color stained Julia's cheeks. "I was hoping to have a word with you about that, but what with the dinner party and attending Almack's, and . . . I forgot."

"Yes, you did." Alec waited for Julia to reply, but she was much too busy herding the girl from the room.

"Go on, Desiree. Tell Mrs. Winston to let me know if she needs anything else." Julia shut the door behind the maid before turning to him. "We have a paltry ten courses for dinner, but Lord Fallington had only eight and no one said a thing. Besides, the turtle soup is excellent, and Mrs. Winston has made—"

"Sit down."

"There's no need to grump, Alec. I am perfectly willing to discuss this with you." Julia glanced at the clock as she slipped into a chair near the door. "But you will have to hurry. The guests will arrive any minute."

"They can wait." He crossed his arms and faced her sternly. "I thought you agreed to give up this preposterous idea of employing the Society's Haymarket ware as respectable servants."

"I did not 'agree' to anything. We simply ceased discussing it. Besides, Desiree is not from the Society." Her smile was plainly condescending. "So you needn't sulk."

"Don't try to pull the wool over my eyes, Julia. That woman is a prostitute and little else."

Julia's eyes sparkled dangerously. "Desiree is *not* a prostitute. She is a young girl, hardly more than seventeen, and in the worst fix. I had to do something."

It galled that she would risk everything, including his wrath, for a woman ripe from the gutters. The injustice rankled like a hot coal. "That does it: there will be no more visits to Whitechapel. You are entirely out of hand."

"Nonsense," she returned, adjusting the blue silk so that it pooled about her feet. "Mrs. Winston and I have complete faith that everything will go smoothly. You'll see."

"I've seen enough." He glared. "I thought you said she was homely?"

Julia raised her brows. "I *said* that she had been persecuted for her appearance. It's not my fault if you assumed that meant she had missing teeth and a sad tendency to freckle."

The fact that he'd pictured just that made him even angrier. "If she was in such a fix, why didn't you just pack her up and send her to the country?"

"She won't accept charity. She wants to make enough money to buy her own cottage—a very commendable goal, I might add. Besides, there was precious little time. Someone was casting out very strong lures to the child and I had to remove her as quickly as possible."

"Who could blame them? Your protégée couldn't wait to thrust those bangles under my nose."

"Exactly my point," she replied, all cool hauteur. "All it would take is one gentleman with a modicum of address and a pretty bauble and Desiree would have been lost before she even knew what happened. She hasn't the sense to open up an umbrella in the rain. And that, dear sir, is why I was forced to take action."

"Damn it, Julia," he burst out, raking a hand through his hair. "You cannot single-handedly help every urchin and guileless child in London!"

"I can try," she returned, pressing her hands together so he would not see them shake. She would not apologize for helping others. Her heart had ached to see the shabby room Desiree had occupied, reminding Julia all too well of her own damp lodgings the year after her father had died. "I did what I must and there is no more to be said."

A different type of heat warmed his eyes as he placed his hands on the arms of her chair and bent to face her, his mouth within inches of hers. "If anything goes awry, you will pay the price. And this time, I will not settle for mere kisses."

Julia swallowed hard and stared at the winking sapphire nestled in his cravat. How could he call those incredible, drugging, sensual onslaughts "mere" anything?

He leaned closer until his breath warmed her cheek. "If our distinguished guests suspect your protégée of being anything other than an innocent kitchen maid, you will pay dearly indeed."

Unable to answer, she gave a jerky nod.

"You will resign from the Society and come willingly to my bed. I want it all, Julia." His voice softened into a husky invitation. "Every delectable inch."

She would not have thought it possible, but he was even more handsome up close, his dark hair falling across his brow, begging to be straightened, his eyes shimmering with passion and anger. Julia's instinct was to retreat, but she was already leaning as far back in her chair as she could.

There was nothing for it but to pretend she wasn't in the least affected by his nearness. Yet her smile trembled. "Desiree will do well. Mrs. Winston and I have worked with her extensively these past two days. No one will suspect a thing."

Alec ran a finger down her cheek, sending a ball of fire along her spine and through her lower limbs. "You had better hope they don't, love."

God save her from unprincipled rakes. Her insides had long since melted, her hands were damp, her heart fluttered like a caged butterfly. At any moment she would burst into flames, consumed by the fires of her own passion until nothing was left but a pile of ashes.

The thought of that lonely pile of ashes made her unaccountably angry, and she managed an admirable glare. "You have no right to make such demands."

"Don't I?" A muscle in his jaw clenched and he spoke in the stiff, cold tones of a stranger. "The only request my grandfather ever made of me was to protect the fortune from Nick's clutches. We set a bargain, you and I.

If I am to abide by your rules, then you will abide by mine."

A lump rose to stick in Julia's throat. "Your grandfather would have understood my intentions. Lady Birlington said he was quite generous and sponsored many charity efforts."

Alec straightened abruptly, pushing himself away from the chair to tower over her. "Is that all you ever think about, your blasted charity work?"

"It was my parents' dream."

"And you? What do *you* dream about, Julia?"

If only he knew. "It is my dream, too."

"My dreams are not so noble as yours." He spoke more quietly now, his voice sifting through the silence like the brush of velvet on bared skin. "But each of us must fight his inclinations. I have relinquished my mistress; what have you given up?"

A hot flood of jealousy made her stiffen. Was that what he wanted? The right to return to his mistress? Before she could form her answer, a soft knock sounded at the door.

Cursing under his breath, Alec turned away as Burroughs entered the room. "Pardon me, my lord, but the Dowager Duchess of Roth and her niece have just arrived and are waiting in the front parlor."

"We will be there immediately," Alec answered shortly. Burroughs bowed and retreated, shutting the door behind him.

Julia struggled with a welter of emotions—fury at Alec's arrogance, hurt at his lack of faith, and a strange thrill of excitement. She told herself she didn't want his attentions, that she didn't crave his touch, but the truth was, she had dreamed of nothing else since the first time she'd seen him almost four years ago. Dangerously handsome and forbidden, he had strolled into the Seftons' ballroom and stolen her heart before she'd realized it. But that did not alter the cold, unpleasant truth: Alec did not love her.

Pride made her stand and meet his gaze with a stubborn scowl. "You needn't worry that I will jeopardize anything. After all, half the money is mine and I would be a fool to let it slip away."

His smile sliced her heart with its coldness. "Ah, yes, the money. Perhaps that is what you dream of as you lie in your cold, lonely bed." His mouth curled unpleasantly. "If you are desperate, there are other ways to secure the fortune. The executors have made it clear that they will immediately award the funds if I get you with child. The thought is very tempting." His gaze slid over her possessively. "Very tempting indeed."

A child? She hadn't even considered that. Wouldn't it be lovely to have a little boy with Alec's gray eyes. . . . What was she thinking? Her husband was telling her he had decided to bed her, not for love, but to meet the approval of a group of men he freely castigated as doddering old fools! Well, he could just find another wife. "I will not bring a child into this world without love."

"What do you know of love?"

Before she could stop herself, she answered, "I've known it these past four years."

A blaze of fury raged across his face. "*Who?*"

Afraid he'd read the answer on her face, Julia spun on her heel and walked to the door. "Our guests are waiting."

His hand closed about her arm and he yanked her against him. "*Who is it?*"

Julia pulled free and met him stare for stare. "Does it matter?"

For a long second he glowered, then he dropped his hold and turned away as if the sight of her disgusted him. Without a word, he crossed to the window and stood with one arm against the frame, his back to her, his head lowered.

Julia struggled to hold back the tears of anger that threatened to spill. Why did she let him affect her so? He was proud, arrogant, and selfish beyond thought. She no longer worshipped Alec from afar. She knew his weaknesses and faults, yet despite them all, she loved him even more than she'd ever thought possible. For his sake as well as her own, she could not allow him to get any closer to her heart than he was now.

Stiffening her resolve, Julia swept from the room. Come heaven or hell, she would see to it that everything went perfectly this evening. The entire house gleamed— the woodwork polished to a new luster, the china ornaments well dusted, and the carpets beaten until they looked new. Already the mouth-watering smell of dinner wafted through the house, evidence of Mrs. Winston's culinary mastery. Buoyed by the scent, Julia gathered her scattered emotions and went to greet their guests.

Everything rested on Desiree's small rounded shoulders. Somehow the thought did not bring Julia any comfort.

Chapter 21

A t Lady Birlington's instigation, Julia had invited as many couples as she could squeeze into the small dining room at Hunterston House. The dinner began well enough, with the guests thoroughly impressed with each other, and satisfied to have been included in such a select gathering. Mrs. Winston conjured up a meal of unsurpassing quality which Burroughs served with an implacable dignity that added an air of formality rarely found outside Buckingham Palace.

While Burroughs served the soup, Desiree lightly tripped in and deposited the first course on the sideboard. Julia watched as the maid left to assist Mrs. Winston in the kitchen. Alec would eat his words before the night was through; Julia was becoming more convinced of it by the minute.

The first course proceeded well, the conversation flowing freely, Desiree performing her duties with flawless grace.

Baron Hewlett put down his spoon and sighed. "Best turtle soup I've ever had."

"I must get the recipe," Lady Chambers said.

"Of course." Julia had always liked the quiet woman, though she thought Lord Chambers something of a simpleton.

Burroughs collected the soup bowls as the aging Duke of Devonshire nodded. "Excellent fare, my lady. Reminds of a dish I was served at the Pavilion, and. . . ." He trailed into silence as Desiree reentered the room holding a steaming china bowl.

Julia frowned. "You were saying, Your Grace?"

He did not answer, merely stared at Desiree as she set down the dish and slipped from the room.

It was quite rude of the man, but Julia supposed she didn't blame him. Desiree's beauty was phenomenal.

The duchess leaned toward Julia. "You'll have to forgive Devonshire. He was up past ten last night. Devastating to a man his age." She cast a cold glare at her husband.

The duke caught her minatory gaze and started, tugging on his collar. "Ah, no. Yes, I mean, yes. Very tired today. Hardly hold my eyes open." He leaned toward his wife and said urgently, "Perhaps we should leave."

She lifted thin brows. "But we just arrived. You can sleep in the carriage on the way home." As if that settled everything, the duchess returned to her meal. Left with a very red face, the duke began casting wild glances toward the door where Desiree had disappeared.

Julia watched him for a moment before sneaking a glance at Alec. He was staring at Devonshire with drawn brows, as if trying to figure out an especially confusing puzzle.

Desiree entered holding a large platter with a steaming goose. The fragrance wafted through the room, making Julia's mouth water.

Lady Birlington's fork clanked against her plate. "Good God! It looks like he's having an apoplexy."

Edmund turned to look at the duke, who was forking food into his mouth as fast as he could, his eyed fixed on his plate as if fearful someone would steal it.

"No, he don't," Edmund said. "Hungry, is all."

"Not him, ninny." Maddie gestured with her spoon. "Chambers over there."

All eyes turned to Lord Chambers. Mouth open, fork suspended in midair, he stared at Desiree. His face shone a pasty white, his thin moustache standing out in dark relief against his pallor.

"Are you well, your lordship?" asked Julia, feeling her first real hint of alarm.

Lady Chambers leaned over and placed a hand on her husband's arm. "Chambers, what on earth is the matter?"

He blinked, color flooding his pale face. "Nothing. Never better. Just . . . thinking, you know. Yes, thinking about the crimped cod." He took a rapid mouthful and gulped. "Best I've ever had. What is this sauce, Lady Hunterston?"

"Rhenish Cream," Julia replied, watching him uneasily. What was happening? Though she had known Desiree's beauty would affect her guests, she had never expected anything like this.

Lady Birlington set down her wineglass. "Well, you may like it, but I think it is much too salty."

A huge clatter arose from the sideboard as a large serving fork clanged to the floor. Desiree's face turned beet red and she hurriedly bobbed a curtsey, casting an anguished glance at Julia. "Pardon, Your Gr—ladyship. It just slipped off the tray."

"Oh . . . my . . . God."

Everyone turned to Edmund. His face flushed, his eyes bulged, his mouth opened and closed. "You . . . she . . . good God, it can't be . . . I mean, how could it be?"

The maid clapped her hands together. "Lord Valmont!" She held up her wrist and fingered a silver bangle. "Look, I still have the bracelet you gave me."

Edmund's gaze widened. "By Jove!"

Desiree looked at the bracelet and a slight frown marred her white brow. "It isn't one of my favorites. I have to wear it over my sleeve so it won't turn my arm green." Her mouth pursed into an enchanting pout. "I was not happy you were trying to cheat me."

If possible, Edmund's face reddened even more. "Nonsense! Don't know what you're talking about! Never saw you before in my life."

Lucien raised his quizzing glass to regard his friend. "Nip farthing to the end, eh, Edmund?"

"Demme, Luce!" Edmund whispered loudly. "I was cheated! I paid a guinea for that trinket."

"What were you doing buying the gel a bracelet?" Lady Birlington's brows arched in astonishment. "I've never heard of buying gifts for other people's servants."

Edmund gulped, casting a wild glance around the table. "Ahm, didn't. Mean to say, wasn't me. Just someone who looked like me."

"With the same name? Impossible!" Lady Birlington scoffed.

Julia gave a breathless laugh. "Amazing, the people who look similar. I met a woman the other day who looked exactly like Princess Caroline."

"Perhaps it *was* Princess Caroline," Lucien suggested. He polished his quizzing glass with his napkin before turning it on Desiree. "She has the most annoying habit of showing up where she is least wanted."

Lady Birlington frowned. "I don't know about you, Edmund, but I would be very uncomfortable to think there was a person who looked like me. Especially if they were using my name and giving away shabby bracelets to people's servants. There ought to be a law against such chicanery."

"Oh, but your ladyship," interjected Desiree, oblivious to Julia's frantic signals, "I'm certain it was Lord Valmont." She turned to Edmund. "I still have the poem you wrote, too."

Lucien dropped his quizzing glass, letting it dangle on a ribbon from his waistcoat. "Edmund! Such unexpected depths."

"Stop it, Luce," hissed Edmund.

Julia wanted to crawl under the table. Nick's evil intentions in placing Desiree in her path were suddenly painfully clear. Tossing caution to the winds, Julia cast an uncertain glance at Alec.

He met her gaze, his face dark and inscrutable. For one instant, she thought she saw a glint of triumph in his smoke gray eyes. The thought infuriated her.

Turning to Burroughs, she said with as much hauteur as she dared, "We are ready for the next course."

The butler bowed. "Yes, my lady." Without giving the maid time to do more than murmur a protest, he firmly led her from the room, leaving the guests in an uncomfortable silence.

Lady Chambers took a sip of wine. "I do so love a well-cooked goose." She regarded her husband over the rim of her glass, a dangerous gleam in her eye. "Don't you, Alfred?"

Color bloomed in his cheeks. "Ah, yes, m'dear," he replied, setting his wineglass down so hard Julia was surprised it didn't shatter.

Lady Birlington nodded. "You are to be commended on the meal, Julia. It's a wonder Mrs. Winston can even cook in the tiny kitchen you have here." She leaned toward Lady Hewlett. "I have tried to convince them to get a larger house, but they will not listen."

"We are quite comfortable where we are," Alec said, though he did not remove his gaze from Julia.

Julia fixed her attention on her plate and refused to look up. How was she to have known every man in the *ton* had such an appreciation for the theatre?

"It might be a comfortable house, but the rooms are not appropriately situated," Lady Birlington said loudly, as if to cow Alec into submission by sheer zeal. "Lord Bentham wanted to paint Julia's portrait here, but there's no room. I finally told him to come to my house and do it there."

Lady Chambers raised her brows. "Bentham is painting your portrait? How lovely."

"He's offered to donate it to the dowager's charity ball next month," Julia said brightly, hoping everyone had forgotten Desiree.

Alec offered no comment. Sitting at the end of the table, he appeared at his ease and relaxed. *Too* relaxed, as if he were already anticipating his victory. She remembered his words during their argument and heat flooded her cheeks. That he should make such demands was unconscionable. Worse, she had the distinct impression he expected her to fulfill them without protest.

Julia's relief was beyond measure when the evening finally ended. Painfully sensible of Alec's threat, she tarried in the vestibule until the last guest left, very aware of her husband's presence. Lucien must have realized something was untoward, for he lingered, casting concerned glances at Julia. When Alec finally escorted his friend to the door, Julia tried to make her escape.

"Julia."

She paused, one foot on the bottom step, and took a deep breath. Pasting a bright smile on her face, she turned. "That went well, didn't it? But so tiring! Goodnight." Julia placed her foot back on the step. To her surprise, he did not argue.

"Yes, it has been a long day."

Julia breathed a sigh of relief and continued up the stairs. She hadn't taken more than a few steps when she realized her error. He was following her—and much too closely.

With every step she took, his footfall echoed. She even fancied she could feel his knee brushing the back of her skirt. As she neared the top of the stairs, her bedroom door loomed in front of her. Julia felt like Joan of Arc facing her executioners, each second bringing her closer to her ultimate end.

Finally, she placed her foot on the top of the landing

and distinctly felt Alec's hand brush hers on the railing. She snatched it away, the touch burning up her arm. She had dreamed that one day Alec and she might share the intimacies of marriage, but not this way. Not as the result of an argument.

Stopping outside her bedroom door, she whirled and faced him, disconcerted to find him not even half a pace behind her. He was so close, she was forced to retreat until the doorknob pressed into the small of her back. "There's no need to go any further. If you wish to yell at me, we might as well do it here."

Alec lifted a hand and placed it on the door frame, his sleeve just brushing her hair. "I am not going to yell."

"The veins in your forehead are bulging."

He placed his other hand on the opposite side of the door frame until he had caged her within his muscular arms. "You can either open the door and enter of your own free accord, or I will pick you up and carry you." His mouth lifted in a rakish grin that sent her heart tumbling. "But it will be one or the other, love."

Julia wet her lips. "A-are you threatening violence?"

"I make no threats." His breath stirred the hair at her temple. "Only promises."

"How can you think . . . as if I would walk right into my room and lie down and . . . you cannot expect me to do such a thing."

His silver gaze rested on her mouth for the longest time before he abruptly straightened from the door and crossed his arms. "I did and I do."

It was ludicrous. Silly. Impossible. Julia crossed her arms and stared back. "I could not possibly do . . . *that*, without love."

Alec's mouth quirked in a devastating smile. "*That*, to many people, *is* love."

She sniffed. "Not to me, it isn't."

"Oh, yes. I had forgotten." His face darkened.

"You've been in love for four years with someone who hasn't deigned to notice. How very noble."

His sneer was more than she could bear. "That is none of your concern."

For a second he appeared astounded, then his scowl returned in full force. His hands closed into fists as, with a fierce curse, he turned on his heel and stalked away, trampling across her heart in the process. Without a backward glance, he strode back down the steps into the study and slammed the door behind him.

Julia placed a hand across her mouth to still the desire to call after him. God knew she was no beauty, and never would be. But she had seen the unmistakable glimmer of desire in his gray gaze on more than one occasion. Like an idiot, she had dared to hope it might blossom into something more, given time and care.

But it was not to be. Shoulders slumped, Julia entered her own room and readied for bed, dressing by rote. Fighting tears, she pulled her nightrail over her head and sat at the dressing table, where she methodically twisted her hair into a heavy braid.

It was depressing to love a man who didn't know the meaning of the word. And she had loved him since she'd first laid eyes on him, even though he'd been so far above her reach, she had never faced her own feelings. Now, seeing him every day, and discovering for herself that he could be kind, gentle, and so much more than he gave himself credit for, was pure torture.

She caught sight of her tear-blurred reflection and sniffed, gathering her resolve. "That's enough of that," she scolded the weakling in the mirror. "They don't call him Devil Hunterston for nothing. He's far from perfect."

Tonight was an excellent example of his shortcomings. He'd bullied her, threatened her and practically forced himself into her room. If she dwelled long enough on the last one, she could almost remove the lingering hint of disappointment that he did not see fit to follow through.

Buoyed by the realization that, of the two, she was the infinitely superior in character, virtue, and eloquence, she climbed into bed. Julia then blew out her candle and whiled away the time waiting to fall asleep by categorizing all her rakehell husband's faults.

Chapter 22

It was almost an hour before Julia heard Alec's tread on the steps. That steady, deliberate walk could only mean he had imbibed far too much.

"I should have made that a condition of the will, too," she muttered. "Next time I make a bargain to marry, I'll add no arguing *or* drinking."

His steps neared. She could picture him, his cravat slightly mussed, a lock of midnight hair across his brow as he fumbled for the doorknob. But his door never opened. Instead, a heavy silence fell in the hall.

Julia tossed back the counterpane and tiptoed to the door. She leaned her ear against it, straining to hear something . . . anything. But other than the sound of her own breathing, she couldn't make out a thing. Seconds stretched into minutes and finally Alec gave a mumbled curse, his voice so close to the other side of the panel that Julia stepped back, her heart pounding. She heard two hasty steps and then the vigorous slam of his door.

Julia sagged against the wooden panel, relief changing rapidly into disappointment, then annoyance. "How rude! Slamming a door in the middle of the night. Rude and insufferable." She returned to her bed, plopped onto the edge, and crossed her arms. "He acts just like a child. Spoiled, is what he is. No wonder. An only child, raised by a grandfather, doted on by a house full of servants. Then he grows up to look like a prince, with those eyes and that hair and those—" She squenched her eyes closed and took a deep breath.

It wasn't fair. Here she was, wide awake and filled with turbulent emotions, while he enjoyed a deep, restful sleep. Well, she was her father's daughter. No one kept her awake when she didn't want him to. Julia stomped to the door, yanked it open, and marched across the hall.

Just as she lifted her hand to deliver a spirited knock, Alec's door opened.

He looked down at her with an inscrutable expression. His broad shoulders filled the opening, his lean, muscular frame encased by a ruby red robe, loosely belted about his narrow waist. She tried to ignore the fact that his bare chest was just at eye level, covered with sensual dark curls.

She tried, but failed miserably.

His gaze traveled from her face to her braid and then lower, halting at the sight of her upraised hand.

Julia realized her fist was still suspended in knocking position. She hurriedly tucked it behind her and lifted her chin a notch. "I just came to tell you it was rude to slam the door."

He leaned against the jamb and crossed his arms, his face now in the shadows. "Did I wake you?"

Insolent cur. "You would have, if I'd been asleep."

His arrogant gaze brushed across her like the touch of a feather, leaving a tingling trail of awareness in its wake. "And so you came to protest, wearing nothing but your nightrail."

Julia looked down. The lace nightgown covered remarkably little, hinting at every curve, allowing the pink of her nipples to peek through. "Oh. I should have stopped for my dressing gown, but I didn't think of it."

It suddenly dawned on her how this must look, banging on his door in the middle of the night wearing nothing but an indecently sheer strip of lace. He must think she was desperate for his company.

The idea fanned her temper more. Crossing her arms over her woefully covered chest, she scowled. "This is my house, too. I can wear whatever I wish. I just wanted you to know that I think you are rude and boorish and. . . ." She trailed off as she noticed the muscles of his chest flex, and wondered what it would feel like to splay her hands across their hardness.

The truth was, he was handsome and desirable, and she wanted him so badly she could barely think. The vaguest hint of a sob closed her throat.

Before she made more of a fool of herself than she already had, she spun on her heel and marched across the passageway, her trembling self-control barely intact. Just as she reached her door, a firm hand closed around her elbow. Warmth settled in her breasts and lower.

"Julia." His breath stirred the hair behind her ear.

"What?" she managed to say in a husky whisper.

His hand grazed her arm with the lightest of touches, his fingers skimming over her too-sensitive skin to her shoulder, where he pushed aside the gossamer lace. "I'm sorry for slamming the door."

The words caressed her, pulsing across her like a hot wind. Julia shivered as sparks of heat spread through her. His hand came to rest on her neck, cupping her throat with a sensuous gesture that pulled her body against his.

For a moment, she leaned against him, his velvet robe pressed against her back. Rivulets of pleasure tingled up her arms, curling her hands into fists. Without another word, she turned into his embrace.

The scent of brandy and sandalwood engulfed her. She tightened her arms about his neck, and clung as if he were a rock in the middle of a storm-ridden sea. *Please, please, just this once, let him want me, too.*

After a long, silent moment, Alec let out his breath and gently pushed her away.

The damp chill of the night immediately made her shiver. What had she been thinking? Hopelessness slammed into her heart and settled in her chest with an aching sob. She had loved him for so long, desired him so much, that just this one second of separation caused an almost physical pain.

"Julia."

The word was both caress and command. Drawing a swift breath, she lifted her gaze.

His eyes darkened. "This has to be your decision." Naked desire reflected in his gaze. "I want you, Julia. All of you." He lowered his mouth to hers, halting just a breath away, his lips hovering but not touching. "Say you want me, too." His voice roughened to crushed velvet, his eyes black with desire. He pulled her close and gently brushed his hips against hers until she could feel the swell of his manhood.

She gasped at the sensations that flickered and sparked, her hands closing over the sinew of his arms. She wanted, needed, to get closer to him. Oblivious to everything but the feel of him against her, she pressed her body to his.

With a strangled curse, he dropped his forehead against hers, his breathing harsh in the silence of the hallway. "God, Julia," he whispered hoarsely. "Tell me you desire this as much as I do."

She clutched at his arms, his robe bunching beneath her insistent hands. "I want you, Alec." When he didn't respond, she closed her eyes, terrified at the urgency of her own desires. "Please, Alec. *Please.*"

Alec drank in the sound of her plea, more intoxicating than any brandy, sweeter than any cordial. He almost laughed to think he'd nearly convinced himself that she did not want him, that she desired someone else. Julia might think she was in love with a worthier man, but she desired *him*.

Tonight there were just the two of them, him and his Julia.

"Alec," she whispered again, this time more urgently, her eyes wet. Her mouth trembled, the sensual line of her lips captivating him. "*Please,*" she whispered. A lone tear escaped from beneath her lashes and slipped over the pale satin of her cheek.

Alec bent to catch it, his mouth following the wet trail, the salty sweetness shredding his control. He cupped her cheek with his hand as he pressed his lips to the curve of her lashes, the straight line of her nose, the wide crest of her forehead.

Her lashes trembled as he gently placed his lips on hers. She stilled at his touch, her mouth moist and soft. He slid his mouth over her bottom lip, maintaining only the barest contact.

She shivered and he captured her mouth again, teasing her lips apart until his tongue grazed the smooth edge of her teeth. She moaned and opened to him, as unknowingly erotic as any woman he had ever known.

The kiss deepened, their tongues mingling. Julia's hands moved frantically over him, tugging and pulling until she'd loosened his robe. Thinking only of getting nearer to the slim body encased in enticing lace, he helped her, pulling his arms from the sleeves and dropping the robe to the floor.

The waft of cool air across his naked back reminded him they were in the hallway. With a muttered oath, he caught her arms and stepped back, breathing hard. "Julia, love. We can't stay out here."

She opened dazed eyes, the green alight with flecks of gold. "What?"

He traced his thumb over her mouth, savoring the wetness. "Not here," he whispered. "The servants."

Julia looked around, her gaze halting when it encoun-

tered his nude form. A delightful blush rose from her
shoulders to her neck and came to fruition on her cheeks.
"I didn't realize we were still in the hallway."

"Come to my room." He closed his arms around her
and took a step backward, toward his open door, already
thinking of the huge bed and how she would look lying
naked on the softness of his counterpane.

"No."

Alec's heart pounded a furious rhythm. "Why not?"
he asked harshly.

She flicked him a sultry glance. "My room is closer."

Before he could do more than blink, she turned,
opened her door, and disappeared, leaving only the enticing scent of cinnamon.

Alec stared. He, who had so much more experience
and knowledge, should have been the one controlling
this seduction. But as he was beginning to realize, there
was no controlling Julia.

She peeked back around the door and crooked a finger. Her braid had loosened until long wisps of honey
silk drifted about her shoulders, clinging to her slender
frame and following the curve of her breast. Alec swallowed with a throat gone dry when he thought of those
strands cleaving to his hands, his face, his chest. Like a
puppet on a string, unable to resist doing as he was bidden, he followed her into her room.

Julia stood before her bed, her hands furiously working the fastenings on her gown. Alec closed the door
and leaned against it and forced his breathing to slow.
The lace nightrail had haunted him for more nights than
he cared to remember and she appeared more wanton
than even his dreams had envisioned. Her long legs were
visible through the material, her creamy skin rivaled the
delicate lace in whiteness, and her breasts, small and
firm, were made just for his hands. Two steps brought
him to her.

Her frantic fingers jerked at the row of buttons that held the delicate lace at the back of her neck. Alec placed his hands over hers. "Don't tear it, love. I may want you to wear it again."

Her hands fell to her sides and she tilted her head down, pulling her hair to one side and allowing him to unfasten the fascinating row of buttons, though her knuckles showed white and her eyes followed him hungrily. As he loosened each button, he placed a kiss on the skin bared before his eyes. From her neck, down her back, to the delicious curve of her bottom, he placed one lingering kiss after another. Her hands trembled, but she didn't move away.

As he loosened the last button, the lace slithered to the floor, a luxurious drift of cobwebs. She turned and Alec caught her curves flush against him. He fought for control. Julia turned her face into his neck, her breath raking his throat, her hair spilling across his arm in a silken fall.

God, but he wanted her as he had wanted no other. He pulled back and stared at her face, at the slant of her mouth, the incredible lashes that framed her sparkling eyes, the firm chin that now trembled ever so slightly. The scent of her need mingled with the spice of the lemon and cinnamon innocence so inherent to her. Within her emerald gaze shone a yearning so clear he had to clench his teeth against the desire to throw her onto the floor and sink into her softness.

But this was no lightskirt, used to the ways of lovemaking. This was Julia, his wife, to protect and covet above all others.

He held her at arm's length, struggling to think. "Julia, I don't want you to be afraid. I cannot promise—"

She launched herself against him, sending him reeling back onto the bed. Her body covered his, her hands everywhere—on his arms, his chest, his hips. All thought fled before her passion. She moaned into his mouth as her breasts pressed against his chest, her nipples hardening with the contact.

He cupped her rounded hips in his hands, pulling her higher until her face was level with his, her body directly over his.

She writhed against him. "Closer," she whispered, her eyes almost black with desire.

"Easy, love," he murmured. "Slow down."

Julia's breath brushed his ear, hot and frantic. Alec closed his eyes, clenching his teeth. With tormenting thoroughness, her hands explored the width of his chest, lingered on his shoulders, and traveled down his arms. He grabbed a fistful of sheet in each hand, willing his unruly body not to bury itself into her.

She placed a kiss wherever her hands strayed, her feather-soft touches fraying his control. Her explorations continued as she trailed her fingers across his stomach. There, she halted. He opened his eyes. She gazed at his manhood.

For an instant he feared he'd frightened her, but she turned to him, her gaze burning.

Without a word, Alec leaned up and pulled her back across him, the fall of her hair enclosing them in a world of sensuous satin. Her hands slipped down his sides, grazing the sensitive skin until he ground his teeth in delicious agony. When her fingers slipped between his legs, he flipped her over to her back and pinned her arms over her head.

"For God's sake, don't do that," he said through clenched teeth. "Not yet."

Moaning, she pressed herself against him, one leg lifting to twine about his. Any chivalrous thoughts fled before his searing passion. Alec positioned himself between her thighs and thrust home.

She surged against him, a cry torn from her lips as her tight wetness closed around him. He caught her gasp of pain in his mouth, urging her past it and on to the pleasure that awaited her. Quickening his pace, he pulled her with him in a tide of passion that built with each stroke.

She wrapped her legs about his hips, matching his fervor with her own. Alec savored the honesty of her reactions, the sweetness of her as she gave herself over to him completely. She held nothing back, committing herself to the act of passion completely.

Just when he thought it impossible to maintain his control, she cried out, gripping his shoulders and arching against him. Shock waves of pleasure pushed him over the edge, into a sea of bliss.

When he could breathe once more, Alec rolled to one side and pulled her against him. She curled up, limp and replete, in his arms. As passionate with her body as she was with her soul, Julia had taken him farther than his wandering lust had ever gone.

He waited for his heart to resume its normal pace. When he finally opened his eyes, she was raised on one elbow, looking at him as if memorizing every feature.

Alec smiled, the daze of fulfillment settling about them like a warm cocoon. In this instant, he felt as if he could accomplish anything. He traced a finger over the elegant line of her collarbone to the hollow of her throat. Her pulse beat a rapid rhythm against his fingertips. "You are a vixen, my love. I think you bit me."

Her gaze flew to his neck and a blush, hot and furious, lifted across the creamy expanse of her breasts to her neck and face. "Sorry."

He chuckled, catching her to him and rolling on his back until she lay on top of him, her head tucked beneath his chin. "Don't look so chagrined. I was only teasing."

She buried her face in the column of his throat and said nothing. After a long silence, she said, "Alec, was that correct?"

Alec tilted her face back until he could see her clearly. "It was perfect."

Julia placed her hands on his chest and regarded him with a frown. "I hoped I'd done it right, but I wasn't sure."

He grinned, tucking a strand of her hair behind her ear. "Oh, yes." He caught a flicker of something in her eyes and frowned. "Julia, did I hurt you?"

New color burnt her cheeks. "Oh, no. It was uncomfortable, but just for a minute." She tilted her head to one side. "Does it always feel like that?"

Alec shook his head. He'd made love with more women than he could remember. Each time he had taken and given pleasure, but never had he experienced the shattering release he'd had with Julia. But it was more than physical pleasure. Julia's response satisfied him on another level, in a way he was unwilling to examine too closely. He kissed her chin. "It is different every time."

Her eyes widened. "*Every* time?"

He grinned and nodded. "And it will only get better."

Julia's gaze darkened as she placed her hand on his stubble-roughened cheek. For a long instant she gazed at him. "Alec, I don't want to fight anymore."

For an instant, he couldn't believe she had capitulated so completely. But there was no predicting Julia. Catching her against him, he chuckled. "Then we won't."

The moment sweetened. In the morning, she'd resign from the Society and they would begin their lives anew. Alec smiled in contentment and kissed her forehead. With a pleased smile, she curled against him.

For a long, peaceful moment, he held her. A strand of her hair tickled his nose and he brushed it aside. As he listened to the steady pace of her heart, he remembered how she'd told him she knew love and had known it for years. He tried to imagine the paragon who deserved such unwavering adoration, but could think of no one.

Alec scowled. He'd be damned if he would stand by and watch his wife yearn for another man. As if she could sense the change in him, Julia shivered.

He pulled the counterpane over her shoulders, tucking it under her chin. Like a child, she snuggled deeper. He smiled bitterly, appreciating the irony. Over the years he'd dallied with countless wives, never once wondering about their husbands. Now, lying in bed with his own wife, he begrudged her the one passion she'd ever had.

Julia sighed in her sleep, turning toward him. The cover slipped and the pale crest of her breast appeared. The chill of the room puckered the nipple and his mouth watered, a stab of lust instantly stiffening him to readiness. The desire to make love to her until she thought of no one but him fixed in his mind, and he rolled onto his elbow to look down at her sleeping face. But the sight of the faint shadows under her eyes halted his burgeoning desire.

With a regretful sigh, he pulled the blanket around them both. There would be time enough tomorrow to discover the depth of their passion. Closing his eyes, Alec drifted off to sleep, content in the knowledge that after tomorrow, Julia would at least be spared the tiring labor of her work with the Society.

Chapter 23

Alec woke to the sounds of the street. Carriages rattled by, vendors hocked their wares, voices called in greeting. He frowned. His room didn't open onto the street . . . of course. He wasn't in his room, but Julia's. Smiling drowsily, Alec reached out an arm to pull her to him.

His hand fell onto tangled sheets and a pillow. He stretched further, all the way to the edge of the bed, but no warm body rested beside his. Instantly awake, he raised himself on an elbow and looked about the room.

Julia's gown still lay on the floor, a forlorn puddle of lace, and her robe was tossed across a chair. Other than the tangle of bedclothing, everything was perfectly neat and strangely empty. Perhaps she'd gone to request breakfast. The idea of his not-so-prim wife serving him breakfast in bed seemed entirely appropriate.

He turned onto his back and placed his hands beneath his head, the cool air brushing against his bared skin. Despite the late night and the amount of brandy he had consumed, he was as refreshed and rested as if he'd slept a week. Perhaps there were benefits to having a woman like Julia for a wife—one who had a compulsion to take care of everything and everybody. Lately, he had thought that she had exempted him from her list of cares.

It was satisfying to see she was capable of expending at least *some* of her boundless attention on him.

The edge of a pillow tickled his ear. He lifted a hand to push it away and caught the lingering scent of their passion. An instant impression of Julia's long legs and her heated response flashed through his mind.

Restless, he piled the pillows behind him and pulled the thin sheet over his lap. When she returned, he would take great delight in showing her how much he loved the morning, when the air held a tang of freshness and the early light dispelled all shadows. A good morning tumble set the mood for the entire day. The memory of her wildness the night before made him count the minutes with growing impatience.

Another quarter of an hour passed, and still no Julia. Where in the hell was she?

Chastising himself for a fool for lying in bed and waiting, he looked about for something to cover his nakedness. The sheets or blanket would wrap around him three times and still drag behind him like a serpent's tail. Alec picked up the lace nightrail and wrapped it experimentally about his hips, but the thin cloth showed more than it hid.

He dropped it to the floor and grabbed the frilled robe from the chair and fastened it about his waist. Layers of ruffles fluffed from his hips to well above his knees, but it would have to do.

Muttering to himself about the inconvenience of being married to an independent woman, Alec opened the door and peered into the hall, hoping against hope that none of his meddling servants were about.

The hall was blessedly empty; nothing but the faint sound of Mrs. Winston's voice floating up the stairs disturbed the early morning peace. Relieved, he opened the door wider and leaned out, scanning the floor for his robe.

"Good morning, my lord." Burroughs stood in the

doorway of Alec's room, the butler's gaze politely directed over his right shoulder. "Chilton found your robe this morning when he brought your wash water. I believe he blamed the incident on her ladyship's page."

Alec's face heated, but he refused to retreat. Tightening his grip on the bunched material at his hip, he nodded. "I'll be sure he knows I left it there."

"Of course, my lord. If you're finished lurking about the hallway, perhaps you would care for some breakfast?"

"I am not *lurking*."

The butler's gaze drifted to Alec's makeshift covering. "As you wish, my lord."

Ignoring the urge to bolt into his room and slam the door behind him, Alec tightened the robe about his hips. "Have you seen Lady Hunterston?"

"Yes, sir. She left early this morning."

"Did she say where she was going?"

"Johnston complained about having to visit Whitechapel, my lord. I would venture to guess she went to one of her meetings." The butler paused, then added in a deferential tone, "Her ladyship appeared somewhat distracted."

So that was where she had gone. Alec had no doubt this morning's journey would be difficult for Julia. As committed as she was to the Society, it would be hard to simply walk away. He frowned. She should have waited for him to accompany her.

From the stairs came Chilton's unmistakable mincing tread.

"Oh, God," Alec muttered. Straightening his shoulders, he marched past Burroughs and into his room, stopping long enough to glare. "Not a word of this to the others."

"I wouldn't think of it, my lord." The faintest hint of amusement lingered in the dry tone.

His good mood long gone, Alec slammed the door.

Despite the fact that Julia had gone to do as he had bidden, it irked him that she could apparently hop out of bed and go traipsing about town as if last night were less than nothing. Hell, *he* was a little shaky this morning. She should be equally affected.

He scowled and threw open the wardrobe, pulled out a shirt, and tossed it onto the bed. How could she just rise and leave without a word? It was the most heartless action he had ever witnessed from his giving and gracious wife. The fact that she'd done it to him only made it worse. Especially since he'd wakened ready to entice her with new pleasures.

Alec poured water into a basin and splashed his face, the warm liquid running down his unshaven jaw. He reached for a towel and caught sight of his reflection. For the first time in weeks, no fatigue shadowed his eyes. He rubbed the roughness of his chin and immediately thought of Julia's mouth against his, her pale arms twined about his neck, her long legs wrapped around his hips.

Naked, she had the body of a sprite: slender and small breasted, as delicate as a wraith. She was a siren, dressed by day in the clothing of the righteous, protected by staid spectacles and a prim manner. But by night, she transformed into a passionate vixen, playful and seductive, but more beautiful and more vibrant than any woman he had ever known. His manhood twitched and rose and Alec cursed Julia's blithe absence yet again.

Mrs. Winston's voice came through the closed door. "Goodness! Someone has gone and mussed the mistress's room. The bedsheets have been torn off the bed."

"His lordship did not sleep in his bed last night," said Chilton, a superior edge to his tone.

"Well, it's about time." Mrs. Winston's giggle raked across Alec's raw nerves. "I vow, I was beginning to think that you were going to have to have a talk with him about his conjugal duties."

If the housekeeper's giggle had raked Alec's nerves, his valet's high-pitched titter sliced them in two. He would not be made sport of in his own house.

He stomped to the door and flung it open. "If you are through gossiping, perhaps one of you would be good enough to see to my breakfast."

Two pairs of astonished eyes fixed on him, but not on his stern face. Instead they locked on his hips, where Julia's robe still hung in many-ruffled splendor. Heat flooded his neck and face.

"My lord," said Chilton, stepping forward, his nose flared in alarm. "I will come immediately and see to your clothing."

"No," Alec said abruptly. The last thing he wanted was a chattering valet to keep him company.

"But, sir, I—"

"I don't need any help dressing."

Mrs. Winston looked pointedly at Alec's ruffled attire, her mouth twitched into a grin. "Maybe not, my lord, but Chilton could at least iron some of the wrinkles out of that."

For an instant even Chilton looked as if he might burst in a spate of wild giggles. It was more than Alec could endure. Red-faced, he retreated into his room and slammed the door. No man should be faced with a horde of merry, impertinent servants at this time of the morning.

He loosened the robe from his hips and tossed it to the floor, kicking it under the bed for good measure. Good God, what was wrong with him? He'd lost his ability to think. Irritation seethed in his stomach, and he knew he'd eat no breakfast this morning. Turning to his wardrobe, he yanked out a pair of breeches and jerked them on.

As he thrust his arm into his shirt, a sudden thought trickled through his annoyance. What if Julia had decided not to give up the Society, after all? God only knew what unpredictable thoughts might have settled in her brain while he lay blissfully asleep at her side. It didn't bear thinking of.

Alec tried to recall her exact words regarding the Society, but couldn't. His memories of the night before had less to do with words and more to do with silken hair, the touch of her skin against his, her seductive scent.

He tugged the shirt into place and buttoned it, hastily tying his cravat. Just to be sure Julia understood her responsibilities, he would go to the Society himself. And if she did not—Alec scowled. He would deal with that when the time came.

Hurrying in earnest, he shoved his feet into his boots and pulled on his coat. Then he ran down the stairs, calling for his carriage.

Julia had worked in the squalid alleyways and filthy streets of Whitechapel too long to consider herself an innocent. Indeed, she had seen far more than any maid should. But nothing had prepared her for the searing passion she had felt with Alec.

She had slept deeply, dreamlessly, only to awaken to find him wrapped about her, his legs entwined with hers, his warm breath against her neck. She had lain there, eyes closed, and savored the moment. Never had she felt more loved or in love. Perhaps one day he would learn to love her in return. Julia had smiled at the thought and snuggled closer, resting her cheek against his broad chest.

For now, she would be content with what he'd given her—a night of pure, delicious, satiating passion. Tears had gathered in her eyes and clogged her throat. It was all so new, so wonderful.

Of course, Alec would not think of their night of passion with any emotion at all. Like all rakes, he would think of it as nothing more than a pleasurable moment, one to be enjoyed and then dismissed.

The thought had made her stir within his comforting hold. Is that what he would do? Awaken and roll away, acting as if nothing had occurred? Would he expect her to act the same—casual and accepting, as if their relationship had not changed? As if she weren't now even more committed to him, even more in love with him?

Julia had pulled away from the warm arms that held her and slipped from the bed. Frowning in his sleep, Alec gathered her pillow close, but did not awaken. As quietly as possible, she dressed, pulling on clothes and shoes at random. She couldn't face him now, not when her love ran so near the surface that with one look at her face, he would know the truth. She needed time to collect her thoughts and arm herself against her own feelings.

One day, he would come to love her. But it would be fatal to rush him. She would woo him gently, teach him the value of true love, the pleasure of caring for others. Perhaps that was the way to reform him, after all.

For now, she needed to calm her tangled feelings. Fortunately, the Society was to meet this morning. Julia had pinned her hair in the predawn darkness and then stopped by the bed to watch Alec sleep. He looked mussed and boyish, his hair falling across his forehead. She reached out and almost touched him, but stopped. Sighing deeply, Julia had slipped silently from the room.

She arrived at Whitechapel just as Lord Burton stepped from his carriage. Full of jovial witticisms, he escorted her into the vicar's office where the rest of the board had collected. The meeting passed in a blur.

Julia tried to keep her mind on the work at hand, but thoughts of the previous night kept flashing before her eyes, interrupting her ability to speak. Twice, she forgot what she was saying in mid-sentence. Flustered, she left as soon as was acceptable, saying a hurried good-bye and whisking out the door.

Halfway down the front steps, she halted, her heart thrumming a painful tattoo. "Alec."

He leaned against the bottom railing, hands stuffed into his pockets. The brim of his hat shadowed his eyes. "I came to take you home."

Julia cast a wary glance over her shoulder, relieved to see that no one had followed her out. "You shouldn't be here."

His jaw clenched. "Perhaps it's time the members of the Society knew you have a husband."

"It is a bit late to decide that." She brushed past him and peered around his phaeton to where Johnston should have been waiting with the coach.

"I told him to leave." Alec's voice sounded at her ear. "Get in, Julia."

"But I wasn't going home. In fact, I won't be home until late. I have errands to run, and a book to return to the lending library, and Lady Birlington specifically requested that I attend her for tea." That should show him she was completely unaffected by last night.

Yet he looked far from pleased, his mouth tight with anger. "Whatever you have to do can wait." He pulled her to his phaeton without giving her time to remonstrate.

Julia took her place with ill grace. "I don't see why you couldn't just wait until I got home."

Alec climbed in beside her and tossed a coin to the boy who'd held the horses. "Because I have no wish for our confounded servants to barge in on us while we settle this once and for all."

"Settle what?"

His gaze rested on her with a decided glint. "*Us.*"

Effectively robbed of speech, Julia could only nod. She waited for him to say more, but he seemed absorbed in guiding the phaeton through the crowded streets.

Finally, after an eternity of stomach-twisting silence, he said, "Julia, about last night—I don't want you to think that . . . you shouldn't. . . ." He stopped, face flushed, his eye pinned straight ahead. "What I mean to say is—"

"Pray do not." It was all too clear what he meant to say. Mouth aquiver, she sniffed miserably. "I understand perfectly."

"No, you don't," he said with a grim glance. "I have never played fast and loose with a virgin, and I am not about to start now."

Fast and loose? They had spent a night of remarkable passion and he described it as "fast and loose?" Her eyes showed an annoying tendency to water in the bright sunshine. "There's no need for you to worry. Last night was all my fault."

He turned to regard her, a puzzled crease between his brows. "Your fault?"

"Yes, but you needn't fear. I don't expect a declaration or anything." Not that she'd refuse one, should he offer.

His face held a distinctive sickly pallor. "A declaration?"

Her heart sank into her stomach like a lead weight, but Julia managed an airy shrug. "Of course. It was just a brief interlude and means nothing to either of us."

His pallor receded behind an angry flush. Staring straight ahead, he asked in a clipped voice, "A brief interlude. Is that how you see it?"

"Oh, yes. Very brief and very . . . well, an interlude." This was all working out perfectly, Julia decided, trying to buoy her flagging spirits. She was effectively alleviating his distress while maintaining what little pride she had left. Yet she couldn't seem to stop her eyes from leaking large, slow drops. She fumbled in her reticule for her handkerchief.

Alec stared straight ahead, too uninterested to notice her plight. He turned the phaeton onto a wide, pleasant street and left the stench and poverty of Whitechapel behind. "Julia, I think you miss the importance of what has occurred. You and I . . . there is a strong physical attraction between us."

"Physical?" Her voice quavered piteously, but he didn't notice.

Color touched his neck and face. "Our bodies are made for one another."

How could he take the incredible beauty of their night of passion and reduce it to a physical explanation? He reminded her of Mr. Tumbolton, trying to fix a mathematical equation to the soul. Some things simply could not be measured.

Pride dried her eyes. "I'm not sure I know what you are talking about, Alec."

His simmering glance sliced through her heart as surely as a sword. "You felt it, too, Julia. I know you did."

"I felt a lot of things," she said, stung. "I'm just not sure I wouldn't have felt them with someone else."

Alec abruptly pulled the horses to, oblivious to the fact that they were in the middle of a crowded thoroughfare. "*What?*"

Her cheeks burned with her own audacity, but she resolutely plowed on. "I haven't had much experience. For all I know, I might feel that way with. . . ." She struggled to find a name and couldn't think of one. Just when she needed it most, her brain had fallen into a deep slumber and refused to be roused. More than likely it was reeling in shock at hearing her say such outrageous things, but she didn't care.

"With whom?" His eyes gleamed beneath the brim of his hat. From behind them, a journeyman began to yell obscenities.

Julia struggled to think of a name. "Oh, I don't know. Nick or someone."

Alec appeared thunderstruck. "*Nick?*"

"Or someone." Damn it, why couldn't she think of a

dashing suitor—someone who was as noble as he was handsome? Surely there must be dozens of them littering the *ton*, yet she could think only of the man beside her.

He stared at her for a long minute before turning back to the horses and urging them to a trot. His movements appeared mechanical, as if he were locked in some sort of inner struggle and scarcely knew what he was doing. "How long have you known Nick?"

It had been Julia's first season as a chaperone . . . the first time she had seen Alec. A tremulous smile lifted her mouth. When she caught Alec's stare, she forced herself to swallow. "Four years ago. A little more, to be exact. Why?"

His face tightened, white lines appearing at the side of his mouth. "I will remind you that you are married to me, madam."

"I'm not likely to forget it."

"Good." With a distinctly unfriendly glance, he asked, "How did the Society take your news this morning?"

The change in topic made her blink. "I think we have settled most of the details," she replied cautiously.

"Then it is done." His hands tightened about the reins. "I know they will miss you as much as you will miss them, but it is for the best."

She paused in returning her handkerchief to her reticule. "I beg your pardon?"

He shot her a short glance that confirmed her worse suspicions. "I said—"

"I know what you said; I just don't understand it. What do you mean, they will *miss* me?"

Confusion flickered in his gray eyes before he frowned. "Do you remember last night, madam?"

"Of course I remember it. You came to my room and we—"

"No," he interrupted, slightly red. "Not that. I meant the dinner party where the beauteous Desiree made such an impression. You agreed that you would give up the Society if she caused a scandal."

It should not have bothered her that Alec thought Desiree beautiful, because the girl was. Yet it hurt to hear him say it aloud. Especially when he had never said such a thing to her. Clearing her throat, Julia said, "But she did *not* cause a scandal."

"Julia, half the men around that table knew who and what that woman was!"

She regarded him with lifted brows. "Did they say anything when they retired to the library for port?"

"No. They stood in miserable silence, afraid to look each other in the eye."

"Well, there. They will be too embarrassed to say anything. You see, nothing will come from it. From now on, I will just keep Desiree belowstairs when there is company."

"It will not be so easy as that."

"Wait and see."

He shook his head. "I am through discussing this. You will cease your association with the Society and have nothing more to do with this ridiculous servant referral business."

"Nonsense. We are all set to launch it next week."

"Damn it! You have seen what happens when you try to pass off one of your women from the Society as a maid. It will not work."

"I would hardly consider Desiree a good example. The women from the Society are from Whitechapel, and none of your acquaintances are likely to know them."

"And if someone does?"

"They will dismiss it as an unlikely coincidence and never again think of it. Few people are as memorable as Desiree."

Alec pulled the phaeton to a halt in front of Hunterston House. "You will find someone else to sponsor this project." He spoke the words slowly, as though using all his strength to contain his anger. "I won't allow you to be involved."

Julia's heart pounded in her dry throat. "You cannot stop me."

"You would disobey me?"

She thought of the hopeless eyes of the women of Whitechapel and steeled herself. "Yes."

Alec stared at her, his breath rapid, his mouth carved into an implacable line. "Very well, madam. Since you are so determined to pursue this path of ruin, then I need no longer concern myself with offending your delicate sensibilities—or anyone else's, for that matter."

"What do you mean?"

"From now on, I will drink, gamble, and do as I please." His mouth curved in a cool smile. "I may even take a mistress."

"But the executors—"

"Will not care, so long as I am discreet. Despite their age, they are men of the world and know how things are done." His silver gaze raked across her. "No one will even lift a brow."

He was right. She had imposed those rules herself, hoping to keep him from the corruptive influences of the gaming hells he normally attended. Jaw clenched against the telltale quiver of her chin, Julia gathered her skirts and clambered down from the phaeton. "Very well, do as you must. But heed me well: no brandy-soaked rake will ever be welcome in my bed. I hope you thoroughly enjoyed last night. It was your last. I want nothing more to do with you."

He regarded her for a long moment, his gaze lightly skimming her face, her mouth, lingering on the curve of her body as intimately as a touch. "We shall see about that." With a tip of his hat, he drove off.

Had she found a rock, she would have thrown it. As it was, she had to be content with kicking the wrought-iron gate as hard as she dared. Limping up the sidewalk, she was appalled to see Mrs. Winston, Burroughs, Chilton, and a very wide-eyed Desiree scurrying from sight.

Wonderful, Julia thought. *Just wonderful.* Sniffing, she made her way through the gauntlet of servantly concern to the safety of her own bedchamber, where she indulged herself thoroughly in a spate of angry tears.

Chapter 24

"**C**ome away from the window," Maddie ordered. "It is rude to scowl at people you don't even know."

Sighing heavily, Julia turned to plop onto Lady Birlington's settee with an unladylike bounce. This last week had stretched her nerves until she felt like one of the ragged pieces of twine Muck always seemed to have tucked in his pockets.

True to his word, Alec had returned to his old ways with a vengeance. Julia was weary from lying awake, listening for the sound of the front door, though she might have spared herself the trouble. He came home with the dawn, singing at the top of his lungs to make sure she knew he was belligerently and faithfully breaking every one of her rules.

Her hands itched to box his ears until they were red and stinging.

More disturbing was his attitude toward her. He still escorted her to every function as if nothing were amiss. And though he hadn't made one move to visit her room, he had begun a steady assault on her defenses, using every excuse possible to touch her.

If they rode in the carriage, his thigh pressed against hers in a most disturbing manner. If they danced, he held her far too close, taking delight in her attempts to put some space between them. Every day, his hands lingered, and his warm breath sent spirals of heat against her neck, her shoulder.

But then, like the fairy tale of old, he would disappear as soon as he'd escorted her home. Her real agony began as she lay awake and imagined him laughing and nuzzling some beautiful courtesan who could contort in all manner of lurid positions and was only too happy to do so for such a heart-wrenchingly handsome man.

"You look red, gel. Perhaps we shouldn't go this evening."

"Oh, no. I'm fine."

"Nonsense. Besides, it wouldn't hurt to stay home one night; we've been gadding about like a pair of geese for a month now," Maddie said with evident satisfaction.

It was true. They had been inundated with invitations. Julia had been astounded at the number that had come her way. As she'd predicted, the episode with Desiree had had remarkably few repercussions—not one of their dinner guests had wished to admit he was conversant with a common actress. When Julia had pointed out that fact to Alec, and that he had perhaps been a bit hasty in his recriminations, he had merely regarded her with a shuttered gaze and shrugged.

Julia picked up a novel from the stack on the table and leafed through it, stopping to read all the heroic passages. Why couldn't Alec be more like the men in these books, men who valiantly pursued the women they loved and pledged eternal devotion? She would wager that "Sir Randolph" would never attempt to explain away lovemaking as a mere "physical attraction."

She sniffed. Thank goodness she was at least spared the embarrassment of rejecting Alec's unwanted advances! Julia had rehearsed the whole episode in her mind, getting as far as when he got down on his knees and begged her forgiveness. At that point, she somehow forgot her pride and threw herself in his arms. But then, he looked so very forlorn on his knees.

Julia tossed the book back on the table. Her imagination was far too active. Alec was no hero. Somewhere, something had gone horribly wrong with his upbringing. If his grandfather were alive today, she would have some very choice words to say to the man.

"For heaven's sake, Julia," Maddie said with a stern frown. "What ails you? You're as blue as megrim. If you are just going to sit there and stare into the distance and scowl, I may as well send for Edmund. He may not be the brightest thing, but at least he has some conversation in him."

For a moment, Julia considered taking Maddie into her confidence, but one look at the shrewd blue eyes, and she balked. "Sorry, Aunt Maddie. I'm just tired."

"Aren't going into a decline, are you? I should call my doctor and have him give you a good purge. Clean you out and let you sleep like a babe. I have one every week. Does me a world of good."

Oh, yes. That would finish off the week in a satisfying blaze of wretchedness. Julia slumped against the settee and stared at the ceiling.

Maddie let out an exasperated sigh. "Do you want a purge or not?"

"No, I don't think it would help." In fact, nothing would help, except a magical genie who could transform her into a raving beauty who was content to sit at home with her hands folded primly in her lap while the whole world marched by.

Alec would like that, Julia thought with disgust. Well, he could just forget it. If a fairy godmother were to suddenly appear and offer her a wish, she would be much more likely to ask for something sensible, like an end to hunger or poverty or—

"For God's sake!" Maddie scowled. "You look like

you swallowed a bee. Speak up! What's Hunsterston done to put you in such a taking?"

The urge to confide was overwhelming. Julia took a deep breath and sat up straighter. "Alec and I have had a disagreement."

"Oh," Maddie said with evident disappointment. "Is that all? Not a day went by that Birlington and I didn't rip up at each other for something or another."

"Really? Who gave in?"

Maddie chuckled, her bright, painted lips parting to reveal patently false teeth. "He never could stand it when I refused to talk to him. Worked every time."

Julia smiled tiredly. She had heard that Lord Birlington had been deeply in love with his wife. Now that she knew Maddie, she could see why. "I'm afraid it's not that way for us."

"Why not?"

"Alec and I did not marry for love."

"Well, you certainly act like lovers. Here you are, moping about like your heart is broken while he's out drinking and carousing like there's no tomorrow."

Julia raised her brows in what she hoped was an innocent gesture. "Oh? I suppose Edmund has been keeping you apprised of Alec's every move."

Maddie did not appear deceived. "Edmund is an empty-headed gabster. But yes, he's mentioned a few things."

Throwing subtlety to the wind, Julia asked in a blunt voice, "Like what?"

"Your husband doesn't seem to be in the muslin line, if that's what you're asking. But he's drinking more than he should. Losing quite a bit at cards, too. If you ask me, he sounds like a man in love."

"Sounds like a fool, to me."

"Not much difference." Maddie regarded her with a shrewd gaze. "Bit of a tangle, eh? You love him but don't want him to know."

"I never said I loved him," Julia said hotly.

"Lud, child, don't flame up at me. I'm only telling you what I see."

A defeated sigh escaped her. "Am I that transparent?"

"Good God, no," Maddie said. "Besides, it wouldn't matter if you were. The last thing men are capable of is looking at a woman and telling what she feels. Don't know why that is, because it ain't as if we don't give them enough hints."

"True. I practically threw myself at him and he . . . didn't reciprocate."

Maddie regarded her with a narrow gaze. "He didn't, did he?"

"No," Julia said miserably. Her limbs felt leaden, her heart hollow. Unbidden, her mouth trembled.

"Now don't go turning all missish on me," Maddie said hastily. She watched as Julia struggled to compose herself, then sighed. "I suppose I should help you. I'm something of a hand with matchmaking. After all, I was the one who introduced Lady Chambers to her husband." A frown crossed Maddie's wrinkled face. "Of course, I always thought he was a dolt. But if she doesn't mind, who am I to say? They seem happy enough."

Julia recalled Lord Chambers' face on seeing Desiree and wondered just how happy he was.

"First things first." Maddie used her cane to rub Ephram's belly. The dog opened one eye and wiggled his tail. "You need to gain Huntertson's attention."

"Oh, I have it. Everything I do makes him angry."

"Well, that's a start. Next, you have to meet him on his level. Make him think you are one of the most exciting, unpredictable women he has ever known. He'll not even look at another woman."

The vision of herself as a mysterious, seductive enchantress held immense appeal. "How do I do that?"

Maddie regarded her with a critical stare. "For one thing, we've got to get you some different clothes."

Julia looked down at her morning dress of pale yellow muslin over a bodice of blue satin. "What's wrong with this? I thought it was charming."

"That's the problem. You don't want to look charming. You want him to nuzzle your neck and try to slip his hand up your—"

"Aunt Maddie! I could never wear anything like that in public."

"Who's talking about in public? And don't try to tell me you don't want his attentions in private. You'd have to be blind or dead not to know your husband has more than his fair share of looks."

Julia was perfectly aware of her husband's physical charms. "What do you think Alec would do if I just admitted I was . . . fond of him?"

"Run like his coattails were afire. Never saw a man more determined to remain uncommitted." Maddie shook her head, the artificial flowers scattered in her wig flopping dramatically. "That's his grandfather's fault. John felt as if he'd ruined things for Alec's mother by coddling her. He was determined not to make the same mistake with his grandson."

"Mrs. Winston told me he was forever ripping up at Alec over the littlest things."

"Barked at him all the time. So much that I don't think the boy knows his own worth." Maddie frowned. "Probably feels worse around a philanthropist like you. Hell, sometimes you make *me* feel like a sham."

"How could Alec think such a thing? Why he's . . . he's so . . . *Alec.*"

"Handsome as Hercules, isn't he?"

It was more than that. It was the fact that he'd brought Muck a toy ship when he thought no one would see; that he allowed Mrs. Winston to call him "Master Alec" without a wince; and that night after night he pretended to drink Burroughs' warmed milk. "Alec can be very kind when he wants to be."

"For your sake, I hope so." Maddie tapped a gnarled finger on the arm of her chair. "I suppose you have shared his bed by now."

Julia blinked.

"Don't look at me like that," Maddie said, though a spot of color touched the parchment of her cheeks. "You've been married almost four months. Ought to have some idea what I'm talking about. And if you don't, then Hunterston is not near the man I took him for."

"We . . . we have . . . if what you mean is—"

"Good gracious, don't enact a Cheltenham tragedy just because I asked a question! I don't know what has made today's generation so missish. In my time, we would have just said it aloud." Maddie cocked a discontented brow. "Well? Have you?"

"Yes. Once."

"Once? Only once? A fine, handsome man like that in your home, and you've only slept with him once? Good God, you don't have ice water in your veins, do you? If I had a man who looked like—" She broke off at Julia's anguished expression. "Well, that's between the two of you. Daresay it's a good thing I don't have such a randy stallion at my disposal. My heart's not as strong as it used to be."

"Neither is mine." Julia blushed when Maddie's mouth quirked in a devilish grin.

"We'll have to start at the beginning. You need some admirers. I noticed the other day Alec don't like it by half when one of those lap dogs you've had trailing after you starts yapping for attention. He stands and stares as if he'd like to march across the room, toss you over his shoulder, and storm out." Maddie regarded the gold knob of her cane with a thoughtful gaze. "Maybe Bridgeton would do. He seems intent on catching your attention."

Julia remembered Alec's bleak reaction at her mention

of Nick. "I don't think that would be a good idea. They hate one another."

"Hmm. Well, we don't want a duel or anything like that. They say Bridgeton has killed more than his fair share." Maddie sighed. "A pity, for he would have been perfect."

Julia didn't respond. Ever since Nick had pointed her in Desiree's direction, she'd expected him to avoid her. Instead, he had an annoying tendency to show up when Alec was not about and play the charming cousin until she longed to slap him.

Ephram growled in his sleep and kicked with his back paws. "There, there," cooed Maddie. She patted him on the head before fixing her gaze back on Julia. "Perhaps Wexford would do, though he does gad about, disappearing for weeks on end and doing God knows what."

"I doubt he would agree. He is Alec's best friend, you know."

"All the more reason for him to flirt with you. But I suppose you are right. What about young Bentham? Still painting your portrait, isn't he?"

Julia nodded. "For the charity auction. I thought it would take hours and hours, but all he did was make a few sketches. It'll be interesting to see if it even looks like me when he's done."

"If Bentham paints it, you can be assured it will be recognizable. He's a talented artist. Handsome, too."

"And infatuated with Therese. He speaks of her all the time." Shortly after the Bastions' rout, Julia had feared he had developed a partiality for her, but he had quickly reverted back to her cousin's circle of admirers. It was rather curious that he wanted to paint her at all.

Maddie waved a hand. "It doesn't matter who he is in love with. All we need is for Alec to *think* he might be interested in you." She nodded with satisfaction. "Now we have a plan of action. First clothes, and then Bentham."

Julia wondered if such silliness would really make a difference. It sounded like a lot of fustian, but in a way it was not much different from Alec's steady attack on her senses with his suggestive touches and simmering glances. She sighed. Silly it might be, but right now it was all she had.

Lucien quirked a brow. "Well, halfling? Are you or aren't you?"

Edmund fingered first one card and then another. After staring at his hand for what seemed to Alec like an eternity, he drew a card and laid it on the table. "There."

Alec drew a card and tossed it beside Edmund's. Usually, he found the more lively company at the gaming hells of the East End far preferable to the stuffy, conventional atmosphere at White's. But tonight, the stultifying club perfectly suited his mood.

Lord Blackmore, a pompous ass who practically lived at White's, scratched his bulbous nose. "Hm. Playing deep, are you?" He squinted at his cards before selecting a discard.

Lucien placed his own hand on the table. "Ah, the fruits of patience. I believe that puts me over the top."

"Damn you, Luce," Alec said without rancor. He tossed his cards aside and refilled his glass. He'd rather lose money to Lucien than to anyone. At least he knew it would go to better use than with some of the ivory turners he'd been playing against this week. He suspected some of them had been cheating—not that he really cared. It had been a relief, losing money. As far as he could see, his grandfather's fortune was little more than a curse.

Alec took a deep swallow of his brandy and grimaced. He was tired of brandy, tired of carousing, tired of everything this evening. The glass curved into his hand and he regarded it gloomily. He wasn't sure why he even bothered to drink. It did little to dull either his anger or his lust.

And oh, how he lusted. Him. The renowned Devil Hunterston—in lust with his own wife. It was laughable.

But worse was the galling knowledge that Julia preferred another man. No, he corrected himself, not just another man, but Nick.

The idea of Julia with Nick ate at him, stalked his waking thoughts, and preyed upon his sleep. The last week had been his own private hell. Yet his desire for Julia grew stronger with each passing day. He reached for the bottle of brandy.

"My, my, my. What have we here?" Nick's smooth voice cut into Alec's thoughts.

"What in the hell do *you* want?" Alec slammed the glass onto the table, heedless of the brandy that sloshed onto the cards.

Blackmore glanced uneasily from one to the other as he dealt the cards for another game. "Easy, Hunterston. It's only Bridgeton."

"There is no 'only Bridgeton,' " Alec replied ungraciously. Not even to Julia. *Especially* not to Julia.

Nick regarded him with a faint smile. "Such affection. You unman me."

The mocking tone lifted the bile in Alec's throat. "Go to hell."

For one delicious instant, an answering flare of anger sparked in the blue eyes. Though it was quickly extinguished, an immediate sense of satisfaction warmed Alec.

Edmund's uneasy laughter broke the silence. "Don't mind him. Alec always trifles when he's jug-bitten."

Nick's smile became a sneer. "I never mind Alec—jug-bitten or not."

Alec put down his cards and made to stand, but Lucien grasped his arm.

"Don't," Lucien said quietly.

Jerking his arm free, Alec subsided into his chair. Though he yearned to do otherwise, Lucien was right. "Say whatever it is you came to say, Nick. I'm busy."

"Such rudeness," he sighed. "And here I came to congratulate you on Julia's recent triumph in reforming London."

Alec sloshed more brandy into his glass. "What are you talking about now?"

Nick raised his brows. "Tsk, tsk. What's the matter, Alec? Doesn't Julia confide in you?"

"My wife confides in me," Alec said succinctly, "each and every night."

Nick's jaw tightened, his eyes blazing to life before he caught himself and pasted a thin smile on his lips. "Perhaps Edmund is familiar with Julia's latest reform efforts."

Edmund lifted a befuddled gaze from his cards. "What?"

"Desiree," said Nick succinctly.

"Oh, my God! Don't remind me! I thought I would die." He turned to Blackmore. "There I was, sitting at Lady H.'s dinner party, when I look up and see this bit of muslin I'd been chasing. Bold as brass she was, carrying in a plate of crimped cod as if she owned the place."

Lord Blackmore appeared properly scandalized. "You don't say? Same thing happened to me once. Sitting there at supper and caught a glimpse of a ragged fellow out in the hall. Coal scuttler or some such thing. Just traipsed in, pretty as you please, asking if he could work. Shocking. Had my butler give him the go."

"This woman didn't wander in. Lady H. hired her as a maid. Forever helping out the plebeians, you know."

"Servants are a deuced nuisance. We've been without a proper footman for a week now. Caught the last one nipping my private stock." Blackmore frowned. "Now that I think on it, my wife mentioned something about Lady Hunterston and servants just the other day. What was it? Oh, yes—I remember." He fished in his pocket and produced a card, handing it to Edmund.

Edmund slowly read the bold lettering. He started, then blanched and sent a harried glance at Alec before cramming the card into his waistcoat.

Alec stared, a horrible thought rising. "What is it?"

"Oh, I think you know," said Nick.

Alec ignored him. "Damn it, Edmund. What is it?"

Edmund shook his head. "Just a card. Nothing special."

"Read it."

A slow flush lifted in Edmund's cheeks. "I already did. No need to read it again. I remember exactly what it says."

Alec glared. "Edmund."

The harassed young man cast a wild glance at Lucien.

Lucien shrugged. "Read it. He'll pummel it out of you if you don't."

Edmund wiped a hand across his damp face and slowly pulled the card free. He cleared his throat and read aloud. "S.W.W. Servant Referral Service. All experienced and highly trained. References provided."

At first, Alec hoped it was a joke, but Nick's satisfied smile told him otherwise.

"Cousin Julia is always a delightful surprise, isn't she?" purred Nick.

Alec glared, relieved to find an object for his anger. "Just what do you mean by that?"

"Merely that I find your wife fascinating."

Lord Blackmore blew out his cheeks. "Easy, Bridgeton. Careful what you say about someone else's wife."

Nick's gaze narrowed on the chubby man. "Oh, but Julia is so much more to me than my cousin's wife."

"Good God, man!" Blackmore shot a startled look at Alec.

But Nick was not finished. His smile heavy with

meaning, he leaned across the table. "Tell me, Alec. Is there fire beneath that prim exterior? I have been dying to discover for myself."

Seeing nothing but a haze of red, Alec leapt across the table. Cards, coins, and markers scattered across the floor. The room erupted into a cacophony of shouts and yells as men began placing bets on the outcome of the fight.

Though Nick was ready for the attack, Alec's fury was unstoppable. His charge carried Nick backward, across a table, and toppled them both to the floor. When Lucien and Edmund finally managed to pull Alec away, Nick lay on the floor, blood dripping from his mouth and nose.

Shaking off Lucien's grasp, Alec looked down at him. "Never, *never* speak my wife's name again."

He turned sharply on his heel and left. Inwardly seething, Nick wiped the blood from his nose with the back of his hand and slowly got to his feet.

Blackmore huffed. "Demmed shame who they let in the club nowadays." He shot a dark look at Nick from under heavy, black brows. "Demmed shame."

One by one, the spectators returned to their game as servants scurried about, resetting tables and bringing out fresh cards and drinks. Nick placed a handkerchief to his nose and winced. He should never have goaded Alec, but the idea of causing dissention in the Hunterston household was too sweet a thought to be ignored. He'd known Julia would not mention her business venture to her strict husband and he'd been right. Alec had been shocked.

Unfortunately, Nick had been caught off guard by the strength of Alec's reaction. It was beginning to appear that Therese was right. Alec did indeed have feelings for his wife. Nick scowled and tucked his handkerchief into his pocket.

Once again, it seemed as if his cousin would win

everything. The thought infuriated Nick. He was through wanting just the money. Now, he wanted it all.

He replaced his hat and bowed to the room, but no one acknowledged him. Nick set his teeth in a smile at the snub, inwardly seething like a bed of embers. It was one more indignity he could lay at Alec's door.

Fortunately for Nick, there were more subtle and infinitely more gratifying ways of reckoning vengeance than fisticuffs. Alec would pay dearly for this little incident—and it would take more than money, now. It might even take the attentions of the fascinating Julia.

The thought calmed him. Alec's wife was unlike any woman he'd ever known, and Nick had known hundreds. They loved his face and craved his affection, but none had ever touched his heart, if he indeed possessed one. Yet there was something about Julia that made him wonder if she could wake his hardened soul back to life.

Chuckling a little at his own folly, Nick waved down a hackney and climbed in. It was nonsense, of course. His soul was as dead as his heart.

Within a remarkably short time, the hackney deposited him at No. 10 Laura Street. Nick hated this part of the city. Full of cits and lawyers, it reminded him too much of the ease with which he himself could fall into obscurity. He climbed a set of rickety stairs and knocked on a faded door.

Thirty minutes later he emerged, a smile once again on his face, his steps jaunty. He located another hackney and ordered it to drive past Hunterston House. As the conveyance creaked up the road, he lifted a corner of the ragged curtain and watched as it came into view.

It wasn't as impressive as Bridgeton Manor, yet Hunterston House held its own charm. For now, it was dark with the exception of one solitary upstairs window. Nick wondered if the irrepressible Julia awaited her husband's return.

He smiled and dropped the curtain. Soon, it would all

belong to him. Satisfied with his work, he thumped his cane on the roof and ordered the hackney toward May-fair, where his palatial residence awaited him in solitary splendor.

Chapter 25

Dawn was just breaking when Alec let himself into Hunterston House. Without waiting to divest himself of his gloves and hat, he took the stairs two at a time and threw open the door to Julia's bedchamber.

Julia sat upright as the door banged against the wall. Hair mussed and cheeks flushed, she clutched the sheet to her and blinked sleepily. "Alec?"

Irritation flared. "Who else would be coming to your room at this time of the morning?"

She frowned and pushed the thick, honey-colored braid over her shoulder. "What's wrong?"

He made an impatient noise and strode to the bed and threw the card onto the counterpane. "What is *this*, madam?"

Julia picked it up and squinted. "Looks like a card. I can't quite make it out, but it looks like 8-4-4 something."

"It says 'S.W.W.' to be correct."

She opened her eyes absurdly wide. "Is that a haberdasher?"

"No, it is not."

"What a pity. Edmund was just telling me the other day that he needed a good—"

"You know very well whose card that is."

Julia sighed, the innocent expression disappearing. "Of course I know whose it is." She held the card at arm's length. "We should have gotten the cream ones, but Aunt Maddie wouldn't have it."

"Lady Birlington was with you when you ordered those?"

"Oh, yes. She argued about the color, the size, and what to write on them. A very helpful woman, Lady Birlington."

Alec raked a hand through his hair. "Good God."

"What's the matter?"

"How can you ask that?"

"Oh, for heaven's sake!" Julia threw back the counterpane and slipped her legs over the edge of the bed. "You are the most absurd man, coming in here ranting and raving about a simple card. You have become more of a prude than Vicar Ashton."

Alec barely heard the words. Julia's nightrail gleamed in the early morning light, the rosy pink satin as luscious as the flesh it covered. Low cut, the scanty bodice hinted at the gentle swell of her breasts while the skirt hugged her body like a second skin, molding to her narrow waist, the delightful curve of her hip, and the long line of her leg.

Alec's heart lodged against his third rib. It was the most disreputable nightrail he had ever seen. "Where in hell did you get that?"

She smoothed her hands over the silk, the thin material tightening across her breasts until the peaks of her nipples were plainly visible. "This? I bought it yesterday." She regarded him through her lashes, a faint smile curving her mouth. "Do you like it?"

He hated it. He hated it for casting such intriguing shadows between her breasts, for caressing the line of her thigh, for making his body ache with frustration and desire.

God help him, but he wanted to rip that pink silk away

and . . . he ground his teeth and forced his attention back to the card now covered by the counterpane. "I came to speak to you about that card, not your shameless attire."

A flush rose along her shoulders and neck until they exactly matched her gown. "I don't think it's shameless. Quite comfortable, really. Except when I turn over, then it slips up and gets all tangled around my waist and between my—"

"For God's sake!" he burst out. If it had been anyone else but Julia, he would have thought she deliberately taunted him.

"You look angry."

Alec raked an impatient hand through his hair. "I suppose I should not be shocked by your choice of nightwear. Any woman who would hand out cards like a common tradesman would think nothing of going naked."

Julia's wide mouth flattened into a frown. "I don't know why you'd care. According to you, we're ruined already."

"There is still a chance, however slim."

"Not with you carousing all over town, drinking and gambling and God knows what."

Alec said stiffly, "Unlike you, my behavior is not outside the realm of acceptable society."

She sniffed and put her slim nose in the air. "That is only because men are not held to such standards as women. If I were to behave in such a manner, I would be cut forthwith."

"How many of those damned cards have you handed out?"

Julia turned a cool, unimpressed stare on him. "As many as I could."

"Good God!"

She ignored his outburst and rose from the bed. Without sparing him so much as a glance, she crossed to the washstand and raised her hands to the fastenings on her gown. The silk pulled across her breasts and outlined every curve and shadow with mouth-watering detail.

Alec tried to swallow, his cravat suddenly much too tight. "What are you doing?"

"Getting dressed. Thanks to you I'm wide awake now, so I might as well get up." As if it were the most natural thing in the world, she began to unlace her nightrail.

Eerily fascinated, Alec watched her slim hands loosen first one and then another ice-pink tie. The ties slithered through the silk with a breathy sigh and dropped to the floor.

For one mad instant, he thought of throwing his pride to the wind, taking her in his arms, and bearing her back to the bed they had once shared. As passionate as she was, he knew he could win her over.

But winning her body wasn't enough. It would never be enough. But that was all she had to give. Her heart belonged to Nick.

Furious and hurt, Alec stuffed his hands in his pockets and wished he had the strength to look away from the enticing display before him.

The nightrail slithered to the floor, a puddle of rose pink exposing a body that made the beauty of the gown pale in comparison. He closed his eyes against that creamy expanse of flesh, those long, lush legs and impudent breasts. His breeches inevitably tightened. "One day, madam," he managed to grit out through clenched teeth, "you will be the death of me."

With a decidedly shaky hand, he slammed the door behind him and went to lock himself in the solitary splendor of his study.

"Lord Edmund Valmont," intoned Burroughs from the door of the breakfast room.

Julia looked up from her pile of correspondence and raised her brows as Edmund rushed past the butler, a rolled newspaper clutched in his hands.

Not only was it unfashionably early, but the young man appeared to have dressed in the dark. His fair curls tangled beneath a hat that looked as if it belonged to one of his servants, and his cravat was but half tied, one long end dangling over his shoulder like a scarf. The buttons of his coat had been thrust through the incorrect holes, and his shoes did not match.

"Heavens, Edmund. What has happened?"

He slid to a stop in the center of the room and cast a wild glance around. "Where's Alec?"

She sniffed and returned to the pile of invitations. "In his study."

Edmund turned to the door. "I have to see him immediately."

"It won't do you any good," she said calmly just as he reached the door. She pushed the salver of invitations and notes aside to put a slice of toast on her plate. "He has locked the door to his study and won't come out. Burroughs said he's in no mood to be bothered."

Julia couldn't help but feel a small amount of satisfaction at that. Maddie had been right. To attract a rake, one had to appeal to him on his own level. It really had been quite exhilarating. For the first time in days, hope buoyed her spirits.

Edmund heaved a defeated sigh and removed his hat, tossing it onto the table. "I'd better wait until he's in a better frame of mind. I should have known it would be bellows to mend after Nick accosted him last night."

Julia stabbed her spoon into the marmalade jar. So that was how Alec had discovered the cards. She had no doubt that the despicable Nick had put the whole incident in the worst light possible.

She slathered marmalade on her toast and decided she was beginning to develop a healthy dislike for that man.

Edmund threw himself in a chair, twisting the paper in his hands.

"Come and have some breakfast, Edmund. Whatever

it is, there's no sense in getting in a dither."

"I can't. I have to see Alec. Perhaps after he's eaten he'll feel more the thing."

Julia doubted it, but didn't reply. As far as she could tell, Alec had been in a bad mood since he'd married her.

Burroughs entered the room with a tray, the steam curling from the silver salvers.

Edmund leapt from his chair. "Bacon! Just the thing. Burroughs, could you take some to Alec? It would make him feel immensely better. Whenever I'm a bit out to let, I find that bacon will set me to rights in a trice."

"Oh?" replied the butler, eyeing Edmund with much the same expression he would have bestowed on a plate of bad meat.

Impervious to slights, Edmund nodded. "I just hold my nose and eat as much of it as I can stand. The next thing you know, I'm out kicking up a lark again. Works like a charm every time."

"How marvelous. Unfortunately, his lordship has decided against breakfast this morning." The butler cast a repressive glance at Julia. "Again."

Julia piled bacon on her plate and added two eggs. Just for good measure, she poured a thick cream sauce over the whole. She always ate when something bothered her. If she and Alec kept going as they were, she'd weigh fifty stone by the end of the year.

Just as she lifted a fork to her mouth, a roar reverberated through the house.

Julia started. "Heavens! What's that?"

Burroughs tilted his head to one side as another roar echoed through the hallway. "I believe, madam, that is his lordship."

As if in answer, the door to the breakfast room slammed open. A potted plant toppled to the floor as Alec stormed in, a newspaper clutched in his hand. Edmund took one look at his grim countenance and retired to the window, trying desperately to secret his own newspaper away in his waistcoat.

Alec advanced on the butler like an avenging angel come to battle evil. "What do you call this?" He tossed the *Morning Post* onto the breakfast table.

Lifting a gloved hand, the butler carefully examined the paper. "I believe it is a newspaper, my lord. I could be mistaken, as someone has ripped the heading from the—"

"It is *yesterday's* paper."

The butler lifted his brows. "Oh, you wished for *today's*?"

"Of course I wanted today's paper!" Alec snapped, hands clenched into fists. "Why would I want to see yesterday's?"

Julia noted he had not changed from last night's attire, his cravat loosened, his jaw shadowed. Rumpled and bloodshot, he still managed to make her knees quaver.

Burroughs sighed. "I'm afraid Miss Desiree is still engaged in ironing today's paper. It was a bit sticky when it arrived this morning."

"Surely it has not taken her all morning to iron a paper. Go and—" Alec broke off as he caught sight of Edmund standing still as a statue beside the curtain. "What are you doing here at this time of the morning?"

"Me? Oh, nothing. Just out for my morning constitutional. Deucedly healthy thing, walking." Edmund patted his rounded stomach with false geniality. "Don't know if you know it or not, but I walk everyday. Walk for miles sometimes. Once I walked all the way to—"

"At this time of the morning?"

"Uhm, yes. Of course. Better for your knees if you do it before nine. I've decided—"

"Is that today's paper?" Alec interrupted.

Edmund looked down at the newspaper crammed half in and half out of his waistcoat. "What? This? Oh, no.

This is yesterday's paper. Must have left it in there and not noticed."

Alec's gaze narrowed. "Give it to me."

For a second Julia thought the young man would refuse, but after a heartfelt sigh, he pulled the crinkled mass from his coat and crossed the room toward Alec. Edmund shot an apologetic glance at Burroughs as he passed. "He was bound to find out, sooner or later."

The butler bowed, and sending an enigmatic glance at Julia, left the room.

Julia frowned. There'd been an unmistakable warning in Burroughs' gaze. She watched with growing trepidation as Alec scanned the front page, his face frozen into a mask. Whatever it was, it was not good.

After an agonizing moment, Edmund burst out, "Good God, Alec. Don't just stand there! What are we to do now? I vow, when I read that article this morning and saw Lady H.'s name, I almost—"

"*My* name?" Dropping her knife, Julia reached over and yanked the paper from Alec.

He made an effort to grab it, but she eluded him and sprang from her chair, crossing to the window to read it in the morning light. Emblazoned across the front page ran the words WELL-KNOWN CHARITY HIDES BROTHEL.

The words danced and swayed before her eyes, and all she could do was catch jumbled phrases. Well-known sponsor . . . Lady Hunterston . . . providing servants-for-hire to many well known . . . hides an exclusive brothel . . . patronized by dukes and members of parliament alike. . . .

The words spun round and round. She barely noticed when Alec retrieved the paper from her nerveless hand.

"Good God," she said faintly.

The door opened. "The Duke of Wexford," Burroughs announced.

Lucien strolled into the room. He checked his stride

when he saw the paper in Alec's hand. "Bloody hell, you've seen it already."

Alec gave a curt nod.

Julia fought her way through a flood of thoughts, each more horrifying than the last. For the first time, she truly feared for Alec's promise to his grandfather.

So far, they had battled innuendoes and whispers. She feared neither. But this, a newspaper article replete with names and sounding so official . . . a lump formed in her throat.

She looked up and found Alec regarding her with an inscrutable expression, the paper clamped between his hands. She wouldn't blame him if he threw it at her.

Taking a deep breath, she said, "The executors will read this."

Alec gave a brief nod, condemning her more thoroughly with that gesture than any words could. A band of misery clamped around her chest, weighting her down. She sank into a chair and tried to think what could be done.

"Don't be so grim, Alec," Edmund urged. "I'll fetch Aunt Maddie. She'll know what to do."

Alec shook his head, his face a frozen mask of condemnation. "The damage is done."

Edmund strode to the door, crushing his hat onto his mussed curls. "We can't just stand here and do nothing. Aunt Maddie is up to every rig and row in town. I'll be back as soon as I've seen her."

Julia listened as Edmund's footsteps faded. The tightness in her chest eased a bit at his words. So far Aunt Maddie had known what to do in every other instance. "Perhaps Lady Birlington can—"

"Not this time." Alec tossed the paper onto the table, his bleak expression fixed on her with damning regard. "The executors will have already read every despicable word by now. You—" He stopped as if unable to go on, his face shuttered against some strong emotion.

She knew what was behind his bleak gaze. Every prediction he'd ever made about her charity work had come true. Because of her stubbornness, her refusal to compromise, they had lost it all.

She tried to swallow and failed. "Alec, maybe if I—"

"*No*. You have done enough." The harsh words echoed.

"Alec," Lucien said, stepping forward to place a hand on his friend's arm. "Julia did not mean any harm."

Burroughs entered carrying a small silver salver on which sat a note. "My lord, this just came from Mr. Pratt. He requests an immediate reply."

Julia watched Alec ripped open the envelope. His face darkened as he read. Finally, he looked at Burroughs. "Tell Mr. Pratt I would be glad to attend a meeting at the executors' convenience."

The butler bowed and left.

Alec cursed and crumpled the note in his hand, the thick paper crackling.

Lucien sighed. "I assume they have seen the article and demand an accounting."

Alec tossed the note into the fire. "They cannot wait to dig their hooks into me."

Julia rubbed her forehead to still the ache growing behind her eyes. It was all so unfair. But she refused to believe that something could not be done. "Alec, perhaps there are some people who can help. Lady Birlington will do what she can, and the board members of the Society might—"

He rounded on her, his anger so intense she drew back. "Forget your damn Society and the inheritance! Don't you understand what this means?"

"Of course I do. It means the fortune is at risk—"

"Damn the money, Julia! It means that you are ruined. Completely and utterly ruined."

"I don't care about that."

"You will. People will turn their backs on you so quickly you will wonder if you ever had their regard to begin with. All those who supported you and nurtured you will treat you as if you were a leper."

She looked down at the newspaper, the hurtful words standing out in bold relief. "I am sure some will believe this, but not all."

"One or two may continue to acknowledge you. But it will not be enough."

"I—"

He cut her off with an anguished gesture. "God, Lucien, explain it to her." Alec turned to the mantel as if the sight of her pained him.

Julia clasped her hands in her lap. It wasn't so much the thought of being shunned, or even of the Society losing its funding that sank her stomach to the floor. It was Alec's dark expression.

Lucien sighed and regarded the tip of his boot. "I believe what Alec is trying to say is that every scandal has a victim, one person who must pay. That is especially true in a situation like this, when so many are caught in the ugly net."

"You think it will be me."

Lucien nodded. "Thanks to the tone of that article."

"But it is untrue. The Society would never . . . I would never. . . ." She sighed, her shoulder slumping. "The fortune—"

"Is gone," Alec said in a clipped voice. "The executors will never allow us to have the money now. We dare not even hope."

She stood and took a step toward him. "Perhaps if I explain how all this happened, they will understand that you, at least, are not to blame."

"Damn it, Julia!" he snarled, turning to her. "Haven't you done enough?"

Her temper leapt to meet his. "You can't give up without even trying!"

He glowered, his eyes dark with emotion. "One of us must face reality."

Julia squared her chin. "I face reality every day, Alec."

"You?" he scoffed with a bitter laugh. "*You*, who squander your love on a man who will never return your affections? If that is your reality, you can keep it."

The words hit her with the force of a cannon shot, stealing her breath and crushing her heart. He knew. He knew she loved him and he despised her.

Her hand dropped to her side. She was unable to speak, unable to breathe.

Lucien's quiet curse broke the silence. "For the love of God, Alec."

Alec ignored him and stalked from the room. Julia heard him calling for the carriage as the door slammed.

Tears rushed in as the shock slipped away, a raw pain in the region of her heart. She leaned against the window and closed her eyes.

Lucien spoke, his voice soft over her shoulder. "Julia, don't. He doesn't mean anything he says right now."

She nodded, unable to do more. Seconds later she heard the door close, and then Lucien, too, was gone.

Chapter 26

"As pleasant as the day is, I suppose we're not just going out for a carriage ride," Lucien said, holding tightly to the seat as Alec sped the phaeton between two lumbering carts.

Alec turned the light vehicle across a busy thoroughfare, narrowly missing an overloaded dray in the middle of the road. "I am going to find a man by the name of Thomas Everard."

"Ah, the author of the libelous article." Lucien glanced at his friend's grim profile. "And just what do you propose to do, once you have located Mr. Everard?"

"Tear out his heart and stuff it in his mouth."

"There is a certain charm to that plan, but I hardly think it will help."

"It will make *me* feel better," Alec said, his brow low.

"Yes, but it may make things much worse for Julia."

Alec's scowl deepened.

Lucien sighed, recognizing the mulish expression. "Allow me to point out a few things. Unless you kill the man, he will write another article. Maybe something about the violent tendencies of the nobility, accompanied by a nice drawing of a snarling Viscount Hunterston pummeling the innocent author."

"I don't give a damn what that cretin writes about

me," Alec said tersely. A heavy coach pulled in front of them and slowed their pace to a near walk.

As Alec cursed, Lucien pulled a cheroot from his pocket and rolled it between forefinger and thumb. He sniffed it appreciatively and cast a sidelong glance at his companion. "If you don't care what Mr. Everard writes, why are we enroute to visit him?"

"Because he besmirched—" Alec broke off, controlling himself with an obvious effort. "It doesn't matter. He will not be writing such lies again."

Ah, so they rode to protect the lady's honor, did they? Lucien grinned and wondered how much of Alec's anger was due to pride, and how much was the cause of a deeper, more serious emotion. He suspected Alec felt much more strongly about his unconventional wife than he realized.

The phaeton pulled up in front of the seedy offices that housed the *Morning Post*. Lucien took the reins while Alec strode inside, returning a short time later holding a torn and bloodied scrap of paper, a hastily scribbled address scrawled across one corner.

Lucien noted the scrape on Alec's knuckles. "Any problems?"

Pulling a handkerchief from his pocket, Alec wrapped it around his hand, a dab of blood staining the fine linen. "No. They were amazingly helpful."

"How fortunate."

Alec nodded. "For them."

Lucien did not vouchsafe a reply. In Alec's current mood, any answer was sure to set off his barely held temper. In mutual silence, they proceeded to No. 10 Laura Street.

Climbing down from the perch, Alec tossed Lucien the reins. "I will not be long."

"Shall I accompany you?"

"No," Alec answered curtly. "This is a private matter between me and Mr. Everard."

Lucien nodded and watched his friend disappear up a narrow stair. Never had he seen Alec so concerned about the opinions of others. Indeed, these last few months had rendered an amazing change that was especially obvious when Alec was with Julia. The very air seemed to crackle with contention.

Chuckling, Lucien lit his cheroot, pulled his hat low, and considered the faded door where his friend had disappeared. All told, it was very amusing.

Half an hour later, Alec returned, slightly mussed, but intact. Despite the fact that a scrape marred his jaw and his chin sported a swollen lump, he appeared remarkably satisfied.

"I see Mr. Everard made an impression," Lucien remarked dryly, gathering the reins.

A lopsided smile curved Alec's bruised mouth, though it did not reach his eyes. "Not near the impression I left on him."

"Did he mention where he received such erroneous information?"

Alec gave a nod, his eyes shadowed. "Nick."

"Of course." Lucien set the phaeton in motion. "I thought I detected your nefarious cousin's hand. How did he manage to work his evil this time? Bribery? Blackmail?"

"Nick purchased Mr. Everard's vowels from a certain gaming establishment. Almost a thousand pounds worth."

"How unfortunate for Mr. Everard."

Alec scowled. "He has dealt with Nick before. Apparently Mr. Everard writes the society news, as well. Nick has used his services to discredit his enemies."

"Bloody hell! You were right about Nick; he is an underhanded villain." Lucien pulled the team to a halt to allow a nursemaid walking her charges across the street. "What do you intend to do now?"

"Mr. Everard will be writing a retraction article," Alec said with a grim smile.

"It will be too little, too late."

"Besides writing a public apology, Mr. Everard has agreed to attend the meeting of the executors tomorrow to report his entire commerce with Nick."

Lucien frowned and set the phaeton in motion once again. "Perhaps we should bring him with us now, in case he changes his mind."

"And do what? Hold him prisoner in the cellar? Only imagine how that would look if it ever came to the attention of the executors."

Heaving a sigh, Lucien nodded. "I suppose you are right. Such an escapade is bound to come to light."

Alec reached into his pocket and pulled out a folded note. "Therefore, I had him write me a vowel for two thousand pounds."

"And now he owes you more than he owes Nick." Lucien grinned as he tooled the carriage along. "Very good, Alec."

"Debtors' prison can be a powerful inducement, especially for something as simple as the truth."

"I would flee the country to escape the hands of both of you."

"I have agreed to pay all his debts if he will tell the truth at the executors' meeting. He can start with a clean slate. I think he was relieved at the idea of being free from Nick."

"Who wouldn't be?"

Alec nodded. "Now the only issue left to resolve is that of my cousin." A dangerous gleam lit the silver eyes.

The sight made Lucien uneasy. "Alec, perhaps you should leave well enough alone. At least until after the meeting tomorrow."

"What I do depends on Julia." Alec clenched his hand into a fist in his pocket, oblivious to the sting of his battered knuckles. "From now on, she will set the course."

"Julia? But why?"

"She is in love with Nick." The words settled around him like noxious ash.

"*What*?"

"Damn it, do not ask me to say it again." He wasn't sure he could.

Lucien edged the phaeton around a mail coach lumbering down the street, his brows low. "Surely you are mistaken."

"She practically confessed it."

"But I would have sworn—" Lucien broke off, casting an uncertain glance his way. "What do you mean, she *practically* confessed?"

"Some time ago, Julia told me she had been in love for a long time—almost four years. That is exactly the length of time she has known Nick. She even remembers the first time she saw him."

"I cannot believe it."

"If you had seen her face, you would know." Alec would never forget Julia's dreamy expression. It was permanently burned into his mind.

"You are wrong. She could have met any number of people four years ago, and—"

"It is Nick, I'm sure of it. I wish to God it were not true." Alec raked an impatient hand through his hair. "Lucien, think. Julia gathers people to her. Not perfect people, but broken ones."

A thoughtful look crossed Lucien's face. "Like Muck and Desiree."

Suddenly tired, Alec leaned back against the squabs. "People like Nick. To a reformer, he must seem irresistible."

Lucien frowned. "Do you think she honestly believes she can reform him?"

"My wife is an eternal optimist. She believes anything is possible."

After a long silence, Lucien shot him a concerned glance. "What will you do?"

Alec couldn't allow himself to even think about what he really wanted to do. Watching her white face as she read that damnable newspaper article had been the most agonizing moment of his life. Alec had felt her pain as clearly as if it had been his own, and his anger had risen against the person who had dared harm her. No matter Julia's feelings for Nick or anyone else, she was his wife, and he would protect her.

The fact that she had not trusted him to find a way clear of this difficulty, but had immediately latched onto Edmund's suggestion to lay the problem in Lady Birlington's lap, had infuriated Alec all the more.

"She is *my* wife, Lucien. I will not let her go."

Lucien regarded him for a long moment before turning back to the road. "I'm still not convinced she cares for Nick any more than she does her other projects, but you know her better than I." He sighed and shook his head. "Perhaps, in time, she will forget him."

Alec did not answer. Julia was not a woman to love lightly. She valued her heart more than that.

The problem was, he was beginning to think he did, too.

"Will ye be wantin' me any time soon, my lady?" Johnston asked.

Julia shook her head. "I will be with Lady Birlington for several hours. You may return at two."

She turned to go up the long walk just as two fashionably dressed women descended Maddie's steps. She vaguely remembered the chubby, sour-faced woman as Lady Harrington. The young woman following in her wake bore such a striking resemblance, Julia knew it must be her daughter.

Noses in the air, eyes straight ahead, they sailed past Julia as if she were invisible.

Lady Harrington said in a sneering voice, "Of course, Eveline, it is exactly what one would expect from such a pretentious snippet. She should have stayed with the chaperones, where she belonged."

The daughter replied with a titter, "I'd say the Devil got his due, wouldn't you?"

Amid a flurry of gaiety, they climbed into their carriage. Julia had known it would be uncomfortable to be ridiculed, but part of her quivered at the harsh laughter.

From behind her, Johnston cleared his throat. "Mistress, for what it's worth, I believe ye and the master have done right by Miss Desiree."

Julia turned in surprise. "Why, thank you, Johnston."

"She may not be the brightest, but there's not a parcel of harm to her. As to what other people think," he scowled in the direction the carriage had disappeared, "don't ye worry none 'bout them. The good ones'll stay by ye through thick and thin, and as fer the rest—well, ye didn't need them anyways."

"Thank you, Johnston. It is very kind of you to say so," Julia replied, choked with emotion.

The door opened again and this time a solitary figure emerged—a young woman dressed in green silk, a gypsy bonnet perched on her fashionably coifed curls, and a painted silk scarf tied under her chin in a rakish bow. Yet despite her lively attire, the woman's pleasant features were marred by a beaky, prominent nose that gave her an air of hawkish intensity. On seeing Julia, she hesitated before continuing down the walk.

Julia's step faltered. Lady Burton. At the Society meetings, Lord Burton rarely spoke of his wife except to mention her social aspirations in a voice of great weariness.

She suddenly realized the article in this morning's paper had exposed her in more ways than one. Once the

Board members realized she had hidden her marriage and was their "anonymous" donor, they would be hurt at her deception.

Julia was so wrapped up in her depressing thoughts that Lady Burton's bow caught her unawares.

"Lady Hunterston, what a pleasure. The Dowager Duchess of Roth cannot say enough about your kindness in assisting with the ball this evening. It should be a great success."

The charity ball. Julia almost groaned. She had forgotten all about it in the events of the morning. She forced herself to return Lady Burton's smile. "I hope you will be attending."

"Of course! I only hope I can persuade Lord Burton to come with me." To Julia's surprise, a twinkle lit the woman's gray eyes. "But you know how he is, almost a hermit. I don't think he'd even go out of doors if it weren't for his charity work."

Julia managed a smile. "Lord Burton has been very supportive of the Society. He frequently mentions you, too. He says you have quite a flair for organizing things."

Lady Burton's cheeks suffused with pink, a pleased smile curving her lips and softening her whole face. "Has he, indeed? I shall have to thank him for his kind words when I return home." She placed her gloved hand on Julia's arm. "Don't let that article from this morning upset you, my dear. Trust Burton and the others to set things to right. They were already discussing it when I left."

Hope swelled in Julia's heart until she remembered Lord Kennybrook's insistence that they start a sausage factory. They were dear old gentlemen, but hardly capable of assisting her at this juncture. Still, she managed a smile. "They are too kind."

"As are you, Lady Hunterston. Well, I must be off. I

look forward to seeing you this evening." With a bow, Lady Burton departed.

Moments later, Julia followed the tall, thin butler into the morning room where Maddie sat by the fire, a blue cashmere shawl draped over her lap. Ephram snored gently on a pillow by her feet as she absently rubbed his stomach with a slippered foot.

She gave an exclamation on seeing Julia. "There you are! Wondered when you'd arrive. Lovett, if anyone else comes, tell them I am out."

"Yes, madam." Bowing, the butler softly closed the door.

Julia crossed to sit on the settee facing Maddie. "I suppose Edmund has already told you."

"The fool came bursting into my dressing room this morning and demanded to know what's to be done."

"What did you tell him?"

"The same thing I'm going to tell you," the old lady said peevishly. "Nothing. Absolutely nothing."

Julia's heart sank. Until that moment, she hadn't realized how much she had counted on Aunt Maddie repairing the damage.

Maddie regarded her with a narrow look. "Have you been cut yet?"

"Just outside your house. Lady Harrington and her daughter."

A stain of angry color rose over Maddie's cheeks. "Of all the nerve! And that woman, positively reeking of the shop. She is the daughter of some cit, you know. They say he is nothing but a merchant from Birmingham, but I never listen to gossip."

"She has always been very pleasant before."

"Ha! She's a buffoon. Insists on visiting me, but I always have Lovett tell her I'm out. They say Harrington only married the old hag to escape debtors' prison. For my part, I'd prefer prison."

Julia had to smile. "You would not prefer prison. You complain when your sheets aren't ironed. I can't imagine what you'd do without sheets."

"I could get used to it quicker than having to converse with that half-wit and her pasty-faced daughter. Makes me bilious just thinking about it."

Ephram growled in his sleep, his little paws twitching. Maddie reached over and scratched his ear until he began to snore. "All the fault of that blasted paper," she grumbled. "I wrote them first thing this morning and canceled my subscription. That should set them straight."

"I don't think it's the paper's fault."

"Who's fault could it be?"

Julia had thought of nothing else on her way here and it was painfully clear. "Nick. It sounds exactly like something he would do. And my handing out all those cards only made it look worse." Julia sighed. "I should have listened to Alec."

"Pshaw. Alec's in no better case. He caused quite a ruckus at White's last night, without any help from you, I might add."

"Last night?"

"He got in a brawl with Nick right in the middle of the card room. It's a wonder they didn't blackball the both of them."

"Alec was in a frightful mood when he returned this morning."

"I daresay." Maddie's sharp gaze rested on Julia's face. "So? Did he like the pink silk?"

Julia felt her blush all the way to her toes. "Yes. At least, I think he did. He got all red in the face and then left."

"Ran like a coward, eh?" Maddie nodded with satisfaction. "That's a good sign. A pity that dratted article appeared this morning."

It was more than a pity, Julia thought miserably. It was a tragedy of Greek proportions. "Alec was furious."

"Surely not with you? Nick is the one he should be shouting at."

Julia picked up one of the decorative pillows from the settee and hugged it to her. "I didn't mention my suspicions about Nick because I feared Alec might search him out and they would come to blows."

"Or worse. I never saw two men more determined to make cakes of themselves, and Nick has too much experience with dueling to make one comfortable."

Julia traced a flower embroidered on the pillow cover. "I wish there were some way we could fix this."

"Oh, we shall come about," Maddie said, adjusting her shawl so that the bottom fringe covered her toes. "Never fear."

"But you said there was nothing to be done."

"No, I didn't," the old woman said testily. "I said you should *do* nothing. That is not the same thing."

Julia set the pillow aside. "I don't suppose you'd care to explain?"

Maddie heaved an exasperated sigh. "Pray, pay attention! It is quite simple, really. You simply go about your business as if nothing has occurred."

"But everyone knows what has happened."

"Of course they do; they will talk of nothing else all day. The next question is how you will react."

"And how will I react?"

"Like a princess, my dear. Refuse to acknowledge the event in any way. Act as if that newspaper is exactly what it is: a scurrilous publication that prints nothing but lies."

"That seems easy enough."

"Oh, no." The old woman's brilliant blue eyes narrowed in warning. "It will take all the nerve you've got and a little more, for there are bound to be a few awkward moments."

"I'm getting good at those," Julia said glumly.

Maddie's mouth twitched into a smile. "The Dowager said tonight's charity ball will be a shocking squeeze. We couldn't ask for a finer opportunity to put a damper on the whole mess."

"I certainly hope we can pull this off. Alec promised his grandfather he would keep the fortune away from Nick."

"Leave it to me." Maddie rubbed Ephram's stomach with the toe of her shoe. "I'll call on Almira this morning and ask for her help. If she comes out in our corner, we need have no fear. Everyone will follow her lead."

Julia's shoulders sagged. "The Dowager may not wish to assist me. The newspaper article was quite explicit."

"Nonsense. Almira knows which way the wind blows; she'll be anxious to help." Maddie's face softened. "You've made quite an impression on her, Julia. On several people, in fact. Don't worry; we'll muddle through this. I don't mean to say there's not been damage, for there has. But we're far from lost."

Julia nodded, trying to reconcile herself to the thought of an entire evening spent under the harsh, knowing stare of the *ton*, tittering behind their gloved hands at her discomfort. Still, if there was even the slightest chance she could help Alec, she would do it, even if it killed her. "Thank you, Aunt Maddie. I was hoping you would see a way through this."

"So I shall. Now tell me, my dear, what do you intend to wear this evening?"

Chapter 27

A s Maddie had predicted, the Dowager Duchess of Roth was outraged at the liberties taken by a newspaper she had no compunction calling a slanderous rag. Furthermore, once Maddie had finished edifying her ladyship about how Julia had been rudely cut by Lady Harrington, a woman they both heartily detested, the Dowager became so incensed she demanded that Julia and Alec be her guests of honor at the charity ball.

As a result, an elegant carriage equipped with the Roth crest arrived at Hunterston House to carry Alec and Julia to the ball as a visible sign of her favor.

Julia brushed a hand over the lush velvet cushions. "Nice carriage."

Alec's gaze flickered across her. "Yes, it is."

It was the most he'd said to her since this morning's scene. Julia folded her hands in her lap and sighed. She couldn't fault him for his anger. She even understood why he blamed her. After all, she hadn't taken his advice on one single thing.

Julia looked out the window and pulled her cloak closer, wishing the evening were already over. Aunt Maddie had seen to every detail of Julia's costume, from the cut of the bodice to the bronze satin slippers festooned with amber crystals. She flexed her foot and winced. Pretty the slippers might be, but they pinched her feet hideously. Drat Nick for forcing her to this measure. She'd take great delight in telling him exactly what she thought of his antics.

The silence lengthened and Julia cast a surreptitious glance at her forbidding husband. He was elegantly dressed in black, an emerald nestled in the snowy folds of his cravat. He stared straight ahead, arms crossed, his mouth an unyielding line. To Julia, he looked every inch the Devil he was named. As she stared, he rubbed his jaw and winced as his hand brushed where a faint bruise lingered.

Mrs. Winston had told her how Alec had gained his bruised jaw. Julia couldn't imagine that pummeling the author of the article had accomplished anything worthwhile, but if it had afforded Alec some relief, then so be it. In her opinion, Mr. Everard deserved more than a punch in the nose for his part in this dastardly plan. Much more.

Julia toyed with the edging of her cloak. "Do you think there will be many people tonight?"

Alec looked at her as if seeing her for the first time, his gaze suddenly narrowing. "Where are your spectacles? You didn't break them, did you?"

She flushed. "No." That was another of Aunt Maddie's suggestions, one Julia was sure she would regret.

Alec frowned and looked as if he would say more, but the coach rumbled up the graceful drive of Roth House. Its lights ablaze, the stately manor shimmered in the twilight. A footman placed a step by the door and Alec assisted her down, his silver gaze brushing across her for an intense moment. Looking quickly away, Julia clutched the cloak tighter and entered the foyer.

The Dowager had spared no expense to ensure her charity ball would be the event of the season. Yards and yards of gold silk swathed the entryway, which was brightly lit with fanciful golden lamps. A deep red ori-

ental rug had been rolled across the marble floor. Julia
felt as she if were arriving in a strange exotic land.

"Your cloak."

Julia gave a start at Alec's voice so close to her ear.
She reached up to untie her cloak and for one horrifying
moment, she wondered what she had been thinking to
let Maddie talk her into this. But it was too late now.
Taking a deep breath, Julia pulled the bow loose and
allowed Alec to slide the cloak from her shoulders.

Cool air immediately chilled her neck and shoulders
and brushed across the tops of her breasts, exposed by
her low décolletage. Alec stilled, his cold gaze raking
down the length of her body. She knew what he saw,
for she'd stared at herself in the mirror a full half hour
before she'd gathered the courage to leave her room,
even wrapped in the concealing cloak.

The dress was simply, but seductively made. Heavy
bronze-colored silk molded her body, outlining the shape
of her breasts, the rounded contours of her hips, the
curve of her thigh. A delicate lace overskirt the color of
heavy cream served to emphasize the sensuous cling of
the silk, drawing the eye to the length of her legs. A
single bronze feather nestled in her curls and wrapped
about her face, brushing silkily across one of her shoulders with every move.

Julia had never worn anything so daring. In one way,
it was terrifying and she wondered if she dared breathe.
In another way, it was exhilarating to think of herself
the center of attention—or so Maddie had assured her.

Alec swore under his breath and held out her cloak.
"Put this back on."

Julia swallowed her disappointment. While she hadn't
expected his mouth to drop open in astonishment, a simple "You look nice" would have been pleasant. Shoring
up her irritation, she turned from him.

"Damn it, Julia." His breath brushed against her ear,

as heated as his temper. "Put your cloak back on before anyone sees you."

Another couple had just entered the foyer and were handing their wraps to the footman.

Julia waved at them and smiled, though she had no idea who they were. "Oops. Too late."

Alec's fingers dug into her elbow as he pulled her to the corner and further from the line of guests. "We will go home and you will change."

"I can't. If I were to appear in two different gowns in one evening it would cause talk, and we don't need more."

Julia recognized the next arrivals as Lord and Lady Eston, and she nodded to them. Lord Eston immediately returned the greeting, his gaze raking over her with approval. Lady Eston turned away, nose in the air, pulling her reluctant husband after her.

The simple brilliance of Maddie's strategy was suddenly plain. If Julia could just win half the people at tonight's ball to her side, perhaps she could turn the tide of this latest disaster. Even if that half was of the male persuasion.

If such silliness would save the fortune for Alec and the Society, she would be a fool not to at least give it a try. She caught Lord Eston's appreciative stare as he waited to greet his hostess. Julia returned his smile with what she hoped was a seductive grin. For a second he looked astonished, and then his face softened into an answering smile.

Well! That wasn't too difficult. One down, two hundred to go. She straightened her shoulders and decided to allow the clinging silk to do its magic.

Alec swore and caught her arm in a powerful grip. "What in the hell are you doing? Trying to prove what that newspaper article said is true?"

She plastered a smile on her face and said in a calm,

rational voice, "My father used to say the best way to take a hit is square on the chin."

"I have had enough hits for one day, madam. You will put your cloak back on and we will return home."

Julia's patience fled. She had as much to lose as he. She yanked free from his hold and planted her fists on her hips, heedless of the way the silk dress crumpled beneath such harsh treatment. "Nonsense. That article wasn't about you; it was about me. If I can stand it, so can you. Aunt Maddie and I have a plan, so stop complaining."

He looked at her bared shoulders. "*This* is a plan?"

"Of course. And a good one, too." She hoped.

"I was a fool to ever put you in the way of that woman." Yet, despite his churlish tone, he did not stop his intense perusal.

As his gaze touched on the curve of her breasts rising over the bronze silk, Julia shivered, her heart thumping an extra beat for good measure. "Aunt Maddie said the *ton* would forgive anything if one were interesting enough and had position or money."

"We only have the money until my meeting with the executors tomorrow."

"But we have it today," she said brightly. "Now all we need is to become interesting."

"Well, you have certainly made a start," Alec said, wondering if he should just toss the cloak over her head and be done with it. But the hopeful glow in her emerald eyes held him in check. She truly believed she could help with such an obvious ploy.

Despite his apprehension, Alec had to admit Maddie had done her work well. No man would look at Julia this evening without wondering if what lay beneath the clinging silk was as luscious as it appeared. Never had her eyes appeared so deep a green, her skin so brilliant, her body more enticing. Worse, the tantalizing scent of cinnamon wafted from her honey-colored ringlets with every move, making him remember their one night of passion in vivid, intense, painful detail.

Alec sighed his defeat and motioned one of the footmen to take the cloak. "In the future, you will ignore *all* of Aunt Maddie's plans. That woman can be dangerous."

Julia awarded him with a brilliant smile before peering around the room, the bronze feather pinned in her hair smacking him across the face. Alec waved it away. "If you are looking for Lady Birlington, she always sits near the refreshment table so she can gawk."

"Oh, no. I wasn't looking for Aunt Maddie. Do you see Nick?" Her voice deepened. "I want a word with him."

The gown suddenly took on new meaning. Her careful preparation was not for him. She had worn the dress for the man she loved.

Something must have shown in his face for she laid her hand on his arm. "Are you well?"

"I was just thinking I should have brought my dueling pistols." Pride lifted the corners of his mouth into a hollow smile. "No doubt all your would-be admirers will want to fight."

A pleased flush tinted her cheeks. "I feel silly in this dress. I'm likely to laugh if I catch sight of myself in the mirror."

From where she stood, her arm almost brushing his, Alec could see the tantalizing rise of her breasts above the bodice. The gown moved with her every breath, a gleam of gold playing across the bronze that drew the eye. Every satiny inch of the sinuous silk begged to be touched. He wanted to slide it up her long, smooth legs, across the luscious curve of her hip and to her narrow waist. He wanted to free her breasts from the bodice and tease them into delicious submission.

He cleared his throat. "No one will laugh, Julia. You look beautiful."

Her eyes widened in surprise and he cursed himself

for being a fool. She didn't wish to hear such drivel from him. He was saved by Lucien's arrival.

"Good God," the duke murmured, stopping in front of Julia. He lifted his quizzing glass and regarded her from bronze feather to slippered feet. "Behold, the moth has become a butterfly."

Julia frowned. "Moths don't become butterflies, Wexford. Caterpillars become butterflies."

His lips twitched and he sent an amused glance toward Alec before bowing. "I beg your pardon, Lady Hunterston. It just seemed rude to call you a caterpillar."

"It was rude to call me a moth, too. Disgusting creatures! One ate a hole in my favorite bonnet last winter."

He chuckled. "Though you look an angel, you are still very much our Julia. I am only surprised Alec will allow you to wear such, ah, fashionable attire, lovely though it is."

Alec scowled at his friend's levity. "It wasn't my idea."

"Lucien, pray do not tease Alec. It was Aunt Maddie's idea. It is either this, or Alec and I can just go home and wait for the executors to take all the money."

Lucien grinned. "I find it hard to imagine you sitting at home and waiting on anything."

Her chin squared in a way that made Alec want to kiss her until she flushed with passion. He leaned forward to murmur in her ear, "You are the most damnable woman, do you know that?"

"So I've heard," she replied, casting him a startled glance before coloring an adorable pink.

Lucien cleared his throat. "Pardon me. We should move out of the entryway. People are starting to stare." He took Julia's arm and led her toward the receiving line. "May I claim the first dance?"

Alec tucked Julia's hand into the crook of his arm, pulling her from Lucien's side. "The first dance is mine."

The Dowager greeted them with telling enthusiasm, thanking Julia loudly for her assistance in planning the ball and auction. Two couples who had maintained a frosty silence behind them visibly thawed at the effusive reception, and even stopped to speak with Julia before entering the ballroom. Alec caught her triumphant look and smiled, sharing her excitement as they followed Lucien.

If the foyer had looked impressive, the ballroom was magnificent. Long swaths of watered silk hung from the ceiling and fastened to the wall with gold cords before collecting on the floor in jewel-toned puddles. Each fastening was adorned with bouquets of gold flowers. The silk began at the far wall as a pale lavender and gradually darkened to midnight, where the golden twinkle of hundreds of candles gave the impression of sunset darkening to a starlit night.

The music swelled over the room and people danced by, swirling gowns of every color imaginable against an army of broad shoulders and black coats. Nodding to Lucien, Alec held out his hand and swept Julia onto the floor. It was difficult to hold her and not ask her about Nick, but he managed, savoring instead the feel of her in his arms, the warmth of her hand in his.

All too soon, it was over and the music ended. Lucien arrived to claim his dance. Alec watched them twirl away, every eye upon them.

By the time supper had finished, Alec had begun to feel a spark of hope. Though some slights were inevitable, it quickly became obvious that Julia had made friends in high places. She had won the rare approval of the established matrons, and was obviously a darling of both Lady Birlington as well as the Dowager Duchess of Roth.

His relief was short lived, however, when he saw the wife of one of the executors sidling up to Julia. Alec quickly headed the woman off, inquiring after her husband and murmuring the proper sympathies when she explained how her husband had succumbed to a putrid sore throat.

Maneuvering the lady into the refreshment room, Alec abandoned her to the care of the Dowager Duchess, who was entertaining anyone who would listen with the latest tales of her unruly page, an urchin who bore a shocking resemblance to her late husband. Feeling as if he had just escaped a hangman's noose, Alec made his way back to the ballroom.

Lucien fell into step beside him. "Nick just arrived."

"Where is he?" Alec asked grimly, certain he would find him languishing over Julia in some secluded corner.

"He went to the card room." Lucien looked across the room to where the objects for the auction were being set out. "I wanted to see Bentham's portrait, but he refuses to allow it be uncovered until the auction begins."

"Oh?" Alec listened with but half an ear as he looked over the crowd, trying to find a bronze plume and a delectable pair of bared shoulders.

Edmund came up, wiping his brow with his handkerchief. "Whatever you do, don't agree to dance with Miss Hepperdon."

Lucien's mouth quirked. "The redhead?"

"Lud, yes," said Edmund with a dark look. "She don't look it, but she's as strong as a horse. She swung me across the room on one of the turns. Bumped me right into Patterson and his wife. Deuced embarrassing." His gaze fell on the dais. "I say, have either of you seen Bentham's painting of Julia? Everyone is agog to see it."

Alec winced. "Damn. I had forgotten that."

"Don't look so grim," Lucien said. "Julia is to be congratulated. Bentham is notoriously selective in choosing his subjects."

Though Lucien was right, Alec did not reply. Every

time he turned around there was yet another man in Julia's life.

It was galling.

A chime rang, signaling the beginning of the auction. The Dowager made a gracious speech about how the charities would benefit, then stepped aside to allow Lord Dunston to proceed with the first item. With a flurry of bids, the auction began.

Alec finally located Julia standing by the dais with Lady Birlington and the Dowager. Maddie, resplendent in orange and green, wore a red wig teased into a wild spate of curls. Her bold coloring made Julia appear that much more elegant.

Relieved that Nick was nowhere in sight, Alec made to move through the crowd toward Julia when Edmund choked, his face an alarming red.

Alec frowned. "Good God, what is it?"

"Nothing. Choked on my wine."

"Your glass is empty."

"Oh." Edmund eyed his empty glass as if it had suddenly appeared in his hand. "Oh, well, yes. I was, uhm, holding a swallow in my mouth."

"Why on earth would you do that?"

"It, ah, warms it and, uhm, makes it . . . sweeter. And . . . more fragrant."

Lucien shook his head. "It's only a quarter past ten, Edmund, and already you are ape-drunk."

"I am not," protested Edmund. He leaned toward Lucien and gave an extensive series of winks and head bobs.

"Confound it, what is wrong with you?" asked Lucien.

Edmund grasped his hair with both hands. "Damn it, Luce! I never met a more thick-headed—" He stopped when he caught Alec's gaze. "There you are! Come and play a hand of whist with me! Do you good to get some air. Too hot in here."

Alec tried to shake himself free of Edmund's insistent hold. The hum of the crowd increased as bids were called in furious order. "Not now."

"But I need you in the card room," said Edmund desperately, clutching Alec's arm even tighter.

"What for?"

"Money. End of the quarter and my pockets are to let. Devilish thing to happen, but I forgot my wallet, too."

Alec scowled and pulled out his wallet, handing Edmund a pile of bills. "Here. Now go."

"That won't do." Edmund flushed, a thoroughly miserable look on his plump face. "Not enough. Maybe you should return home and fetch some more."

"Damn it, Edmund! What are you about?" Beside him, Alec heard Lucien give a startled exclamation. "What is it?"

Lucien didn't answer, but stared at the next item presented for bidding. There, standing on an easel, was Bentham's portrait of Julia.

Alec's throat went dry.

Bentham had painted Julia reclining on a couch amidst a sea of blue silk. Muck, improbably dressed as Cupid, leaned against a footstool and stared up at her with adoring eyes. A fan partly covered her face, though there was no mistaking her green eyes or the delicate arch of her sable brows. Alec's gaze drifted past the fan and beyond, his hands clenching into fists as he realized what had so shocked Lucien.

Bentham had painted Julia nude.

Chapter 28

J ulia leaned forward and squinted at the portrait. "I thought Bentham was going to paint *me*."

"It *is* you," Maddie snapped, her parchment skin flushed an unbecoming red. "That scoundrel painted you in the nude."

Squinting again, Julia could barely make out the flesh-toned figure reclined on the couch. As soon as she saw the green eyes peering over the fan, she started. "Heavens!" She glanced around at the sea of blurry faces. "Perhaps no one will notice."

"How could a person not notice *that*? A few more inches and it would be life sized." Even as Maddie spoke, people were beginning to point. "Demme. There's nothing for it but a forward attack."

The old woman peered through the crowd, finally focusing on the narrow-shouldered young man beside Therese. "You!" she called, thumping her cane. "What is the meaning of this?"

Bentham glanced uncertainly at Therese, then cleared his throat and said in a loud voice, "Lady Hunterston requested that I paint her in the nude. I protested, of course, but the beauty of the composition was such that I was powerless to demur."

Julia had never heard such obvious drivel in her entire

331

life. A fine painter Bentham might be, but as an actor, he was a dismal failure. Even Desiree, a depressing example of thespian ability, would have pronounced the lines with more finesse. Unfortunately, Bentham's allegation was so startling Julia doubted anyone but herself noticed anything amiss. Someone other than the dreamy-eyed artist had to be behind this newest effort to cause a scandal.

Julia's gaze narrowed on Therese. Her cousin glowed. Her perfect rosebud mouth curved in a smug grin, and she could not have appeared more pleased.

Maddie scowled. "I hope Bentham knows what he's gotten himself into. Hunterston looks ready to split someone open."

Alec stood not far from the dais, his face a frozen mask of anger. He stared at Bentham as if trying to decide which bone to break first. Julia stiffened her resolve at the sight. If she didn't act soon, the whole place would erupt.

She walked up to the painting and peered closely. "A pity it doesn't look like me."

Bentham's face reddened. "Of course it looks like you."

"The face is mine, that's true." She looked down at her bosom where it pressed against the bronze silk, then returned her gaze to the painting's rounded, more robust charms. "Unfortunately, the rest is less than accurate. Too bad. I always wished I were a bit more curved."

The Dowager Duchess bent to peer at the painting. "Very true, Lady Hunterston. And you are certainly thinner than this woman." She straightened, her brows arched high. "It appears Bentham has mistakenly placed your head on someone else's body."

Bentham started to protest, but a sudden move from Alec made him retreat a hasty step. Before Alec could follow, Lucien placed a restraining hand on his arm.

Lady Birlington peered over Julia's shoulder. "Humph. Missed your feet, too. Don't know who he painted, but they have tiny feet." She glared around the room. "All women with big bosoms and tiny feet must step forward immediately."

A wave of laughter arose, during which a dashing young blade called out, "By all means, Lady Birlington, let them come to me for examination."

The tension dissipated from the room as the laughter subsided. Julia heaved a tiny sigh of relief and leaned toward the picture once again until her nose almost touched the canvas. "There's a mole, too. Right here on her hip. I don't have one of those. The only person I know who has a mole there is—" She halted, her color rising. She cast a swift glance at Therese. "*Well.*"

Had she shouted her suspicions aloud, they could not have been clearer.

Edmund stared at Therese, his eyes wide. "And she ain't even married." His voice carried all too clearly.

Therese paled. "It is not me. Any fool can see that it is Julia."

Bentham took an impulsive step forward. "Lady Hunterston is—"

"Bentham!" Maddie's voice rang out. "Do you wish me to bring this disgraceful episode to the ears of your mother?"

The young man blanched and shot a desperate glance at Therese. But she was no longer attending him, her gaze fixed on Julia.

"Well?" asked Maddie in a testy voice. "Do you or don't you? I'm sure Lucinda would be very interested to hear of your shameful antics while she is in the country."

"No! No, there is no need." Bentham looked around the room, but not one friendly face turned his way. He reached an impulsive hand toward Therese, but she turned away, jerking her arm from his grasp.

Bentham stared after her, stark misery in his pale blue eyes. Hands clenched into fists, he turned to the Dowager and made a jerky bow. "Your Grace, I will take my leave of you now. I apologize for any harm my mistake has caused."

Julia felt an instant of pity. Dreamy-eyed and weak-chinned, he'd stood no chance against Therese's beauty.

The Dowager waved him on. "Of course, of course." Bentham bowed and left the room, casting one last, anguished glance at Therese.

"This certainly has been interesting," said the Dowager. She regarded the painting critically. "Perhaps I should purchase it for my drawing room, whoever it is."

"Two hundred pounds," Alec ground out.

Julia blinked. "But it isn't even me!"

"*Two hundred pounds*," he repeated, his glance dismissing her.

She knew it was pride that made him offer, yet she couldn't help but be relieved. The thought of the portrait hanging in someone else's home, a constant topic of countless dinner conversations, made her queasy.

The Dowager nodded. "Very proper, Lord Hunterston. The eyes do bear a shocking resemblance to your wife's. I won't even bid against you. You may have the portrait with my blessing."

From the other side of the room came Nick's lazy drawl. "Three hundred pounds."

The Dowager gawked. "Goodness!"

Alec bit off a muffled curse. "Four hundred."

Oblivious to the growing tension, the Dowager clapped. "Well done, Hunterston. I knew you loved the arts."

Nick strolled forward, stopping to deliver a mocking bow to Julia. One of his eyes sported a deep bruise, no doubt a trophy from his argument with Alec at White's the previous night. "Your servant, Cousin."

Julia gave him the smallest nod possible. He might or

might not have planned this debacle, but she had no doubt he was enjoying it to the fullest.

Smiling, he turned to the Dowager. "I believe Alec has discovered he loves the arts far more than he thought possible. Unfortunately for him, I share a similar affection."

"*Five* hundred." Alec glared.

Nick laughed gently. "You have just bid against yourself."

Alec did not flinch. "*Six* hundred."

A ripple of amazement spread through the crowd. Julia had never seen Alec so furiously intense. Arms crossed, feet planted apart, he gave the impression of tightly coiled temper ready to leap into action.

"My, my. So determined," murmured Nick. He assessed Alec for a moment. "But I'm afraid I cannot allow such a rare and beautiful opportunity to pass." He turned to the painting and his quizzing glass lingered an indecent time on the curve of the hips. "I must have it for my bedchamber. *Eight* hundred."

Silence reigned as all eyes turned to Alec. "One thousand pounds."

Even Julia gaped, but Alec stood impervious, his furious gaze locked with Nick's.

The Dowager swept forward. "How generous of you to donate so freely to our charity auction, Lord Hunterston. Surely Lord Bridgeton will concede your right to own such a beautiful painting."

Flicking an imaginary piece of lint from his cuff, Nick shrugged. "It is only a painting."

With a gracious nod, the Dowager signaled Lord Dunston to proceed with the next item. And though people showed an annoying tendency to watch Alec and Nick, the bidding resumed once more.

Julia almost sighed her relief aloud when Nick finally lost interest in the proceedings and melted into the crowd.

The auction went on for another hour, but Julia was only aware of Alec's brooding presence behind her. Discourse was impossible with so many people surrounding them, so Julia was thankful when the last bid was recorded.

When the musicians struck up a waltz at the Dowager's signal, Alec held out his hand and led Julia into the dance. The instant they could speak without being overheard, he shot her a hard glance and pulled her close. "I should strangle Nick for his insolence."

"I'm not convinced your cousin had anything to do with the portrait."

Alec's mouth thinned. "How can you say that? He planned the entire thing."

"No, he took advantage of the situation. It appeared to me as if Therese had orchestrated the whole thing. I have a feeling he was just as surprised as you."

"I am well aware of your *feelings*, madam." Alec's hand tightened on hers. "I do not care for them."

A mortified blush ran from her ears all the way to her toes. He rejected her love so easily, without hesitation. Struggling to swallow the hurt, she tried to increase the distance between them.

His grip tightened even more and he crushed her against him, impervious to the dancers swirling about them, watching and whispering. "Are you so anxious to be rid of me, love? Perhaps you would rather be dancing with Nick?"

All of the day's disastrous events swelled into anger. Anger with Nick and Therese for plotting against her, anger with the people who had stood by and watched her public embarrassment with avid attention, anger with Alec for mocking the one thing she had left—her love for him.

Squaring her chin, she stared at him. "At least Nick would have the good manners not to maul me on the dance floor."

For an instant his face froze, then he abruptly ceased dancing. "If that is the way you feel, madam, then I will no longer burden you with my presence." Without another word, he dropped her hand, turned on his heel and made his way through the ballroom.

Julia stood alone. Pitying stares and sly smiles surged past as the dancers feasted on her humiliation. How could Alec treat her so? She steeled herself not to betray any emotion as she made her way through the horde of twirling couples.

Despite her best intentions, her emotions clogged her throat and blurred her sight. Deeply weary and strung as thin as a cobweb, she had only sheer determination to hold back her tears as she struggled to the edge of the floor.

Suddenly Nick stood before her, taking her hand and bowing. "How kind of Alec, to remember you promised me this dance." His gloved hand closed warmly over hers as his arm encircled her waist. "Shall we?"

Julia hesitated, but he persisted, murmuring, "Come, Julia. Show them you are not to be so cavalierly treated."

She managed a jerky nod and allowed Nick to swirl her back into the pattern of the dance, her thoughts settling into a muddle of hurt and anger.

"Everyone is watching you, my dear," Nick said. "You must smile if you wish to disappoint the curiosity seekers."

"Why would you care? I'm surprised you are even dancing with me, especially after Alec popped your cork at White's."

A flash of anger tightened his features before retreating behind a polished smile. "Last night was a simple disagreement, nothing more." His hand gently squeezed hers. "I do not hold Alec's faults against you, my dear. I think of you as very . . . separate people."

Julia had to bite her lip to keep it from quivering. "You still haven't told me why you are helping me now,

Nick. I don't mean to be rude, but I don't trust you."

He laughed. "Perhaps I suffer from the same quixotic impulses that plague my cousin. But it does not matter. The important thing is that you do not allow anyone to suspect you were harmed by Alec's rudeness."

Julia lifted her chin. "I don't care what anyone thinks about me."

"Bravo, Cousin. That is exactly the attitude we must project. Suppose we discuss something more near and dear to your heart. Tell me, how does your urchin progress? I notice you did not bring him with you tonight."

"He has a slight cough." Julia relaxed slightly, thinking of Muck's fuzzy smile as he drifted off to sleep, one of Mrs. Winston's famous mustard plasters warming his chest.

"And the lovely Desiree?"

Julia frowned. "I've been meaning to speak with you about that. You knew she would be recognized."

"Oh, I counted on it." His hand tightened on hers, but he did not attempt to close the space between them. "You would be wise to cultivate my favor, Julia. Once I have the fortune, I might grant some funds for your projects."

"Oh?' she asked, all polite disbelief.

His mouth curved in an indolent smile. "In exchange, of course, for certain favors."

"Don't be too sure you are getting the fortune, Nick. Alec and I have a meeting with the executors tomorrow. Once we explain everything, they will realize none of this has been our fault." At least, that's what she hoped would happen. Perhaps she could convince some of the members of the Society to speak with the executors on their behalf.

Nick's smug voice cut through her thoughts. "I fear it will do little good. Though I did not plan tonight's entertainment, it was the final nail in a very well-built coffin."

"Once the executors hear about your part in this, they will not allow you near the money, either."

"Ah, but you don't know them as I do. My grandfather became a strict, stern man in his dotage. He surrounded himself with philanthropists with no taste for life and less understanding of the misfortunes of it." Nick shrugged. "They will be especially offended to read the newspaper article suggesting you had less than pure motives in pursuing charity work."

"I can't believe they would heed such drivel. I will speak with them myself and explain everything."

"Once word of the painting reaches their ears, I would be very surprised if they allowed you to speak at all."

Thankfully, the dance ended before Julia had to respond. Her face ached from maintaining the fake smile. "Thank you for coming to my rescue, Nick. Now, if you'll excuse me, I must find Aunt Maddie."

His gaze went past her, a flicker of surprise crossing his face just as a hand touched her arm.

Julia turned to find Lady Burton beside her. The woman's proud face softened slightly. "Lady Hunterston, I was hoping to catch you this evening. Lord Burton and I wanted to invite you and Lord Hunterston to visit us at Burton Park this fall when the leaves change."

Lady Burton spoke loudly, much louder than necessary. Julia glanced about and found others marking their conversation. With a flush of gratitude, she smiled. "Lord Burton has spoken many times of the park and how beautiful it is. We would love to attend."

"Excellent." Lady Burton patted Julia's hand and smiled, her gray eyes twinkling. "He'll be pleased to hear you will be joining us." Nodding pleasantly, she left on the arm of her nephew.

Julia turned to look for Lady Birlington and Nick caught her arm. "Tell me, Cousin, do you have much discourse with Lord and Lady Burton?"

Surprised, Julia shook off his hand. "Some. Her husband is one of the members of the Society. I spoke with Lady Burton today for the first time, though I must say she has been excessively kind."

A faint crease appeared between his brows. "Has she?"

Julia searched the crowd, her heart pounding every time she saw a dark head rise above the crowd, though none proved to be her recalcitrant husband.

Nick placed her hand in the crook of his arm and led her to a chair. "If you are looking for Alec, he disappeared into the game room just as our waltz ended."

"I wasn't looking for anyone," she said stiffly, hoping Alec had seen her dancing with his cousin. It would serve Alec right if she hung on Nick's arm for the rest of the evening.

"Would you like some refreshment, Julia? At least allow me to make amends by procuring a glass of ratafia for your enjoyment." He offered a rueful smile that for a moment made her think of Alec. "It is all I ask."

Julia sighed. She supposed it would not hurt to sit another few minutes. Alec was nowhere to be seen and she had caught a glimpse of Lady Birlington deep in conversation with the Dowager. "Oh, very well. I'd prefer sherry, though."

He bowed. "As you wish, my dear. When I return, we will toast the executors and their making the best choice possible." With a final smile, he disappeared in the direction of the refreshment room.

Tonight had been a total waste, Julia thought. Despite its promising beginning, everything had gone wrong. There was no reason to stay. She would seek out Aunt Maddie, make her excuses, and bring this painful evening to an end.

Nick returned and handed her a glass. "There was no sherry to be had, so I was forced to concede to the ratafia, after all."

She took a sip and grimaced. "Too sweet."

"Drink it nonetheless. We must get some color back into those cheeks." He lifted a hand to her face but Julia pulled away.

"Mind yourself, Nick. We are in public."

"And if we were in private?"

"You'd have two black eyes instead of one," she said promptly, taking another swallow. The quicker she emptied her glass, the quicker she could escape.

Nick chuckled. "You never rattle, do you?"

Julia ignored him and took another sip of the ratafia. For the first time since this morning, she felt calm and relaxed, as if she had no cares, no concerns. Perhaps she should go in search of Alec and tell him how silly their argument was.

But no. Alec didn't want her.

The thought brought an unexpected flood of tears. She took a swift drink to wash away the lump that lodged in her throat. There was less than a swallow left, the last mouthful unexpectedly bitter. Julia shivered.

Nick leaned forward, his chair much too close. "I have been meaning to tell you how lovely you look without those infernal spectacles."

Though his forwardness irked her, a pleasant feeling of lassitude washed all negative thoughts away. "I wish I'd worn them tonight. I almost didn't realize that picture was of me."

"I was amazed at how quickly you dispatched Therese." Nick's voice came close to her ear, his arm brushing her shoulder. "Rarely have I had such a worthy adversary." He lifted her hand and placed a kiss on her wrist.

Julia knew she should retrieve her hand, but her arm seemed laden with an invisible weight. She blinked fuzzily and watched with almost detached interest as the ratafia glass slipped from her other hand.

Nick caught it as it fell. "Perhaps you need some fresh air, my dear."

Yes, that was what she needed. Fresh air to blow away the cobwebs that had descended over her brain. Julia stood and almost stumbled, her knees buckling beneath her. Nick grasped her arm and held her upright, his other arm slipping about her waist.

Julia leaned against him. "It's so hot in here. I can't breathe."

"Hold onto me. We don't have far to go."

She was vaguely aware that he led her toward the balcony. It seemed as if the ballroom had narrowed into a long, thin tunnel of blue. Faces peered at her, whispers echoed like shouts. Julia concentrated on placing one heavy foot in front of the other.

Finally, after what seemed like an hour, they reached the balcony and the cool night air blew across her, chilling her through the thin silk. But the cobwebs did not go away. Instead, they increased until she was forced to lean against Nick, all her efforts focused on staying upright.

The world tilted first one way, then the other. "Good God. What's wrong with me?" Her words sounded slurred to her own ears.

His breath stirred the hair at her forehead, his arms tight about her. "Nothing but a touch of laudanum."

Somewhere far away, the words sounded an alarm. But Julia didn't have the energy to do more than mumble a protest.

"Come, Julia," he murmured against her hair. "We have only a little further to go." He placed an arm about her and half led her, half carried her into the garden and down a path. At some point they reached a coach, the jangle of the traces loud in the silence. The lights from the house seemed far, far away. Nick spoke a quiet command to his coachman.

"Nick," said a sharp voice from the direction of the garden. "What are you doing here?"

Julia focused on the silver figure and made out Therese's furious face.

"I am taking my cousin home," he said calmly as if discussing the weather or the placement of a cravat pin. "She is not feeling well."

Therese examined Julia. "She is drunk!"

He chuckled and stroked Julia's hair with a strangely gentle gesture. "Go away, Therese. I have everything well in hand."

"It looks like it," she sneered. "What are you going to do with her?"

Nick shrugged, the movement causing Julia's cheek to rub against his coat. He turned to his coachman who stood silently waiting. "Open the door."

"Yes, my lord."

The door opened and Nick lifted Julia onto the seat. She didn't even have the strength to hold her head upright, but let it loll against the squabs. In the darkness, the voices outside the coach seemed even louder, echoing inside her head with painful clarity.

"If you take her with you, I will tell everyone what you have done."

"Tell whomever you like, Therese. I will be on my way to Langley before you even reach the ballroom."

Therese unleashed a furious screech. "Langley? That's where we first—"

"Spare me your maudlin memories. My hunting box will be perfect. It is private, nestled away where no one will find us."

A sob rose in the night, followed by another. "Damn you, Nick. You cannot treat me this way! After all I did!"

He sighed. "I suppose you are talking about that little trick with the portrait. It was overdone, but effective.

Just how did you manage to convince a coward like Bentham to put himself at such risk?"

The sobs ceased abruptly. "That is no concern of yours."

"Ah, but I think it is," Nick said in a horrifyingly quiet tone.

"Y-you promised to marry *me*."

"No, my dear. That is an illusion you created." There was a pause before he added, "Besides, I have found other, more delectable prey."

Julia felt his hand reach through the darkness to caress her cheek. For an instant she was glad she was too drugged to feel anything more than distracted revulsion, for she would surely have wretched.

Therese shrieked. The unmistakable sound of a scuffle followed, only to end with the crack of a harsh slap. Hysterical sobbing filled the night.

Nick called to his footman. "Lady Frant has had too much to drink. Take her back to the ballroom and deliver her to her mother."

Without waiting to see if his orders were obeyed, he swung into the coach beside Julia and settled her in his lap, tucking her in with a cloak as if she were a child.

All too soon, the cocoon of warmth, combined with the swaying motion of the coach, sent Julia tumbling helplessly into a black, dreamless sleep.

Chapter 29

"There you are." Lucien's voice came from the balcony steps.

Alec turned from where he had been leaning against a tree, fighting for a semblance of control. "What do you want?" The cool bubbling of the fountain had done much to soothe his anger, but not the vast ache that had taken the place of his heart.

Lucien pulled out a cheroot and lit it, his eyes hard in the flare of light. "What in the hell were you doing, to leave Julia like that?"

Alec set his jaw. "I was angry." Angry, furious, jealous . . . hell, he'd experienced more emotions this evening than he'd realized he possessed. And all because of the unavoidable fact that his wife loved another. The thought weighted his shoulders like a sack of stone.

Lucien made a sound of disgust. "Oh, yes. And you have such reason to be angry. Your wife has taken in a child, saved a woman destined for ruin, transformed your household into a living, breathing home, and squandered your funds on charity. I'm surprised you aren't calling for her head on a platter."

"You don't know the half of it. She's incorrigible, impertinent and—"

"You love her."

The ache swelled into something more and he had to swallow before he could speak. "Julia doesn't believe Nick had anything to do with this latest debacle."

Lucien shrugged. "She wouldn't. In fact, I'm surprised she hasn't found him a position in your house. He'd make a hell of a butler if you could keep him from the liquor cabinet."

"This is not a laughing matter!"

"I don't think it is," Lucien said shortly. "If you had seen Julia's face when you left her in the middle of the dance floor, you would agree."

Remorse ripped at his tenuous control, but Alec subdued it. He hadn't meant to cause her pain, but he seemed unable to look at her without experiencing the agonizing burn of jealousy. And that, he admitted, was what had made him stalk from the dance floor like the cad he was.

Alec raked a hand through his hair, emptiness holding his heart in an icy grip. All his life he'd been selfish and intemperate, caught up in the pursuit of empty pleasures until he'd met a spirited, no-nonsense American reformer who believed she could change the world. And she had changed the world—his world. Now, he could no longer imagine life without her and the realization frightened him to death.

A pain akin to fire lanced through him. He loved Julia. There was no denying it any longer. But . . . did she love him? Was it even possible after the way he'd treated her? Or had Nick managed to convince Julia, with her boundless passion, that he could offer her more than her own foolish husband?

Alec fisted his hands and stared into the darkness.

From behind him, Lucien asked, "Alec, you must do something to right this."

Alec roused himself with an effort. "There's nothing to do. I lost my temper. I've been so fixated on winning the inheritance, keeping it from Nick that I didn't see— "He rubbed a hand over his face. "I've been a fool, Lucien. A damned fool."

"We agree on that, at least," Lucien said in a grim voice. "Your grandfather would have been pleased beyond thought to know you were in love with someone other than yourself. I'm not sure that isn't what he had in mind to begin with."

Was that possible? The conditions of the will had seemed improbable, bizarre even. But frankly, it didn't matter. At the moment, all he could think about was the fact that his wife loved another man.

Lucien sighed. "I know you promised your grandfather you would try to keep the fortune from Nick, but . . . isn't Julia more important than the money?"

Julia was more important than everything. "Luce, she . . . she doesn't want me." The words burned his throat, but he choked them out anyway. "She wants Nick."

Lucien frowned. "Bloody hell."

"I know. But the signs are all there. He's forever around and she defends him every chance she gets. Even tonight, she said Nick didn't even know about the portrait, that it was all Therese's doing."

Lucien dropped to a bench by the fountain, his brow

lowered. After a moment, he said, "Alec, she could be right. Therese holds sway over Bentham, not Nick. Furthermore—"

One of the bushes sprang to life, the leaves rustling violently. Edmund stumbled into the clearing. "Thank God you are here, Alec!" The younger man's voice held an unmistakable note of panic. "Julia's disappeared with Nick. Aunt Maddie said for you to come at once."

The world spun crazily for one mad moment. Alec was running before he knew it, pounding down the pathway and bursting into the ballroom. Without a word to those he pushed aside, he made his way to Lady Birlington.

"Demme, Hunterston," she hissed when he reached her. "Didn't that silly nephew of mine tell you not to make a scene?"

"Where is she?"

Maddie's chin quivered and, for the first time since Alec had known her, she appeared all of her seventy years. Clenching her gnarled hand about the cane, she gathered herself and scowled through her tears. "We don't know. Nick escorted her to the balcony ten minutes ago or longer."

Edmund added, "They were mighty chummy, too. He had his arm about her waist and she was leaning against him like—"

Maddie thumped her cane near enough to Edmund's foot that he jumped. "Not another word! I won't have my own family telling tales!"

"But Aunt Maddie, I saw them myself! Julia walked right by me and didn't even say a word! She looked—"

Alec whirled on Maddie. "Damn it, why didn't you stop them?"

The brilliant blue eyes sparkled. "Why didn't *you* stop

them? She's *your* wife!" Maddie sniffed, her lips quivered. "I would have stopped them if I could, but I'm not as young as I once was. By the time I got to the balcony, they were gone."

"And then Therese—" Edmund stopped and turned a bright red. "But no one believed her."

"Believed what?"

Edmund eyed Maddie's cane. "Not sayin'. Would sound bad and m'aunt says—"

Alec curled his fist in Edmund's lapels and lifted him up on his toes. "No one believed *what*?"

Edmund gulped and began talking so fast his words tripped over one another. "Th-Therese burst into the ball-room screeching th-that Nick had lied to her, p-promised to marry her. She was hysterical, s-sobbing th-that he'd stolen Julia away to his hunting l-lodge." Edmund's hand gripped Alec's wrists. "That's a-all she said, Alec. I swear."

Suddenly aware of the look of panic on Edmund's face, Alec loosened his grip. "I'm sorry."

"No need to apologize." Edmund straightened his cra-vat. "All to pieces, worrying about Julia. I perfectly under-stand."

Lucien quirked a brow. "Do you think Therese was telling the truth?"

Edmund nodded. "Bound to be. Made a regular cake of herself, crying all over the place." He leaned forward and said earnestly, "Alec, I think it's a trap. Nick knows you will come after her. He had to know Therese would tell, too. She's not very circumspect."

Alec gave a cool nod though his heart slammed against his ribs in a furious beat. "Then he's won one battle." He turned to call for his carriage, but Lucien caught his arm.

"You should know something. I heard Grenville say just this evening that Nick was on the verge of ruin. He is desperate and will do whatever he must to get the fortune."

Alec shook off the restraining hand. "I don't have a choice." All that mattered was Julia. He prayed he would not be too late.

Julia awoke slowly, her mouth dry and bitter, her head aching furiously.

"I was beginning to think you would never awaken."

She blinked toward Nick's voice. His large form loomed before her, his golden hair lit by firelight. She struggled to sit upright on a small settee, hampered by her gown which had twisted about her ankles.

"Don't try to move too swiftly," he said. "It takes some time for the effects of the laudanum to wear off."

Laudanum. Memories flooded back and with it came all of the fear she had been too drugged to feel. Heart pounding in her throat, Julia rested her head against the back of the settee. *Before I do anything, I must regain my wits.*

Accordingly, she took a long, slow breath and examined the room. Low and wide, it was decorated in masculine tones, with heavy, dark furniture flanked by a huge, stone fireplace. "Where are we?"

Nick made an expansive gesture. "Welcome to my private hunting box. The only thing my mother ever left me worth possessing."

"It's very nice." Her voice creaked like the hinge on an old door and she placed a hand to her throat.

A frown flickered across his face. He crossed to the table and filled a cup from a pitcher. "Here, drink this."

She regarded it with suspicion but made no move to take it. "What is it?"

Nick smiled and took a deep drink from the cup before offering it to her again. "Only water. Nothing more, I assure you."

Julia took the cup, her hand trembling with even that small effort. "It was very nice of your mother to leave you such a pleasant retreat."

"It once belonged to an elderly nobleman. I often wonder how many times my mother serviced him in order to gain it. She was a whore, you know."

He said it in the most commonplace of voices, but Julia saw the flash of emotion in his blue eyes. In a way, Nick was very like the children from the Society. Hurt repeatedly, they became tough and rebellious, ready to handle life's worst and often seeking out that very thing as if to test themselves. "It is still very nice she left it to you."

Nick shrugged and looked around the room. "It was all she had to give." His gaze returned to Julia. "But we are not here to speak of my mother."

"Oh?" Julia pushed her hair back from her face. It had long since fallen from the pins and streamed over her shoulders in a tangled mess. "Why are we here?"

His hooded gaze followed her every move. "Perhaps I have decided I care nothing about the fortune and want only you."

Julia raised her brows in polite disbelief.

Nick chuckled. "Always the pragmatist, aren't you? But you are correct. No woman can outshine seventy thousand pounds a year."

"Not many men, either." Though Alec had managed to. He was worth much, much more. Her throat tightened as she recalled his anger at the ball. *God, please, don't let that be our last conversation ever. I have so much to tell him, so many things to explain and—No. I can't think about this now. It hurts too much.* She smoothed her skirts over her knees, her palms damp. "You . . . you know Alec will find us." Provided, of course, he chose to come after her.

"Oh, I am counting on it." Nick leaned an arm on the mantle, picked up the iron poker, and stirred the flames to a higher level. "I would be most disappointed if he did not."

Realization dawned. "You want him to miss the meeting with the executors."

He smiled.

"You had this planned all along!"

"My only worry was how to lure you away from Alec long enough to give you the ratafia. Then you two staged that brilliant row in the middle of the dance floor. Heaven, shall we say, has smiled on this venture."

Though Julia felt better by the minute, her head still throbbed a relentless beat. "Heaven is not smiling now."

"Ah, but it is. Imagine how it will look to the executors: Alec will chase after his wife who has, to all intents, run off with another man, while they meet to discuss whether he has stayed free of scandal. The answer should be obvious, even to that bunch of ninnies." His smile widened. "I have destroyed any influence you may have had with the executors. Now, they will think you an adulteress and worse."

She sniffed. "I've never even met the executors."

Nick's gaze flickered, an odd smile on his lips. "I beg to differ."

"What do you m—"

"But let us move on to the second act, shall we? We have already closed the curtain on the first, exciting as it was."

"What is the second act?"

"It will be brilliant, I assure you." Nick replaced the poker and came to stand near her, his handsome face alight with true amusement. "Alec will come breathing the fire of the righteous and I . . ." Nick's smile chilled her. He crossed to a small table and picked up an elaborate box. The carved lid lifted to display a set of dueling pistols. "Alec and I have a score to settle. One long overdue."

Cold fear clutched her stomach. "What would that solve?"

"Everything." He shut the box carefully, his pale hand lingering on the lid and the gleaming mother of pearl inlay. "When my esteemed cousin arrives, he will have no choice but to fight me." Nick slid his hand over the box with an almost loving gesture. "I have never lost a duel."

Julia swallowed at his calm, certain voice. "Never?"

"Not once."

"You cannot have fought very many, then."

He quirked a brow. "Dueling is much more accepted on the continent. I fought my first one when I was only thirteen."

Julia tried to swallow, but couldn't. "So young."

"Yes. He insulted my mother, called her a whore." Nick shrugged. "Sometimes the truth is so unpalatable that it should never be said aloud."

She wet her dry lips, the elaborate box seeming more menacing with every word Nick spoke. "Alec will not fight you. I-I cannot imagine he would agree to such foolishness."

"How can he refuse? I left the ball with his willing wife." Nick's smile turned cruel. "Thanks to you, Alec will have no choice."

Julia's heart sank. She could picture how she must have looked, leaving the ballroom, Nick's arm about her waist. Her cheeks burned at the thought. Tears threatened, but she held them at bay. There would be plenty of time for that once this drama was played out. She had forever to regret what would never be. Right now, she had to think. "Nick, don't do this. I know, in your heart, you don't want to hurt anyone."

His smile slipped. "You know nothing about my heart."

"But I do. I-I've spoken to you. Listened to you. You might not care about many people, but I think you once cared for your mother. That means something. And I think you must have cared what your grandfather thought too and—"

"Enough!" he said harshly, his expression shuttered. His mouth was white with anger. "I didn't bring you here to listen to your theories on reforming lost souls, especially mine. There are more amusing ways to while away the time."

Before she knew what he was about, he was beside her on the settee. His arm rested along the back, his fingers brushing against her shoulder in a suggestive manner. His broad shoulders blocked the warmth of the fire. Julia averted her gaze and glanced around the room. There had to be some safe topic of conversation that would enthrall him until she could figure a way out of this mess.

Her gaze fell on the table, covered with a cold repast. "Perhaps we should eat."

He took one of her hands in his. "I have ever found innocence appealing. There is something unique in knowing one is first." He leaned closer, slipping an arm about her shoulders, his fingers lightly caressing her bared skin.

"Would I be your first? Or did my quixotic cousin manage to charm his way into your bed?"

Julia stood, heedless of the way it made her head spin. Whatever demons haunted Nick, they were out in full force tonight. "What we need is some food," she suggested brightly, crossing to the table and slipping into the farthest chair.

Nick watched her through half closed eyes. "You cannot put me off forever, Julia."

"You can't wish to ravish me on an empty stomach. It could cause indigestion." She began piling mounds of cold ham and sliced apples on her plate. Just for good measure, she took three pieces of bread and slathered them with butter, ignoring the quaver of her stomach at the sight.

He watched her for an amused moment before joining her at the table, claiming the chair beside hers. "Very well, but it only prolongs the moment. I *will* seduce you. If not now, then after Alec has been dispatched."

Julia tamped down terror at Nick's calm assumption. "Alec won't come. You've made one mistake; he doesn't care about me."

"Have you looked at yourself in the mirror lately?" He leaned forward and traced the back of his hand down her cheek. "Those lips were made for sinning."

Julia stuffed her mouth full of buttered bread. No man could kiss a woman with a mouth full of buttered bread. She hoped she looked every bit as repulsive as she felt.

After an astonished moment, Nick threw back his head and laughed.

It wasn't exactly the response she'd hoped for, but it was better than unbridled lust. The only problem she had now was what to do with all the bread in her mouth. Her stomach still roiled from the laudanum and her throat was tight with fear.

Chuckling, he said, "You always manage to surprise me. That is a rare quality indeed."

Julia attempted to swallow. The lump stuck in her throat and refused to move. She choked, her eyes watering as the lump seemed to grow and grow.

A flicker of irritation crossed his face. "Pray do not try that old trick."

She wanted to tell him she was not playacting, but she could make no noise, could barely move for trying to breathe.

As her distress increased, Nick's amusement faded. "Good God, Julia!"

Though the roar in her ears, she heard his voice as if from a great distance. He thumped her firmly on the back, then again and again. After what seemed an eternity, the lump finally went down and sweet air rushed to fill her lungs. Coughing and sputtering, she wiped her eyes. Cursing, Nick poured her a glass of ale and handed it to her.

After several sips, her breathing settled into a more normal rhythm. She looked at Nick with a thankful sigh. "You saved my life."

His eyes widened just an instant, uncertainty flickering across his face, but he quickly banished it. "Do not make me out to be a hero."

"But you are."

"Really?" He captured her hand and pressed it to his mouth, his eyes languorous. "Then show me your appreciation."

Julia tried to regain her hand, but he held tight. "Oh, just stop it!" she said, suddenly tired with the whole debacle. All she had wanted was to sponsor a charity and look what had happened. She'd married a man who could not love her and been kidnapped by another who was determined to disgrace her, and now she'd almost died. Worse, it would have been the most ignominious kind of death—choking on buttered bread.

Her life was not going at all the way it should, and she was tired and sore and angry. She pulled on her hand. "Leave me be. My head hurts."

He refused to relinquish his hold. "Julia, my love. You are a pragmatic woman. As such, you should be thinking ahead. Once Alec has lost the fortune, he will be unable to fund these projects of yours. I, on the other hand, will have more money than I know what to do with." Nick turned her hand over and placed a warm kiss on her wrist. "I'm not interested in marriage, of course, even once you are a widow. But perhaps we can reach an agreement, one more suitable to *both* of our interests."

"I don't bargain with men who plan on killing my husband. He may be difficult, but he is my husband, after all." *And I love him dearly.* She managed to keep her voice light, though her heart was anything but.

Nick chuckled, his fingers tightening on her wrist. "I see I shall have to be more plain in my intentions." He yanked her from her chair and into his lap, her back scraping painfully across the edge of the table.

"Release me!"

His arms clamped around her, his hands tangling at her waist in the bronze silk of her gown. There was a determination in his gaze she could not deny. He was going to have her one way or another. Fine, Julia decided, her patience at an end, her anger roused as never before. Without another word, she wrapped her arm about Nick's neck and kissed him. She didn't just gently press her mouth to his, but avidly sought his kiss, arching against him.

Anything to keep his attention off her other hand, which had just closed around the metal cover for the ham dish. The cover hit his head with a distinct gong sound, and for an instant, she thought his eyes crossed. Then he sagged forward and tumbled both of them to the floor. Julia's cheek hit the edge of the chair, and black spots wavered in front of her eyes.

She blinked them away and as soon as Nick's grip loosened, she scrambled upright and made a mad dash for the door. Before she gained her freedom, hands closed around her waist, yanking her back. Julia kicked with all her might, but her slippered feet did nothing to the booted shins they met.

Nick's hands bit cruelly into her arms as he turned her to face him. Blood dripped from his forehead and ran down his neck to darken his cravat with a red stain. "Stop it," he hissed, his eyes sparking blue flames. "I don't wish to hurt you." He shook her with each word, his fury palpable.

Julia grit her teeth. "Leave me be!"

He yanked her to him, his eyes blazing into hers, his hands like iron bands on her bare arms as he hissed through his teeth, "The next time you attempt something that foolish, I will forget you are a woman. Do you understand?"

She nodded and curled her hands into fists.

"Sit down." He almost threw her from him.

As soon as he released her, she swung at him with all her might, her fist connecting with his eye.

His head jerked back from the blow and he stumbled, tripped over a stool and fell. The punch did little more than anger him, for he rolled immediately to his feet and started after her, bellowing his rage.

But that second of freedom was all Julia needed, for she was out the door and into the hallway, running as fast as she could. From behind her came the thud of his booted feet, each step bringing him closer. Julia saw the huge oak door ahead and grabbed the handle, flinging it open . . . and dashed right into Alec's outstretched arms.

Chapter 30

❧❧❧

"**M**y, my. What a charming tableau." Nick's voice rang cold and furious.

The pale dawn light gleamed along the barrel of a cocked pistol. Alec tightened his hold on Julia, his heart racing as he savored the feel of her in his arms. Her enticing scent drifted around him as he fought the desire to sink his face into her hair and never let her go.

There would be time for that later. Right now, he had a dog to neuter. "Bridgeton, I—" The growing light touched Nick's face where blood glistened. With a heart grown even colder by fear, Alec managed to rasp out, "What happened to you?"

Nick's gaze flickered to Julia, though he said with a careless shrug, "I ate something that disagreed with me."

Alec said a short prayer of thanks that Lucien kept such fine horseflesh. Had it not been for Wexford's lightly sprung chaise and prime set of chestnuts, Alec would have been too late. "A pity it didn't kill you," Alec returned coldly. "Nick, my wife and I would like to return home now."

Nick's gaze flickered insolently over Julia. "Neither you nor your *wife* has a say in this matter."

Alec ground his teeth. Damn it all, he had not thought to be at such a disadvantage. But then, he hadn't foreseen Julia bursting through the door in terror just as he approached it. At this very moment, the pistol from the box beneath the seat of Luce's chaise was resting in the pocket of Alec's greatcoat. It was their one and only hope.

Nick gestured with his pistol. "Escort her inside."

Julia pulled back from Alec's embrace to stare up at him. A smile trembled on her wide mouth. "I was afraid you wouldn't find me."

Alec refused to think what might have happened if he'd been a moment later. He drank in the sight of her. Her hair tumbled about her shoulders in a mass of tangles and framed her pale, strained face, the jaunty feather long gone. Her eyes shimmered above an angry cut along the curve of her cheek.

Lifting a hand, he gently wiped away the thin trickle of blood. Anger seethed through him and he glared over her head at Nick. "You will pay for this, Bridgeton."

"Probably. But not today." Nick aimed the pistol at Julia.

Fury clenched Alec's jaw. "This is between us. Let Julia go."

"So she can alert the authorities? That wouldn't be wise. Besides . . ." Nick's gaze flickered insolently over Julia, lingering on her breasts. "I have plans for her."

Alec leapt at Nick, but Julia held his arm.

"Alec, *no.*"

Her voice poured icy cold over the red-hot rage that possessed him. He found himself looking into her eyes, lost in the calm warmth he found there. His mind worked once again and he examined her delicate features. Was she disappointed to discover Nick's true character? Had her heart, so tender and true, been crushed by that horrible and unpalatable truth?

A swell of sympathy cut through the brittle edges of his own pain. He knew the agony of unreturned love, knew the disappointment of looking into someone's eyes and seeing nothing but the reflection of another. He wanted so to ask her how she fared, yet before he could say a word, she leaned forward and whispered, "I hate to sound spiritless, but we should do as he asks."

Alec squeezed her hand. She was right; now was not the time. "Lead the way."

She returned to the hunting box, casting a reproachful glance at Nick as she went.

On entering, Alec noted the overturned chairs and an upended metal dome beneath the table. Fear clutched his throat. "Did he—"

"No." A flicker of humor quirked her mouth. "I didn't give him a chance."

Relief flooded him. Thank God she had been spared. Unable to stop, Alec caught her to him and rested his cheek against her silken hair.

"Charming," came Nick's mocking voice. "Pray be seated."

It was all Alec could do to keep himself in check. But one look at Julia's pale face and he loosened his hold and led her to the settee. Once there, Alec pulled her back into his arms.

Nick shut the door and approached the fireplace. Resting his shoulder against the mantle, he regarded them with a somber stare, the pistol never wavering.

Alec forced himself to meet his cousin's gaze. "You should get something for that cut. It's bleeding profusely."

Nick cast a dark glance at Julia. "I am sure it is."

She sniffed. "Nick and I had a disagreement."

Though she appeared angry, Alec was relieved to see no other emotion on her expressive features. Was it possible that Lucien was right? That Julia's heart had not been touched by his corrupt cousin, but only her ready sympathy? But whom, then, had she loved for four long, anguished years?

Nick gingerly touched the lump on his forehead. "I have to commend you, Cousin. Your wife is as exciting as she is lovely." His insolent gaze rested on Julia and Alec's hands curled into fists.

Julia tugged on his arm. "Pray, don't let him provoke you! He *wants* to fight a duel."

"Silence!" Nick's face darkened and he turned to Alec. "You have no choice. You either fight or . . ." The pistol lifted in a suggestive manner toward Julia.

Alec's hands itched for the feel of his own pistol, still tucked safely away in his pocket, but he dared not risk Julia's safety. "The executors will never release the funds to you after this."

"Why not? The will stipulated nothing concerning my behavior." A satisfied smile curved Nick's mouth. "Only yours."

Julia leaned forward. "Forget this silly duel and let us go."

"I can't, my dear. Alec will not let me leave here alive." The blue gaze flickered to Alec. "Will you, dear cousin?"

Alec met the cold stare with one of his own. "You will never again harm Julia."

She tugged urgently on his coat. "Alec, Nick saved my

life." At Alec's disbelieving look, she added, "I was choking on some bread and he saved me."

To Alec's amazement, Nick shifted, looking decidedly
uncomfortable. Catching Alec's gaze, Nick shrugged.
"She is no use to me dead."

"I would be of just as much use to you dead as alive,"
Julia corrected. "You used me to get Alec here; that was
my one and only purpose. Though you may wish us to
think otherwise, it says something that you didn't let me
die when you had the chance."

Nick's face reddened. "Enough of this! Alec, it is time
to bring this farce to an end. I have a lovely brace of pistols for our meeting. Shall we take this outside?"

Alec rose.

"No, Alec!" Julia caught his hand, rising to stand beside
him. "He has never lost."

"Neither have I." Alec removed his greatcoat and
slipped it around Julia. Her eyes widened when she felt the
weight of the pistol in the pocket. He leaned close under
the pretext of kissing her cheek to whisper, "Get away
when you can."

She sent him a mutinous glare, but held her tongue.

Placing a hand on Julia's elbow, Alec led her past Nick.
Just as she drew even with him, she stumbled, her foot
catching the long hem of the coat.

Nick had been reaching for a narrow box carrying the
dueling pistols when Julia fell. He immediately reached
out a hand to steady her, the barrel of his weapon momentarily lowering.

It was the moment Alec had been waiting for. He
lunged, knocking Nick's pistol from his hand. It skittered
across the floor, spinning wildly and coming to rest by the
hearth.

Nick dove after the lost weapon, Alec right behind him. End over end, the two men scrambled wildly. Julia started forward, the weighted swing of the greatcoat reminding her of her own hidden weapon.

Slipping her hand into the pocket, her fingers closed over the cold metal. The men fought on, oblivious to their surroundings, to her, to everything. Taking a great breath, she moved to stand by the decorated box that held the dueling pistols.

Hand shaking, she pulled her own pistol from the greatcoat pocket, pointed it at a great metal caldron that hung beside the fireplace and, squinting, took aim and fired.

She missed the cauldron by several feet, the bullet striking the hearth mere inches from the two men. A shower of dust and shale exploded into the air, raining white powder and shards of stone across the men and the floor.

Alec and Nick froze, then turned toward her, their faces a comic mix of hope and terror. Before either could move, Julia discarded her weapon and retrieved one of the dueling pistols from the box. She pointed it at Nick.

He started for the lost pistol that lay so close at hand, but Julia cocked her weapon.

He froze at the loud click.

"Thank you," she said. "I don't want to shoot you, but I will if I must."

Nick gracefully gained his feet, hands held palm up. "Easy, Julia," he said, a worried fold to his brow. "It fires easily. More easily than you might think."

Alec grinned, touching his eye where a bruise was beginning to appear. "Bridgeton, you should have thought of that before. Now that Julia—"

"Sit down." She waved the gun toward the settee. "*Both* of you."

Alec's smile disappeared. "Julia! Surely you don't mean—"

"*Sit down.*"

Wearing identical scowls, the two men sat on opposite ends of the settee like offended mastiffs. Julia hid a sigh of relief. Anything was better than the raw fury she'd seen in their faces moments earlier. "This has gone far enough." She turned to Nick. "Your plan has a serious flaw."

He frowned. Blood dripped from his nose and marked a path down the side of his face. He looked tired, annoyed and thoroughly disgusted. "Impossible. I thought of every circumstance."

"You keep seeing yourself as competing with Alec for your grandfather's money. But you are also Alec's heir: the next living male relative. You cannot kill a man and then inherit from him, even in a duel."

Nick's mouth opened, but no words came out. He looked from Julia to Alec, then back again. After a long moment, he slumped against the back of the settee. "I'll be damned," he said softly. "I'll be double damned."

Julia almost felt sorry for him. She turned to Alec. "And as for you, you have spent years believing Nick to be something he's not."

Alec scowled. "You can't expect me to—"

She cut him off with a wave of the pistol. "Nick, tell Alec about the missing money from your youth."

"What is there to tell?"

"The truth."

For a long moment she thought he'd refuse, but he shrugged, his gaze hooded and intent. "Alec, I did not steal Grandfather's precious money."

"You expect me to believe that now?"

"Call it the romanticism of youth or some such folly, but I had one or two morals back then. Now . . . " His gaze dropped to his scraped and bruised hand. "It is the bad blood, you know. There is no escaping it."

Alec did not speak for a long moment. Finally, he burst out, "Grandfather said you admitted everything!"

"Grandfather never even gave me a chance to speak." Nick regarded his cousin with a flat stare. "You know how he was."

Alec raked a hand through his hair, his brow creased. "If you didn't take the money, who did?"

"Mrs. Winston believes it was Nick's mother," Julia offered.

Alec frowned. "She was at Bridgeton House the week before the money was discovered missing, but I never thought . . . " Dismayed, Alec turned to his cousin. "Is that what happened?"

Nick sneered. "It is possible, I suppose. She was not above common thievery."

"Why didn't you say something?"

"What? That my mother was a whore and a thief and I sincerely hoped you didn't think I was like her?" Nick's lip curled. "Don't be foolish."

Looking at Alec's stunned expression, Julia's sympathy overcame her exasperation. Alec had a lot of his grandfather's pride; she could see the struggle in his face even now. "Alec, if anyone knows the importance of family, it is you. You know how it was when your grandfather died."

Alec nodded once.

"Imagine how things have been for Nick."

"Please," Nick spat. "I don't want your pity."

"You're not getting it," Julia said sharply. "I feel many things for you, but pity is not on the list."

A faint smile tugged Nick's mouth. "I apologize," he said with false meekness.

She had to fight a desire to answer that faint smile. Instead, she sniffed. "I was merely pointing out to my beloved husband that it is possible that you deserve another chance. Just one."

Nick looked at Alec. "I would, of course, leave the country. Forever."

Julia thought this over. "What about Italy? I hear it's quite lovely this time of year."

Humor twinkled in the depths of Nick's eyes. "I have always found the climate beneficial."

Alec growled. "I am not happy with this. He still kidnapped you."

"And saved my life." She pushed a strand of hair from her forehead and sighed. "What would you have me do, Alec? He hasn't harmed anyone."

"Damnation! He abducted you, attempted to cheat me of the fortune, cause a scandal, drugged you and—"

"Very well." Nick stood and adjusted his cravat. He regarded Alec with a cool smile. "So have me arrested."

Alec glowered and Nick laughed softly. "No, I didn't think so. You would not submit your lovely wife's name to the scrutiny of a trial, would you? Fortunately, my only intention now is to put the events of this lamentable night behind me. Julia, it has been . . . not pleasant, but interesting." He bowed, then faced Alec. "As for you, Cousin, I hope you know this wasn't personal."

Alec's expression didn't change.

Nick's smile faded. "Perhaps what I should say is that it shouldn't have been personal but I, unfortunately, allowed it to be so. For what it's worth, I am sorry." He gathered his coat and hat, and turned to the door.

"Wait!" Alec stood.

Nick stopped, one hand on the knob.

Alec's hands clenched and unclenched. "Where will you go?"

Julia understood his struggle. Somewhere inside of the depraved man before him was the cousin he had once idolized. Idolized and wrongly accused.

Nick's grin flickered. "To Italy and then on to hell."

Julia's ready sympathy stirred. "Alec, we should help him make a clean start."

Silence met her as Alec stared at her. Slowly, almost reverently, he took her hand and placed a kiss on the palm before he turned to Nick. "Sell Bridgeton House to me."

Nick's face darkened. "No. It's all I have."

"If you flee now, it will be auctioned off to satisfy your creditors. Sell it to me instead. I'll pay you what it is worth."

"How do you know I won't use your own largesse to ruin you?"

"I will accept your word."

Pain flickered in Nick's eyes. "Damn you. Damn you to hell. My solicitor will contact you within the week." He opened the door, and then hesitated. Finally, he turned back around. "Do me a favor, Alec."

"What?"

"Go to the meeting with the solicitors."

"It is too late."

Nick smiled, his eyes glinting. "Go and take Julia with you." Without another word, he left, closing the door softly behind him.

Julia breathed a sigh of relief as she listened to his measured tread fade. Her wrist ached from holding the heavy pistol.

Alec's warm hand closed over hers. "Allow me to return this weapon to its proper place." He placed the gun on the table, then yanked her into his arms. "You and I need to have a talk about the impropriety of pointing a weapon at your husband."

"It wasn't loaded. It went off when Nick dropped the box."

A dangerous glint lit Alec's gaze. "Always full of surprises, aren't you?"

There was no mistaking the admiration in his voice. A heated flush rippled up her back and danced along her already jangled nerves. Heaven help her, but she was too tired, too hungry and too much in love to deal with any more excitement. "We've had a very adventurous evening, haven't we?"

His lips quivered for a moment before he grinned. "As usual, you have managed to wrap the whole in a nice, neat packet."

Julia noted the bruises on his face. A thin sluice of blood marred his well-shaped mouth. "Heavens, Alec. Look at your mouth!" She crossed to the table and dipped a napkin in the water pitcher and brought it back to the settee. "Sit down."

He obediently sat, but his gaze remained on her.

She dabbed at the cut, forcing herself to focus on his mouth, though that in itself was torture. She knew the feel of his lips against hers, the sensuous heat of his breath across her neck. Her stomach fluttered in excitement.

Alec caught her hand, halting her ministrations. "Julia, why did you let Nick go?"

His deep voice seemed a caress in itself. Julia kept her eyes trained on the bruise on his jaw. "I didn't have a choice. If you had killed him, there would have been some sort of inquiry, perhaps even gaol. I need you here." She swallowed and added, "With me."

His fingers tightened on her hand. Swirls of silver lit the gray of his eyes, mesmerizing in their brilliance.

Slowly, ever so softly, he said, "My God," he breathed. "I almost missed it. You love *me*."

Whatever declaration she'd hoped to hear, that wasn't it. Disappointed, she jerked her arm free. "Of course I love you. I wouldn't have agreed to marry you if I didn't."

He regained his hold on her hand. "But you said you had been in love for four years!"

"Yes. With you, you fool. Who else would I have been in love with?"

"Nick."

Julia knew it was impolite to gape, but she couldn't help it. "Heavens, what made you think that?"

"You said you'd known him for four years."

"I've known a lot of people for four years. That's when I came to England."

Alec looked stunned.

Julia offered a wan smile. "I daresay you don't remember the first time we met, but it was at the Seftons' ball. You came in late, slightly drunk. Your cravat was crooked, too. You looked so handsome I dropped my fan and you picked it up and handed it back to me. You didn't say anything, but you smiled." She examined his face. "I still treasure that smile."

A pained expression darkened his eyes. "I don't remember."

"Of course you don't. You were badly dipped and I was hardly a memorable person." She chuckled. "At least, I wasn't then. Seems I can hardly sneeze now without causing some fuss."

"Whatever you do, don't sneeze in that dress."

She glanced down. Through the opening of the great-coat she could see where her dashing gown had twisted, her bosom nearly exposed. Blushing, she attempted to right the material. "I told Maddie I shouldn't wear this blasted thing but she—"

His hand covered hers, his fingers brushing against her breasts. "Julia."

She stilled, suddenly intent on the top button of the greatcoat. His shadow fell over her as he stood.

Alec lifted her chin with a gentle hand. "Julia, listen to me. This isn't easy, but . . . Julia, I love you."

Her breath froze in her lungs.

He continued, oblivious. "I wish I could say I've loved you for years, too, but I haven't. All I know is that I love you now, and always will."

Julia wanted to believe him, but she couldn't. She'd seen his kindnesses with the servants, and some part of her wondered how much he classified her with them—as a responsibility.

She pushed his hand away and forced a smile. "It has been a very hectic night. Perhaps we should talk about this another time."

He caught her wrist and jerked her against him. "Damn it, Julia. Look at me. Really look at me. *I love you*."

Julia squinted up at him. She wanted to believe him so badly. "Say it again."

"*I. Love. You*." His wonderful, amazing eyes gleamed a misty warm gray, clearly reflecting his love.

"You really do," she said, amazed.

He made an exasperated noise. "Haven't I just said it a thousand times?"

"No. Only four."

Alec chuckled. "I am still ahead of you." He slipped an arm about her waist and pulled her closer, the hard length of his thigh pressed intimately against her. "And I plan on staying that way. You may spread your care and concern all over London, to every urchin and fallen woman you meet. But I intend to be very selfish about your love. It is all mine."

He kissed her gently at first, then with increasing passion. Julia flung her arms around him and held him close, reveling in the beating of his heart, the warmth of his touch, the sensuous heat of his mouth.

Through the passionate haze, the clock on the mantle chimed a gentle melody. Julia started and pushed away. "Alec! The meeting!"

He gathered her back against him. "Forget it, Julia. It's unlikely we could make it in time. Besides, they will have already made their decision—"

"We have to try! I can't believe there's still not some hope, not after all we've been through." She disengaged herself from his embrace. "Please, Alec."

He lifted his brows as he tugged his coat more closely about her. "Still thinking of the other half of London you have yet to save?"

"No," she said with mock severity. "I'm just thinking of you and your debts. You offered to buy Bridgeton House from Nick, not to mention the shocking amount you bid on that silly portrait of Bentham's. I'd hate to see you sent to Fleet Prison because you don't have the necessary funds."

Alec grinned and kissed her nose. "Think how well the portrait will look in the dining room of Bridgeton House."

"I didn't know you'd want such a grand residence."

"I don't, but we will need somewhere to put our children and—as Mrs. Winston keeps telling me—our house is much too small."

To Alec's intense satisfaction, her blush lasted most of the way back to London.

Hand in hand, Alec and Julia climbed the steps of the office of Pratt, Pratt and Son and made their way into the foyer. Alec knew they must both look a sight after their arduous night, but he felt as fresh as a yearling at his first race.

Muffled voices sounded behind the thick, oaken door. He placed a kiss on Julia's forehead. "Wait for me here. I won't be long."

She refused to relinquish her hold, her jaw mulish. "I want to go with you."

Alec smiled, cupping her face with his hands. He couldn't seem to stop touching her, running his fingers over her creamy skin, sinking his hands into her silken curls. "I know you do. But this is my battle, not yours."

Reluctant to the end, she released his hand only to call out as he reached the door, "Alec?"

He turned and waited.

She twisted her hands together, doubt and concern clouding her eyes. "Good luck."

He returned to give her one last kiss. When they were both breathless, he broke away. "Wait for me here."

Unable to do more than nod, Julia watched him straighten his cravat and enter the room.

Time passed with agonizing slowness. For a while she paced the foyer, stopping by the closed door to listen to the blurred murmur of conversation. Once she heard voices raised in reproach, and she had to fist her hands to keep from bursting through the door.

After a seeming eternity, Alec emerged, his face pale and drawn.

Her heart ached and tears filled her eyes. They'd lost the fortune. She wished she could ease his pain. She touched his sleeve. "Alec, I'm so sorry. If only I could have—"

He pulled her to him, the faint scent of sandalwood enveloping her. Julia closed her eyes and burrowed deeper. She was surrounded by him, by his strength, his concern, and his love. It was heaven.

"Julia, my dear," sounded a voice behind her. Julia pulled away from Alec's embrace and turned. There, strolling from the room, was Lord Kennybrook. He stopped when he saw her face. "Good God! What happened to you, my dear?"

Julia could only stare. "What . . . why are you here, my lord?"

"Never mind that! You've a gash on your cheek and your gown is torn." He shot a hard glance at Alec from under thick brows. "Damn it, Hunterston. You have to take better care of her." He turned to call over his shoulder, "Burton! Come and see who has joined us. Looks like hell, but she seems sound."

Lord Burton waddled forward. "Good thing, too. Hate to have to drag Alec back into that den of wolves just to teach him a lesson." He bowed over Julia's limp hand, his brown eyes twinkling. "Bet you're surprised to see us, eh?"

She nodded, trying to comprehend. "Why *are* you here?" A sudden thought occurred. "Did you come to testify before the executors on our behalf?"

"Testify?" Kennybrook puffed out his cheeks. "Lord Burton and I are *on* the Board of Executors, my dear."

Julia turned to Alec. "I thought you said they were a bunch of—"

"Intelligent, well-meaning gentlemen," finished Alec smoothly.

Kennybrook snorted. "I'd wager you've called us more than that, young man. While I don't blame you, I'd be just as pleased not to know about it."

Julia shook her head, wondering if she had heard aright. "How did you become executors?"

Kennybrook waved a hand. "Oh, Burton and I knew Alec's grandfather since Cambridge."

Lord Burton chuckled. "We were a trio of scamps back them. Kicked up every lark you can name." He waggled his brows. "Maybe even a few you can't."

"Lord, yes," agreed Kennybrook with a wistful sigh. "But then John got married and we saw less and less of him."

"Until he became involved in the Society," Burton said.

Lord Kennybrook pulled a cigar from his coat and rolled it between his fingers. "You never met him, my dear. But John was the anonymous benefactor whose support we lost just as you joined us. Very generous with his blunt, you know."

Burton's face fell. "It was one of his favorite charities."

Alec shook his head and Julia noted the white lines about his mouth. "You should be proud of him," she said softly.

His mouth curved in a bitter smile. "He never told me any of this."

"Why should he?" expostulated Kennybrook. "He wasn't one to brag on his generosity. You are just fortunate he thought to make me and Burton executors." He glanced around to make sure they were alone before whispering loudly, "The rest of 'em are the biggest bunch of bores I've ever seen."

"Heavens, yes," agreed Burton. "We had the devil of a

time trying to keep them from tossing Alec out on his ear."

Kennybrook clamped the unlit cigar between his teeth. "It was close, but we pulled through. It was a sheer stroke of genius to have Wexford bring Lady Birlington and the Dowager Duchess to proclaim your innocence."

"Lucien was here?" asked Alec, startled.

Burton folded his hands across his waistcoat. "He was waiting on the steps when we arrived. Marie helped, too."

Julia blinked. "Did she?"

Burton beamed, his face softening. "Marie may not be as genteel as some would wish, but she has a big heart. Once she found out it was bellows to mend with the two of you, she went out and collected Therese—practically dragged the silly chit all the way here."

Kennybrook grimaced. "Of course, then we had to listen to the shrillest caterwauling I've ever heard. She cried and bleated about how Nick had told her he would marry her if she helped him trick you out of the funds. When she got to the part where she'd led young Bentham into painting that portrait, it was all I could do to keep a civil tongue in my head."

Burton grunted his agreement. "Silly wench. Made me sick to even look at her. It was all going swimmingly, but that newspaperman sealed it all."

"I wondered if Mr. Everard had made his appearance," Alec said, his mouth curving in a slight smile.

"Oh, yes," Kennybrook said. "He explained the whole story about the article and how Nick had finagled him into printing it. Burton and I vouched for the integrity of the Society, of course, and that put an end to that." He sighed happily. "All in all, it went rather well."

Julia rubbed her forehead. "Are you saying the fortune is still Alec's?"

"No," Alec said quickly, turning her to face him. His eyes gleamed with warmth. "It is *ours*, Julia. Yours and mine."

"By Jove," Kennybrook chuckled, "you've something of your grandfather in you, after all. Mind, I had my doubts, especially when you colored up like a rose when I told you to begin your family and put an end to this scandal nonsense."

Julia had to bite her lip to keep from laughing. "That was you?"

Kennybrook beamed. "Who else?"

Burton patted his friend's shoulder. "We are both anxious to be named godfathers. Much more to our liking than this executor nonsense."

"Yes, fewer meetings." Kennybrook waggled his shaggy brows. "So what's next, Lady Hunterston?"

Julia rested her head against her husband's shoulder and sighed happily. The whole world seemed brighter, more lovely than she'd ever thought possible. "I thought perhaps we might expand the Society to include men, as well as women. And children, too."

Alec's arm settled about her shoulders. "I, sir, plan to keep the books from now on."

"Well," blustered Kennybrook, looking pleased. "That is quite a thought."

Lord Burton's brow lowered. "Speaking of children—"

"Yes, sir," replied Alec, his hand warm on Julia's elbow. "We will start working on that right away. In fact, if you don't mind, we'll take our leave of you now."

"Alec," Julia gasped, her cheeks heating.

Kennybrook gave a sharp crack of laughter. "Take her away, my boy! But see to it she moves those damnable meetings back to a normal time. I'm too old to see the dawn." With a wave of his hand, he dismissed them.

Alec bundled Julia into the chaise. He settled her against him and urged the horses to a swift trot. Once they were home, he would have Mrs. Winston draw them a bath while Chilton packed his wife's clothes for the move across the hallway. Julia would be right where she belonged, in his arms night after night. Alec grinned and glanced at his bride.

Julia sat, her hands twisting about the folds of the coat, a frown resting on her brow.

Concern tightened his chest. "What's wrong, my love?"

"I thought you hated children."

"Who said that?" he said, astounded.

"Mrs. Winston. She said you haven't liked children since you were seventeen and the maid—"

"One day," he interrupted with as great an amount of dignity as he could muster. "I am going to have a long talk with that woman."

"Take my advice." Julia patted his arm and leaned her head against his shoulder. "Be sure you have a comfortable chair."

Chuckling, he wrapped an arm around her and took her home.

Epilogue

London, 1815

Sunlight warmed the early spring grass at Hyde Park, warming the new buds, and filling the air with the scent of dozens of fresh blooms.

A large, grand carriage creaked down one of the wider, more sedate paths. Inside, Lady Birlington thunked her cane on the floor. "Edmund, stop gawking!"

"I wasn't gawking! I was trying to see how many—that's two, three." He leaned out the window, counting on his fingers. "And another—Good God!" He fell back into his seat, a bemused expression on his face. "There are *four!*"

"I know there are four! I can count 'em as well as you. Now order the coachman to stop. I'm not getting any younger and Lady Hunterston will be gone before I can speak with her. I need her to send me a new housekeeper from her Society. Poor Mrs. Beel fell down the stairs last week and will be out of service for weeks. Meanwhile, Julia sent a woman to the Duchess of Devonshire for just that purpose and she is impeccable. Even I was impressed."

Edmund knocked on the roof and the coachman immediately pulled up beside a walkway where a short line of fresh-faced children and starched maids walked up a wide, sunny path, the wind stirring ribbons and bows. In the front strode a handsome couple, the man tall and dark, the woman slender with golden brown hair. In the woman's arms was yet another infant, this one tinier than the other.

Lady Birlington leaned out the window. "Lord and Lady Hunterston! Just the people I most wished to see."

Alec, who'd been walking at the front of the line, his arm solicitously tucked through Julia's, looked surprised. "Lady Birlington, how are you? Julia and I just returned from—"

"Yes, yes." Lady Birlington pinned her gaze on Julia. "Lady Hunterston, pray hand that mewling infant to someone and come and speak to me. I've a favor to ask."

Julia smiled and then handed the gurgling baby to Alec, saying in a low voice, "Here. I suppose you'll have to hold her now."

"It's about time," he said gravely, taking the child with practiced confidence. "I thought I'd have to trip you to get my turn."

"I'm not that bad."

He merely raised his brows.

She laughed. "Enjoy it while you can; I'll want her back after I finish speaking with Mad Maddie." Julia slid a finger over the baby's soft cheek. "Marianne, do not let your father get too used to carrying you. That's a mother's privilege."

Lady Birlington knocked on the carriage door with her cane. "Julia, I am getting sun burned! Leave that child and come here. You may return to moon over her as soon as we're through."

"Coming!" Julia called. She gave her husband a droll look and made her way to the carriage.

Alec watched her go, admiring the gentle sway of her hips as she walked. As she reached the carriage, Edmund appeared around the back. He sent a harried glance at Lady Birlington and then, apparently satisfied he'd escaped undetected, scampered to Alec's side, hiding behind some foliage on the off chance she might catch sight of him.

"Whew! Thank God we ran into you!" Edmund said, looking much happier now that he was away from Lady Birlington. "I couldn't take another moment. Was thinking of slitting my own throat but this is much easier." He peered at the infant in Alec's arms. "Is that one yours?"

"Julia and I just adopted her."

Edmund shook his head and frowned. "Not saying she's not a pretty little thing, for she is, but why would you wish to adopt her? People bound to say she's your by-blow."

"I don't care what people say. Marianne needed a family and we needed children. Seemed a good match. As Julia says, there are all those bed chambers at Bridgeton House—"

Edmund made a choking noise. "You're going to fill *all* of them?"

Alec laughed. "Perhaps." Smiling, he touched the baby's nose. Little Marianne gurgled a laugh that sent a grin straight to Alec's heart.

Edmund bent closer. "She's a merry one."

Marianne's wide blue gaze locked onto Edmund's face.

She stared at him intently, then slowly, her lip began to tremble, her eyes began to water, and her face turned red.

Edmund looked so alarmed that Alec had to laugh. He shifted Marianne so that her gaze settled on him once more and her smile returned instantly. "Easy, Edmund. She's not old enough yet to value your charm as she ought."

"I never was any good with children. Don't think I'll have any of my own."

"That's a pity. We are quite happy with the two we've chosen so far." He smiled as Marianne's tiny fist closed over his finger.

"Two?" Edmund looked down the line of nannies and children. "I see four."

"This babe and John, who you see at the end of the line, are ours."

"John, eh? After your grandfather?"

Alec nodded. He caught John's attention where the young boy stood beside his governess, and winked. The boy smiled and winked back, all with an air of solemnity that made Alec chuckle.

Edmund looked impressed. "He's a composed one. How old is he?"

"Seven."

"And yet he acts as if he's ready to have his own establishment! Who are the other two?" Edmund gestured to the babies sitting snug in the arms of two maids. "Just trying them on for size?"

"No, those are Lucien's sons."

"Arabella had twins?"

Alec nodded.

"I must take him some cheroots to celebrate. I take it they're in town?"

"They arrived last week with her brother in tow. I hear Robert and Liza have had a falling out of some sort and the two barely speak."

Edmund scrunched his nose. "Must make for awkward suppers."

"Perhaps they will come around. People sometimes do." Marianne cooed loudly and Alec shifted the baby to his shoulder.

Edmund watched, fascinated. "I never thought of you as a family man."

"I didn't, either." He hadn't thought of himself as many things until Julia had come into his life. "It took me a while, I'll admit. At first, I was just trying to help Julia, but then . . ." He leaned his cheek against Marianne's fine hair and the sweet scent of lavender rose from the baby's skin.

Across from him, Julia caught his gaze and for a long moment, they shared a smile.

Life with Julia had been far more gratifying than he'd expected. And more exciting, too. He never knew what might happen from one day to the next, yet every day had been both filled and fulfilling. "Ever hear anything from that villain, Bridgeton? I suppose he's still traveling the continent."

Alec hesitated, then shrugged. He'd heard a rumor that Nick had returned to England and was even now residing in Bath. Alec didn't know if there was any truth to the rumor, but he didn't care enough to find out.

Whenever he thought of his cousin, it was with an uncomfortable combination of disdain and regret. Alec only hoped that one day Nick might find someone to love, someone who would give him the strength to turn back into the man he used to be.

Julia finished speaking to Lady Birlington and reached up to shake the old woman's hand through the carriage window. The wind lifted the edges of Julia's skirts and swirled them playfully around her ankles, then traveled over Alec, wisping Marianne's fine hair, and on down the line of children. Lucien's sons gurgled with laughter and opened their hands wide as the wind swept by, as if to catch it. John watched the little ones with a faint smile, his brown hair ruffled.

Alec's heart swelled. This was what life with Julia was about—family and happiness, comfort and love. All things he'd never really known before.

"Edmund!" Lady Birlington called. "What on earth are you doing with Hunterston? And don't pretend you're not there, hiding in the shrubbery, for I can see your shoes!"

"Coming, Aunt Maddie!" Edmund answered. He cast an exasperated glance at Alec. "Wish I could walk with you. Much more fun than sharing a seat with Aunt Maddie's pug. That evil wretch bit me twice last week and all she did was tell me not to tease him. As if I didn't have better things to do!"

Still muttering, Edmund scampered back to Lady Birlington's carriage, pausing to say something to Julia on the way.

Julia laughed and joined Alec on the walkway. She held out her arms and he dutifully deposited Marianne into them, then glanced back and beckoned John. Seconds later, the little boy's hand clasped in his, Julia tucked against his side, they continued their walk. "What did Edmund say?"

"He begged that we think twice about filling *all* of the rooms at Bridgeton House as he still needs a few places to hide from his aunt and we're one of his last bastions."

"How selfish of him!"

"So I told him. Then he said that he supposed he wouldn't mind sharing a room with John, but no one else. Apparently, Marianne rattled him too much."

Alec laughed. "Yes, but John probably won't want to share a room with Edmund. The man is two shoes shy of a pair."

Julia smiled and tilted her head to rest it on her husband's shoulder. "Fortunately for everyone concerned, I'm willing to leave *one* guest room unoccupied at Bridgeton House."

"Only one?"

She smiled up into his eyes, cradling a fat and sleepy Marianne. "We owe it to your grandfather to fill his house with laughter. Can you think of a better way?"

Laughing softly, he hugged her. No, he couldn't think of a better way. Life with Julia was all he wanted, now and forever. Smiling, he rested his chin on her hair as they continued their walk, the sun lighting the way.

The seductive allure of *New York Times*
bestselling author

KAREN
HAWKINS

HOW TO TREAT A LADY
978-0-06-051405-1

To save her family from ruin, Harriet Ward invented a wealthy
fiance. But now the bank wants proof of the man's existence.

AND THE BRIDE WORE PLAID
978-0-06-051408-2

Devon St. John vows he will never give up his beloved
freedom—even when a temptress's impulsive kiss casts a
tantalizing spell . . .

LADY IN RED
978-0-06-058406-1

Marcus St. John must recover a lost family heirloom from the
irritatingly beautiful Miss Honoria Baker-Sneed.

HER MASTER AND COMMANDER
978-0-06-058408-5

Prudence Thistlewaite wants nothing to do with her wickedly
handsome, ill-tempered neighbor Captain Tristan Llevanth.

HER OFFICER AND GENTLEMAN
978-0-06-058414-6

Considered unmarriageable at twenty-five Lady Elizabeth
discovers the delicious ache of desire when she meets
Christian Llevanth.

Next month, don't miss these exciting new love stories only from Avon Books

Between the Devil and Desire by Lorraine Heath
Olivia, Duchess of Lovingdon, would never associate with such a rogue as Jack Dodger, a wealthy gentleman's club owner. Yet when Jack is named sole heir to the duke's personal possessions, Olivia is forced to share her beloved home with this despicable, yet desirable man . . .

Simply Irresistible by Rachel Gibson
Georgeanne Howard leaves her fiancé at the altar when she realizes she can't marry a man old enough to be her grandfather, no matter how rich he is. Hockey superstar John Kowalsky unknowingly helps her escape, and only later does he realize he has absconded with his boss's bride.

The Highland Groom by Sarah Gabriel
To claim her inheritance, Fiona MacCarran must marry a wealthy Highlander, and soon. Arriving in the misty Highlands as a schoolteacher, she despairs of finding an acceptable groom . . . until she meets Dougal MacGregor.

Wild by Margo Maguire
For Grace Hawthorne, the new stranger is unlike any man she has ever known. Proud, defiant, and mesmerizingly masculine, he flouts convention and refuses to enter into proper society. Is he the real Anthony Maddox, heir to a glittering earldom? Or an arrogant imposter, sworn to claim what doesn't belong to him?

AVON

978-0-06-157912-7

978-0-06-146850-6

978-0-06-137325-1

978-0-06-157823-6

978-0-06-145101-0

978-0-06-136624-6

Avon Romances

the best in
exceptional authors and unforgettable novels!

Unforgettable, enthralling love stories,
sparkling with passion and adventure
from Romance's bestselling authors

HOW TO PROPOSE TO A PRINCE   *by Kathryn Caskie*
978-0-06-112487-7

NEVER TRUST A SCOUNDREL   *by Gayle Callen*
978-0-06-123505-4

A NOTORIOUS PROPOSITION   *by Adele Ashworth*
978-0-06-112858-5

UNDER YOUR SPELL   *by Lois Greiman*
978-0-06-119136-7

IN BED WITH THE DEVIL   *by Lorraine Heath*
978-0-06-135557-8

THE MISTRESS DIARIES   *by Julianne MacLean*
978-0-06-145684-8

THE DEVIL WEARS TARTAN   *by Karen Ranney*
978-0-06-125242-6

BOLD DESTINY   *by Jane Feather*
978-0-380-75808-1

LIKE NO OTHER LOVER   *by Julie Anne Long*
978-0-06-134159-5

NEVER DARE A DUKE   *by Gayle Callen*
978-0-06-123506-1